MONKEY KING

A shape-shifting trickster on a kung-fu quest for eternal life, Sun Wukong, or Monkey King, is one of the most memorable superheroes in world literature. High-spirited and omni-talented, he amasses dazzling weapons and skills on his journey to immortality: a gold-hooped staff that can grow as tall as the sky and shrink to the size of a needle; the ability to travel 108,000 miles in a single somersault. A master of subterfuge, he can transform himself into whomever or whatever he chooses and turn each of his body's 84,000 hairs into an army of clones. But his penchant for mischief repeatedly gets him into trouble, and when he raids Heaven's Orchard of Immortal Peaches and gorges himself on the elixirs of the gods, the Buddha pins him beneath a mountain, freeing him only five hundred years later for a chance to redeem himself: He is to protect the pious monk Tripitaka on his fourteen-year journey to India in search of precious Buddhist sutras that will bring enlightenment to the Chinese empire.

Joined by two other fallen immortals—Pigsy, a rice-loving pig able to fly with its ears, and Sandy, a depressive man-eating river-sand monster—Monkey King undergoes eighty-one trials, doing battle with Red Boy, Princess Jade-Face, the Monstress Dowager, and all manner of dragons, ogres, wizards, and femmes fatales, navigating the perils of Fire-Cloud Cave, the River of Flowing Sand, the Water-Crystal Palace, and Casserole Mountain, and being serially captured, lacquered, sautéed, steamed, and liquefied, but always hatching an ingenious plan to get himself and his fellow pilgrims out of their latest jam.

One of the all-time great fantasy novels, *Monkey King: Journey to the West* is at once a rollicking adventure, a comic satire of Chinese bureaucracy, and a spring of spiritual insight.

Acclaim for Julia Lovell's translation of
Monkey King

"The best English edition of the classic Chinese fantasy novel I have ever read. If you wish to understand why *Monkey King* has been a fixture in Chinese popular culture for no fewer than five centuries, then look no further."　　　—Minjie Chen, *Los Angeles Review of Books*

"A fun, accessible book that will attract readers to a text that may otherwise seem obscure and imposing."　　　—*The Wall Street Journal*

"Exhibit[s] a rollicking exuberance."　　　—*The Washington Post*

"A vivacious delight: a genuinely very funny book is given its full due."　　　—*Foreign Policy*

"[A] brilliant new translation."　　　—*South China Morning Post*

"[An] engaging translation . . . All who have loved *Robin Hood*, or Tolkien, or J. K. Rowling, or the superheroes [Gene Luen] Yang pings in his foreword, will find similar friends in Monkey, Tripitaka, Pigsy (the Friar Tuck of Asia) and Sandy."　　　—*Asian Review of Books*

"A translation that's really funny . . . [It] is a delight and a tour de force."　　　—*Asian Books Blog*

"A joy to read . . . The stories flow from the book beautifully, and we can't wait to find out what trouble Monkey gets into next, and how he gets out of it."　　　—*International Examiner*

"Fantastically funny . . . Lovell is to be commended."　　　—*The Mountain Times*

"This new translation . . . breathes fresh life, humor, wit, and charm into the sixteenth-century classic. . . . If you did not know that this was an abridged version . . . you never would. . . . [It] is exactly as long as it needs to be, with the fat cut and the story paced perfectly. . . . [Lovell] has injected the book with energy, spice, and humor." —*Books and Bao*

"Lovell does an admirable job condensing the original text . . . while capturing the essence of Chinese fantastical storytelling and parody. Readers . . . will get a kick out of this madcap fable." —*Publishers Weekly*

"This new edition should more than satisfy anyone interested in reading not only a highly praised classic of Chinese literature, but also one of the most influential fantasy narratives in the world." —*Booklist*

"A magnificent new translation of one of the funniest, most subversive satires ever written." —Junot Díaz

"A new translation of *Monkey King* is a cause for joy! Imaginative and mischievous, exhilarating and timeless, this sixteenth-century superhero saga is a delight to readers of all ages." —Yiyun Li

"Uproarious and action-filled, this highly readable new translation captures the most beloved of Chinese characters in all his impossible charm. Irrepressible and irresistible, Monkey speaks to us across the centuries, and here makes us laugh anew." —Gish Jen

"An exhilarating new translation of my favorite of all the classic Chinese novels—a great, wild epic that expands and fires one's imagination." —Ha Jin

"A fantastic retelling, easily on par with Neil Gaiman's *Norse Mythology*. *Monkey King* has never been so much fun; I friggin' loved it."
—Peter Clines, *New York Times* bestselling author of *Paradox Bound*

"What a delight that this exhilarating translation of the timeless classic will entertain generations to come."
—Marie Lu, #1 *New York Times* bestselling author of *Legend, The Young Elites,* and *Skyhunter*

PENGUIN CLASSICS  DELUXE EDITION

MONKEY KING

Wu Cheng'en (c. 1505–1580) was a Ming Dynasty poet about whom little is known, although he is believed to be the author of *Journey to the West*, which he published anonymously. He lived much of his life as a hermit.

Julia Lovell is the translator of *The Real Story of Ah-Q and Other Tales of China: The Complete Fiction of Lu Xun* and the author of *Maoism* and *The Opium War*. She is a professor of modern China at Birkbeck College, University of London, and writes about China for *The Guardian*, *Financial Times*, *The New York Times*, and *The Wall Street Journal*. She lives in Cambridge, England.

Gene Luen Yang is a MacArthur "genius," the National Ambassador for Young People's Literature, and the author of the half-million-copy *New York Times* bestselling graphic novel and National Book Award finalist *American Born Chinese*. He lives in San Jose, California.

WU CHENG'EN

Monkey King

JOURNEY TO THE WEST

Translated with an Introduction and Notes by
JULIA LOVELL

Foreword by
GENE LUEN YANG

PENGUIN BOOKS

PENGUIN BOOKS

An imprint of Penguin Random House LLC

penguinrandomhouse.com

Previously published in the United States of America by Penguin Books,
an imprint of Penguin Random House LLC, 2021
This edition published 2022

Map by Laura Hartman Maestro

ISBN 9780143136309 (paperback)

THE LIBRARY OF CONGRESS HAS CATALOGED THE HARDCOVER EDITION AS FOLLOWS:
Names: Wu, Cheng'en, approximately 1500–approximately 1582, author. |
Lovell, Julia, 1975– translator. | Yang, Gene Luen, writer of foreword.
Title: Monkey King / Wu Cheng'en; translated with an
introduction by Julia Lovell ; foreword by Gene Luen Yang.
Other titles: Xi you ji. English
Description: New York: Penguin Books, [2021] | Includes bibliographical references.
Identifiers: LCCN 2020048511 (print) | LCCN 2020048512 (ebook) |
ISBN 9780143107187 (hardcover) | ISBN 9781101600979 (ebook)
Classification: LCC PL2697 .H7513 2021 (print) |
LCC PL2697 (ebook) | DDC 895.13/46—dc23
LC record available at https://lccn.loc.gov/2020048511
LC ebook record available at https://lccn.loc.gov/2020048512

Printed in the United States of America
5th Printing

Set in Sabon LT Pro

Contents

MONKEY KING

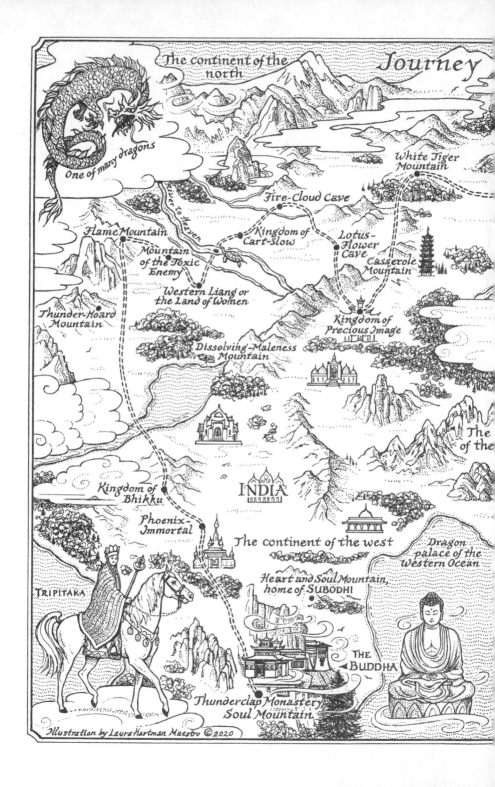

The continent of the north

Journey

One of many dragons

White Tiger Mountain

River to Heaven

Fire-Cloud Cave

Flame Mountain

Kingdom of Cart-Slow

Lotus-Flower Cave

Mountain of the Toxic Enemy

Casserole Mountain

Western Liang or the Land of Women

Thunder-Hoard Mountain

Kingdom of Precious Image

Dissolving-Maleness Mountain

The of the

Kingdom of Bhikku

INDIA

Phoenix-Immortal

The continent of the west

Dragon palace of the Western Ocean

TRIPITAKA

Heart and Soul Mountain, home of SUBODHI

THE BUDDHA

Thunderclap Monastery, Soul Mountain

Illustration by Laura Hartman Maestro © 2020

to the West

SANDY

Tushita Palace

West Gate of Heaven

Jade Emperor's Hall
of Divine Mists

PIGSY

South Gate
of Heaven

River of
Flowing Sand

Village of
Gao

CHINA

TIBET

Serpent's Coil
Mountain

Five-Phases
Mountain

CHANG'AN

MONKEY KING

continent
south

Water-Crystal Palace
(Dragon palace of the
Eastern Ocean)

The land of Aolai

Flower-
Fruit
Mountain

The continent of the
east

Mount Potālaka, home
of GUANYIN

Palace of Hell

(These lands are somewhat mythical.)

Foreword

I first heard about the monkey king from my mom.

When I was a kid, my mother used to tell me Chinese folktales before bedtime. My mother is an immigrant. She was born in mainland China and eventually made her way to the United States for graduate school.

She told me those stories so that I wouldn't forget the culture that she had left. Even though I hadn't ever experienced that culture firsthand, she wanted me to remember it.

Of all her stories, my favorites by far were about Sun Wukong, the monkey king. Here was a monkey who was so good at kung fu that his fighting skills leveled up to superpowers. He could call a cloud down from the sky and ride it like a surfboard. He could change his shape into anything he wanted. He could grow and shrink with the slightest thought. And he could clone himself by plucking hairs from his head and then breathing on them. How cool was that?

Eventually, though, I moved on to other kinds of heroes. One day when I was in the fifth grade, my mom took me to our local bookstore in San Jose, California. There I bought my first American comic book off a spinner rack in the corner of the store. Superman, Spider-Man, and Captain America soon replaced Monkey King in my heart.

I became obsessed with comic books. I loved them so much

that I went on to pursue a career in comics. Today I am a professional graphic novelist. My most well-known book is *American Born Chinese*, published in 2006. Monkey King is one of my protagonists, but the book isn't a direct adaptation of my mother's stories. Sun Wukong occupies too high a pedestal in my mind. I wouldn't dream of attempting a project like that.

Instead, I invited Monkey King into my story so that I could talk about the uneasiness of growing up Asian in America. The character I knew from my childhood expressed his emotions without reservation. I needed him to emote on my pages.

For research, I tracked down an English translation of *Journey to the West*, the centuries-old Chinese classic that first told the monkey king's story. Reading it was the first time I encountered him on my own, without the filter of my mother.

Turns out, my mother was pretty faithful. As I read it, I realized that American superheroes hadn't replaced Sun Wukong in my heart after all. Superman, Spider-Man, and Captain America were simply Western expressions of everything I loved about the monkey king.

Superman's epic battle with Doomsday echoes Monkey King's epic battle with Red Boy. Spider-Man's struggle against his own ego in the bowels of a pro-wrestling arena echoes Monkey King's struggle against his own ego in the bowels of a mountain of rock. Captain America's friendship with the Hulk, a thickset former foe, echoes Monkey King's friendship with Pigsy, a thickset former foe.

This story about a monkey with superpowers has lasted for centuries because it captures something essential about our experience. Sun Wukong might be a monkey, but his anger, anxiety, and arrogance are all too human. We all know what it feels like to be disrespected. We all know what it's like to lose control. We've all yearned for spiritual enlightenment. And we all know that the effort needed for enlightenment sometimes feels like a golden band that can squeeze the life out of us at any time, without warning.

The monkey king's story reverberates across continents and cultures. *Journey to the West* is the very definition of timeless.

And that's why new translations like the one you're about to read are so important. They brush off the dust so that we can rediscover what is lasting.

My mother now has Alzheimer's. She's forgotten all of the stories she used to tell me when I was young, but I remember. In many ways, I've built my entire career on those moments before bedtime. With every comic book and graphic novel that I create, I am trying to recapture the wonder I felt when my mother would regale me with tales of Sun Wukong, the monkey king. I hope reading this book fills you with that same wonder.

Because I want you to remember, too.

GENE LUEN YANG

Introduction

Monkey King, or *Journey to the West* (c. 1580), is one of the masterworks of Chinese fiction. It recounts a Tang-dynasty monk's quest for Buddhist scriptures in the seventh century, accompanied by an omnitalented kung fu monkey king called Sun Wukong, one of the most memorable reprobates in world literature; a rice-loving divine pig able to fly with its ears; and a depressive man-eating river-sand monster. It is a cornerstone text of Chinese fiction, and an index to early modern Chinese culture, thought, and history; its stature in East Asian literature may be compared with that of *The Canterbury Tales* or *Don Quixote* in European letters.

The novel commences with a spirited prologue—seven chapters long—recounting Monkey's many attempts to achieve immortal sagehood, in the course of which he acquires knowledge and weapons that will serve him well through the rest of the book: these include the ability to perform "cloud-somersaults" that carry him 108,000 miles in one leap, and a gold-hooped staff that can grow as tall as the sky and shrink to the size of a needle. He becomes a master of subterfuge by learning to transform himself into seventy-two different varieties of creature (though for some reason his disguises are occasionally unable to magic away his tail or scarlet buttocks). He studies freezing spells and how to turn each of the eighty-four thousand hairs on his body into other animals (including clones of himself) or objects. Yet time and again he is brought low by his irrepressible naughtiness. Finally, after taking up a bureaucratic sinecure in the Heavenly government of the Jade Emperor, he commits the unforgivable crime of gorging himself on the peaches, wine, and elixirs of immortality. Following an epic battle between Monkey and the armies of Heaven, the Buddha pins Monkey beneath the Five-Phases Mountain.

Five hundred years later, one of the founding emperors of the Tang dynasty, Taizong, dispatches a pious monk, Tripitaka, to India in search of precious Buddhist sutras that will bring virtue and enlightenment to the Chinese empire. On Tripitaka's way through China, the Buddha releases Monkey from beneath his mountain so that he can atone for his sins by protecting the monk on his journey. Joined by two more disciples, the pig spirit (Pigsy) and the sand monster (Sandy), both fallen immortals also, they advance westward through the wildernesses of the Silk Road: the territories now known as Xinjiang, Tibet, Nepal, and finally India. In the course of their travels, they encounter murderous Buddhists, perfidious Taoists, expanses of rotten persimmons, and monsters of all shapes and sizes (femmes fatales, rhinoceroses, iguanas, scorpions). They are serially captured, tied up, lacquered, sautéed, steamed, and impregnated, and come very close to being diced, boiled, liquidized, pickled, cured, and seduced by various fiends. Eventually, after eighty-one such calamities, the pilgrims reach Thunderclap Monastery, the stronghold of the Buddha in India, and are rewarded with armfuls of sutras and posts in the Buddha's government of immortals.

Most of the "official" version of the novel as it circulates today—one hundred chapters long—was published in 1592 by an entrepreneurial press in Nanjing, east China. But it sprang from a much older set of stories and legends about Tripitaka (c. 602–664), an indisputably remarkable historical individual.[1] After taking holy orders at the age of twelve, he acquired a Chinese

Buddhist education, learned Sanskrit, and grew impatient with the errors and omissions of the translations of Buddhist scriptures that had so far reached China. In the late 620s he resolved to travel to India himself and bring back to China original texts. Without permission from the emperor, he set off across the deserts and freezing mountains of China's far northwest, surviving bandits, pirates, demanding monarchs, and an assassin-guide. After some fifteen years of traveling around India, studying religion and logic, philosophy and metaphysics, he returned to China loaded with books, statues, and manuscripts.

Even before Tripitaka's death, his life was shrouded in myth; in subsequent centuries it was adapted and readapted by oral storytellers in increasingly outlandish ways. Although Tripitaka himself left behind a rather matter-of-fact account of his travels—preoccupied more with recording mango and millet cultivars, soil quality, and local textiles than with fantastical trials and monstrous obstacles—the odyssey over the centuries blurred into mythology, until almost nothing of Tripitaka's own record of the journey was left in the fictions and dramas told about it.[2] By the retellings of the thirteenth century, Tripitaka had acquired a Monkey disciple, a delinquent-turned-Buddhist bodyguard; across the next three hundred years, this character would come to dominate the narrative. In prose and drama of the fourteenth and fifteenth centuries, the stories told about Tripitaka and his charismatic Monkey disciple came to resemble a fictional Rolodex, from which writers and entertainers across East Asia could take and retell their favorite episodes. (One of the novel's episodes—set in the kingdom of Cart-Slow—is recounted in detail by a fourteenth-century Korean primer of colloquial Chinese.) The precise origins of many of these stories are very hard to pinpoint. No one particularly agrees on the inspiration for Monkey: one interpretation traces him back to a legendarily lecherous White Ape; another to a simian water demon whose troublemaking led him to be pinned beneath Turtle

Mountain; another again to Hanuman, the sage companion of Rama in Hindu mythology.[3]

It has proven similarly difficult to confidently identify the author or editor who selected and organized these stories into the one-hundred-chapter version that quickly became one of the "master novels" (*qishu*) of late imperial Chinese fiction. Despite the obvious popularity of the text, neither the publisher, editor, or prefacer of the 1592 edition knew—or were willing to admit they knew—who had produced the book. For in the sixteenth century (and arguably until the twentieth century), fiction was a disreputable pastime; few respectable literati would want to be publicly associated with it. The literal translation of the Chinese term for fiction—*xiaoshuo* (lesser discourses)—captures this sense of cultural disdain. The best evidence we have points to authorship by one Wu Cheng'en (c. 1506–1582), the son of a silk-shop clerk from east China. Like many of his educated peers, Wu repeatedly failed to pass the civil service exams—the fiercely competitive entrée to a government post and conventional social status. For much of his life, he scraped a living writing elaborate, poetic birthday greetings. When the demands of this literary odd-jobbing permitted, he wrote ghost stories, humorous fiction, and poetry.[4] After centuries of posthumous obscurity, he shot to fame when Hu Shi—a celebrity intellectual of the early twentieth century—wrote an essay identifying Wu as author of the hitherto anonymous novel. Although there was no more obvious candidate, Hu Shi's proof was little more than circumstantial. A local guide from Wu's native place, Huai'an, listed a *Journey to the West* among Wu's oeuvre (though we cannot be sure whether this is the novel or a different piece of travel writing) and described him as "a man of exceptional intelligence and many talents . . . able to compose poetry and prose at a stroke of the brush; he also excelled in humor and satire." The novel happens to contain many turns of phrase particular to the Huai'an dialect. By Wu's own admission, he was addicted to entertaining tales of the supernatural. The mystery of *Journey to the West*'s authorship will probably never be resolved. The best we can say is that sometime in the sixteenth century, a talented writer with a passion for literary impishness and descriptive poetry knitted existing characters and stories together with episodes of his own creation into a single novel.

Whoever wrote or compiled it, the book reflects the dynamic literary milieu of sixteenth-century China. The Ming dynasty (1368–1644) had begun in high tyrannical style; the dynasty's founder and his son were ruthless, centralizing dictators who unleashed large-scale purges on the court and bureaucracy. As the dynasty proceeded, the penalties for displeasing later emperors remained terrifying. The throne's secret police tortured those suspected of anti-imperial insurrection; court beatings were dealt out to officials found wanting. Between 1642 and 1644 alone, three high-ranking ministers were driven to suicide by imperial will. But from the middle of the sixteenth to the seventeenth centuries, the dynasty's violent autocracy coexisted with political and institutional paralysis—the Wanli emperor (r. 1573–1620) avoided court audiences for thirty years. Despite the terrors of the Ming political system, the actual limits to central control left room for an extraordinary cultural florescence. While China's population expanded threefold, education and literacy surged amid a boom in publishing. During the sixteenth century, printed books for the first time exceeded manuscript copies; Ming China housed, at any one time, more books than the rest of the world put together. The growth in population fueled unprecedented migrations and a new, free-flowing traffic of information and ideas. This enhanced "mobility of economic and social opportunity translated into a corresponding mobility of consciousness," argues Andrew Plaks, a historian of the Ming novel.[5] Popular literary forms flourished, as vernacular fiction and drama—both, in the traditional hierarchies of Chinese literature, generically subservient to poetry—began claiming the earthier realms of everyday human experience as acceptable raw material for art. In addition to *Journey to the West*, another three of the six "master novels" of imperial China were completed during the Ming dynasty: *The Romance of the Three Kingdoms*, a recounting of the civil war into which China plunged after the fall of the Han dynasty in AD 220; *The Water Margin*, a picaresque tale of twelfth-century outlaws; and *The Plum in the Golden Vase*, a sexually explicit chronicle of intrigue in a wealthy Ming household. Although the vernacular of *Journey to the West* is a long way from contemporary spoken Chinese, it is relaxed, expansive, and lively when compared with laconic, highly compressed, allusive classical Chinese. A 1620 preface to a collection of vernacular stories communicated the emotional immediacy of the medium:

> Just ask the storytellers to demonstrate in public their art of description: they will gladden you, astonish you, move you to sad tears, rouse you to song and dance; they will prompt you to draw a sword, bow in reverence, cut off a head, or donate money. The fainthearted will be made brave, the debauched chaste, the unkind compassionate, the obtuse ashamed. A man may well intone the Classic of Filial Piety and the Analects of Confucius every day, yet he will not be moved so quickly nor so profoundly as by these storytellers. Can anything less accessible achieve such effect?[6]

In philosophy, Neo-Confucian scholars such as Wang Yangming grew preoccupied with the workings of the individual mind, arguing that all—no matter how humble their background—are born with a capacity for innate knowledge; even uneducated commoners could attain enlightenment. The implicit egalitarianism of this argument opened the door to the kind of down-to-earth characterizations of the vernacular novels that flourished through the late Ming dynasty. Populated by gods, demons, emperors, bureaucrats, monks, animals, woodsmen, bandits, and farmers, *Journey to the West* presents an epic, multivocal account of imperial China.[7] The cultivation of the self by highly imperfect beings is a central theme of the novel, on which more will be said below.

Expressive of the intellectual fluidity of its time, the novel has generated diverse readings: Buddhist, Confucian, Taoist, comic, satirical. It tells us something, too, about popular Ming geographies of China's western frontier, belying the old cliché of imperial China as self-sufficient, isolationist, xenophobic. *Journey to the West*—an odyssey out of China, to attain the wisdom of Indian Buddhist civilization—tells a different story: one of Chinese fascination with foreign exotica. The pilgrims regularly express wonderment at the glittering city-states they encounter on their way west. Very broadly, interpretations of the novel divide between two camps: critics who see *Journey to the West* as a religious allegory for the human condition and those who see it as good-humored supernatural slapstick. The one clear conclusion that can be drawn from the many exegeses of the past five hundred years is that the book is a gloriously open text: one that has lent itself to multiple explanations and constant adaptation.

Evidence for the second view—of *Journey to the West* as fantastical farce—is abundant. (It cannot be entirely coincidental that the title's word for "journey"—*you*—can also mean "play."[8]) Monkey, the hero of the piece, sets the tone, as the embodiment of mischief in motion: always on the move, always transforming, always with an ingenious plan to get himself and his fellow pilgrims out of their latest jam. (In Chinese literary culture, religion, and folklore, the monkey is often the playful or cunning shadow of human character, though it is also capable of great devotion and piety.[9]) Despite the redoubtable challenges that Monkey faces throughout the novel's one hundred chapters—crossing two oceans on an uncertain quest for enlightenment, battling dozens of monsters and immortals, keeping a peevish and constantly hungry

Tripitaka safe and happy—he remains permanently bent on fun, ready to taunt Taoist masters, dragon kings, sundry human rulers, the sovereigns of Heaven and Hell, the celestial court, the Buddhist pantheon. Whenever things look bad, a joke restores Monkey—physically and mentally. Through the book's prologue, recounting his especially reckless early career, Monkey has the comic artlessness of an impulsive child. Without a thought for the consequences, he guzzles Heaven's immortal peaches, wines, and elixirs, thereby wrecking the festivity of the millennium and triggering a Heavenly declaration of war. "Bad! Very bad!" is the closest he gets to introspection afterward. "Run away! Run away!" There is an absurd ingenuousness to Pigsy, too. Bombastically boastful, focused on instant personal gratification, ready to abandon the pilgrimage at any setback, he is susceptible to any demon bearing a bowl of fried noodles. He also possesses an extraordinary capacity for power-napping—most impressively during his second fight with the Yellow-Robe demon, where he abandons Sandy, dives into a clump of grass, and immediately falls asleep for the rest of the day, conveniently missing the rest of a disastrous defeat. Monkey and Pigsy are not the only characters with an appetite for play: the monsters that the pilgrims encounter also delight in games and tricks (albeit ones with a deadly outcome: the eating of Tripitaka).

The novel zings with physical and verbal humor. Consider Monkey's unstoppable sassiness in the face of exceptional perils and torments, exemplified by this exchange with an immortal messenger disguised as a woodcutter, bringing news of some appalling mountain trolls:

> "Deep in this mountain lies the Lotus-Flower Cave, home to two monsters determined to have you for dinner."
>
> "What luck!" responded Monkey cheerfully. "Do you know how they plan to eat us?"

"I beg your pardon?" asked the nonplussed woodcutter.

"I see you are inexperienced in such matters. If they start with the head, I'll be dead in one bite—all good. After that, they can fry, sauté, braise, or boil me—it wouldn't matter one bit. But if they start with my feet, well, I might still be alive even when they get to my pelvis. And that would be—literally—a pain."

"You're overthinking this. The monsters will catch you, pop you in a steamer, then eat you whole."

"Better still! Just a touch of stuffiness, then it'll all be over."

"Beware, flippant monkey! Beware! These monsters have five treasures of incomparable magic power. Beware!"

The book's quick-fire exchanges drive the characterization—especially the rivalry between Monkey and Pigsy. Even when the two of them are in mortal danger (for example, imprisoned in Golden Horn and Silver Horn's cave, being prepared for the steamer) they jeopardize the escape plan by snarking at each other.

The book is often an action-packed situation comedy. In a recurring joke (resembling the miscalculations of supervillains in James Bond films), the pilgrims' various demonic captors time and again fail to eat Tripitaka before Monkey can rescue him because they are too busy debating whether to steam, salt, or pickle him, or because—like good Confucians—they are determined to invite their esteemed parents to share the feast. Monkey's most formidable adversary—King Bull Demon—breaks off mid-battle to don a duck-green silk dinner jacket and head to a short-notice banquet, thereby enabling Monkey to finagle a magic fan off Bull Demon's wife. And, of course, Monkey's shape-shifting facilitates regular buffoonery, especially when he impersonates consorts in order to prank their monstrous spouses.

The book projects a vibrant vision of the supernatural: in the virtuosity of Monkey's transformations (especially his ability to smuggle himself into his enemies' stomachs and perform kung fu on their vital organs), in the spectacular special effects of immortal battles, in the movement among human, animal, and spirit worlds. This is at the same time a savage, vengeful universe, in which beautiful women are disguised fox- or scorpion-spirits and can be destroyed with impunity. The novel is also full—and we return to its playfulness here—of the nonsensically arbitrary rules of fantasy. Why can Monkey disguise himself as an entirely convincing piece of cloth or a seven-inch caterpillar but not lose his tail or red bottom when he becomes a goblin? Why does the swallowing calabash not care whether the respondent answers to his real name or not? In its obsession with immortals' and demons' technical capabilities—including Monkey's ability to manufacture armies of simulacra by chewing his armpit hair to a pulp— the novel is a first cousin to the weaponized plots of Hollywood superhero movies, even though these two narrative traditions are separated by hundreds of years and thousands of miles.

Journey to the West offers a tongue-in-cheek ethnography of sixteenth-century Chinese imaginations of the spirit realm. The immortals and monsters that fill the novel are reassuringly like us. Their bureaucracies and governments replicate those of the human world: they carefully submit petitions to the correct supernatural department; a person cannot expire until the underworld civil servant on duty has checked the mortality schedules in the ledgers of life and death. Like officials all over the world, the Buddha's subordinates guarding Thunderclap Monastery demand a bribe of Tripitaka and his disciples before giving them access to the scriptures. All problems, all situations—from cosmic injustices, via baleful monkey-demons, down to the precise amount (in inches and drops) of rainfall due—can be dealt with through filing a complaint with the Heavenly government or by issuing an imperial edict. This idea that the afterlife will closely resemble life on earth still resonates today, in contemporary burial practices.

In the premodern past, well-to-do Chinese people would want to be buried with objects—real or simulacra—from the human world that they assumed would be useful in the afterlife: money, furniture, clothes, jewelry. And today, funerary shops sell paper copies of Prada handbags, BMW keys, and credit cards. Every nonhuman realm that appears in the book—celestial, infernal, monstrous, fishy—is organized along mortal hierarchies, while ministers in the human world pull strings in Hell. And demons and deities grapple with the same domestic and interpersonal complexities as ordinary people: Monkey runs into serious problems when he antagonizes the whole fiendish family—mother, father, uncle—of the fire-breathing Red Boy; the otherwise invincible King Bull Demon is run ragged by dividing his attention between his first wife and his new concubine.

The comedy can take on a harder, more political edge. Sixteenth-century China was subject to egregious tyranny under a series of emperors of questionable competence, and it is easy to read criticism of misrule into many of the novel's portrayals of power.[10] No one in authority comes off well. The Jade Emperor is a capricious dictator prone to issuing draconian punishments; Buddha and Guanyin—supposedly renowned for their compassion—help trick Monkey into wearing the headache hoop and regularly dispatch immortals to harass the pilgrims. The book genuflects to the greatness of the Tang empire but reminds readers that its "son of Heaven"—the emperor Taizong—killed two of his brothers. Just about every king the pilgrims encounter is gullible, dim-witted, cowardly, and brutal. Virtue and honesty reside far more often in ordinary people: the water-seller who accumulates wealth in the underworld through his good works; the wronged Li Cuilian who isn't afraid to tell the emperor his taste in interior decor is terrible. The narrative's mix of registers—marketplace repartee, pompous officialese, lyric poetry, folksy proverbializing—captures a complex weave of Chinese society, politics, and religious belief.

The book's undermining of hierarchies and external appearances is replicated on the pilgrimage. It is the handsome, educated
Tripitaka who is the weakest link, trembling and weeping at the
least trial, failing to recognize demons, and punishing Monkey
for his hypervigilance. The three disciples—all of them disgraced,
hideous immortals—are, at least relative to their master, reposi-
tories of resourcefulness. "We're ugly but useful," as they often
say to the terrified humans they encounter. (Demons, by contrast,
often disguise themselves as beautiful women, handsome men,
and dignified priests.) To the end, the pilgrims are not saints but
rather plausibly fractious individuals. Perhaps reflective of the
growing mobility of sixteenth-century society, the book is full of
boundary-crossing and form-changing: the pilgrims travel out of
China; immortals become monsters and then immortals again;
Taoist priests are demons; monkeys are enlightened; the emperor's
own envoy rubs a mud mask mixed with pig's urine onto his face
to transform into a simian disciple. Those chosen to accompany
Tripitaka on his quest are not the great and the good but rather
humble, benighted creatures, all of whom attain immortality at
the book's conclusion.

The satire plays with gender roles, too. In the Land of Women,
the disciples are forced to see the world through female eyes and
submit at least temporarily to a female-dominated society—
implicitly urging the Ming-era reader to contemplate the discom-
forts of being a woman in male-dominated China. Pigsy and
Tripitaka are within an hour reduced to moaning wrecks by only
the very beginnings of childbirth. Traveling through the country,
the male pilgrims have a brief taste of everyday life in a public
sphere run by the opposite sex: being ogled by passersby and
forced into marriage by those more powerful than they are.

Since its publication, however, literary interpreters of *Journey
to the West* have argued that the book is far more than fantastical
comedy, that its significance is overwhelmingly spiritual.[11] It is, of

course, a book about a Buddhist pilgrimage, in search of scriptures of enlightenment, and is littered with exhortations to Buddhist virtue. References to Taoism are also ubiquitous: Monkey's fabulous talents come from Taoist techniques of self-cultivation, and the celestial government is ruled by the Taoist Jade Emperor and his pantheon. Confucianism is less institutionalized in the book, but no less present in the way that its values saturate social relationships. The humans and monsters encountered throughout the book are staunchly Confucian in their devotion to rulers and families. Tripitaka is arguably more Confucian than Buddhist, in regularly declaiming his loyalty to the Tang emperor. From Boqin the hunter to King Golden Horn the mountain demon, the novel is full of filial piety: to fathers, mothers, brothers. Its mix of references to the three teachings expresses the syncretism of late imperial religious belief. "The most commonly accepted opinion of those who are at all educated among the Chinese," observed the Italian priest Matteo Ricci, who lived in China between 1582 and 1610, "is that these three laws or cults really coalesce into one creed."[12]

Beneath these surface references, the novel has also been read as an allegory expressing the metaphysical concerns of the late Ming dynasty—especially the preoccupation of Neo-Confucian and Chan Buddhist thinkers with the workings of the mind. (This may have been done to make its disreputable aspects more palatable to educated readers—just as medieval Europe created an allegorical framework to provide moralized readings of works like Ovid's *Metamorphosis*.) The pilgrims, according to this reading, each represent different facets of human nature: Pigsy, sensuality; Sandy, morose phlegmatism; Tripitaka, timorousness; and Monkey, the mutability of human genius in need of discipline (namely, the trials of the pilgrimage) to realize its potential for good. The earliest Buddhist sutras translated into Chinese analogized the human mind as a monkey: restless, erratic, volatile. By the end of the first millennium AD, the phrase "monkey of the mind" had become a stock literary allusion. The author of the preface to the 1592 edition thus interpreted Monkey as being "the spirit of the heart and mind. . . . Demons are born of the mind, and they are also subdued by the mind. That is the reason for subduing the mind in order to subdue demons. . . . This indeed is how the Way is accomplished and plainly allegorized in this book."[13] A second preface, published in the late 1600s, agreed:

> Although the book is exceedingly strange . . . its general importance may be stated in one sentence: it is only about the retrieving or releasing of one's mind. For whether we act like demons or become Buddha is all dependent on this mind. Released, this mind becomes the erroneous mind. . . . An example of this is when the Mind Monkey calls himself a king, a sage, to disturb greatly the Celestial Palace. When this mind is retrieved, it will be the true mind, and once the true mind appears, it can extinguish demons. . . . There is no place that its movement and transformation cannot reach.[14]

The Mind Monkey's chaotic pursuit of self-gratification leads to his initial downfall: imprisonment for five hundred years. "With discipline," the prologue concludes, "he might become a force for supernatural good; without it, he was pure animal—a wrecking ball in Heaven." One subsequent theme of the novel is how to harness Monkey's extraordinary talents to maximize benefit to those he encounters—hence Guanyin's placing of the hoop on Monkey's head to control the Mind Monkey, and Monkey's destruction in chapter 14 of the six robbers named after human senses and temptations. Collecting the sutras is not the ultimate purpose of the pilgrimage. Monkey could fly to India and return in the blink of an eye, but this would not teach him self-restraint. The fundamental objective of the quest is to train and steady

Monkey's mind through the vicissitudes of the journey. The bizarrely grisly scene in which Monkey pulls out a mass of hearts from his chest in front of the King of Bhikku plays with the idea of the changeable, multivalent mind—for Chinese uses the same word for heart and mind (*xin*). And Monkey is indeed tempered as he progresses west. By the final chapters, he is noticeably more serene, benevolent, and protective of life, rescuing 1,111 little boys in Bhikku and saving the inhabitants of Phoenix-Immortal from starvation.

Certain peculiarities of the quest's geography support the supposition that the journey is primarily a mental or spiritual, and not a physical, one (an aspect once more shared with European medieval romances). The landscape through which the pilgrims travel never changes much; the same religions are encountered and the Chinese celestial hierarchy continues to hold sway; everyone seems to speak Chinese—or, at least, there is never any mention of the pilgrims struggling with foreign languages. But the book is too open to support a single allegorical interpretation. Although the travelers' quest is ostensibly spiritual, the book is profoundly irreverent toward religious and moral authority. Hypocritical Neo-Confucians, covetous Buddhists, and libidinous Taoists—all are mocked; at one point, Monkey even urinates on the hand of the Buddha. The satire and indignity to which the book subjects representatives of all three religions indicates the novel is not interested in cheerleading for any of the faiths. The baseness of most of the rulers encountered makes a mockery of Confucian loyalty to the sovereign. The Taoists of the kingdom of Cart-Slow are the butt of the novel's standout piece of physical comedy, when Monkey, Pigsy, and Sandy trick them into drinking urine, while shoving effigies of Taoist immortals into a nearby toilet (or "Bureau of Rice Reincarnation," as Monkey renames it). At no point in the story is Tripitaka a particularly fine advertisement for Buddhist piety. After almost ninety chapters of trembling and sobbing, he remains grumbling and fearful even in the Western Heaven—Monkey has to shove him into the bottomless boat so that he can be ferried to the other shore of enlightenment. And nirvana has its problems, too. The Buddha and his representatives turn out to be ambivalent characters, demanding bribes before handing over the scriptures for which the pilgrims suffered so much and manufacturing another challenge for arbitrary arithmetical reasons. Read within the context of a highly didactic Chinese literary tradition, *Journey to the West* stands out for its spiritual and political subversion, for its imperfectly eccentric characters, and for its refusal to fit any single interpretation.

This book about shape-shifting has itself shape-shifted. Almost as soon as it had been arranged into a literary novel, it slipped back into the cycle of literary transmigration from which it had come. Over the past five centuries, dozens of adaptations have appeared, across print, theater, film, music, dance, and fine arts. Sequels, extensions, and rewritings began in the first half of the seventeenth century. The earliest—*The Continuation of the Journey to the West*—seems to have objected to earlier versions' indulgence toward Monkey's misbehavior and dilution of the pilgrimage's religious message. It obliges Monkey and his fellow disciples to return to China on foot, judging that they were still unworthy of canonization at the end of their outward journey. The Buddha further confiscates all of the pilgrims' weapons, forcing them to overcome all incidental trials through moral, not physical, strength. Eventually, Monkey discovers that reciting spells in Sanskrit is more effective than bashing demons. In another sequel—from the 1640s, probably—Sun Wukong is swallowed whole by a mackerel named Desire; the novel satirizes China's self-seeking educated classes for ignoring the cataclysmic state of the country (which at the time of writing was teetering on the edge of dynastic collapse and regime change). The year 1909 also spawned three sequels. In one—*The New Journey to the West*—the Buddha sends the pilgrims back to China thirteen hundred years after their journey westward, to find out about the country's new religion: westernization. Beginning their investigation in Shanghai, the pilgrims experience various modern mishaps: Monkey misidentifies a bicycle as the fire wheel on which his old antagonist Nezha used to travel and mistakes a bus and an official for monsters. Tripitaka and Pigsy become opium-den addicts, while the secret police try to recruit Monkey into their ranks. The novel uses the time travelers' disorientation to evoke the whirlwind of transformations that China—on the threshold of revolution—was undergoing.[15]

Adaptations and rereadings of *Journey to the West* have proliferated in periods of exceptional political and social turmoil (in the two examples above, the fall of the Ming and Qing dynasties respectively). The anarchic mischief of the story and characters, it seems, has resonated particularly in times of turbulence. Logically enough, the past hundred years, a century of protracted revolutionary unrest for China, have seen regular reworkings of the novel.

In the 1910s and 1920s, the intellectual radicals of China's New Culture Movement sought to replace classical Chinese literature with vernacular writing that—they believed—would forge a national consciousness and enable China to stand up to Japan and powerful nation-states in the West. Although they themselves took to writing in a westernized prose barely comprehensible to many ordinary readers, they also celebrated as inspirational archetypes the classics of pre-twentieth-century fiction (which until that point had languished at the bottom of the hierarchy of literary genres, far below poetry and essays). Eager to break with what they viewed as an elitist tradition, they embraced *Journey to the West* as a revolutionary precedent for the vernacular fiction they yearned to popularize. For centuries, argued the cultural reformer Hu Shi,

> The novel has been destroyed by Taoists, Buddhists, and Confucian scholars. Taoists claim it as a manual of alchemy. Buddhists say it's Chan philosophy. Scholars say it's a Neo-Confucian guide to rectifying the mind and the will. All these readings are inimical to the obviously absurd, playful spirit of *Journey to the West* . . . which has its origins in folk myths and legends. . . . *Journey to the West* is simply a delightful, absurd piece of fiction—there's no subtle underpinning to its message.[16]

During the Mao era (1949–1976), when anything old or foreign could be denounced as counterrevolutionary treason, Monkey and *Journey to the West* were strikingly exempted from attack. In 1954, one of the top literary publishers of the People's Republic of China (PRC) produced an authoritative, annotated edition of the one-hundred-chapter novel (the edition still stands, and is the basis of this translation). Drama and film adaptations, and picture-book abridgments mushroomed. Skirting over the importance of religion (the "opium of the people," according to Marx) in the novel, literary critics toiled to fit the book into a Communist framework of revolution: the vindictive Jade Emperor represented the oppressive ruling class; the demons and monsters were his lackeys—landlords and local bullies.[17] Monkey—no longer a playful picaro—was reinvented as a revolutionary who "dares to act and dares to do things."[18] He could be easily imagined as a legendary stand-in for Mao: just as Monkey sprang invincible from his roasting in Laozi's brazier, Mao was idealized as strengthened by decades of political and military vicissitudes. In the early 1950s, while other myths and legends from the "old society" were denounced as superstitious dross, Monkey's rebellion against Heaven was condoned as "healthy and good," for he represented "the infinite power" of the peasant class defying their rulers.[19]

In 1955, Zhou Enlai—premier of the PRC and one of Mao's savviest culture-shapers—commissioned a stage adaptation of the story that focused on the prologue describing Monkey's epic insurrection: *Great Havoc in Heaven*. But Zhou wanted refinements to the story: more emphasis on Monkey's "resistance to oppression," on the evil schemes of Heaven, and on the "working-class wisdom" that Monkey deploys to defeat the celestial ruling class. This new version recast Monkey's rebellion not as a hedonistic quest for self-gratification but rather as a righteous defiance of ruling-class privilege; the analogy between Monkey's and Mao's struggles was further underlined by importing into the script military terminology from the civil war that the Communists had just fought and won against their rivals the Nationalists. The play excised Monkey's defeat by the Buddha, ending instead with Monkey expelling the Jade Emperor from his palace and toasting his victory with his simian comrades.[20] In the early 1960s, the prologue story was also adapted into a two-hour hit animation (but was banned during the Cultural Revolution, due to a perceived resemblance between the Jade Emperor and Mao—both had a mole on their chin).[21]

To Mao—an anarchist in his early twenties—the havoc-wreaking instincts of Sun Wukong were a lifelong inspiration, and by the early 1960s he publicly identified himself with Monkey. Furious with comrades who had rewound his disastrous plans for radical political, economic, and cultural transformation of China, Mao pointedly invoked the pilgrims' encounter with the White-Bone Demon in a 1961 poem:

> Wind and thunder rise up,
> An evil spirit is born from a pile of white bones.

The monk is one of the ignorant masses, but can still be taught,
While the evil spirit generates calamity.
The Golden Monkey swings his enormous cudgel
And cleanses the universe of a myriad miles of dust.
Today, with the return of evil miasmal mists
We acclaim Sun Wukong, the great sage.[22]

The demon—who disguises herself in turn as a beautiful girl and her kindly old parents—stood for conservative traitors in China and the Soviet Union pretending to be faithful revolutionaries; the visionary Monkey—determined to smash the demon—for Mao; the other pilgrims for ordinary people, insufficiently clear-sighted to spot the counterrevolutionary schemes around them.[23]

While plotting the Cultural Revolution—an attack on domestic critics of his radical policies—in the months running up to spring 1966, Mao turned once again to Monkey to incite Red Guard attacks on the party establishment: "We need more Sun Wukongs . . . to disrupt the heavenly palace."[24] Mao's bowdlerized version of *Journey to the West* as a parable of violent insurrection proved to be an effective tool of education. The young generation brought up in the early years of the PRC—exposed to the story and characters in politicized adaptations of the original—lapped up the message of heroic insurrection. Coming of age in 1966, in time for the start of the Cultural Revolution, many self-identified as "monkey kings" in response to Mao's call to rebel against the party. One of the founding Red Guards, Luo Xiaohai, openly admitted his fascination with Monkey: "I loved his defiant attitude toward pompous authority figures . . . the quintessential act of rebellion." When Mao pronounced that "if the central leadership of the Party were revisionist" he would "call on monkey kings from the grassroots to make havoc against heaven," teenagers like Luo pledged to be "monkey kings," to "turn the old world upside down, smash it to pieces, create chaos, and make a huge mess. The messier, the better." These young people would learn for themselves the punitive consequences of unchecked power, when Mao sent in the army to suppress the civil war that he unleashed during the Cultural Revolution.[25] It can be no coincidence that during the Cultural Revolution—a time when most books, even Marx's, were proscribed—picture books of the White-Bone Demon story were constantly in print. Certain sensitive details were excised, though—such as the pilgrims begging, since Buddhist monks were denounced under Mao as "social parasites."[26]

At yet another moment of rupture—China's emergence in the 1990s from socialist planning after the trauma of the 1989 crackdown on pro-democracy protests—a fresh reinvention of *Journey to the West* mesmerized Chinese youth. *A Chinese Odyssey*, a Hong Kong production released in 1995, became a cult classic—and generated dozens of fan fictions—among mainland college students. The adaptation seized imaginations for its portrayal of Sun Wukong not as an indomitable revolutionary this time, but rather as a chaotic gangster tormented by frustrations and anxieties. Liberally supplemented by slapstick, often scurrilous humor, the presentation of Monkey as a helpless drifter chimed with the disillusioned, aimless irreverence being popularized in mainland films and fiction of the late 1980s and 1990s. A 2008 internet review spelled out the ways in which young people trying to make their way in a nominally Communist party-state identified with the hapless Monkey of *A Chinese Odyssey*: "A young guy who is talented but does not respect rules [Monkey] loathes the big and important cause that he is assigned [the pilgrimage to India]. He especially cannot bear the nagging preaching of his teacher [Tripitaka], but the rules and regulations in the world [Guanyin] won't let him go." As an internet comment on a 2015 movie remake puts it: "Every Chinese person will fall in love with Monkey. Each generation has its own Monkey."[27]

Journey to the West even has an unexpected purchase on the childhood memories of Britons and Australians growing up in the 1980s, when a Japanese TV version—translated as *Monkey*—became a cult hit. (Japanese culture has also generated many adaptations of *Journey to the West*—*Saiyuki* in Japanese—including the long-running franchise *Dragon Ball*.) The production values were poor and the dubbing worse, but the playful strangeness and abundant kung fu seized youthful imaginations—at a time when, in the UK at least, general awareness of Chinese culture was minimal. In the United States, the novel's plot and characters have spawned operas, comics, and a boxing style. Gene Luen Yang's prizewinning 2006 graphic novel *American Born Chinese* used an introspective rewriting of Monkey's story to reflect on the transformations and distortions that Chinese Americans undergo to conform with white US culture.[28] It may even be that the revelatory moment of *Kung Fu Panda*—the titular panda's discovery that the canonical "dragon scroll" is blank—is lifted from the Buddha's gifting of wordless scrolls in the penultimate chapter of *Journey to the West*.

JULIA LOVELL

NOTES

1. See Glen Dudbridge, *The Hsi-yu Chi: A Study of Antecedents to the Sixteenth-Century Chinese Novel* (Cambridge: Cambridge University Press, 1970) and the introduction to Anthony Yu's first volume of his translation of the novel, *The Journey to the West* (Chicago: University of Chicago Press, 2012), for an excellent survey of the novel's antecedents.
2. For Tripitaka's account, see *The Great Tang Dynasty Record of the Western Regions* translated by Li Rongxi (Berkeley: Numata Center for Buddhist Translation and Research, 1996).

3. See, for example, Dudbridge, *The Hsi-yu Chi,* and Lu Xun, *A Brief History of Chinese Fiction* translated by Yang Hsien-yi and Gladys Yang (Beijing: Foreign Languages Press, 1964).

4. Liu Ts'un-yan, "Wu Ch'eng-en," in *Dictionary of Ming Biography 1368–1644,* L. Carrington Goodrich and Chaoying Fang, eds. (New York: Columbia University Press, 1976), 1479–1483.

5. Andrew Plaks, *The Four Masterworks of the Ming Novel: Ssu ta ch'i-shu* (Princeton: Princeton University Press, 1987), 16–17.

6. Cited in Yan Liang, "When High Culture Embraces the Low: Reading Xiyou ji as Popular Fiction in Chinese Society," unpublished PhD diss. (University of California Santa Barbara, 2008), 131.

7. For its heteroglossia, *Journey to the West* bears logical comparison with Rabelais's near-contemporary work *Gargantua and Pantagruel,* the gleeful carnivalesque of which was explored by the Russian critic Mikhail Bakhtin in his 1965 study *Rabelais and His World* (translated by Hélène Iswolsky, Cambridge, Mass.: MIT Press, 1968).

8. For an excellent development of this idea, see Chiung-yun Evelyn Liu, "Scriptures and Bodies: Jest and Meaning in the Religious Journeys in Xiyou ji," unpublished PhD diss. (Harvard University, 2008).

9. My thanks to Roel Sterckx for these insights. See also Roel Sterckx, Martina Siebert, and Dagmar Schäfer, eds., *Animals Through Chinese History* (Cambridge: Cambridge University Press, 2019).

10. For more on this reading, see Vincent Yang, "A Masterpiece of Dissemblance," *Monumenta Serica* 60.1: 151–194.

11. For an example of this reading, see Plaks, *The Four Masterworks.*

12. Timothy Brook, "Rethinking Syncretism: The Unity of the Three Teachings and Their Joint Worship in Late-Imperial China," *Journey of Chinese Religions* 12, no. 1: 13.

13. Cited in Yu, "Introduction," *Journey to the West* Volume 1, 27. Translation slightly modified.

14. Cited in Yu, "Introduction," 28–29. Translation slightly modified.

15. Qiancheng Li, "Transformations of Monkey: Xiyou ji Sequels and the Inward Turn" in *Snake's Legs: Sequels, Continuations, Rewritings, and Derivations and Chinese Fiction,* Martin W. Huang, ed. (Honolulu: University of Hawai'i Press, 2004) 46–74.

16. Hu Shi, *Zhongguo zhanghui xiaoshuo kaozheng* (Shanghai: Shanghai shudian), 366–367.

17. See anon., ed., *Xiyouji yanjiu lunwenji* (Beijing: Zuojia chubanshe, 1957).

18. Rudolf G. Wagner, *The Contemporary Chinese Historical Drama: Four Studies* (Berkeley: University of California Press, 1990), 145.

19. Hongmei Sun, *Transforming Monkey: Adaptation and Representation of a Chinese Epic* (Seattle: University of Washington Press, 2018), 65–67.
20. Sun, *Transforming Monkey*, 67–69.
21. Liang, "When High Culture Embraces the Low," 281.
22. For another translation, see Mao Zedong, "Reply to Comrade Guo Moruo," November 17, 1961, www.marxists.org/reference/archive /mao/selected-works/poems/poems31.htm.
23. Wagner, *The Contemporary Chinese Historical Drama*, 139–235.
24. Cited in Julia Lovell, *Maoism: A Global History* (London: Bodley Head, 2019), 54–55 (see also further discussion).
25. Liang, "When High Culture Embraces the Low," 290–291.
26. Wagner, *The Contemporary Chinese Historical Drama*, 162.
27. Sun, *Transforming Monkey*, 96, 116; see also discussion in Liang, "When High Culture Embraces the Low," 312–327.
28. Sun, *Transforming Monkey*, 135–167.

A Note on the Translation

This translation—from the one-hundred-chapter version of the book, republished in 1954 by Zuojia chubanshe—aims to bring out the many voices of the novel. I was greatly helped by reference to previous translations, above all Anthony Yu's complete translation (*Journey to the West*) published by the University of Chicago Press between 1977 and 1983, and by Arthur Waley's abridgment, *Monkey* (1945). Two considerations drove the decision to undertake a new translation. First, language changes. The most recent complete version—W.J.F. Jenner's Beijing Foreign Languages Press edition—was commissioned and completed thirty years ago, in the 1980s. Second, the sheer length of the original—a full translation stretches to four large volumes—makes an abridged version an appealing option for teachers, students, and general readers. Waley's version still has great charm and dynamism; because his names for Tripitaka's pilgrims are so well known, I have adopted them here. But it left much scope for translating episodes that it had cut out.

This version comes to about a quarter of the length of the original. I have reduced the novel in two ways. First, although I have translated the book's opening and concluding chapters—which set up and conclude the quest—almost entirely, I have omitted outright some of the episodes describing parts of the pilgrims' journey. The structure of the book lends itself easily to this approach, for the scripture quest is made up of a succession of incidents, most of which are unconnected by narrative threads. Some are only a chapter long, others more extensive. These omission decisions have often been difficult, for there are many fantastical and significant episodes that could not be fitted in: the Buddha's scheme, early in the pilgrimage, to seduce the lustful Pigsy with a household of beautiful women; a monastery of larcenous monks; the appearance of an evil monkey doppelgänger whom Monkey must destroy; a den of soccer-playing spider fiends. I have tried, wherever possible, to ensure that the themes and character traits that appear in omitted episodes are covered in those I included: the temptations of the senses; Monkey's struggles with multiple selves; the novel's extraordinary, inventive fantasy.

I have also sometimes reduced and compressed individual chapters. The Chinese original shows its roots in oral storytelling by regularly recapitulating elements of the story so far, inheriting the fear of the marketplace raconteur that listeners might have wandered off then returned between scenes or simply forgotten key plot twists. To speed up the narrative, I have almost always left these repetitions out. The Chinese features a great many descriptive poems, which embroider on situations, landscapes, and battles. Again, in the interests of narrative economy and pace, I have for the most part omitted these, except for where they are an integral part of the plot. I have, however, often incorporated their descriptive elements into the surrounding prose.

Literary translators have two responsibilities: to the original text and to readers of the target language. Whichever languages translators work between, satisfying both constituencies can be difficult, but when working between two literary cultures as remote chronologically and geographically as sixteenth-century China and the twenty-first-century Anglophone world, the challenges are redoubtable. Sometimes, a translator has to sacrifice technical, linguistic fidelity to be true to the overall tone of a text.

Wordplays—ubiquitous in *Journey to the West*—are difficult to translate without explanatory footnotes that problematically slow down the delivery of the joke. Where I decided to omit these puns, I sometimes tried to compensate by enhancing the humor of other parts of the narrative or dialogue. In places, therefore, this version might read as a reworking as well as a translation; my hope throughout has been to communicate to contemporary English readers the dynamism, imagination, philosophy, and comedy of the original.

I'm very grateful to John Siciliano and his editorial team for meticulously guiding the manuscript through publication. I would like to thank warmly Desmund Cheung, Craig Clunas, Hao Ji, Liang Yan, Liu Chiung-yun, Tian Yuan Tan, Edward Wilson-Lee, and Vincent Yang for their generous assistance with planning and completing the abridgement and introduction. Hao Ji and Liu Chiung-yun provided invaluable guidance for the map of the pilgrims' route. Many thanks to Julith Jedamus, Thelma Lovell, and Robert Macfarlane for reading and commenting on the manuscript. I also benefited from invaluable conversations about early medieval Asia and early modern religious texts with Rebecca Darley, Kate Franklin, and Kat Hill.

JULIA LOVELL

Suggestions for Further Reading

Cynthia J. Brokaw and Kai-wing Chow, eds., *Printing and Book Culture in Late Imperial China* (Berkeley: University of California Press, 2005).

Glen Dudbridge, *The Hsi-yu Chi: A Study of Antecedents to the Sixteenth-Century Chinese Novel* (Cambridge: Cambridge University Press, 1970).

Liangyan Ge, *Out of the Margins: The Rise of Chinese Vernacular Fiction* (Honolulu: University of Hawai'i Press, 2001).

Robert E. Hegel, "China I: Until 1900," in *Encyclopedia of the Novel*, ed. Paul Schellinger (Chicago: Fitzroy Dearborn, 1998), vol. 1, 205–11.

Qiancheng Li, *Fictions of Enlightenment: Journey to the West, Tower of Myriad Mirrors, and Dream of the Red Chamber* (Honolulu: University of Hawai'i Press, 2004).

Frederick W. Mote, *Imperial China 900–1800* (Cambridge, Mass.: Harvard University Press, 2003).

Andrew H. Plaks, *The Four Masterworks of the Ming Novel: Ssu ta ch'i-shu* (Princeton: Princeton University Press, 1987).

David L. Rolston, ed., *How to Read the Chinese Novel* (Princeton: Princeton University Press, 1990).

Hongmei Sun, *Transforming Monkey: Adaptation and Representation of a Chinese Epic* (Seattle: University of Washington Press, 2018).

Sally Hovey Wriggins, *The Silk Road Journey with Xuanzang* (Boulder, Colo.: Westview, 2004).

Wu Cheng'en, *The Journey to the West*, rev. ed., 4 vol. (Chicago: University of Chicago Press, 2012).

Vincent Yang, "A Masterpiece of Dissemblance," *Monumenta Serica* 60.1: 151–194.

Principal Characters

Aoguang: Dragon King of the Eastern Ocean

Buddha: founder of the Buddhist faith

King Bull Demon: once Monkey's sworn brother, later his most formidable antagonist

Chen Guangrui: Tripitaka's father, a brilliant scholar and official of the Tang empire

Cui Jue: a minister under Emperor Taizong's father (who founded the Tang dynasty)

Erlang: nephew of the Jade Emperor who captures Monkey

Gold Star of Venus: the Jade Emperor's peace envoy who summons Monkey to Heaven

Golden-Headed Guardian: one of the chief deities appointed by Guanyin to protect Tripitaka on the pilgrimage to the west

Guanyin: one of the Buddha's Bodhisattvas (an enlightened being with oversight of the mortal world) responsible for assisting the pilgrimage to the west; renowned for her compassion, but regularly generates adversity for Monkey

Hui'an: Guanyin's disciple, son of heavenly general King Li Jing

Princess Iron-Fan: owner of the magic Palm-Leaf Fan that can control the blaze of Flame Mountain; first wife of King Bull Demon and mother of Red Boy

Princess Jade-Face: daughter of a fabulously wealthy fox king; second wife of King Bull Demon

Jade Emperor: monarch of the Taoist Heaven

Laozi: founder and chief deity of Taoism

King Li Jing: a heavenly general who volunteers to subdue the rebellious Monkey

Liu Boqin: the hunter who rescues Tripitaka from one of his first perils and leads him to the imprisoned Monkey

Liu Hong: the bandit who murders and impersonates Chen Guangrui

Monkey (also known as Beautiful Monkey King and Sun Wukong): a magic kung fu monkey

Nezha: son of King Li Jing, Taoist prince who tries and fails to subdue Monkey

Pigsy (also known as Zhu Wuneng): former Marshal of the Heavenly River, a fallen immortal who becomes one of Tripitaka's disciples; a skilled fighter, but overly susceptible to food, beautiful demons, and napping opportunities

Queen Mother of the Jade Pool: wife of the Jade Emperor and hostess of the Great Grand Festival of Immortal Peaches, which Monkey sabotages

Red Boy: monstrous son of King Bull Demon and Princess Iron-Fan; a master of the art of demonic flames, but eventually captured by Guanyin and retrained as her attendant

Sandy (also known as Sha Wujing): former General of Curtain-Drawing in Heaven, banished by the Jade Emperor for smashing a crystal cup; one of Tripitaka's disciples on the journey to the west

Star Lord Orionis: one of the Jade Emperor's deities who helps the pilgrims dispatch a redoubtable scorpion-spirit

Subodhi: the immortal Patriarch of the West who teaches Monkey the secrets of eternal life, multiple transformations, and cloud-somersaulting

Taizong: the second emperor of the Tang dynasty whose trip to the underworld generates an empire-wide quest for Buddhist virtue

Tripitaka (also known as Xuanzang, Riverflow, and, finally, the Sandalwood Buddha): the brilliant, virtuous monk who leads the pilgrimage to the west.

True Immortal of Wish Fulfillment: the vengeful uncle of Red Boy who jealously guards the magic water of Abortion Spring

Wei Zheng: prime minister of Taizong, also a trusted functionary of Heaven with excellent connections in Hell

Yama: King of the Underworld

Yin Wenjiao: daughter of Yin Kaishan and mother of Tripitaka

Yin Kaishan: one of Taizong's chief ministers, father of Yin Wenjiao

Lord Yellow-Robe: a man-eating horror who captures Tripitaka and Sandy; in reality, the Wood-Wolf Star taking on monstrous mortal form in order to conduct a clandestine liaison with another Taoist deity, the Jade Lady

Chapter One

After Pan Gu created the universe, by separating earth and sky with his mighty ax, the world was divided into four continents, in the north, south, east, and west. Our story takes place in the east.

By a great ocean lay a land called Aolai, within which was a mountain called Flower-Fruit, home to sundry immortals. What a mountain it was: of crimson ridges and strange boulders, phoenixes and unicorns, evergreen grasses and immortal peaches. And on its peak sat a divine stone, thirty-six and a half feet high, twenty-four in circumference.

Since creation, this rock had been nourished by heaven and earth, the sun and the moon, until it was divinely inspired with an immortal embryo, and one day gave birth to a stone egg, about as large as a ball. After exposure to the air, it turned into a stone monkey, with perfectly sculpted features and limbs. This monkey learned to climb and run, then bowed in all four directions of the compass. Two golden rays shone from his eyes all the way to the Palace of the Polestar, startling the benevolent sage of Heaven, the Jade Emperor, while he sat on his throne in the Hall of Divine Mists surrounded by his immortal ministers. The emperor ordered two of his generals, Thousand-Mile Eye and Follow-the-Wind Ear, to look out of the South Gate of Heaven and locate the source of this light. "Your humble servants," they soon reported back, "have traced it back to Flower-Fruit Mountain, in the small country of Aolai on the eastern continent, where a rock has given birth to an egg, which has turned into a stone monkey, whose golden eyes have dazzled even Your Majesty. But now the monkey has paused for some refreshment, and the blaze has dimmed."

"The creatures of the mortal world are all born from heaven and earth," the Jade Emperor remarked tolerantly. "Nothing they do can surprise us."

The monkey gamboled over the mountains, eating grass, drinking from streams, picking mountain flowers, hunting for fruit; he kept company with wolves and snakes, tigers and panthers, befriended deer and antelope, and swore brotherhood with macaques and apes. At night, he slept below cliffs; at sunrise, he wandered through mountains and caves, with no sense of the passing of time.

One sweltering morning, he sheltered from the heat with a crowd of monkeys in the shade of some pines; they swung from branch to branch, built sand pagodas, and chased dragonflies and lizards. Afterward, bathing in a mountain stream, they noticed how its current seemed to tumble like rolling melons and wondered where it was coming from. "As we don't have anything particular to do today," one of them suggested, "let's follow the stream to its origin." With shrieks of happy agreement, they all scrambled up the mountain to a great curtain of a waterfall.

The monkeys clapped their hands in delight. "Whoever dares pass through the waterfall to discover the source of the water, and returns alive, can be our king."

After three calls for a volunteer, the stone monkey suddenly jumped out of the crowd. "I'll go!" This excellent monkey closed his eyes, crouched, then sprang with one bound through the sheet of water. Once on the other side, he opened his eyes. Before him was a gleaming iron bridge, under which flowed the source of the stream. From the bridge, he could see into a beautiful cave residence: cushioned with moss, hung with stalactites, furnished with carved benches and beds, and equipped with pans and stoves. In the middle of the bridge hung a stone tablet on which was written, in large, regular calligraphy, the following address:

HEAVENLY WATER-CURTAIN CAVE
THE BLESSED LAND OF
FLOWER-FRUIT MOUNTAIN

The stone monkey leaped back out through the waterfall. "Fantastic luck!" he whooped.

"What's it like inside?" the other monkeys crowded around to ask. "How deep is the water?"

"It's the perfect place for us to make our home, an ideal refuge from Heaven's fits of temper," explained the stone monkey, and described the wonders of Water-Curtain Cave. "It could easily hold thousands of us. Let's move in straightaway."

"You go first and we'll follow behind!" yelped the others.

Once more, the stone monkey crouched, shut his eyes, and sprang through the water. "Come on!" he called. The braver of the monkeys immediately followed; the more nervous ones tweaked their ears, scratched their cheeks, stretched, and chattered a good deal before eventually leaping onto the bridge and into the cave. Once there, they were soon snatching at bowls, fighting over stoves and beds, and dragging things back and forth—for such is the mischief of monkeys. There was not a moment's peace until they'd fretted themselves into exhaustion.

The stone monkey spoke again: "A monkey stands and falls by his word.* You promised that whoever dared pass through the waterfall and returned safely would be king. So what are you waiting for?"

*The original Chinese is a quotation from Confucius, *The Analects*.

Without a murmur of dissent, the monkeys immediately bowed and wished their new king a long, long life. Their new ruler quickly dropped his old name—Stone Monkey—in favor of Beautiful Monkey King and appointed a few of the monkeys to ministerial and civil service positions. The monkeys then devoted themselves to exploring the delights of Flower-Fruit Mountain by day and returning to Water-Curtain Cave at night.

The Beautiful Monkey King lived this happy, innocent life for somewhere between three and four hundred years. Then one day, while banqueting with the other monkeys, he suddenly became melancholy and began to weep. "What has upset our great king?" clamored the others.

"I fear for the future," the monkey king explained with a sigh.

"But we live in bliss," said his subjects, laughing, "slaves of neither the unicorn, the phoenix, nor man. Why are you worrying about the future?"

"Life is good now," the monkey king said, "but eventually we will grow old and fall into the clutches of Yama, King of the Underworld."

While the monkey masses—instantly fearful—buried their faces in their hands and mewled piteously, a long-armed ape jumped out of the crowd: "Our great king's new sense of mortality suggests the beginnings of a religious calling. Only three types of creature can escape King Yama and his wheel of life and death: Buddhas, immortals, and holy sages."

"Where are they to be found?" asked the monkey king.

"In ancient caves on divine mountains."

"I leave immediately," declared the monkey king. "Even if my quest takes me to the very end of the world, I will return with the secret of eternal life."

All the monkeys applauded wildly. "Marvelous! First, though, we will gather fruits from far away for a huge send-off feast." The next day was taken up with preparing and consuming this banquet, an extraordinary spread of plums, cherries, lychees, pears, dates, peaches, strawberries, almonds, walnuts, chestnuts, hazelnuts, tangerines, sugarcane, persimmons and pomegranates, and coconut and grape wine. The monkey king sat at the head of the tables, with his subjects approaching in turn, in strict order of age and rank, to toast him with wine, flowers, and fruit.

The following day, the monkey king rose early. "Make me a dry pinewood raft, little monkeys, and fetch me a bamboo pole and some fruit for the journey." When all was ready, he hopped onto the raft and, pushing off with all his might, set off across the ocean. He was in luck, for a strong southeasterly wind blew him directly to the northwest coast of the southern continent. When his bamboo pole told him he was in shallow water, he abandoned the raft for the shoreline, where he encountered humans hunting for fish, wild geese, clams, and dredging salt.

He ran at them, making strange faces, and they dropped their baskets and nets and scattered in terror. The monkey king grabbed the slowest of them and stripped him of his clothes. After dressing in them, Monkey made a tour of the continent's towns and cities, studying human manners and speech. Eight or nine years passed. Monkey remained determined to seek the formula for eternal life, while the humans who surrounded him sought only money and fame, without a thought for their own mortality; no one cared what became of him.

Eventually, Monkey came to the Western Ocean. Still in search of immortals, he built himself another raft and floated across to the western continent. In time, he approached a beautiful, jagged mountain, thickly forested at its base and luxuriant with flowers, grasses, mosses, bamboo, and pines—an ideal hermit's refuge. Unconcerned about the danger of wolves, snakes, tigers, or leopards, Monkey climbed up to look around. When he reached the top, he suddenly heard a human voice singing deep within a copse of trees.

I sleep till dawn then wander the wood,
cutting creepers for my livelihood.
When I've gathered as much as I can hold,
I stroll singing through the market till it's sold.
I trade my load for wine and rice,
and never haggle over the price.
Living without ambition or conceit,
only immortals and Taoists will I meet.

"At last!" the monkey king rejoiced to himself. Skipping through the forest, he came face-to-face with a woodcutter busy at work, dressed in a large conical hat made of young bamboo, a cotton-gauze tunic with a silk sash, and straw sandals. "Salutations, immortal!" Monkey hailed him.

The flustered woodcutter dropped his ax. "Hush! I am a poor, ignorant man unable even to feed or clothe myself."

"Why, then, do you sing about immortals?" Monkey asked him.

The woodcutter laughed. "Oh, that. A neighbor of mine, an immortal as it happens, taught the song to me, to cheer me up when life was getting me down. A moment ago, I started worrying about something, so I sang it. I didn't know anyone was listening."

"Why don't you become his disciple? You could learn the secret of eternal life."

"I've not had an easy life," the woodcutter explained. "My father died when I was seven or eight. I'm an only child, and have been my mother's sole support ever since. And now that she's getting old, she needs me all the more. All we have is the rice and tea I get in exchange for my firewood. I can't abandon her for a religious life."

"Well, I'm sure you will be rewarded in later life for your filial devotion. In the meantime, though, could you point the way to the immortal's house, so that I can pay him a visit?"

"It's not far. This is Heart and Soul Mountain. About seven or eight miles to the south, you'll come to the Cave of the Tilted Moon and Three Stars, the home of an immortal called Subodhi, who has trained many disciples, and currently has thirty or forty studying under him."

Monkey tugged at the woodcutter. "Come with me! You won't regret it."

"Did you not listen to anything I said just now?" he answered, exasperated. "I've wood to chop. On your way now."

So Monkey left the woodcutter and found the path to the south. After seven or eight miles, a heavenly cave dwelling came into sight, shrouded in mists and light, framed by an emerald-green forest of bamboo and cypress and by moss-covered hanging cliffs. Cranes, phoenixes, apes, deer, lions, and elephants roamed about. The entrance was tightly sealed and the place seemed uninhabited, but a huge stone slab—thirty feet tall by eight feet wide—told Monkey that the woodcutter had spoken the truth: THE CAVE OF THE TILTED MOON AND THREE STARS, HEART AND SOUL MOUNTAIN. Not daring to knock, Monkey loitered on a nearby pine, nibbling some nuts.

After a very short while, the door creaked open and a young immortal of exceptionally refined looks emerged. He wore a robe with loose, billowing sleeves; his hair was bound with silk cords. "Who's making all that noise?"

Jumping down from the tree, Monkey bowed. "I didn't mean to disturb you. I'm here to learn the secret of eternal life."

"You seek the Way, you say?" The young man smiled. "Our master just told me to look outside the front door for a new student."

"That would be me!" exclaimed Monkey.

"Come on, then," the young man said, ushering him inside.

Monkey followed the youth deep into the cave, past story upon story and row upon row of jeweled pavilions, towers, and arches, until they reached the foot of a jade platform, on top of which sat Subodhi, the famous Patriarch of the West; thirty trainee immortals sat on the ground below. "Master!" Monkey gasped, launching into a frenzy of kowtows.

"Tell me your name and where you're from," Subodhi asked, "before you smash your head beyond repair."

"I come from Water-Curtain Cave on Flower-Fruit Mountain in the land of Aolai on the eastern continent."

"Throw him out!" Subodhi roared. "Liars can't learn enlightenment! Two oceans and the southern continent lie between here and Aolai."

Monkey resumed his kowtowing, this time at double speed. "It's true!" he protested. "My journey here took more than ten years."

"Hmpf," conceded Subodhi. "That sounds about right. So what's your name? Who were your parents?"

"I have no parents," Monkey replied.

"Were you born from a tree, then?"

"All I can remember is an immortal rock on Flower-Fruit Mountain. One year, it split open, and there I was."

"I see," considered Subodhi, hiding his delight at this revelation. "So you were born of heaven and earth. Get up and walk about, so I can look at you." Monkey scampered this way and that. "You're not exactly classically handsome," Subodhi said, laughing, "but you look exactly as a monkey reared on fruit and nuts ought to. I'll give you a surname: Sun. Written one way, it means monkey. But I'll drop the animal radical, leaving us with the *Sun* that means child."

Monkey burbled with glee. "A surname! I've got a surname! But can I have a given name also, so that you can easily call me hither and thither?"

"The given names of my disciples rotate within a cycle of twelve characters."

"And those twelve characters are?"

"Broad, *guang*; great, *da*; wise, *zhi*; intelligent, *hui*; true, *zhen*; obedient, *ru*; of nature, *xing*; of the sea, *hai*; outstanding, *ying*; awoken, *wu*; rounded, *yuan*; enlightened, *jue*. As you fall into the tenth, 'awoken,' *wu*, I will call you Sun Wukong: Sun-who-has-awoken-to-emptiness. Happy with that?"

"Sun Wukong!" Monkey chortled. "I love it!"

The name spoke an important truth: for at the beginning of everything, there were no names—only emptiness. To advance from emptiness, living creatures must first become aware of it.

And if you wish to know what Monkey learned next, you must read on.

Chapter Two

While Monkey pranced delightedly about, Subodhi ordered the congregation to take him away and teach him some basic rules of hygiene and etiquette. The disciples found Monkey a place in the corridor where he could sleep, and the following morning he began to learn from his fellow students how to speak and behave. Day in, day out, they discussed scriptures and doctrines; he practiced calligraphy and burned incense. In his spare time, he swept the ground and weeded the gardens, tended to the trees and flowers, gathered wood and lit fires, and fetched water and carried drinks. Six or seven perfectly contented years slipped by. Eventually, Subodhi climbed back onto his rostrum and summoned his immortals for a lecture on doctrine: a synthesis of Taoism, Buddhism, and Confucianism.

In the audience, Wukong began fidgeting, even dancing, with enthusiasm. Subodhi singled him out for a scolding: "Why can't you stand still and listen?"

"Forgive me! I was too excited by what you were saying."

"Seeing as you're clever enough to understand my lecture, can you tell me how long you've lived in our cave?"

"I fear I've completely lost track of time," Monkey replied. "All I know is that the peach trees on the mountain have fruited seven times."

"If you've eaten your way through seven peach seasons, you

must have been here for seven years. What is it that you want to learn from me?"

"A little Taoism would do nicely, Master."

"There are three hundred and sixty subcategories of Taoism; each can lead to enlightenment. Which do you wish to study?"

"Whichever you think best," Monkey answered.

"How about the division of Art?" suggested Subodhi.

"What would that involve?"

"Summoning immortals, divining with yarrow stalks, and learning to pursue good and shun evil."

"Will it make me live forever?" Monkey wanted to know.

"Not a chance," Subodhi replied.

"Then I'll have nothing to do with it," Monkey responded.

"How about the division of the Schools, then? That would cover the Confucians, the Buddhists, the Taoists, the Yin-and-Yangists, the Mohists, and the Physicians. It's mainly reading scriptures and chanting prayers."

"Is this the road to immortality?"

"If it's immortality you seek, this division is about as useful as building a pillar in a wall."

"I'm not fluent in your Taoist argot. What do you mean by that?"

"If you want a house to last, you gird the walls with pillars. All the same, one day the house will fall into ruin; such is the way of the material world."

"Then I'll have nothing to do with the Schools, either."

"How about the division of Silence?" the Patriarch now suggested. "You learn fasting and abstinence, quietism and inaction, meditating cross-legged, vows of silence and vegetarianism, yoga and solitary retreats."

"But will it make me immortal?"

"It will make you no stronger than an unfired brick on the kiln."

"Another circumlocution! Now what do you mean?"

"An unfired brick may look like a brick, but it has not yet been hardened by fire and water. It will disintegrate at the first heavy rainfall."

"Not for me, then!"

"Can I interest you in Action? This one will keep you busy. You have to gather the yin to nourish the yang, bend the bow and tread the arrow, rub the navel to induce the *qi*. There's also a certain amount of alchemical experimentation involved: burning rushes, forging cauldrons, swallowing red lead, and drinking virgins' menstrual blood, boys' urine, and married women's breast milk. That kind of thing."

"Surely that will bring immortality?"

"To gain immortality from such a method is as easy as fishing the moon out of the water."

"Not again! Speak plainly."

"When the moon is high, it leaves a reflection in the water, but you can't actually fish it out, for it is only an illusion."

"No thanks!" Monkey snorted.

The exasperated Subodhi now jumped off his rostrum. "You monkey, you!" he shouted. "Nothing's good enough!" He hit Monkey three times on the head with a ruler, then walked back to his room, hands behind his back, and shut the door, ignoring the rest of his horrified audience.

"Where are your manners?" the other disciples berated Monkey. "Master Subodhi offered you all sorts of doctrines; why did you reply so rudely? Now you've gone and offended him. Who knows when he'll come out again?"

Unfazed, Monkey smiled from ear to ear, for he had instantly understood Subodhi's hidden meaning. By hitting him three times, his teacher was surely telling him to visit at the third watch—around midnight. By folding his hands behind his back and shutting the main doors, he was instructing Monkey to come by the back entrance so that he could be taught in secret.

Monkey was irrepressibly cheerful all day, whiling away the hours with his fellow students at the entrance to the cave, impatiently awaiting nightfall. At dusk, he lay down to sleep with the others, pretended to close his eyes, and steadied his breathing. Since there was no watchman in the mountains to beat the hour, Monkey could only guess the time from the number of breaths he had taken. When he estimated that the appointed hour had come, he quietly got up, dressed, opened the door, and stole away from the group of sleeping disciples.

Guided by a clear moon and the darting glow of fireflies, he made his way to the back door into Subodhi's room, which he discovered was open. "So I was right!" he congratulated himself. He slipped in and kneeled by Subodhi's bed, where the master was curled up asleep, facing the wall. Soon, Subodhi awoke, stretched his legs, and murmured a poem:

> The Way is mysterious,
> and the golden elixir rare.
> If you reveal magic to an imperfect being
> your words will be empty and your tongue dry!

Monkey took this as his cue to speak: "I'm waiting."

Subodhi pulled on his clothes, then sat back down cross-legged. "Monkey! What are you doing here?"

"You told me to come through the back door at the third watch, for a lesson in enlightenment."

"This chap truly is a child of heaven and earth," Subodhi rejoiced to himself. "How else could he have unriddled me so easily?"

"I have come alone," Monkey went on, "in the hope that Master will teach me the Way of Immortality."

"This is your destiny," Subodhi replied. "Come close and listen."
Monkey kowtowed his thanks, washed his ears out, and kneeled
to hear Subodhi's secret life-preserving precepts.

Thus Monkey was blessed with understanding. After memoriz-
ing the magic formula and kowtowing fulsome thanks to Subodhi,
he returned quietly to his own bed as the sun rose. The moment he
sat down, he shook off his coverlet. "It's morning! Time to get up!"
His fellow students had slept through all that had happened to
Monkey during the night. As the weeks and months went by, he
outwardly played the class fool, while secretly practicing what he
had learned in noontime breathing exercises.

Another three years passed before Subodhi reappeared to teach
his disciples. He spoke of academic debates and parables and of
external self-cultivation. "Where's Monkey?" he suddenly asked.

Monkey kneeled before him. "Here I am!"

"What have you been working on of late?"

"The basics of immortality: the nature and origins of all things."

"In that case, you have already penetrated the divine substance
of matter. But beware of the peril of the three calamities."

Monkey mulled this over for a while. "Master is surely mistaken," he eventually responded. "I thought that anyone who has
learned the Way and is rich in virtue will live as long as Heaven
itself. Neither fire, nor water, nor illness can harm him. What
three calamities do you speak of?"

"What you have learned is not ordinary magic. You have stolen
the creative power of heaven and earth itself, and penetrated the
dark formulae of the sun and the moon. Ghosts and spirits will
seek to bring you down. Although you have extended your life,
in five hundred years' time Heaven will unleash the calamity of
thunder at you. You must seek wisdom to prevent this peril. Succeed and you will live as long as Heaven itself. Fail and you will
die. In another five hundred years, Heaven will rain the calamity
of the cold, dark fire of yin. It burns from the soles of your feet to

the cavity of your heart. It will reduce your entrails to ashes and your limbs to ruins. Your millennium of hard work will then be as dust and nothingness. After another five hundred years, Heaven will set the calamity of wind onto you. This is no earthly wind. It enters through the fontanels, blows through the six internal organs, midriff, and nine orifices. Your flesh and bones will dissolve and your body will disintegrate. You see, then, why I recommend avoiding these calamities."

Monkey's fur stood on end. "Tell me how to escape these horrors!"

"Normally, this would be perfectly simple. But as you are an unusual specimen, I fear I cannot teach you."

"I've a head at the top and feet at the bottom, nine apertures, four limbs, five viscera, and six internal organs. How am I unusual?"

"You bear a superficial resemblance to humans, but your cheeks are abnormally flat." (Monkeys have rather angular faces, with sunken cheeks and pointed muzzles.)

Monkey patted his face combatively. "Appearances can be deceptive. My cheek pouches have storage capacity on the inside. I demand parity."

"Fair enough," considered Subodhi. "Which escape do you want to learn? There's the Art of the Big Dipper, which involves thirty-six transformations, or the Art of the Earthly Multitude, which involves seventy-two."

"The more the merrier," reflected Monkey. "I'll take the second."

"Come over here, then, and I will tell you the formula."

No one knows what Subodhi whispered into Monkey's ear. But our hero was someone who could learn a hundred things from a single explanation. He immediately memorized the magic and, after practicing on his own, mastered the seventy-two transformations.

One day, as the community was enjoying the scenery at dusk in front of the Cave of the Tilted Moon and Three Stars, Subodhi suddenly turned to Monkey. "How are you getting on?"

"Thanks to you, I am now fully perfected. I can float and fly, as light as mist."

"Let's see you do it."

Anxious to show off, Monkey somersaulted some sixty feet into the air. In the time it would take to eat a meal, he had covered three miles. He returned and stood before Subodhi. "I call this cloud-galloping."

Subodhi snorted. "Cloud-crawling, more like. Any self-respecting immortal can fit in a tour of the four oceans between breakfast and dinner. *That's* cloud-galloping. In fact, given that it took you most of the day to travel just three miles, cloud-crawling is an overstatement."

"What you describe is fiendishly hard!"

"Nothing in this world is hard. It is only the mind that makes it so."

"If you're going to help me, then do it properly. Please teach me how to cloud-gallop."

"Immortals begin a cloud-gallop by stamping their feet," Subodhi explained. "But when you took off just now, you jumped. So I'll give you a lift-off that suits you: the cloud-somersault."

Subodhi taught him a magic sign and spell. "Now clench your fists, shake your body, and jump. A single somersault will carry you 108,000 miles."

The crowd of disciples giggled. "Lucky Monkey! If you master this, you can get a job as an express courier. You'll always be able to make a living."

As dusk was now turning to darkness, master and disciples went back inside the cave. But Monkey stayed up all night until he had mastered the cloud-somersault. Day in, day out, he reveled in the freedom of his new immortality.

One day, as spring was giving way to summer, Subodhi's disciples gathered under a pine tree to chat. "You must have some extraordinary karma stored up from a previous existence," the others said to Monkey. "The other day, Master whispered instructions to you for avoiding the three calamities. Have you got the hang of them?"

"Thanks to Subodhi's teaching and practicing hard," Monkey said, smiling, "I know what I'm doing."

"Show and tell, then."

Monkey decided to make an exhibition of himself. "What do you want me to turn into?"

"How about a pine tree?" Monkey made the magic sign, recited the spell, and became a pine tree: tall, straight, and elegant, without the slightest simian semblance. The disciples laughed and clapped. "Marvelous monkey!"

The hullabaloo roused Subodhi, who hurried out with his staff. "Who's making all this racket?"

The disciples immediately hushed themselves while Monkey resumed his original form. "We were just chatting, Master."

"You should be ashamed of yourselves!" roared Subodhi. "Those seeking the Way should not open their mouths so freely, for fear of scattering their vital forces or causing arguments through loose talk. What were you shouting and laughing about, anyway?"

"Monkey was entertaining us with a transformation," the disciples confessed. "We asked him to turn into a pine tree and our cheering disturbed you, Master. Please forgive us."

"Go away, all of you. Except you, Sun Wukong: come here!" Once the others had scattered, a proper scolding began. "What do you think you're doing, turning into a pine tree? Why did you show them what you can do? If you saw someone with exceptional powers, wouldn't you want them, too? Sooner or later, your fellow disciples will ask you for the magic. If you're weak enough not to refuse them, you'll spill the secret. If you don't tell them, they might force it out of you. You are no longer safe here."

"Please forgive me!" begged Monkey, kowtowing.

"No hard feelings. But you must leave."

Monkey's eyes filled with tears. "Where are you sending me?"

"You must go back to where you came from. You won't last long here."

Monkey was overcome with regret. "I have been away from home for twenty years. Though I yearn to see my former subjects again, I hate to leave you before I have repaid your kindness to me."

"Forget it," said the Patriarch. "Just don't drag me into any of your messes."

Seeing that there was no point in arguing, Monkey took respectful leave of Subodhi and his fellow disciples.

Before Monkey departed, Subodhi remade his earlier point more forcefully. "After you leave this place, you're bound to get up to no good. I don't care what villainy you perpetrate; just don't tell anyone that you were my disciple. If you breathe a word of what I did for you, I'll flay your wretched monkey carcass, grind your bones to dust, and banish your soul permanently to the Place of Ninefold Darkness. And I'll only be getting started."

"Right you are. If anyone asks, I'll tell them I'm self-taught." Monkey launched into a cloud-somersault eastward. Soon enough, he landed back on Flower-Fruit Mountain, rejoicing at how easy his return was, compared with his arduous outward journey.

Just as he was trying to work out which path to take back to Water-Curtain Cave, he heard the cries of cranes and monkeys echoing about him. "I'm back, little ones!" he called.

From out of rocky enclaves, grasses, flowers, and trees, thousands of monkeys of different sizes leaped out and surrounded their king. "Why were you gone so long? A cruel demon has attacked Water-Curtain Cave, stolen our possessions, and kidnapped our children."

"Who is this insolent fiend?" raged Monkey. "Tell me everything, and I'll settle his hash."

"He calls himself the Monstrous King of Chaos, and he lives north of here."

"How far?"

"We don't know. He arrives like the clouds and departs like the mist, wind, rain, thunder, and lightning."

"Very well. Amuse yourselves while I go and find him."

Monkey cloud-somersaulted northward, landing on top of a rugged, precipitous mountain. As he surveyed the area, he heard voices. Coming down to investigate, he discovered a number of imps dancing about in front of a cliffside establishment named Watery-Innard Cave. They fled as soon as Monkey appeared. "Stay where you are!" he commanded. "I've a message for you to pass on. I am the King of Water-Curtain Cave on Flower-Fruit Mountain, due south of here. Because this Havoc Monster, or what have you, of yours has repeatedly terrorized my people, I've come to settle the score."

The imps rushed into the cave. "O great king!" they wailed. "Catastrophe!"

"What are you talking about?" the Monstrous King—for it was he—asked. After the fiends reported their encounter outside the cave, their sovereign laughed: "Those monkeys are always saying they have a king who left them to study the Way. So he's back at last, it seems. How is he dressed, and what weapons does he have?"

"None that we can see. He's bareheaded and is wearing a red robe tied with a yellow sash and black boots. He doesn't resemble your regular Buddhist or Taoist. But he's certainly making quite a racket out there."

"Bring me my armor and my weapon," instructed the monster. Once dressed for combat, he exited the cave with his retinue of goblins. "So where's this King of Water-Curtain Cave?" he bellowed.

Monkey gazed upon a demon thirty feet high, with a waist as thick as ten arm-spans and brandishing a sharp, bright sword. He wore a black silk robe, a black iron breastplate pulled tight with leather straps, and ornately decorated boots; his black helmet glinted in the sunlight. This, in sum, was the Monster of Havoc, and he did not look like a pushover.

"Behold Monkey!" Monkey introduced himself.

Finally locating Monkey on the ground beneath him, the monster laughed. "You're less than four feet tall and unarmed. How dare you challenge me?"

"Reckless fiend!" Monkey yelled back. "Think I look small? I can grow in the blink of an eye. And as for a weapon: I can hook the moon down from the sky. Eat my fist!" He sprang up and began showering the monster's face with blows.

The monster blocked them with one hand. "Look, gnome, I'd be a laughingstock if I were to kill you with my sword. I'll lay down my weapon and we can have a boxing match instead."

"Gladly!" cheered Monkey, and the two set to hammering each other. In this kind of combat, long arms sometimes throw inaccurate punches; short-range strikes can be more precise. Monkey pummeled his opponent's ribs and made a direct hit in the crotch. Knocked off balance, his opponent picked up his huge steel sword again and hacked away at Monkey, who smartly stepped back and out of range.

Realizing that the fight was getting serious, Monkey deployed the Body Beyond the Body Magic: he plucked a handful of hairs, chewed them to pieces, then spat them out, shouting "Change!" The hairs transformed into two or three hundred little monkeys, who crowded around their adversary. When someone becomes an immortal, you see, he can transform his spirit at will. Now that Monkey was an adept in the Way, every single one of the eighty-four thousand hairs on his body could change into whatever form he wanted. His mini-monkeys were so sharp-eyed and agile that the monster couldn't get his sword near them. Back and forth they weaved and darted until the monster was completely surrounded. Some squeezed, some tugged, some jabbed at his crotch, while others pulled at his feet, tore his hair, gouged at his eyes, tweaked his nose, and generally befuddled him. While this was going on, the real Monkey managed to grab the monster's sword, advance through the mass of little monkeys, and slice the monster's head in two. Monkey then led his army into the cave, where they slaughtered all the imps. The conquest complete, Monkey shook himself and the hairs returned to his body.

About forty monkeys, however, retained their shape—for they had been kidnapped here from Flower-Fruit Mountain—and tearfully explained themselves to the monkey king. "These stone pots and bowls"—they gestured around the cave—"he also stole from us."

"Then we will take them with us," pronounced Monkey, who then set fire to the cave and burned it to ashes. "Let's head home," he told his followers. "Close your eyes and don't be afraid."

That marvelous monkey muttered a spell, swept up the others in a wind-propelled cloud, and landed smoothly back on Flower-Fruit Mountain. "Open your eyes, little ones." Immediately recognizing their old home, the delighted monkeys rushed into the cave and lined up with the others before Monkey. They held a celebratory banquet of fruits and wine, during which Monkey regaled them with the story of how he had defeated the monster.

"Where were you all that time, great king?" they wanted to know next. "How did you learn this magic?"

Monkey gave them an unexpurgated version of his travels— including Subodhi's imparting of immortality.

"What luck!" applauded the monkeys, toasting their king with bowls of coconut-and-grape wine, divine flowers and fruit.

Chapter Three

After Monkey's triumphal homecoming, he taught the little monkeys how to sharpen bamboo sticks into spears and file wood into knives; how to set out flags and banners; how to patrol, advance, retreat, and pitch camp. But after playing at war for a while, he mused: "What if we really had to go into battle? What if humans or birds or beasts accused us of plotting to rebel, and raised an army to destroy us? Armed only with bamboo poles and wooden swords, how could we fight them? We must have proper swords and spears."

"You are indeed farsighted," the other monkeys chattered. "But where can we get such things?"

Four monkey elders—two red-buttocked females and two long-armed apes—now stepped forward with a suggestion. "Easily done. East of this mountain, across two hundred miles of water, lies the frontier of Aolai. There, a king rules over a city with a huge army; he must have craftsmen skilled in all kinds of metalwork. You could get weapons there, Your Majesty, then teach us how to use them to protect ourselves forever."

Monkey thought this a wonderful idea. "Off you go and play," he told his subjects. "I'll be back soon."

With one cloud-somersault, he crossed the two hundred miles of water in a split second and approached a densely populated city with wide streets, large marketplaces, and thousands of houses.

"This place must be awash with weapons," he mused. "I suppose I could go and buy them. But stealing them through sorcery would be better." Making a sign and reciting a spell, he inhaled deeply, then blew out a gale that scoured the city with a sandstorm. Rulers and subjects fled inside their houses and bolted their doors shut. With the coast cleared, Monkey landed his cloud and rushed through the palace gate straight to the armory. There he found vast stores of every kind of weapon: knives, spears, swords, halberds, battle-axes, bows, arrows, and so on. "But how am I to get all this home? Time for some more body division, I think." Plucking out another handful of hairs, he once more chewed them to a pulp, then spat them out, recited a magic spell, and shouted, "Change!" The fragments of hair turned into one hundred thousand little monkeys, all grabbing at weapons. After emptying the armory, they jumped back onto the cloud and Monkey carried them home on another gale.

Busy playing outside the cave when this army suddenly roared up, the Flower-Fruit monkeys fled for cover. Monkey promptly retrieved his hairs and made a pile of weapons. "Come and choose!" he shouted to his subjects, who ran back out to learn what was going on. Once Monkey had explained his latest marvel, the troop of monkeys spent the rest of the day playing with their new toys.

The next day, after their usual marching drill, Monkey summoned them together and made a roll call of forty-seven thousand monkey soldiers. The size of this army awed the mountain's many wild beasts: its wolves, snakes, tigers, leopards, mouse-deer, roe deer, river deer, foxes, badgers, lions, elephants, bears, antelope, wild boar, mountain oxen, gazelles, and green rhinoceroses. Every demon king from the mountain's seventy-two caves came to pay homage to the monkey king. Each year they presented tribute—golden drums, colorful flags, helmets—and answered Monkey's summons. Some provided military service; others supplies. Together, they turned Flower-Fruit Mountain into a fortress of formidable military discipline.

One day, though, Monkey had a thought. "While you are all very quick now with all kinds of weapons, I'm finding this cutlass of mine very cumbersome."

The four wise monkeys again stepped forward. "You are an immortal, Your Majesty. Ordinary weapons are not the thing for you. Can you travel underwater?"

"I have mastered seventy-two transformations," explained Monkey. "I can cloud-somersault, turn invisible, and apparate. I can soar to heaven and bore down into the earth. I can saunter across the sun and the moon without casting a shadow; I can pass through metal and stone. Water cannot drown me, fire cannot burn me. Is there anything I can't do?"

"Marvelous. For the water beneath this iron bridge flows directly to the palace of the dragon king of the Eastern Ocean. Why don't you go and ask him for a weapon?"

Monkey thought this an excellent plan. "Back soon."

Bouncing onto the bridge, he invoked the magic of aquatic restriction, then threw himself into the water, which obligingly parted for him, and headed straight to the bottom of the Eastern Ocean. Along the way he met a sea-spirit patrol, who asked him his name so that he could be announced to the dragon king. "I am Monkey, the immortal sage of Flower-Fruit Mountain and a close neighbor of your king. I'm frankly surprised you need to ask."

As soon as the patrol reported Monkey's arrival to the Water-Crystal Palace, the Dragon King Aoguang mustered a welcoming party of his sons, grandsons, prawn soldiers, and crab generals to greet their visitor. Once they had all processed back inside the palace for formal introductions, and tea had been served, the dragon king asked Monkey about himself: how he learned the Way and what powers it had given him.

"My body is birthless and deathless," Monkey informed him. "I've taught my subjects to defend our cave in the mountains, but find myself without a decent weapon. I understand that my honorable neighbor here has far more magic weapons than he can possibly use, so I've come to ask for one."

Sensing this was not a request he could refuse, the dragon king immediately ordered one of his commanders (who happened to be a perch) to present Monkey with a large cutlass.

"Not really my thing," Monkey demurred. "Try me with something else."

The dragon king next ordered another subordinate, one Captain Mackerel, to bring out a nine-pronged fork with the help of an eel porter.

Monkey picked it up, then set it down again. "Too light!"

"But it weighs 3,600 pounds," the Dragon King pointed out, laughing. Monkey wanted nothing to do with it. By now, the dragon king was starting to feel distinctly uneasy about his uninvited guest. He asked Commander Bream and Brigadier Carp to bring out a vast halberd weighing 7,200 pounds.

After trying out a few moves, Monkey plunged it into the ground between them. "Flimsy!"

"This is the heaviest weapon in the palace," protested the unnerved dragon king.

"Think I was born yesterday?" Monkey giggled. "Everyone knows the Dragon King Aoguang's not short of treasures. Go and have a proper look around your armory. If I see something I like, I'll give you a fair price."

Just as the dragon king was reaching his wit's end, the dragon queen and her daughter slipped out from behind the throne. "This monkey is clearly not someone to be trifled with," they whispered to the king. "How about giving him the magic iron from the Heavenly River? These last few days, it's been glowing mysteriously and exuding propitious vapors. A sign, perhaps?"

The dragon king said, "But that's the measure that Yu the Great used to tame the floods, to fix the depths of rivers and seas. What good will it do this monkey?"

"Who cares?" said the queen. "Just hand it over and get rid of him." Seeing her point, the dragon king told Monkey about his wife's suggestion.

"I'll take a look," conceded Monkey. "Bring it out."

"You'll need to view it in its current resting place," the dragon king explained. "It's too heavy to lift." He led his demanding visitor into the ocean treasury, from which myriad golden rays were emanating. The king pointed: "That's it."

Monkey went over to investigate. It was a radiant iron pillar, more than fifty feet tall* and as thick as a barrel. "It's got potential," he mused. "A little too wide and a little too long, though." The moment he said this, the pillar grew several feet shorter and several inches thinner. "Smaller!" he commanded. It promptly shrank some more. The delighted Monkey now took it out of the treasury to examine it properly: it was a black iron rod, weighing 13,500 pounds, with a golden ring on either end. An inscription next to one of the rings read: OBEDIENT GOLDEN-HOOPED STAFF. "A weapon that will do my bidding!" exulted Monkey. "Smaller still!" he commanded, tossing the iron from hand to hand. It now shrank to twenty feet long, and to the diameter of a rice bowl.

As Monkey lunged, parried, and twirled his way back into the Water-Crystal Palace, the dragon king and his princes trembled with fear. Turtles and tortoises retreated into their shells, while fish, shrimp, and crabs all fled for cover. "Thanks, worthy neigh-

---

*The original here says "more than twenty feet," but given how much shrinking Monkey subjects the iron to over the ensuing sentences, at the end of which the staff is about twenty feet long, I judged that the first number had to be an error, and therefore increased it to fifty.

bor," Monkey said, beaming at the dragon king while inviting himself to sit back down in the throne hall.

"Don't mention it," quavered his host.

"This lump of iron isn't bad," Monkey continued. "Not bad at all. But I do have one further request."

"You do?"

"Now that I've adopted this magic staff, I feel rather underdressed. If you could rustle up some armor to go with it, I'd be much obliged."

"I'm most dreadfully sorry, but I don't have anything suitable."

"I don't want to be a bother to someone else. I'll sit out here till you come up with the goods."

"I suggest you try another ocean. You might have more luck there."

"But I've settled in so nicely here. If you're sure you don't have anything for me to wear, perhaps you'd like me to test out my new staff on you."

"Desist, I beg you!" yelped the dragon king. "Perhaps my brothers Aoqin in the Southern Ocean, Aoshun in the Northern Ocean, and Aorun in the Western Ocean could dig something up."

"Too far!" Monkey declared. "As the saying goes: a dragon king in the hand is worth three in the bush."

"Of course," stammered the dragon king. "No need at all for you to go there yourself. I will summon them immediately with my iron drum and golden bell."

"What are you waiting for?"

Moments after the alligator general had struck the bell and the turtle marshal beaten the drum, the three dragon brothers converged on the entrance to the Water-Crystal Palace. Aoguang hurried out to meet them.

"What emergency did you bring us here for?" Aoqin asked his older brother.

"It's like this," Aoguang replied. "Earlier today, a so-called immortal sage from Flower-Fruit Mountain, claiming to be a neighbor of mine, turned up demanding a weapon. I finally managed to fob him off with the magic iron pillar from the Heavenly River, but he's now refusing to leave until I give him some armor, too. I don't have a thing to give him, which is why I called you here. Do you have anything that will do, so that I can get rid of him?"

"Let's call up our armies and apprehend him!" spluttered the outraged Aoqin.

"Hopeless," Aoguang countered. "One tap of that magic iron will finish us all."

Aorun argued for the path of least resistance: "Let's find him some armor, send him on his way, then make a formal complaint to Heaven, which can punish him as it sees fit."

"Good plan," chimed Aoshun. "I have here a pair of cloud-hopping shoes in lotus-colored silk."

"And I happen to have with me a golden chain-mail cuirass," added Aorun.

"I can throw in a purple-gold phoenix-feather cap," offered Aoqin.

Delighted, Aoguang now ushered them into the palace to meet his unruly visitor. Monkey put on his shoes, his chain-mail cuirass, and his helmet and mock-fought his way out of the palace with his iron staff, yelling "Sorry for the trouble" as he went. Most unsettled by the whole encounter, the four dragons embarked upon a consultation process about lodging an official complaint with the Heavenly authorities. But we need not concern ourselves with that for the time being.

Parting the waters again, Monkey swept back onto the iron bridge, where his subjects were eagerly awaiting his return. When they saw their king suddenly leap out of the waves, perfectly dry and in his glittering new costume, they kneeled in awe. Monkey sat triumphantly on his throne with the iron staff propped up before him. Not knowing any better, his monkeys crowded around, anxious to try it themselves. Like dragonflies trying to shake a tree, they couldn't move it even a fraction of an inch. "How did Your Majesty carry it all the way here?" they chattered in wonder.

"Every object has its master," said Monkey, smiling and picking it up. "For thousands of years, this piece of iron lay in the ocean treasury fixing the depth of the Heavenly River until, a few days ago, it began giving off light. It has a name—the Obedient Golden-Hooped Staff—and it does whatever I say. When I first laid eyes on it, it was fifty feet long and as thick as a barrel, but it shrank as soon as I told it to. Stand to one side, while I tell it to transform. Smaller!" In an instant, the staff had shrunk to the size of an embroidery needle, which Monkey tucked inside his ear.

"More magic!" bayed the amazed monkeys.

Their king placed the staff on the palm of his hand: "Bigger!" he shouted. It immediately became a twenty-foot pillar that was a couple of feet in diameter. Monkey now tried a touch of cosmic imitation. Bounding out of the cave, he cried "Grow!" and promptly shot up to one hundred thousand feet tall. His head resembled the craggy summit of Mount Tai, with flashing eyes and a butcher's-bowl mouth full of razor teeth. His staff reached up to the thirty-third story of Heaven, and down to the eighteenth level of Hell. Tigers, leopards, wolves, snakes, and the demon kings of the seventy-two caves all emerged to kowtow in terror. A moment later, Monkey undid the magic, shrank the staff down to the size of a needle, tucked it inside his ear again, and sashayed back inside the cave.

The assembled company now sat down to a magnificent banquet, amid fluttering banners and banging gongs. After feasting on a hundred delicacies, all washed down with coconut and grape wine, they returned to their military training. Monkey promoted his four wise monkeys: the two red-buttocked females were named marshals, the long-armed apes generals, in charge of building fortifications, pitching camp, and distributing rewards and punishments. With the day-to-day business thus taken care of, Monkey spent his days riding mist and clouds, sauntering over oceans, and touring mountains. His displays of magic made him powerful, talented friends. He swore brotherhood with six great kings: Bull Demon, Dragon-Monster, Roc-Fiend, Lion-Camel, Macaque, and Giant-Ape. Every day they gathered in Water-Curtain Cave, discussing civil and military affairs over cups of wine, singing, dancing, roaming the world, and living their best lives.

One day, Monkey instructed his four commanders to arrange a banquet for the seven brothers: oxen and horses were slaughtered, sacrifices were offered to heaven and earth, assorted imps were ordered to sing and dance, and everyone proceeded to get thoroughly drunk. After seeing his six compadres off, Monkey lay down under the shade of a pine tree and, a moment later, nodded off, surrounded by a hushed, protective circle of his subjects. As he slept, Monkey dreamed that two silent individuals, holding an official summons on which his full name—Sun Wukong—was written, tied him up and lugged him to the edge of a city. Still groggy with drink, Monkey half discerned an iron sign: WELCOME TO HELL. This brought him to his senses. "Why have you dragged me to the Kingdom of Death?" he demanded.

"You've reached the end of your allotted span," his escorts informed him. "Our orders are to bring you here."

Monkey was outraged: "I have transcended the Three Realms and the Five Phases and am no longer under King Yama's jurisdiction. Why has your idiot sovereign had me arrested?"

Ignoring the protest, the two soul-policemen went on trying to pull him inside. Now in a proper fury, Monkey pulled the magic iron staff out from behind his ear. With one wave, it grew into a cudgel, and Monkey smashed his guards to a pulp. He untied himself and charged into the city, spinning his staff this way and that. Bull-headed and horse-faced demons fled in terror, while ghost soldiers rushed to alert the Palace of Hell. "Disaster, Your

Majesties!" they reported. "An outrageous monkey is about to smash his way into the palace!"

Thoroughly alarmed, the ten kings of the Underworld went out to investigate. "Tell us your name," they called to the furious Monkey.

"How dare you not know who I am?" raged Monkey. "How dare you have me arrested?"

"A—a clerical error, perhaps," the infernal kings replied falteringly.

"Know then," thundered Monkey, "that I am Sun Wukong, Heaven-born sage of Water-Curtain Cave on Flower-Fruit Mountain. Now who the hell are you?"

The ten kings bowed. "We are the emperors of darkness, the ten underworld kings of the wheel of karma."

"Tell me your names or I'll beat you senseless." They did not withhold the information. "Well, if you're all such powerful kings, with superior intellects and the like, how can you have made such a mistake? For I, Monkey, have learned the Way of Immortality and will live as long as Heaven itself. What business do you have with me?"

"Calm yourself," soothed the kings. "Lots of people have the same surname as you. It's probably a simple case of mistaken identity."

"Rubbish!" Monkey retorted. "The warrant never lies. I want to see the register of births and deaths this very minute."

The ten kings invited him into the palace to take a look.

Keeping a firm hold on his staff, Monkey sat himself down in the middle of the palace, while the ten kings ordered a judge from the records department to produce the ledgers for his perusal. The legal official scuttled off and soon returned with a pile of volumes, including the registers for the ten species of living creatures. Monkey went through them one by one: the register of the hairless and the short-haired; the hairy; the feathered; the crawling; and the scaly—no mention of our Monkey. Monkey, you see, was hard to classify. He shared some points of resemblance with humans, but not enough to be categorized alongside them; though his hair was on the short side, he did not belong to the kingdom of the hairless and the short-haired; although he was animal-like in appearance, he did not answer to the unicorn; though he was known to fly, he was not accountable to the phoenix. He was eventually located in his own separate ledger, which Monkey personally examined, finding his name under the entry for Soul Number 1350, with the clarification: "Stone monkey born of Heaven. Lifespan: 342 years. A good death." "I can't remember how old I actually am," Monkey said. "I just want to delete my name. Pass me a brush." The judge quickly found one and loaded it with ink, and Monkey crossed out not only his name but also every name in the monkey section of the ledgers. "So that's that," he announced, tossing the register away. "So long!" And he smashed his way back out of Hell. Glad to keep as great a distance as possible between themselves and Monkey, the ten kings agreed to consult the Pope of Darkness, in his residence in the Emerald Cloud Palace, about filing a formal complaint in Heaven.

As he bashed his way out of the infernal city, Monkey tripped on a clump of grass. Suddenly waking up, he realized it had all been a dream. "How much did you drink at the banquet?" his subjects asked him as he stretched. "You slept through till morning." Monkey told them what had happened in his dream and how he had persuaded the kings of the underworld to cross all their names off the ledger of death, at which news his subjects kowtowed with ecstatic gratitude. And from that point on, most mountain monkeys never got old, for the Underworld no longer had their names and addresses.

Let us turn now to the court of the Jade Emperor, where—at the morning session in the Hall of Divine Mists in the Golden-

Turreted Cloud Palace—a Taoist immortal named Qiu Hongji had just stepped out of the ranks of the Heavenly ministers and announced the arrival of the Dragon King Aoguang, to present a memorial. Bidding him enter, the Jade Emperor read the petition handed to him by a page boy:

Your unworthy subject Aoguang begs to inform his imperial eminence that a bogus immortal of Water-Curtain Cave on Flower-Fruit Mountain, by the name of Sun Wukong (also known as Monkey), has been harassing this small, weak dragon. He broke into my palace, demanded a weapon using threats of grievous bodily harm, then again used intimidation to extort a suit of armor. He terrorized my watery relatives and sundry turtles and alligators. After presenting him with a magic iron staff, a golden phoenix-feather helmet, a suit of chain-mail, and cloud-shoes, my brothers and I—dragon kings, all—saw him off with all due courtesy. But still he terrorized us with magic and violence and didn't say a proper thank you. As we ourselves are no match for him, we respectfully beg you to apprehend this demon to restore peace and prosperity to the ocean bed. Humbly yours, etc., etc.

"You may return to your ocean," the Jade Emperor replied. "We'll deal with this miscreant." Bowing his head in thanks, the dragon king departed.

Directly afterward, further visitors were announced: "The Minister of Hell and the Pope of Darkness also wish to present a memorial." This time the Jade Girl, the emperor's director of communications, delivered the document to the emperor. It went like this:

Heaven is for gods and earth for ghosts; birth and death proceed cyclically, for such is the immutable order of nature. Today, however, a Heaven-born demonic monkey, one Sun Wukong of

Water-Curtain Cave on Flower-Fruit Mountain, ferociously resisted arrest. He beat to death two spectral policemen and trauma-
tized the ten Merciful Kings of Hell. After making the most awful
fuss in the Infernal Palace, he forced us to erase his name on the
register of death and banned us from arresting any of his monkey
relatives, thereby making a shambles of the wheel of reincarnation. I humbly beg you to subdue this demon and restore peace
and security in the Underworld. Respectfully yours, etc., etc.

"You may return to the Underworld," the Jade Emperor pronounced. "We'll deal with this miscreant." The hellish heads of
state retired, with thanks.

His Celestial Majesty now questioned his officials about this
infamous monkey. "When was he born, and when did he start
making trouble like this? How has he become so powerful?"

"This creature," related Thousand-Mile Eye and Follow-the-
Wind Ear, "began life some three hundred years ago as a stone
monkey born of Heaven. After a perfectly ordinary start in life,
he somehow learned the Way of Immortality and is now able to
terrorize dragons and tigers and bully the Underworld into delet-
ing him from their ledgers of death."

"So which," responded the Jade Emperor, "of my divine generals will descend to earth to capture him?"

"Majesty," the Spirit of Longevity from Venus ventured, "given
that this monkey is a child of heaven and earth, of the sun and
the moon, that he walks on two feet, and has attained immortality, I propose that we treat him as we would a human. I humbly
suggest you offer him an amnesty, summon him to Heaven and
give him a government job. Once he's inside the system, he'll have
to behave. If he accepts, we can bamboozle him with sinecures; if
he refuses, we can apprehend him. In any case, such a strategy
will save us a military campaign and bring an unruly immortal
to heel."

"Excellent!" rejoiced the Jade Emperor, ordering a nearby constellation to scribble out the amnesty and appointing the Gold
Star of Venus as his peace envoy.

Landing his auspicious cloud in front of Water-Curtain Cave,
Gold Star announced himself and his mission to the crowd of
monkeys: "I am the representative of the Jade Emperor, who in-
vites your king to join the Heavenly civil service. Run along now
and tell him." The message bounced along a chain of monkey
minions; by the time it reached their king deep inside the cave it
had become: "An old man outside with a piece of paper on his
back says come up to Heaven."

"Ha!" exclaimed Monkey. "I was just thinking the other day
how much I'd like to do that. Send him in!" Once inside, Gold
Star introduced himself formally and repeated his invitation.
"Don't mind if I do, chum!" said Monkey, beaming. "But let's
feast first."

"As I'm on imperial business," protested Gold Star, "I daren't
delay. Let us ascend to Heaven directly. Once the Jade Emperor
has given you your Very Important Job, we'll have plenty of time
to chat."

"Sorry you'll leave empty-bellied." Monkey shrugged and
called his four generals over: "Keep the little monkeys at their
training. Meantime, I'll have a sniff around Heaven and see
whether you can all come, too." He then hopped onto Gold Star's
personal cloud, and they rose into the sky.

Chapter Four

Thanks to Monkey's exceptional skill at cloud-somersaulting, he soon left Gold Star far behind him and arrived first at the South Gate of Heaven. But when he tried to enter, his way was blocked by the spears, swords, and halberds of nine gold-armored divine warriors guarding the entrance. "That Gold Star's a fraud!" griped an outraged Monkey. "He told me I was an honored guest!" At this moment, the panting Gold Star caught up. "You told me the Jade Emperor was going to give me an amnesty," Monkey railed at him. "So why are these goons blocking my way?"

"Calm down," Gold Star soothed, laughing. "As this is your first time in Heaven, our guards have no idea who you are. They daren't let just anyone in. Once you've met the Jade Emperor, been officially registered as an immortal, and given a government job, you can come and go as you please."

"I'm not going," Monkey said sulkily.

"Come on," said Gold Star, yanking him toward the gate. "Let us through, Guardians!" he called out. "I bring with me, on the orders of the Jade Emperor, an immortal from the world below." When the guards stepped back, lowering their weapons, Monkey decided to trust Gold Star and walked slowly in through the green-tiled, jade-studded portal.

Heaven, Monkey had to admit, was quite something. Rainbows of golden light shimmered through purple mists, evergreen grasses, and ever-blooming flowers. Multicolored phoenixes soared around the thirty-three palaces, while the seventy-two ceremonial halls teemed with jade unicorns. The inner halls were propped up by huge pillars coiled with scarlet-whiskered, gold-scaled dragons. Officials glittering with gold and precious stones rustled back and forth in robes of crimson gauze. When the drums of Heaven sounded, Monkey followed ten thousand courtiers through a gold-studded jade door to the emperor's throne room, the Hall of Divine Mists. Topped by extravagantly decorated eaves and ferocious-looking carved animal guardians, the hall was roofed by a vast, brilliant dome of purple-gold, beneath which goddesses fluttered fans and crystal platters were heaped with elixirs. Earth paled in comparison.

Gold Star led Monkey directly up to an audience with the emperor. While his escort was busy prostrating himself, Wukong stood disrespectfully upright. "In accordance with the emperor's decree," announced Gold Star, "I bring you the bogus immortal."

"And he is . . . ?" asked the Jade Emperor.

"You're looking at him!" Monkey now piped up, finally making a perfunctory bow.

The attendant officials paled in horror. "What a savage!" they murmured. "Death's too good for him."

"The bogus immortal," the Jade Emperor pronounced, "has not yet learned manners. We will pardon him this time." Next, the emperor asked if there were any staff vacancies that Monkey could fill. A Star Spirit from Immortal Resources reported that while there were no openings in any of the ministries, the stables did need a supervisor. "I hereby appoint you Imperial Groom," announced the Jade Emperor. The assembled courtiers chorused their thanks, while Monkey whooped his. The emperor then dispatched the Star Spirit of Jupiter to escort Monkey to the stables to take up his new appointment.

Elated at his latest professional development, Monkey began

by taking his duties very seriously. He gathered together his team (administrators, accountants, stable hands) and made a detailed survey of the current state of stable management. There were, he inventoried, a thousand heavenly horses, made up of thirty-three extraordinary breeds (Wind Chasers, Distance Devourers, Light Leapers, Red Rabbits, and the like), all with thunderous gallops and inexhaustible stamina for riding mist and clouds. Monkey painstakingly oversaw the accountants who sourced supplies; the laborers who washed, groomed, fed, and watered the horses; the deputies and assistants who kept everything else running smoothly. Monkey petted and coaxed the horses by day and watched over them by night. If they wanted to sleep, they were woken and fed; if they wanted to gallop, they were brought back to the trough. Within two weeks he had broken them all in.

One day, when all was quiet in the stables, Monkey's colleagues held a welcome banquet for their new supervisor. While the others were merrily drinking away, Monkey suddenly set down his cup. "What grade am I in the civil service here?"

"You don't have one," his colleagues replied.

"You mean I'm too high up for the grade system?" Monkey asked.

"Quite the opposite. You're so low-ranking you're off the bottom of the scale. You've done a famous job since starting in the stables, but you'll never get more than a grudging 'not bad' from the higher-ups. If the horses lose any weight, senior management will tan your hide. And if they get injured under your watch, you'll be severely punished."

"So that's what they think of Monkey!" the Imperial Groom exploded. "Don't they know I'm the King of Flower-Fruit Mountain? How have they hoodwinked me into looking after their smelly horses? I'm off!" Pushing over his desk, he took the iron out from behind his ear, shook it out to the thickness of a cudgel, and barged his way out of the South Gate. Knowing that Monkey was now on the immortal payroll, the sentries didn't dare arrest him.

Within an instant, his cloud landed back on Flower-Fruit Mountain, where the four generals and the monstrous monarchs were busy with their usual drills. "My children!" he cried. "Monkey's back!"

The monkey masses swept their king back onto his throne and conjured up a feast. "You've been in Heaven more than ten years," they acclaimed him. "What glories have you achieved in this time?"

"Ten years? I've been away barely a fortnight."

"One day in Heaven," his acolytes advised him, "is equivalent to a year on earth. What ministry did they give you?"

"Don't ask!" Monkey waved his hands dismissively. "That pathetic Jade Emperor is the worst—couldn't recognize genius if it punched him in the nose. He made me his groom—can you believe it? It was fun to begin with, but when my colleagues told me how low-ranking the job was, I got so mad I smashed up the lousy banquet they were holding for me and came straight back here. They can keep their rotten job."

"Marvelous! Superb!" cried the little monkeys. "Why would you want to look after their stinky horses when you can be king of this cave? You monkeys in the kitchen, hurry up with that welcome-home wine! Our king needs cheering up!"

In the middle of the banquet, two visitors were announced: a pair of rhinoceros-horned demon kings. As soon as Monkey had them shown in, they rushed up to prostrate themselves. "Having heard about your Heavenly appointment and that you'd returned covered in glory, we wish to congratulate you with this red and yellow robe and to offer our faithful service." Monkey happily slipped on the robe, accepted the adulation of the entire banqueting hall, and appointed the demon kings his frontline commanders.

"Just as a matter of interest, what post *did* Heaven give you?" the new arrivals asked.

"That crummy Jade Emperor made me his groom," grumbled Monkey.

"What?" The demon kings seemed astonished. "How could an omnipotent magic monkey be made to look after horses? You are the Great Sage Equal to Heaven!"

Monkey thought this was the best thing ever. "Quick as you can," he ordered his generals, "make me a flag saying 'The Great Sage Equal to Heaven' and mount it on a bamboo pole. No more of this 'Great King' rubbish. And tell my brothers the monstrous monarchs, too."

Back in Heaven, the following day the Heavenly Preceptor—a celestial master by the name of Zhang Daoling—led two stable administrators up to the throne. "Your Majesty," they reported, prostrating themselves, "your new groom absconded from the Heavenly Palace yesterday, complaining that the job he had been given was unworthy of him." At that very moment, the Guardians of the South Gate also appeared to report on Monkey's brusque exit.

"Back to your posts, all of you," the Jade Emperor declared. "We will dispatch an expedition to capture this monster."

The Heavenly King Li Jing and his third son, Prince Nezha, immediately stepped forward. "Your talentless subjects volunteer for this task."

Gratified, the emperor appointed King Li his Monster-Quashing Marshal and ordered father and son to enlist an army to descend to the realm below.

The two immortals turned their palace into the campaign headquarters, where they appointed a god named Mighty-Spirit to direct the frontline operations, General Fish-Belly to bring up the rear, and the Commander of Sprites to maintain troop morale. The force passed out of the South Gate and headed straight for Flower-Fruit Mountain, where the immortals selected a flat stretch of terrain to make camp and told Mighty-Spirit to formally declare war. After buckling on his armor and taking up his Ax of Virtue, Mighty-Spirit approached Water-Curtain Cave, in front of which he could see crowds of horrors—wolves, snakes, tigers, leopards, and the like—leaping, roaring, and waving swords and spears.

"Damnable beasts!" bellowed Mighty-Spirit. "Tell that stable hand of yours that the Great General of Highest Heaven has come, on the orders of the Jade Emperor, to subdue him. If he does not surrender instantly, we will annihilate the lot of you."

"Oh, calamity!" wailed Monkey's creatures, scurrying back inside the cave.

"Whatever's wrong?" asked Monkey. His subjects repeated the gist of Mighty-Spirit's announcement. "Bring me my fighting clothes!" he demanded. Pulling on his purple-gold helmet, his golden armor, and his cloud shoes, he seized his golden-hooped staff and led his troops out of the cave, where he positioned them for battle. Taking in Monkey's resplendent battle dress, burning eyes, and bared fangs, Mighty-Spirit had to admit that his antagonist did not look in the least ready to be subdued.

"Rude and unreasonable monkey!" roared Mighty-Spirit nonetheless. "Do you know who I am?"

"How could I, you dim-witted deity?" Monkey shot back. "We've never met. Identify yourself!"

"How can you not recognize me, you lying ape? Why, I am none other than Mighty-Spirit, frontline commander under Heavenly King Li Jing, from the Divine Empyrean, under orders from the Jade Emperor to bring you to heel. Take off your armor and surrender, or we will exterminate every creature on this mountain.

If you put up the slightest resistance, I will instantly turn you into salted vegetable powder!"

"You're the rude and unreasonable one!" riposted Monkey. "I'd have finished you off already if I didn't need you to take a message back for me. Run back to Heaven and tell that Jade Emperor of yours that he made a big mistake sending me to look after his mangy horses. Read this banner"—he gestured at the GREAT SAGE EQUAL TO HEAVEN notice—"and get the measure of my genius. If your emperor gives me a promotion worthy of my abilities, I'll call off my armies and peace will reign in heaven and earth. But if he doesn't deliver, I'll make things pretty hot for him in the Hall of Divine Mists."

Mighty-Spirit gave three scornful barks of laughter. "You insolent ape. So now you think you're the equal of Heaven, do you? Eat my ax!" Aiming at Monkey's head, he took a massive swing, which Monkey serenely parried with his staff.

The battle was on: they clashed to the left and to the right; they confused each other by generating cloud and fog; they splattered each other with mud and sand. Although Mighty-Spirit's ax cut like a phoenix swooping through flowers, it was no match for the iron staff that the self-styled Great Sage whirled about him. Monkey took advantage of Mighty-Spirit's exhaustion to aim a direct blow to his adversary's head; though Mighty-Spirit blocked it, his ax handle split from the impact and he fled the battlefield. "Useless pustule!" crowed Monkey after him. "I'll let you live this time, but mind you pass on my message! Get a move on!"

Returning to camp, Mighty-Spirit kneeled before King Li. "This stable hand has quite some powers," he panted. "I'm afraid I was unable to defeat him."

"You're a disgrace!" raged the king. "Off with your head!"

"Calm yourself, Father," advised Nezha. "Let me go and get the measure of this monkey."

Allowing himself to be swayed, King Li banished Mighty-Spirit

MONKEY KING   43

to await court-martial, while Nezha strapped on his armor and charged off to Water-Curtain Cave, where he interrupted Monkey in the middle of dismissing his troops. Nezha's baby face belied his prowess as a warrior; he was extraordinarily agile—able to fly, leap, and transform at will—and was armed, moreover, with six magic weapons.

"Who's this dumpling?" Monkey asked. "What business do you have with me?"

"Monstrous monkey!" shouted Nezha. "How dare you not recognize me? For I am Prince Nezha, third son of Heavenly King Li. I am here on the orders of the Jade Emperor to capture you."

This made Monkey laugh a good deal. "Does your mother know you're out, little princeykins? How many baby teeth have you lost already? I'll spare you this time—for the sake of your adorable chubby cheeks. Just read the banner—if you've learned to read yet—and tell the Jade Emperor to give me a proper job. If he gives me a promotion, I'll forget we got off to such a bad start. If not, I'll take my quarrel to the emperor's own throne room. And I'll be bringing my staff, too."

Reading the banner, Nezha was even more provoked. "Extraordinary impudence! Prepare for a pounding!"

"Fine by me," said Monkey nonchalantly. "Swing away."

The furious Nezha turned into a monster with three heads and six arms, each holding a different weapon: a demon-beheading sword, a demon-hacking knife, a demon-strangling rope, a demon-taming pestle, a wheel of fire, and an embroidered ball. Witnessing this transformation, Monkey did feel a slight twinge of alarm. "So this whippersnapper has a few tricks up his six sleeves. Nothing to worry about, though. Time for a little monkey magic." Monkey also became a creature of three heads and six arms; his golden-hooped staff divided into three, one for each pair of hands. After no clear victor emerged from the initial clashes, the prince multiplied his six weapons into tens of thousands; Monkey did the same with his staffs. The local monstrous monarchs scurried inside their caves and slammed their doors behind them.

After thirty rounds, though, Monkey's quick wits prevailed: in the thick of the fight, he pulled out a strand of hair and transformed it into a perfect likeness of himself. While Nezha was fooled by the specious Monkey, the real one leaped up from behind and hit him hard on the left arm. Reeling from the unexpected blow, Nezha turned and fled back to the camp.

Having seen everything from the front of his battle formation, King Li was about to rush into the fray himself when Nezha pulled him back. "This stable hand *does* know a thing or two about fighting. He even managed to wound me on the shoulder."

"How can we possibly defeat him?" Nezha's father quailed.

"He's planted a banner outside his cave, declaring that he is the Great Sage Equal to Heaven," explained Nezha. "If the emperor gives him that job, he says he'll agree to a truce. If not, he'll take his fight to the emperor's throne room."

"Let's pass his ultimatum on to the emperor," King Li ruled. "We can always send in reinforcements if the emperor's against détente."

Meanwhile, the creatures of Flower-Fruit Mountain were celebrating Monkey's famous victories with a first-rate feast. "Now that I'm the Great Sage Equal to Heaven," he said to his sworn brothers, "why don't you rename yourselves, too?"

"Good idea!" exclaimed King Bull Demon. "I'll call myself Great Sage Parallel with Heaven." Dragon-Monster opted for Ocean-Covering Great Sage, Roc-Fiend for Heaven-Merging Great Sage, Lion-Camel for Mountain-Moving Great Sage, Macaque for Fast-as-the-Wind Great Sage, and Giant-Ape for God-Routing Great Sage. For at that moment, these seven monsters could call themselves—and do—exactly what they pleased. After a day of revelry, each retired to his cave.

Meanwhile, King Li and Prince Nezha were reporting on the

war to the Jade Emperor. "We were, in truth, surprised by the abilities of this monkey and beg for more soldiers to destroy him."

"How powerful can one monkey be," wondered the Jade Emperor, "that reinforcements are required?"

"We apologize for our treacherous failure, but this demonic monkey's iron staff first defeated Mighty-Spirit," Nezha explained, "then wounded me on the arm." He next reported Monkey's demand for a promotion.

"Outrageous!" snapped the Jade Emperor. "Have him executed forthwith!"

Gold Star now stepped forward. "This baneful monkey knows how to bluster, but not when to stop. I suspect that even if we commit more troops, he won't be easily defeated, and the campaign will exhaust our armies. Why doesn't Your Majesty bring him around with another amnesty and give him an honorary title?"

"What sort of thing do you have in mind?" the emperor asked.

"Let him call himself Great Sage Equal to Heaven—a nonstipendiary post with no duties. That way, we'll keep him tame and tethered here, and peace will be restored."

"Very well," agreed the emperor, and dispatched Gold Star with a second amnesty.

Heading straight for Water-Curtain Cave, Gold Star found the area somewhat changed. The entire mountain was thick with every species of monster, armed to the teeth and spitting with aggression. As soon as they saw Gold Star, they made as if to attack him. "Chieftains," the shaken envoy placated them, "please tell your Great Sage that I come from the Jade Emperor with a special invitation."

The mob of demons pelted into the cave to report to Monkey: "That old man from up above's back with another invite."

"And not a moment too soon!" exclaimed Monkey. "They treated me shabbily before, but I expect they've learned their lesson now." He told his lieutenants to wave banners and beat drums and generally put on a good show for their visitor. Pulling his red and yellow robe on over his armor, Monkey led his followers to the mouth of the cave. "In you come, old chap!" he hailed Gold Star, who immediately followed Monkey inside.

"I understand," Gold Star began, "that because the Great Sage felt his previous posting was unworthy of him, he went absent without leave from the imperial stables. But all officials have to start at the bottom and rise through the ranks, so you really had no reason to complain. After you defeated Nezha, the prince reported back to the Jade Emperor that you wished to be appointed Great Sage Equal to Heaven. The other generals wouldn't hear of it, but I stuck my neck out for you and persuaded the emperor to invite you back to take up your Great Sageship. What do you say?"

"Thanks ever so!" Monkey beamed. "And sorry for all the trouble. But are you sure it'll go through?"

"I had the title approved before I left. Any problems this time, you can take them up with me directly."

Gold Star once more refused Monkey's offer of a banquet, and the two of them headed back to Heaven on a cloud. The Guardians of the South Gate this time welcomed Monkey with hands folded in front of their chests, and he and Gold Star entered the Hall of Divine Mists. "As ordered," announced Gold Star, prostrating himself, "I have brought the rebellious stable hand back."

"I hereby proclaim you 'Great Sage Equal to Heaven,'" the emperor told Monkey. "But this time, behave." Monkey gave a huge whoop of thanks, and the Jade Emperor ordered two officials from the maintenance department to build the new appointment a mansion to the right of the Orchard of Immortal Peaches. The palace was to house two optimistically named departments— the Ministries of Peace and Quiet and of the Spirit of Calm. The emperor deputized a handful of Taoist deities to serve as Monkey's aides, gifted him with two bottles of imperial wine and ten gold flowers, and ordered him to work on his self-control. Monkey retreated to his palace, where he promptly opened the bottles of wine and drank the lot with his new colleagues. Then, after seeing them all off back to their own palaces, he settled down to live exactly as he pleased.

But did he live happily ever after? Read on to find out.

Chapter Five

Now we must remind you that the Great Sage Equal to Heaven was, when all was said and done, still a monkey demon. He had no idea about rank or salary—all he knew, or cared about, was that he was on the Heavenly Register of Officials. His departmental aides waited on him hand and foot, day and night; as long as he got three square meals and a good night's sleep, he was happy. In his unlimited free time, he cloud-toured other palaces and grew friendly with a constellation of heavenly luminaries: stars, generals, and guardians.

Monkey's burgeoning social network did not go unnoticed, and one morning at court a Taoist immortal brought it to the attention of the Jade Emperor. "With nothing else to occupy him, the Great Sage Equal to Heaven has taken to hobnobbing with stars. All this overfamiliarity and indolence, I fear, will lead to trouble, and erode hierarchy and order. He needs to be given something to do, to keep him out of mischief."

The Jade Emperor immediately summoned Monkey, who bounded amiably into the throne room. "Have you got a treat for me? A promotion, perhaps?"

"I understand," the Jade Emperor told him, "that you have too much time on your hands. So I'm going to give you a job. From now on, you're the caretaker of the Orchard of Immortal Peaches. Don't disappoint me."

Monkey gave his time-honored whoop of thanks and left.

Eager to get started, he went straight into the orchard but was soon stopped by a local gardening spirit, who wanted to know what he was doing there. "The Jade Emperor's just put me in charge," Monkey explained, "so I'm here to get the measure of the place." Immediately saluting his new superior, the spirit summoned the orchard's staff—the maintenance staff who weeded between the trees, watered and pruned them, and swept up the leaves—to give him a tour.

A wonderful sight awaited Monkey. Each tree—personally planted by the Queen Mother of the Jade Pool—was smothered in deep pink blossoms and groaned with golden fruit. "There are thirty-six hundred trees in total," the spirit explained. "The front group of twelve hundred bear small flowers and fruit. Their fruit ripen once every three thousand years. Anyone who eats one will become an immortal, with a light, strong body. The twelve hundred in the middle bear dense flowers and sweet fruit. Their fruit ripen once every six thousand years. Anyone who eats one will float up to Heaven and never grow old. The twelve hundred at the back bear fruit with purple veins and pale yellow stones, ripening once every nine thousand years. Anyone who eats one will live as long as heaven and earth, the sun and the moon." Delighted by his new workplace, Monkey inspected all the trees and pavilions before returning home. Every three days or so he visited to enjoy the scenery, and entirely gave up his footloose socializing.

One day, noticing that more than half the peaches on the older trees had ripened, he grew desperate to try them. But because his personal aides and the immortal gardeners were always close by, there was never a convenient moment to snaffle one—until a plan suddenly came to him. "Wait outside for me, would you?" he asked them. "I feel like taking a nap in this pavilion." Once his immortal attendants had retreated, Monkey scampered up a large tree and devoured as many of the biggest, ripest, juiciest peaches as he wanted (not a small number). He then jumped down and summoned his retinue to escort him home. Every few days, he would gorge himself on peaches, using the same ruse.

Time passed in this delicious way until one morning the Queen Mother decided to host a Great Grand Festival of Immortal Peaches in her Palace of the Jade Pool and ordered her immortal ladies-in-waiting—Red Gown, Blue Gown, White Gown, Black Gown, Purple Gown, Yellow Gown, and Green Gown—to pick peaches for the event. As they approached the orchard gate, they spotted the local spirit, his gardeners, and Monkey's aides standing outside and explained the purpose of their visit. "Hold on," the spirit replied. "There's been a change of management around here. The Jade Emperor has put the Great Sage Equal to Heaven in charge and we have to report to him before opening the gate."

"Where is he right now?" asked one of the ladies.

"Inside, napping in a pavilion."

"Then we'll go and find him. We mustn't keep our mistress waiting."

The spirit escorted them in, but only Monkey's robe and cap were to be found inside the pavilion—for after removing them to climb up and pilfer a few peaches, our Great Sage had shrunk himself to two inches tall and was busy snoozing amid the dense foliage at the crown of a tree. "What should we do?" asked one of the ladies.

"The Great Sage often wanders off," advised one of his aides. "He must have left to meet a friend. You go ahead and pick your peaches; we'll let him know you were here." Weaving in and out of the trees, the ladies-in-waiting managed to pick two baskets from the trees at the front and three from the middle rows, but there were hardly any peaches on the trees at the back—and these thin pickings were green and hard, for of course Monkey had eaten all the ripe fruit.

After a long, hard search, they finally spotted a red and white

peach on a south-facing branch. Green Gown pulled it near, then—
after Red Gown had picked the fruit—let the branch snap back
into position. As chance would have it, tiny Monkey had been
sleeping on that very branch, and the twanging motion startled him
awake. He instantly grew back to his normal size, pulled the iron
out from behind his ear, and grew it to the thickness of a cudgel.
"How dare you steal my peaches, you disgusting fiends!" he roared.

The seven ladies huddled together in terror. "Don't be angry,
Great Sage," they begged. "We're the Queen Mother's ladies-in-
waiting. She sent us to pick peaches for her festival. Because the
orchard spirit couldn't find you, we decided to get on with picking
the peaches. Forgive us!"

Monkey's rage instantly melted into delight. "Enchanting
news. And who, may I ask, has the Queen Mother invited?"

"From past experience: the Buddha, the Bodhisattvas, the holy
monks and the arhats of the west, Guanyin from the South Pole,
the Holy Emperor of Highest Mercy from the East, the ancient
immortals of the Ten Continents and Three Islands, the Dark
Spirit of the North Pole, and the Great Immortal of the Yellow
Horn of the Imperial Center. Then there'll be the Five Elders from
the Five Quarters, the Star Spirits of the Five Poles, the Three Pure
Ones, the Four Emperors, the Heavenly Deva of the Great Monad,
and everyone else from the Upper Eight Caves. From the Middle
Eight Caves, she'll have invited the Jade Emperor, the Nine He-
roes, the Spirits of Seas and Mountains, and then the Pope of
Darkness, and the Earthly Immortals from the Lower Eight
Caves. Pretty much anyone who's anyone."

"And how about me?" Monkey smiled.

"She's not mentioned you as such."

"I am the Great Sage Equal to Heaven, you know," explained
Monkey. "The party won't be the same without me."

"We only know about past protocol. We don't know what will
happen this time."

"Fair enough," said Monkey. "You take it easy here for a bit, while I go and find out whether Monkey's on the guest list."

Monkey made a sign with his fingers, chanted a spell, and used immobilization magic to freeze the seven ladies-in-waiting beneath the peach trees. He then hopped onto an auspicious cloud and headed straight for the Jade Pool. As he approached the venue of the Peach Festival, the Barefoot Spirit ran straight into him. A cunning plan for hoodwinking his way into the banquet immediately formed in Monkey's mind. "Where are you going, dear Barefoot?" he asked.

"Why, to the peach banquet, of course."

"Just as well I bumped into you, then. Knowing how fast I am at cloud-somersaulting, the Jade Emperor told me to make a circuit of all the main thoroughfares into Heaven, to tell guests to go first to a rehearsal of ceremonies in the Hall of Perfect Brightness."

"Strange," ruminated Barefoot. "The rehearsal's usually at the Jade Pool. I wonder why they've changed it this year." But because he was an honest, trusting sort of immortal, Barefoot turned his own hallowed cloud around and made for the Hall of Perfect Brightness instead.

Monkey now chanted another spell to transform himself into an exact likeness of Barefoot, landed next to the Palace of the Jade Pool, and entered with a catlike tread. The palace's ornamented interior was heavy with the most marvelous fragrances. A banqueting table—inlaid with multihued gold—was piled high with delicacies: dragon livers, phoenix marrow, bear paws, and orangutan lips. No guests had arrived yet. Just as the Great Sage was busy goggling at the scene before him, he suddenly smelled exquisitely aromatic wine. Spotting in a corridor leading off the main hall some immortal stewards distilling some alcoholic ambrosia, the Great Sage felt his monkey mouth begin to water uncontrollably; he simply had to have some. But how to get past the brewery staff? Magic was the answer, as usual. He pulled out a few of his hairs, chewed them into pieces, spat them out, recited a spell, and changed them into a swarm of nap-inducing insects. The instant they crawled over the stewards' faces, the servants crumpled to the ground and nodded off. After guzzling the choicest items from the table, Monkey skipped into the corridor and glugged to his heart's content.

Although now as drunk as a skunk, he remained lucid enough to reflect upon his actions. "Not good! Not good at all! Once the guests arrive, they'll lay into me for spoiling their banquet. Best to go home and sleep it off." Careening this way and that, Monkey soon took a wrong turn and found himself in front of the Heavenly Palace of Tushita—home of Laozi, the Taoist patriarch. "How in heaven did I end up here? No matter. I've been meaning to call on Laozi for ages, and now here I am—might as well say hello." Clattering in, he found the place deserted—for Laozi was elsewhere, giving a lecture to assembled worthies in the three-tiered Pavilion of Vermilion Mound Elixir. Heading straight for the potions room, Monkey found five calabashes suspended over a lit oven, each containing fully smelted elixir. "Top stuff!" rejoiced Monkey. "I've wanted to get my hands on some of this for ages. Since Laozi's not around to ask, I'll have a little taste—just for research, of course." He tipped the contents of the gourds down his throat, as if he were gobbling up fried beans.

The elixir immediately woke him from his intoxication and enabled him to make a sober analysis of the situation. "Bad! Very bad! If the Jade Emperor finds out about this, he'll skin me alive. What to do? Run away! Run away! Down to earth, where I'll go back to being a king." In the interest of discretion, he chose the West Gate rather than the South Gate out of Heaven (having taken the precaution of making himself invisible first) and landed on Flower-Fruit Mountain. "I'm back, little ones!" he announced.

The throng of monkeys and cave demons—then in the middle

of their military training—dropped their weapons in surprise and kneeled. "You were enjoying yourself so much in Heaven, you forgot all about us," they said reproachfully.

"But I've only been gone half a year!" Monkey laughed, sweeping back onto his throne.

"Remember that one day in Heaven is a year on earth," his generals reminded him. "You've been gone well over a century. What job did the Jade Emperor give you this time?"

"This time," Monkey reported, "the Jade Emperor saw sense and appointed me Great Sage Equal to Heaven. He built me a palace and gave me two departments and a ministerial staff. But it turned out that I had nothing to do, so they put me in charge of the Orchard of Immortal Peaches. When the Queen Mother failed to invite me to a banquet, I broke into her palace and secretly guzzled all the food and wine for the feast. Then I stumbled by mistake into Laozi's palace, and since he wasn't around I polished off all his elixirs. After that, I decided to lie low for a while. So here I am."

Elated by this update, Monkey's monstrous audience assembled fruits and wine for a welcome-home banquet. After filling a stone bowl with coconut wine, they proffered it respectfully to Monkey. The Great Sage took a gulp and grimaced. "That is disgusting!"

"Coconut wine, it's true, bears no comparison to the food and wine of the immortals," replied two of his generals. "But as they say: east, west, home's best. This is the local brew."

"I spotted many more jars of that scrumptious wine at the Queen Mother's place this morning," said Monkey. "Give me a moment and I'll filch another few bottles. After half a cup, you'll all become immortals." While the monkeys practically effervesced with anticipation, the Great Sage bounced out of the cave and again under cover of invisibility somersaulted back to the Festival of Immortal Peaches, where he found the winemakers still snoring soundly. Tucking two large bottles under each armpit and taking another few in each hand, he spun his cloud around and returned to Water-Curtain Cave, where thanks to the wine of immortality, a thoroughly good time was had by all.

Back to the ladies-in-waiting now. When Monkey's immobilizing magic finally wore off, after a whole day, they went straight to the Queen Mother to explain why they were so late. "How many peaches did you manage to pick?" the Queen Mother asked.

"Only two baskets of small peaches and three baskets of middle-sized peaches," her ladies replied. "When we looked in the back of the orchard, there was just one big peach. We suspect that the Great Sage has eaten all the rest. While we were looking for peaches, he suddenly popped up out of nowhere and threatened to beat us. He also wanted to know who had been invited to the banquet. When we didn't mention his name, he immobilized us all. We've no idea where he went next."

The Queen Mother immediately went to inform the Jade Emperor. But before she could complete her report, the crowd of winemakers turned up to file their own complaint. "An unidentified individual has sabotaged the Festival of Immortal Peaches by drinking the jade wine and eating the hundred delicacies."

Finally, in marched Laozi, who got quickly to the point: "Person or persons unknown have stolen the top-quality elixir I was smelting for your Majesty's personal use."

While the Jade Emperor reeled at this catalog of theft, the departmental aides from Monkey's mansion turned up. "The Great Sage hasn't been seen since yesterday. We've no idea where he is."

Just as the emperor was putting two and two together, the Barefoot Immortal prostrated himself before the throne. "I ran into the Great Sage Equal to Heaven yesterday while on my way to the Queen Mother's festival. He told me that the Jade Emperor had ordered all the guests to attend a rehearsal in the Hall of Perfect Brightness, but no one was there when I turned up."

The Jade Emperor's astonishment grew further. "This fellow falsifies my decrees and deceives my ministers. Tell the Spirit of Public Security to get to the bottom of this."

The divine detective immediately began his investigation and soon returned with a thick dossier of evidence. "The criminal responsible for wreaking havoc," he concluded, "is none other than the Great Sage Equal to Heaven." Outraged, the Jade Emperor ordered his Four Great Heavenly Kings to assist Heavenly King Li and Prince Nezha in bringing Monkey to heel. Together, they mobilized the Twenty-Eight Constellations, the Nine Luminaries, the Twelve Heavenly Branches, the Guards of the Five Quarters, most of the Heavenly officer corps, plus one hundred thousand celestial infantry. Dust and fog billowing about them, this vast expeditionary force descended to earth, encircling Flower-Fruit Mountain so tightly that not even a drop of water could slip through, and spread eighteen cosmic nets to make aerial escape impossible. The Nine Luminaries led their troops in a vanguard attack on the entrance to the cave, where they discovered an enormous throng of monkeys of all sizes prancing about and generally having a fine time.

"Puny demons!" roared one of the spirits. "Where is your leader? We are gods dispatched to subdue the rebellious monkey. Tell him to surrender immediately. The merest whisper of resistance and we'll turn the lot of you into baboon butter."

The panicked monkeys rushed into the cave to report the uninvited guests: "Calamity, Great Sage! Nine fierce gods are outside saying they've come to subdue you."

Just then, Monkey was enjoying a few cups of heavenly wine with seventy-six of his closest friends. He seemed perfectly unfazed by the news of what was going on outside. "Drink your wine while it's warm," he proverbialized. "Never mind the brewing storm."

Another cohort of fiends charged over. "Those rough gods say they're about to break down the door."

"Seek not worldly fame or gain," the Great Sage continued. "Except wine and verse, all is in vain."

Now a third gaggle of monkeys barreled up. "They've smashed in the door and are fighting their way into the cave."

At this, Monkey lost his temper. "How rude! And after I'd treated them so nicely!" He ordered the Rhinoceros-Horned Monster Kings to lead the other monstrous monarchs into battle, while he and his generals brought up the rear.

After the vanguard was quickly bogged down in an ambush set by the Nine Luminaries at the mouth of the iron bridge, Monkey extended his staff to twenty feet and threw himself into the fight. "Make way for Monkey!"

The Nine Luminaries were instantly beaten into retreat. "You stole the immortal peaches and the immortal wine, you wrecked the Peach Festival, then swiped Laozi's immortal elixirs and plundered the divine brewery a second time," they shouted at him after regrouping. "What do you have to say for yourself?"

"Stuff happens!" Monkey laughed back. "What of it?"

"The Jade Emperor has ordered your capture. Surrender now, and your people will live. If not, we will raze this mountain to the ground."

The threat enraged Monkey out of his nonchalance. "Enough of your hot air, you pesky gods—meet my staff!"

Even with the Nine Luminaries leaping simultaneously at him, Monkey easily fought them to exhaustion. One by one, they fled the battlefield and returned to camp, dragging their weapons behind them. "He's got guts, this monkey," they admitted to King Li, who now dispatched the Four Heavenly Kings and the Twenty-Eight Constellations into battle. Monkey serenely arranged the monstrous monarchs and four generals in formation outside the cave, where battle resumed at dawn. After a day of epic, murderous combat, the Heavenly army had taken all the monstrous monarchs captive; only the four generals and the monkey minions managed to escape back inside the cave. Monkey, meanwhile, single-handedly held the Four Heavenly Kings, King Li, and Prince Nezha at bay in a duel in midair. As dusk fell, he pulled out a handful of hairs, chewed them up, and changed them into thousands of specious Monkeys, each with their own golden-hooped staff; together, they beat the Heavenly commanders into retreat.

The victorious Monkey retrieved his hairs, rushed back into the cave, and delivered a philosophical speech to his troops, whose morale had been battered by the capture of the monstrous monarchs. "Victory and defeat are the lot of all armies. To kill ten thousand enemies, you may have to sacrifice three thousand of your own. On the bright side, our losses were all tigers, leopards, wolves, snakes, and badgers. We monkeys are safe and sound. Stay strong! My body division magic has temporarily beaten our enemies back, but they are still camped at the bottom of our mountain. We must eat, sleep, and be vigilant. When morning comes, I will avenge our comrades by capturing Heaven's generals with a fantastic magic trick." And after a few bowls of coconut wine, all the monkeys fell asleep.

Chapter Six

Before things had started to go so wrong in Heaven, the Queen Mother had invited the great compassionate Bodhisattva Guanyin from Mount Potalaka in the South Sea to the Peach Festival. But when Guanyin, with her senior disciple, Hui'an, arrived at the Jade Pool, they found everything in disarray. After a handful of busily gossiping immortals had given her a sketchy account of what had happened, she went straight off to see the Jade Emperor, who was seated on his dais next to Laozi, with the Queen Mother behind the throne.

"So what's this business about the Peach Festival?" Guanyin asked, after exchanging greetings with the three of them.

"Usually it's the highlight of the social calendar," complained the Jade Emperor, "but this year that demonic monkey has spoiled the whole thing. We've had to cancel all the invitations."

"And where did this demonic monkey spring from?" Guanyin next wanted to know.

The Jade Emperor explained Monkey's backstory: his emergence from a stone egg on top of Flower-Fruit Mountain, his radiating shafts of golden light as far as the Palace of the Polestar, and so on. "We didn't think anything of it at the time, but then he went on to make a real pest of himself, bullying dragons, getting himself and his minions deleted from the registers of life and death. My first thought was to take him captive, but the Spirit of

Longevity thought he might have potential as an immortal. Hoping to civilize this magic monkey, we therefore summoned him to Heaven and put him in charge of the imperial stables. After he absconded, claiming the job was unworthy of him, we offered him an amnesty and an honorary title, Great Sage Equal to Heaven. To keep him out of trouble, we put him in charge of the Orchard of Immortal Peaches. But he ate all the biggest peaches (without permission, I might add), smuggled himself into the peach banquet (to which he had *not* been invited) disguised as Barefoot here, polished off all the food and wine, stole Laozi's elixirs, and thieved some more wine to share with his goblins down below. Since we are not amused, we have dispatched one hundred thousand soldiers with cosmic nets to bring him to heel. We're still awaiting news from the battlefield."

Guanyin now told Hui'an—who also happened to be the second son of King Li, the heavenly general—to go to Flower-Fruit Mountain. "Help out on the battlefield, if they need it. Then come back and tell us exactly what's going on."

Approaching by cloud as dawn broke, Hui'an found the mountain thickly shrouded in overlapping nets, guarded by sentries shouting passwords at one another. "It's Hui'an, second prince of King Li, Guanyin's senior disciple," he told them. "I've been sent to inquire about the state of play here." Once the message had been passed on to the king, the sentries were ordered to open the net and admit Hui'an, who immediately went to kowtow before his father and the other commanders.

"What are you doing here, my boy?" asked King Li.

Hui'an explained his mission: "Since no one in Heaven had heard anything about the campaign for a while, the Bodhisattva dispatched your stupid, unworthy son to bring news." King Li recounted the events of the previous day and explained that although they had captured some wolves, snakes, tigers, leopards, and badgers, all the monkeys were still at large.

At this moment, a sentry appeared. "The Great Sage is outside the camp with an army of feral monkeys, all baying for a fight."

The heavenly kings immediately set to discussing battle formations. "Guanyin said I should lend a hand, if necessary," Hui'an interrupted. "Why don't I go and size up this Great Sage?"

King Li accepted his offer. "I'm sure you've learned a lot from Guanyin. But do be careful."

Cinching his embroidered robe and grasping an iron staff, Hui'an leaped out of the camp. "Where is this Great Sage Equal to Heaven?" he hollered.

"None other," replied Monkey, raising his own staff. "Who dares ask?"

"I am Hui'an, the second son of King Li, senior disciple of the Bodhisattva Guanyin of the South Sea."

"What are you doing here?"

"Guanyin sent me to find out what was going on. Given what a nuisance you've been, I've decided to arrest you."

"Big talk from a little squirt," responded the Great Sage. "But don't leave just yet. I want to introduce you to this staff of mine."

The two of them fought like whirlwinds until eventually Hui'an's arms and shoulders began to ache. With one last weak swing of his staff, he fled back inside the camp to report his defeat. "That monkey is extraordinary!" he panted. Shaken by this latest setback, King Li dashed off a request to the Jade Emperor for reinforcements and sent Hui'an and another king back up to Heaven to deliver the message. An instant later, the two of them were in front of Guanyin and the Jade Emperor, who tore open the note asking for backup.

"Ha!" the emperor snorted. "Can this monkey really be powerful enough to defeat one hundred thousand celestial soldiers? Who else can we send?"

"How about your nephew, Erlang, from the River Guan?" Guanyin suggested. "The one who killed six monsters and whose followers include the Brothers of Plum Mountain and twelve hundred plant-headed spirits. These days, he only takes on special missions."

Dashing off another order, the Jade Emperor sent it to Erlang by express cloud. The envoy recapped the state of play with Monkey and the Jade Emperor's request for Erlang's assistance: "Success will result in promotions and rewards all around."

Erlang instantly accepted the challenge and summoned his followers. After a quick mission briefing, they harnessed hawks and dogs, primed bows, and set out across the Eastern Ocean on a particularly violent gale. In the twinkling of an eye, all landed on Flower-Fruit Mountain and were let into the cosmic nets. "I'm ready for this monkey," Erlang said, smiling at the expedition's commanders. "If he gets the better of me, my blood brothers will lend a hand. Just make sure that the cosmic nets are left open at the top. King Li, please stand by in midair holding a demon-reflecting mirror. Should he be defeated, I fear that he will try to flee—the mirror will reveal his whereabouts."

Erlang now led his people out of the camp: his blood brothers from Plum Mountain were to goad Monkey into a fight, while the plant-headed spirits were to hold the defensive line and ready the dogs and hawks for battle. At the entrance to Water-Curtain Cave, Erlang found a tidy column of monkeys beneath a banner that read THE GREAT SAGE EQUAL TO HEAVEN. "The nerve of the creature!" spluttered Erlang.

"Save your outrage for later," urged his brothers. "Just challenge him!"

Meanwhile, a monkey sentry had reported Erlang's arrival to the monkey king, who pulled on his best armor and charged out of the cave to size up his new adversary. Erlang cut a remarkable figure: exquisite features, bright eyes, shoulder-grazing earlobes. He wore a robe of pale yellow goose down, with a jade belt and gold boots. A crescent bow hung from his waist; his hands played with a tri-pointed lance.

"Where did you come from, shrimp?" Monkey taunted, spinning his staff.

"What a question!" roared Erlang. "I am Erlang, maternal nephew of the Jade Emperor, King of Extremely Obvious Brilliance by Imperial Appointment. I'm here on His Majesty's orders, you mutinous macaque, to bring you to justice. Lost the will to live yet?"

"I do have a vague memory," Monkey mused, "of the Jade Emperor's marriage to a mortal by the name of Yang. I presume you're their undersized offspring. One touch of my staff will turn you into pip-squeak pâté, but I bear you no grudge and I'd like to spare your life. Off you trot now. Tell your Four Heavenly Kings to come instead."

Erlang responded to the invitation by aiming at Monkey's head and bringing his lance down hard. Dodging the blow, Monkey returned the compliment with his own staff. This murderously close duel raged through three hundred clashes; deputies on both sides waved banners and beat drums. With no clear winner emerging, Erlang decided to mobilize some magic, suddenly towering a hundred thousand feet tall. Monkey instantly replicated the trick. Noticing that the monkey generals were distracted by this display, Erlang's blood brothers ordered the plant-headed spirits to release hawks, hounds, and arrows at the entrance of Water-Curtain Cave. Caught off guard, several thousand little monkeys were captured while the rest scattered, shrieking, like a nest of dozing birds startled by a cat.

Knocked off balance by the flight of his followers, Monkey shrank back to his real size, pursued by Erlang. Trying to flee into the cave, he was blocked by Erlang's six blood brothers. Panicking, Monkey pinched his staff to the size of an embroidery needle, tucked it inside his ear, changed into a sparrow, and perched on a treetop. "Where did he go?" exclaimed the discombobulated brothers.

Keeping a cool head, Erlang saw through Monkey's transformation with his magic third eye. Discarding his weapons, Erlang turned into a falcon and rushed at the sparrow, which soared upward, now as a cormorant. Erlang smartly became a large sea crane, drilling into the clouds with its bill. The Great Sage changed direction, plunging into a stream as a fish. Erlang—now a fish hawk—skimmed over the surface of the water. Monkey swam off in the opposite direction, leaving a trail of bubbles. "There's something odd about that fish," mused Erlang. "It has the look of a carp but no red tail. There's something of the bream about it, but it has no gill bristles. And why did it make off as soon as it saw me? I smell Monkey!" Just as Erlang's beak dipped into the water, Monkey flung himself onto the bank as a water snake and slithered off into the grass. Erlang turned into a vermilion-headed gray crane and pounced with his pincerlike beak at the fake snake, which promptly became a spotted bustard, perched stupidly amid the knotweed. Seeing that Monkey had transformed strategically into such a degraded creature—the spotted bustard is the lowest and most promiscuous of birds, mating carelessly with phoenixes, hawks, and crows—Erlang refused to go anywhere near him. Returning to his true form, he shot the bustard with his pellet bow, sending the bird hurtling off balance.

After rolling down the mountain a way, Monkey laid low for a while, then transformed into a small temple to the local spirit: his mouth became the entrance, his teeth the doors, his tongue the statue of the Bodhisattva, his eyes the windows. His tail proved a puzzler, though, until he eventually decided to stick it up in the air as a flagpole. The approaching Erlang sized up the shrine with that useful third eye of his. "That monkey's trying to fool me again. I've seen plenty of temples in my time, but never one with a flagpole. If I go in, he'll gobble me up. I'd better smash the windows and kick the door in." Anticipating that this would hurt, Monkey sprang into the air and disappeared again.

As Erlang looked around him, his six blood brothers caught up; after briefing them quickly, Erlang told the others to keep a lookout while he went to check on King Li and his demon-reflecting mirror on the cloud tops. "Have you seen that Monkey?" Erlang hollered.

King Li shone his mirror in all directions, then laughed. "I see him! He's made himself invisible and is on his way to your own stomping ground, the River Guan." Erlang hurried off in pursuit.

As soon as he reached the Guan, Monkey changed himself into an exact likeness of Erlang, received the obeisances of Erlang's subordinates, and set to officiating in his nemesis's own temple. Not long after, however, the real Erlang arrived, and his officials rushed out to see the doppelgänger. "Has a so-named Great Sage Equal to Heaven been here?" Erlang wanted to know.

"No, no one of that name. But there is another version of you inside."

After the real Erlang charged at his impersonator, Monkey took his true form. "Welcome to the Temple of Monkey!" Erlang struck at Monkey's face with his tri-pointed lance, but Monkey dodged, and the two of them jousted their way back to Flower-Fruit Mountain.

Back in Heaven, the Jade Emperor and his court were wondering why they had heard no news of Monkey for some while. Guanyin suggested they go out to see for themselves. "Good idea," agreed the Jade Emperor, and sent for his carriage. From the South Gate, they could see Erlang battling Monkey within the cosmic nets, with King Li and Nezha floating on top, holding the demon-reflecting mirror.

"Erlang has Monkey surrounded, if not quite in the bag," concluded Guanyin. "Time for me to give him a hand."

"How?" Laozi asked.

"I'll throw my willow vase at him. It will stun him long enough for Erlang to apprehend him."

Laozi was doubtful. "If he gets his iron staff to it, he'll smash it to bits. I've a better idea." Rolling up his sleeve, he shook a bracelet off his left wrist. "This steel circlet is infused with ingenious magic, impervious to fire and water, and can trap all manner of creatures."

Dropped from Heaven, the snare hit Monkey squarely on the head as the battle with Erlang and his brothers was reaching a fever pitch. Losing his balance, Monkey stumbled and fell. As he tried to pick himself up, one of Erlang's small dogs bit him on the calf. "Get lost and chomp on your master!" Monkey cursed. Before he knew it, Erlang and his brothers had pinned him down, trussed him with ropes, and punctured his shoulder blade to prevent him from transforming again.

Laozi retrieved his circlet and suggested that the Jade Emperor and his retinue return to the Hall of Divine Mists, while the expeditionary forces congratulated themselves on a job well done and packed up for home. In no time at all, the triumphant commanders returned to Heaven, caroling songs of victory. Erlang was richly rewarded—with a hundred golden flowers, bottles of wine, tablets of elixir, and countless other treasures—and sent back home. The felon, the Jade Emperor decreed, was to be taken to the Demon Execution Block and chopped into small pieces, to put an end, once and for all, to Monkey's grandiloquent tricks.

Chapter Seven

The Heavenly executioners tied Monkey to the Demon-Defeating Pillar on top of the Demon Execution Block. There, they chopped him with a knife, minced him with a hatchet, stabbed him with a spear, and slashed him with a sword—all without the slightest effect. The Star Spirit of the South Pole ordered the Immortal Fire Department to roast him with fire, but that cut no ice, either; then he had the Immortal Thunder Department strike him with thunder-bolts; again, Monkey was not bothered. "This Monkey is unfath-omably powerful," the executioners reported back to the Jade Emperor. "We've tried everything, but he's still alive."

"What are we to do?" asked the Jade Emperor.

"This monkey," Laozi explained, "ate the peaches and drank the wine of immortality, and swallowed five calabashes of elixir. I expect that the contents of his stomach have been smelted into a magical mass that, united with his constitution, has made him almost indestructible. Let me slow-cook him in the Brazier of Eight Trigrams to extract the elixir; once that's done, he'll crum-ble to ashes." The Jade Emperor told his security forces to hand Monkey over to Laozi, who took him directly to Tushita Palace. There, Laozi untied Monkey, pulled the knife out from his shoul-der blade, and pushed him into the brazier, telling his attendant to stoke up a strong blaze. Smoke billowed inside the brazier, leaving Monkey's eyes permanently red and inflamed.

Forty-nine days rushed by, and Laozi's braising was complete. As soon as Monkey heard the oven door open, he sprang out, rubbing his eyes, kicked the brazier over, and charged out of the potions chamber. Laozi's attendants and the Security Department escort rushed to restrain Monkey, but—febrile after his confinement—he was too much for all of them. Laozi himself tried to apprehend Monkey but was shoved aside while Monkey made his escape. Taking his magic staff out of his ear, Monkey turned it into a cudgel and went on such a rampage that the Nine Luminaries and Four Heavenly Kings preferred to stay at home and pretend they couldn't hear anything. The slow-cooking, it seems, had only further refined Monkey's powers. With discipline, he might become a force for supernatural good; without it, he was pure animal—a wrecking ball in Heaven.

All this hullabaloo soon came to the attention of the Jade Emperor, who promptly sent a pair of his ministers west to ask the Buddha to vanquish this problem monkey. The two made straight for Thunderclap Monastery on Soul Mountain, where—after the usual exchange of courtesies—they were ushered in to see the Buddha, and their whole sorry tale tumbled out. "You're our only hope," they pleaded.

"Look after the monastery," the Buddha told his Bodhisattvas, "and make sure no one slacks off their yoga. I've got a demon to exorcise." He and his two senior disciples then traveled directly to the Jade Emperor's palace, outside which they discovered the untamable Monkey noisily encircled by thirty-six thunder gods. "Put down your weapons," the Buddha ordered the thunder gods, "and tell the Great Sage to come and talk to me."

After receiving the message, Monkey walked cantankerously over to the Buddha. "Who are you? Can't you see I'm in the middle of a battle?"

The Buddha laughed. "I am the venerable Gautama Buddha from the Land of Ultimate Bliss in the West. I have just learned

of your rebellion against Heaven. Where were you born? When
did you learn the Way? Why are you making such a nuisance of
yourself?"

For reasons best known to himself, Monkey chose to answer
in free verse:

Born of heaven and earth, infused with immortal magic,
I am a monkey from Flower-Fruit Mountain.
After making my home in Water-Curtain Cave,
I sought instruction in the mysteries of eternal life
And mastered the art of infinite transformations.
Since earth was too small for me,
I set my heart on the Jade Heaven.
No one can reign forever in the Hall of Divine Mists,
Just as king succeeds king in the human world.
True heroes dare to fight and win.
Strength is honor; and none are stronger than I. Yield to Monkey!

The Buddha was unimpressed by this performance. "You're
just a magic monkey," he snorted. "How dare you presume to
usurp the throne of the Jade Emperor? He has been cultivating
himself since he was a boy, 1,750 eons ago. An eon lasts 129,600
years. Do the math—that's how long it takes to master the Infinite
Way. You, on the other hand, are merely an animal with preten-
sions to humanity. How dare you boast and curse like this? Repent, before you throw your life and talents away."

"I don't care how old he is," Monkey retorted. "He should give
someone else a turn as emperor. Me, for example. Tell him to get
lost and give me his palace, and that'll be an end to it. If not, I'll
make a rumpus he'll never forget."

The Buddha tried a different tack. "So you're immortal and
fluent in the art of infinite transformation. What other skills can
you bring to the role of emperor?"

"I can travel 108,000 miles in one cloud-somersault. Why, I'm grossly overqualified for the job!"

"Very well," said the Buddha, "I'll make a bet with you. If you can somersault out of the palm of my right hand, then you win. I'll tell the Jade Emperor to move in with me and turn Heaven over to you. But if you can't, then you'll go back to being a monster in the world below. It'll take you centuries to get anywhere near Heaven again."

Monkey laughed to himself. *This Buddha's an idiot. His palm's less than a foot wide. How could I fail?* "You swear?" he asked out loud.

"I swear," confirmed the Buddha, opening his palm out like a lotus leaf.

"Back in a jiffy!" Monkey shouted, leaving behind only a vapor trail. All the while, the Buddha kept his Eye of Wisdom on him, watching as Monkey whirled forward like a pinwheel until he suddenly encountered five flesh-pink pillars surrounded by green air. *Looks like this is the end of the road. Hello, Hall of Divine Mists, good-bye, Jade Emperor. The Buddha promised!* Then Monkey had a second thought: *I should leave my mark, in case the Buddha tries to be slippery about it.* Pulling out a hair, he changed it—with a breath of magic air—into a thick writing brush soaked in ink and scrawled in large letters on the middle pillar: THE GREAT SAGE EQUAL TO HEAVEN WAS HERE. His inscription complete, he retrieved his hair and—I'm very sorry to say—deposited a stream of bubbling monkey pee at the base of the first pillar. With a reversal of his cloud-somersault, he was back to where he had started, standing on the Buddha's palm. "Mission accomplished. Tell the Jade Emperor to pack up."

"You never left my palm, urinous ape!" the Buddha roared.

"Don't be thick," retorted Monkey. "I went to the edge of Heaven, where I found five flesh-pink pillars surrounded by green air. I even left a little memento: come with me and I'll show you."

"No need," the Buddha responded. "A glance down will suf-
fice."

Looking down, Monkey found—as promised—the words THE
GREAT SAGE EQUAL TO HEAVEN WAS HERE written on the Buddha's middle digit and a reek of monkey piss at the fork of the
index finger. "What—what sorcery is this?" he gasped. "I don't
believe it! Let me have another go."

But as our hero squatted for a second somersault, the Buddha
flicked Monkey out of the West Gate of Heaven and back to earth.
The Buddha's five fingers became the five phases—metal, wood,
water, fire, and earth—of Five-Phases Mountain, pinning Monkey
beneath. "Hurray!" the assembled deities clapped and cheered.
Their monkey-extirpation job done, the Buddha and his disciples
were about to leave when the Jade Emperor's chariot—canopied
with jewels, drawn by eight bright phoenixes, escorted by won-
drous music, and broadcasting blossoms and incense—drew up.

"You have saved us with your blessed presence!" the emperor
effused to the Buddha. "Please stay for the Great Banquet of
Heavenly Peace so we can thank you properly."

"Oh, it was nothing," said the Buddha modestly. "I am your
humble servant. My powers pale in comparison to yours."

The golden gates to the Jade Capitol, the Palace of Primal Mystery, and the Institute of Penetrating Light were thrown open, and
the Buddha was invited to sit on the emperor's own dais. Some
eleven thousand deities feasted on dragon livers, phoenix marrow,
jade juice, and immortal peaches. There were divine dancing girls,
there were zithers, there were gifts (including two pears and an
auspicious purple fungus), and many, many toasts.

They were all blind drunk when an imperial inspector arrived
to report that Monkey's head was sticking out from underneath
the mountain. "No matter," said the Buddha. He fished out of his
sleeve a plaque on which was inscribed in gold the Buddhist man-
tra OM MANI PADME HUM and told one of his disciples to fix it

to a piece of rock on the top of the Five-Phases Mountain. The mountain immediately struck deep root, leaving just enough room for Monkey to breathe and move his paws about a bit.

The Buddha and his disciples now bid farewell to the Jade Emperor and his gods. Compassionate as ever, the Buddha, before returning to the west, appointed some protective spirits to guard the Five-Phases Mountain. When the prisoner was hungry, he explained, they should feed him iron pellets; when he was thirsty, he was to be given molten copper. When he had served his time, someone would release him, so that the baneful monkey could atone for his hubris by serving the Buddha. His liberator would be—one prediction went—a priest from the future Tang empire.

But as to when this person might come, the prophecy said nothing.

Chapter Eight

Some five hundred earth years passed. One day, back in Thunderclap Monastery in the Western Heaven, the Buddha called together his assorted arhats, guardians, Bodhisattvas, monks, and nuns for a lecture on scripture, over some fruits and flowers. "The morals of the populations of the four continents vary greatly," he concluded. "The inhabitants of the continent of the east are peaceful and decent. Those in the north kill a good deal, but they do so for survival's sake. They're rough but not malicious. Though the inhabitants of the west are not first-rate illuminates, they live long, abstemious lives. But the inhabitants of the southern continent, I'm afraid, are a lecherous, wicked, and violent lot, bubbling over with poison and spite. I have here three caskets of scriptures, 15,144 scrolls in total, which teach truth and goodness. One set speaks of Heaven, one of Earth, and one of the damned. I would like to send them to the Land of the East on the southern continent, but I fear the creatures there are currently too stupid and profane to appreciate them. I need someone to travel east and find a true believer—a scripture pilgrim—willing to cross a thousand mountains and myriad rivers to come and fetch these scriptures back east and convert the people there to the boundless blessings of Buddhism. Do I have a volunteer?"

Guanyin bowed three times before the Buddha. Her skin was like jade and her lips bright red; her dark hair was piled into a dark, smooth chignon. She was dressed in a white silk robe and a velvet skirt, and her wrists jangled with scented bracelets. "I am unworthy but willing. Please instruct me."

The Buddha was delighted, for Guanyin possessed extraordinary powers—above all her compassion. "You must take especial care on this mission," he advised her. "You must travel low enough that you can see which mountains and rivers you pass, and give the scripture pilgrim precise directions to Thunderclap Monastery. The going will be tough for this true believer of ours, and I therefore have five treasures that you can use to help him." Two of his disciples brought out an embroidered robe and a nine-ringed monk's staff. "You can give these two items to the pilgrim for his personal use. This robe will prevent him from tumbling back into the wheel of life and death. This staff will protect him from harm." The Buddha also gave Guanyin three circlets. "These are the tightening hoops, and each obeys a different spell. Should you meet along the way a monster with extraordinary magic powers, you should convert him and persuade him to become the scripture pilgrim's disciple. If he gives you any trouble, put one of these hoops on his head, where it will immediately attach itself. Recite the spell that goes with it, and his eyes and head will swell and ache so badly that he'll think his brains are about to burst out. That should lead him back to the way of truth and virtue."

On taking her leave of the Buddha, Guanyin called her trusty disciple Hui'an to accompany her, for he possessed an iron staff weighing a thousand pounds, handy for pulverizing any incidental demons. Pausing only to take tea with the caretaker of the Taoist temple at the foot of Soul Mountain, whom she told to expect a scripture pilgrim in a couple of years' time, they soared eastward at low altitude.

Presently, the two of them passed over the River of Flowing Sand: a turbulent, deserted body of water, some eight hundred miles wide, its banks fringed with withered grass. "How will our pilgrim, a weak mortal, cross this vast river?" Guanyin wondered.

Just as the Bodhisattva was pondering the desolate immensity of the river, a hideous monster leaped out of the waves. He had a sinewy, greenish-black body and wild, scarlet hair. His eyes burned like stoves and razor-sharp teeth protruded from a blood-stained mouth. He charged, bellowing, at Guanyin until Hui'an blocked him, and the two of them dueled ferociously on the river-bank. "Who dares defy me?" demanded the fiend.

"I am the second son of King Li," Hui'an replied.

The monster suddenly seemed to recognize his opponent. "Didn't you use to be the disciple of Guanyin? What are you doing here?"

"Following Guanyin, of course. She's just over there."

Hearing this, the fiend could not apologize enough. Putting away his staff, he allowed Hui'an to apprehend him and take him over to Guanyin. "Forgive me," he begged, bowing. "I was once the General of Curtain-Drawing in the Hall of Divine Mists. Because I carelessly broke a crystal cup one Peach Festival, the Jade Emperor punished me with eight hundred lashes, banished me to earth, and changed me into my present form. Every seventh day, he sends a flying sword to pierce my torso over a hundred times. It wears a person out. That's why I'm a little highly strung. And the cold and hunger are so unbearable that every couple of days, I have to come out to eat a passerby. Fancy meeting you in a place like this!"

"You were banished here," Guanyin replied, "because of the crime you committed in Heaven. And now you're just making things worse by eating people. Look, the Buddha's sent me to the Land of the East to find a pilgrim to seek scriptures from the Western Heaven. Why don't you join the mission—become the pilgrim's disciple on his journey to the west? I'll have a word with the flying sword to leave you alone. If you complete the pilgrimage, you'll atone for your crime and can go back to your old job in Heaven. What do you say?"

"It sounds good in principle," mused the fiend. "But I see a potential problem. I've eaten more people than I can remember, including the odd pilgrim traveling west for scriptures. Because everything sinks to the bottom of Flowing Sand, I throw all my victims' heads into the river. But the skulls of the nine pilgrims floated back to the surface, so I threaded them onto a rope to fiddle with when I was at a loose end. I'm afraid that due to the river's bad reputation, pilgrims won't come this way anymore— and there go my prospects."

"Nonsense. Wear the skulls as a necklace. When the true scripture pilgrim comes, there's sure to be a use for them."

"In that case, count me in." The Bodhisattva touched his head and gave him holy orders. Taking inspiration from the river, she gave him the surname Sha (sand) and the religious name Wujing, "awakened to purity"—Sandy, for short. He then saw Guanyin over the river, swore off eating humans, and waited for the scripture pilgrim to arrive.

Guanyin carried on eastward with Hui'an. After traveling some way, they encountered a tall mountain shrouded in a miasma too disgusting to pass through. Just as they were about to hitch a lift on a cloud, a second hideous monster jumped out at them. He had a snout riddled with holes like a lotus seed pod, his ears fanned out like palm leaves, and his yellow eyes gleamed between. His fangs were as sharp as steel files, within a gaping mouth as wide as a braising dish. He wore a golden cap, and his armor was secured with what resembled snakeskin straps. Without pausing for niceties, he charged over and made to smash his weapon—a rake with teeth like dragon's claws—down on Guanyin's head.

Hui'an was ready for him, though, and blocked the blow. "Hands off my teacher!" he yelled.

"If it's a fight you're after," the monster shouted back, "it's yours!" A tremendous, if messy, battle began, with mud, dust, sand, and rocks spraying everywhere. At the climax of the struggle, Guanyin dropped some lotus flowers between them. "How dare you bamboozle me with blossoms?" the fiend snorted. "Who are you, anyway?"

"I am the disciple of Guanyin, insolent fleshpot," Hui'an replied. "She was the one who dropped the lotus on you."

"Guanyin?" asked the demon. "Guanyin of the South Seas, who sweeps away the three calamities and the eight catastrophes?"

"Who else?" replied Hui'an.

The fiend threw down his rake and bowed. "Where is she? Could I trouble you to introduce me?" Hui'an pointed upward. "Forgive me!" cried the fiend, kowtowing to Guanyin, who descended to join them.

"Where are you from, pig-fiend, and why did you attack us?" she demanded.

"I am neither pig nor fiend," the pig-fiend replied. "I was once Marshal of the Heavenly River. But after I got drunk and propositioned Chang'e, Goddess of the Moon, the Jade Emperor had me beaten with two thousand hammer blows and banished me to the mortal world. Just as my spirit was seeking reincarnation, it took a wrong turn and found its way into a sow's womb—hence the snout and ears. I bit the sow to death, pulverized the rest of the litter, then made this mountain my stronghold and whiled away the time eating people. Fancy running into you here. Could you see your way to saving me?"

"If you wish to have a future, think of the future," expounded Guanyin. "You broke the law in Heaven and now compound the sin with your murdering ways."

"Future!" the fiend spluttered. "So what was I supposed to eat—the wind? If you submit to the law, you'll be beaten to death; if you submit to the Buddha, you'll starve to death. Off with you both! I'll stick to catching stray travelers, the plumper and juicier the better. I don't mind how many crimes I commit, as long as I get to eat them."

Guanyin tried another tack. "Fortune favors the virtuous. Food will find its way to the good. And there are plenty of edible plants; why do you have to feast on humans?"

This argument finally gained some traction with the fiend. "I *would* like to be a better pig. But how can I atone for my crimes against Heaven?"

"The Buddha has ordered me to find a pilgrim in the east who will travel west to seek scriptures. Why don't you go with him as a disciple? You'll atone for your sins and get out of your current dead end."

"Count me in!" exclaimed the fiend, and Guanyin touched his head and gave him holy orders. Taking inspiration from his physical appearance, she gave him the surname Zhu (pig) and the religious name Wuneng, "awakening to power"—Pigsy for short. On converting to Buddhism, Pigsy gave up meat and spices, and awaited the arrival of the scripture pilgrim.

As Guanyin and Hui'an rushed on, they ran into a mewling jade dragon. "Who are you, and what is wrong?" Guanyin asked.

"I am the son of Aorun, Dragon King of the Western Ocean. Because I accidentally set fire to our palace and some pearls were lost in the blaze, my father denounced me to Heaven for being unfilial. The Jade Emperor had me hung up and whipped, and in a few days' time I will be executed. Please save me, Guanyin!"

The Bodhisattva and her disciple immediately dashed up to Heaven to intervene with the Jade Emperor. "While traveling east, on a mission from the Buddha to find a pilgrim to seek scriptures in the west, I've encountered a disorderly dragon awaiting execution. I beg you to spare his life so that he can carry my pilgrim to the Buddha." The Jade Emperor promptly agreed to the pardon and allowed the dragon to go off with Guanyin, who sent him to live in a mountain stream. She ordered him to turn into a white horse when the pilgrim passed by, and to expiate his crimes on the journey to the west.

Not long after Guanyin and Hui'an had resumed their journey eastward, they encountered a blaze of golden light and radiant mists. "It's coming from Five-Phases Mountain," Hui'an reported, "from a plaque inscribed by the Buddha himself."

"So this must be where the Great Sage Equal to Heaven, who made such a nuisance of himself at the Great Grand Festival of Immortal Peaches, is imprisoned," mused Guanyin. On reading the inscription—OM MANI PADME HUM—Guanyin was moved to improvise a short poem:

The reckless monkey regrets his rashness.
He wrecked the festival of peaches,
and ran amok through Tushita Palace.
He saw off one hundred thousand troops and terrorized Heaven,
before the Buddha pinned him down.
When will he be freed to make use of his talents?

"Hey!" yelled Monkey from underneath the mountain. "Who's up there reciting poetry about my shortcomings?"

Guanyin came down the mountain to seek him out. Monkey's spirit guards greeted her politely, then took her to see the prisoner, who was trapped inside a stone casket, able to speak but not move. "Do you recognize me, Monkey?"

"Of course," he replied, opening wide his smoke-reddened eyes. "Thanks for looking in. You're my first visitor in five hundred years. And time passes slowly when you're stuck beneath a mountain with only iron pellets to eat. What brings you this way?"

"I was just passing. The Buddha's sent me east to find a pilgrim to seek scriptures in the west."

"That double-dealing Buddha tricked me under this mountain," Monkey complained. "Please let me out."

Guanyin frowned. "You did some terrible things five hundred years ago. If I release you, you'll just go back to your bad habits."

"I've seen the error of my ways!" protested Monkey. "Show me compassion and I'll embrace Buddhism."

Guanyin thawed on hearing this. "If you really mean it, I'll send my pilgrim from the east to rescue you. You'll become his disciple and practice Buddhism all the way to the west. Promise?"

"I swear!"

"Very well, then. Before I leave, I will give you a religious name."

"I already have one," Monkey reminded her. "Sun Wukong: Sun-who-has-awoken-to-emptiness."

"Excellent." Guanyin smiled. "I've already appointed two other disciples, and their names also contain *wu*, awakened. You'll make quite a trio. Well, no time for chitchat. I must be off."

Within a few days, Guanyin and Hui'an reached Chang'an, capital of the Tang empire, and, disguising themselves as shabby monks, entered the city at dusk. They wandered down a main street until they found the temple of a local spirit. The shrine's incumbents—the spirit and its guardians—immediately prostrated themselves, then hurried out to summon all the other nearby deities (the god of the city, of the soil, and sundry other temple spirits), who also rushed over to bow and scrape. "This visit is top secret," Guanyin told them all. "I'm here on the Buddha's orders, to find a pilgrim to bring scriptures back from the west. I need to stay in one of your temples for a few days. I'll head back as soon as I've found my pilgrim." The local spirit moved in with the city god for a while, to make room for Guanyin and Hui'an, while the other deities returned to their residences. The search for a pilgrim was about to begin at last.

Chapter Nine

Let me tell you now about Chang'an, which generations and dynasties of kings and emperors have made their capital, in the northwest province of Shaanxi. It was a city of great beauty, spread across three counties threaded with rivers and carpeted with flowers. When Guanyin arrived, the emperor Taizong—second of the Tang dynasty—had been on the throne for thirteen years. The country was at peace and people of the entire world declared themselves his subjects.

At court one day, Taizong's prime minister Wei Zheng made a suggestion to the emperor. "We should copy the practice of earlier dynasties and hold examinations to recruit the best scholars and administrators to run the government." And so Taizong sent out an empire-wide edict: Any man, of whatever background, who could write well and was fluent enough in the Confucian classics to have passed the three basic literary qualifications should come to Chang'an to take the imperial civil service exam.

When a gentleman called Guangrui from Haizhou learned of the imminent exam session, he immediately asked his mother's permission to attend. "If I were lucky enough to earn an official posting, it would enhance our family's reputation, and benefit my future wife and sons."

"You're ready for this," his mother—a lady surnamed Zhang—agreed. "But take care, and come back as soon as you've been

given a job." Guangrui reached Chang'an just in time for the start
of the exams and, when the results came out, discovered that he
had come in first. After receiving a certificate signed by the emperor himself, he was toured on horseback through the streets of
the capital for three whole days.

The procession passed by the house of Yin Kaishan, one of
Taizong's chief ministers, who had a captivatingly pretty, unmar-
ried daughter called Wenjiao. At the very moment that Guangrui
passed beneath, Wenjiao was about to drop an embroidered ball
from a decorated tower; whomever it chanced to hit would be
her husband. The moment she laid eyes on Guangrui, Wenjiao
could see that he was an exceptional young man, a first impres-
sion corroborated by his ranking top in the civil service exam.
Not coincidentally, the embroidered ball scored a direct hit against
Guangrui's black silk hat. A symphony of pipes and flutes erupted,
and an army of maidservants rushed out of the building, grabbed
the bridle of Guangrui's horse, and welcomed the examination
star into the house of his future in-laws. Yin Kaishan and his wife
immediately summoned guests and a master of ceremonies, and
married the young lady off to Guangrui. The new couple bowed
to heaven and earth, to each other, and to the girl's parents. The
minister gave a huge banquet and, after an evening's revelry, the
new couple retired hand in hand to the bridal chamber.

At court early the next day, Taizong and his officials appointed
Guangrui governor of Jiangzhou and ordered him to leave straightaway to take up the post. After thanking the emperor, Guangrui
informed his wife and in-laws, and the newlyweds headed off to
begin a new life. As they left Chang'an, spring was in the air: a
gentle breeze and rain were encouraging green shoots and rosy
blossoms. Since the road to Jiangzhou passed by Haizhou, Guangrui paid a visit to his old home, where he and his wife bowed to
his mother. "Congratulations!" Mrs. Zhang exclaimed. "A job
and a wife!" After Guangrui explained how it had all come about,

he invited his mother to accompany them to his new posting. She happily accepted, and the three of them set out again.

After a few days on the road, they put up at the Myriad Flowers Inn. That evening, Guangrui's mother suddenly fell ill and asked to rest for a couple of days before they continued on their way. The following morning, Guangrui bought a live golden carp from a hawker outside the inn, with a view to having it cooked for his mother. Just as he was about to order it to be gutted, he noticed it blinking its eyes energetically. "I heard somewhere that this is a sign of supernatural abilities," he observed, and—after asking for directions from the fisherman—returned it to the river where it had been caught.

Although his mother was pleased to learn what Guangrui had done, she still did not feel well enough to travel, especially as it was the hottest time of the year. "Could you rent me some lodgings here, while you carry on to Jiangzhou? You can come and fetch me in autumn, when it's cooler." After some deliberation, Guangrui and Wenjiao secured her a room, left her some money, and resumed their journey.

Soon they came to the River Hong and hired two boatmen— named Liu Hong and Li Biao—to take them across. At this point, a calamity predetermined by a previous existence overtook Guangrui. Liu Hong was immediately infatuated by the beauty of Wenjiao—by her pale, moonlike face, dark eyes, tiny red mouth, and willowy waist—and hatched a wicked plot with Li Biao. After punting the boat to a deserted part of the river, in the middle of the night they killed the couple's servant, then beat Guangrui to death and threw both bodies into the water. When Wenjiao tried to hurl herself into the river after her dead husband, Liu Hong wrapped his arms tightly around her. "Do what I say or I'll cut you to pieces." Unable, for the time being, to think of a better plan, Wenjiao submitted, while Liu Hong ferried the three of them to the other side of the river. Leaving the boat with Li Biao, Liu Hong put on Guangrui's cap and robe and proceeded to Jiangzhou with Wenjiao, where he passed himself off as the new governor.

While the corpse of the servant floated away on the current, Guangrui sank to the bottom of the river, where his body was spotted by a spirit patrol and shown to the dragon king. "My benefactor!" the dragon exclaimed. "One good turn deserves another. I will save his life." He forthwith made an official request to the municipal deity and local spirit to hand over Guangrui's soul to his patrol, who then led it back to the dragon's palace. "Who are you?" asked the dragon. "Why were you beaten to death?" After Guangrui had spilled out his tragic tale, the dragon revealed who he was. "I was the golden carp you released a few days ago. I'm determined to help you out of your predicament." He then placed a preservative pearl in the mouth of Guangrui's corpse, to prevent it from rotting while he worked to reunite it with the governor's soul, and gave Guangrui a temporary posting, and a splendid banquet, in his Department of Water.

Meanwhile, Wenjiao was tormented by murderous loathing of Liu Hong but, because she was pregnant, had to yield to her captor. The staff at Jiangzhou were all taken in by the bogus "Guangrui," and held a grand welcoming feast for their new governor. Time flew by, and one day, when Liu Hong was far away on official business and Wenjiao was thinking sadly about her mother-in-law and husband, she was suddenly overwhelmed with fatigue and collapsed with agonizing stomach cramps. While she was giving birth, a voice whispered to her: "I am the Star Spirit of the South Pole. Guanyin sends you this baby, for he is an exceptional child and one day will be famous throughout China. But when that bandit returns, he will try to kill the boy. You must protect him. The dragon king has rescued your husband, and one day your family will be reunited and your injustices avenged. Remember everything that I've told you. Now wake up!" Coming to from her stupor, Wenjiao hugged her baby, recalling the spirit's words. But she could not think of how to protect him, and when Liu Hong returned he ordered her to drown the baby. "It's too late to go out to the river tonight," Wenjiao argued. "Wait till tomorrow."

As luck would have it, the following morning Liu Hong was sent away on urgent business. *Liu Hong will kill the baby as soon as he returns,* Wenjiao thought. *I might as well leave him in the river and hope that Heaven will take pity and send someone to rescue him.* To help identify him in the future, she bit her finger and wrote a letter in blood giving the name of his parents and the reasons she had abandoned the child, then bit off the child's left little toe. She wrapped the baby in her underclothes and, when no one was around, slipped out to the river near the governor's house. Weeping bitterly, she was about to throw the child into the river when she spotted a plank near the riverbank. After praying to Heaven, she tied the baby to the wood, tucked the letter next to his chest, and pushed the plank down the river. Having watched it drift away, she returned tearfully to the house.

The plank drifted on the current until it reached the Temple of the Golden Mountain, whose abbot—named Faming—had achieved immortality through the pursuit of religious truth. While meditating, he heard a baby crying and discovered the child on the plank by the riverbank. The abbot immediately rescued him and read the letter tucked inside his swaddling. He named the baby Riverflow, found someone to care for him, and carefully hid the letter of identification. The years flew by and Riverflow turned eighteen, at which point the abbot asked him to become a monk, giving him the religious name Xuanzang.

One fine spring day, as the temple's monks debated the finer points of Zen under the shade of some pine trees, a good-for-nothing who was wrong-footed by the subtlety of Xuanzang's questions lashed out at him: "You bastard! You don't even know who your mother and father are!"

His eyes smarting with tears, Xuanzang kneeled before the abbot and begged him to reveal the names of his parents. Faming brought Xuanzang to his room, where the abbot took down from a beam a small box containing the letter and undergarment from eighteen years earlier, then passed both to the young man. As soon as Xuanzang had read the letter, he kneeled, weeping, before the abbot. "Even as I owe my very survival to you, my teacher, I must avenge the wrongs suffered by my parents. Permit me to seek out my mother, and I will beg for funds to rebuild our temple to repay your kindness."

"Take the letter and the cloth," instructed the abbot, "and visit the residence of the governor of Jiangzhou as a mendicant—you'll find your mother there."

Xuanzang went directly to Jiangzhou. Heaven had ordained the reunion of mother and son, for on the day that he visited the governor's house, Liu Hong was once more out on business. That morning, Wenjiao was thinking about the dream she had had the previous night, in which a waning moon had become full once more, when she heard someone reciting Buddhist scriptures and crying for alms outside the house. As soon as she could, Wenjiao slipped out to invite Xuanzang in. Studying him closely while she served him rice and vegetables, she noticed a remarkable resemblance to her husband. She then dismissed her maid so that she could question him more closely. "What is your name? When did you leave your family to become a monk?"

"I never knew my family," Xuanzang replied. "My father was murdered and my mother taken captive by his killer. My abbot told me that I would find my mother here, in this house."

"And what are the names of your parents?" Wenjiao asked.

"My mother is called Yin Wenjiao and my father Chen Guangrui. My childhood name was Riverflow, but since becoming a monk, I've been called Xuanzang."

"I am Yin Wenjiao," his mother revealed. "Can you prove your identity?"

Xuanzang burst into tears and produced the letter and the undergarment in which he was once swaddled. Wenjiao instantly saw that they were genuine and the two of them fell, weeping, into each other's arms. "But you must leave immediately!" Wenjiao begged him. "If Liu Hong finds you here, he'll kill you. Tomorrow, I will feign illness and insist on visiting your temple to donate shoes for the monks. We can talk more then."

The next day, still light-headed with joy and anxiety, Wenjiao took to her bed, pretending to be ill. Liu Hong asked her what was wrong. "When I was younger, I promised to donate a hundred pairs of shoes to Buddhist monks. Five days ago, I had a dream in which a monk holding a knife demanded the shoes, and my illness began the following morning."

"What a trifle!" sneered Liu Hong, and told his stewards to order a hundred families in the city to each deliver a pair of monk's shoes within five days.

"Which local temple should I donate them to?" asked Wenjiao, when the shoes were ready.

"There's Golden Mountain and Burned Mountain," replied Liu Hong. "Either would be fine."

"I've heard good things about the Temple of the Golden Mountain," Wenjiao observed guilelessly. "I'll take them there." Liu Hong commissioned a boat, and Wenjiao and a trusted companion set off for the temple.

Meanwhile, Xuanzang had returned to Golden Mountain and told the abbot everything. Not long after, Wenjiao arrived. After receiving a warm welcome from the monks, she prayed and distributed the shoes. Once everyone else had left the hall of worship, Xuanzang kneeled next to her. Wenjiao asked him to take his shoes and socks off; she immediately saw that his left little toe was missing, and they once more tearfully hugged each other, then she thanked the abbot for looking after Xuanzang.

"But I worry the murderer will hear about your reunion," Faming warned Wenjiao. "You must leave immediately, for your own protection."

"Take this incense ring," Wenjiao instructed Xuanzang, "and go to Hongzhou, some fifteen hundred miles northwest of here. There, you will find the Myriad Flowers Inn. Ask for an old lady by the surname of Zhang—your father's mother and your grandmother. The ring will prove who you are. Then go on to the capital of the Tang empire—to the house of my father and your grandfather, Chief Minister Yin, to the left of the emperor's palace. Give him this letter and ask him to have the emperor send soldiers to arrest and execute Liu Hong, to avenge your father. Then, at last, you can rescue me. I must go now, in case that villain gets suspicious."

After Wenjiao's boat had departed back to Jiangzhou, Xuanzang immediately set out for Hongzhou and made inquiries about a Mrs. Zhang at the Myriad Flowers Inn. "Oh, yes," recalled the innkeeper. "She went blind and ran out of money. She became a beggar and now lives in a derelict potter's kiln near the south gate of the city. I could never understand why we heard nothing more of the son who left her here."

Xuanzang immediately sought out his grandmother. "You sound so like my son, Guangrui," she said, sighing.

"I'm his son," Xuanzang told her. "Wenjiao, your daughter-in-law, is my mother."

"But why didn't your parents come back for me?"

"My father was murdered by bandits," Xuanzang revealed. "And one of them forced my mother to become his wife."

"How did you find me?" she asked.

"My mother sent me, with this incense ring."

Mrs. Zhang now wept freely. "My son died for the sake of

wealth and reputation! Thinking that he had abandoned me, I cried myself blind for him. At last, Heaven has sent you to find me."

"Take pity on us," Xuanzang prayed, "and restore my grandmother's vision." He then licked his grandmother's eyes and her sight returned.

"You're the very image of Guangrui!" the old lady exclaimed, feeling a mixture of joy and sorrow. Xuanzang took her back to the Myriad Flowers Inn, rented her a room, and left her some money, promising to be back in a month.

Xuanzang then traveled directly on to Chang'an, where he made straight for the mansion of Yin Kaishan. When the doorman announced the arrival of a monk claiming to be a relative, the chief minister was puzzled, for he knew of no monks in the family, until his wife intervened: "Last night, I dreamed that Wenjiao came back to us. Could this be a letter at last from our son-in-law?"

After Xuanzang was shown in, he kneeled, weeping, before his grandparents and handed over his mother's letter to them. As soon as Yin had read it, he burst into tears. "This is our grandson," he explained to his bewildered wife. "Our son-in-law was murdered by bandits, and one of them forced Wenjiao to become his wife." When Mrs. Yin also began to cry, her husband soothed her: "I will tell the emperor and personally lead an expedition against the murderers."

As soon as the emperor learned what had happened, he called up sixty thousand soldiers, who marched to Jiangzhou under Yin Kaishan's command. After obtaining the cooperation of the local forces, the imperial troops surrounded the governor's house before daybreak, broke in, and apprehended Liu Hong before he could get out of bed. Yin Kaishan now asked his daughter to come to him, but overwhelmed with shame at what had happened to her, she wanted to kill herself first. Xuanzang rushed to dissuade her: "How can I live, if you die?" Her father also tried to comfort her.

"A widow should join her husband in death," she sorrowed. "After my husband was murdered, I had to yield to his murderer. Only thoughts of my child kept me alive. But now that my son is grown and my father has taken revenge on this murderer, how can I face my family? I must die, for my husband's sake."

"None of this was your fault," reasoned her father. "Why should you feel ashamed?" Father and daughter burst into tears and hugged each other; Xuanzang watched, also weeping.

"No more sadness," Yin Kaishan told them, wiping his eyes. "I'm going to deal with our criminal." Proceeding to the execution ground, he discovered that a local official had also arrested Li Biao, Liu Hong's accomplice. Yin Kaishan ordered both bandits to be flogged a hundred times. Then each signed a confession to the murder of Guangrui. Li Biao was nailed to a wooden frame and cut to pieces in the marketplace, after which his head was displayed on a pole. Liu Hong was taken to the exact spot on the River Hong where he had beaten Guangrui to death; there, his heart and liver were gouged out of him while he was still alive. Wenjiao, her father, and her son then stood on the bank, casting the two organs into the river as libations, while a eulogy to Guangrui was burned.

Their sobs resonated deep underwater and the eulogy—transmitted to the afterlife through burning—was delivered to the dragon king. "Wonderful news!" the monarch told Guangrui. "Your wife, son, and father-in-law are all making sacrifices to you on the riverbank. Now is the moment to return your soul to your family. I will send you back with a wish-granting pearl, ten bales of mermaid silk, and a pearl-encrusted jade belt." Guangrui, of course, could not thank the dragon king enough. After a fond farewell, the king ordered an aquatic patrol to take Guangrui's body up to the surface of the river and unite it with his soul.

Meanwhile, Wenjiao was so overwhelmed by grief that she would have drowned herself there and then if Xuanzang had not held on tightly to her. As they were struggling with each other, Guangrui's body floated up to the bank. Immediately recognizing her dead husband, Wenjiao cried all the harder. Then Guangrui uncurled his fists and stretched out his legs. A moment later, to the amazement of everyone gathered on the bank, he climbed onto the bank and sat down. "What are you all doing here?" he asked, gazing at his wife, his father-in-law, and a young monk all sobbing their hearts out.

Wenjiao told him everything that had happened and introduced him to his son. "What are *you* doing here?" she asked him back. "I thought you were beaten to death by bandits some nineteen years ago."

"That golden carp I bought then released at Myriad Flowers Inn," Guangrui explained, "turned out to be the local dragon king, and he rescued and preserved me after I'd been murdered, as well as presenting me with the marvelous gifts I have with me now. How wonderful to see you all again, after such misfortune. And I have a son!"

After a grand banquet to celebrate, the family and the expeditionary force returned to Chang'an, passing by the Myriad Flowers Inn en route to pick up Xuanzang's grandmother. That very day, magpies set to chattering loudly behind the inn. Just as she was wondering if this was a portent of sorts, her son and grandson rushed in. She and Guangrui burst into tears and embraced. After exchanging all their news of the last eighteen years, Guangrui paid the inn's bill and the entire family was reunited in the mansion of Yin Kaishan. The following day, the minister reported everything that had happened to the emperor, who promptly appointed Guangrui to be Subchancellor of the Grand Secretariat, a key executive post in the court. Xuanzang was sent to the Temple of Immense Blessings to continue his religious studies. And as for Wenjiao: Wenjiao quietly committed suicide after all.

Chapter Ten

We travel now to another riverbank, this time near Chang'an, to eavesdrop on an exchange between two friends—a local fisherman and a woodcutter who lived in the mountains nearby. Although neither had had any luck in the civil service exam, they both had more than a smattering of education, and tottering home one evening after more wine than was perhaps good for them, they began to quarrel amicably about which were more beautiful—mountains or rivers. To decide the matter, they engaged in a poetry duel—each exchanging poems to extol the beauty of their preferred natural feature. One would praise seagulls and crabs; the other craggy peaks and mountain tea. Finally, the mountain lover, one Li Ding, made a more practical point about life on the river. "Working on the water is a treacherous business. Anything could happen to you."

"Not if you're me," answered his friend, Zhang Shao. "I know a fortune-teller on West Gate Street in Chang'an—he's never wrong. I give him a golden carp every day and he predicts where I should cast. Every day I net pounds of fish and shrimp. I'll sell tomorrow's catch in the city, buy some wine, and treat you to a drink or six later." And the two went their separate ways.

In China, though, even the riverbanks have ears, and an aquatic patrol in the river caught the last part of their conversation. "Catastrophe!" the sentry reported breathlessly to the local dragon king. "I overheard a fisherman saying there's a fortune-teller in Chang'an who tells him exactly where to fish. If he carries on at this rate, all our relatives will soon be exterminated."

The dragon king was all for charging into Chang'an and killing the fortune-teller. But his family and ministers—a miscellany of shrimp, crab, shad, mandarin fish, and carp—counseled restraint. "Don't trust everything you hear. If you burst onto the streets of Chang'an just as you are, with your usual retinue of cloud and rain, the locals will be terrified and Heaven won't like it. Why don't you enter in disguise and investigate the situation first? If it is as that fisherman says, you can slay the fortune-teller; if not, then you won't have killed an innocent person."

Seeing something in what they said, the dragon king put away his sword and told the clouds and the rain that they wouldn't be needed this time. He then jumped onto the bank, turned into a tall, handsome scholar in a jade-colored silk robe, and made straight for West Gate Street in Chang'an. There, he encountered a large, noisy throng. Somewhere within the crowd, a confident voice rang out: "If you're born in the year of the dragon, expect internal vitality. For those tigers out there: face and fate are pulling in different directions. Flamboyant Jupiter's got a nasty surprise for you . . ." *That's the fellow*, the dragon king thought, jostling his way to the front of the crowd. The fortune-teller's shop was lined with exquisite calligraphy and paintings and furnished with the tools of the trade: crystal balls, astrological trays, occult numbers, and duck-shaped incense burners. The shop sign read: YUAN SHOUCHENG—DIVINE DIVINING. The dragon king went in and sat down.

"How can I help you?" the fortune-teller asked after serving his new client tea.

"I would like a weather forecast for tomorrow," the dragon king requested.

Master Yuan consulted the divination sticks up his sleeve.

"Clouds will confuse the peaks. Mists will shroud the treetops. Those wishing for rain will not be disappointed."

"What time and how much will it rain?" the dragon king pressed him.

"Clouds will appear at the hour of the Dragon. Thunder will sound at the hour of the Serpent. The rain will commence at the hour of the Horse and end at the hour of the Sheep. In total, three feet, three inches, and forty-eight drops of water will fall."

"I hope you're not joking," responded the dragon king. "If all is exactly as you say, I will thank you for your forecast with fifty ounces of gold. If not, I will expose you as a fraud, break down your door, tear up your sign, and drive you out of Chang'an."

"As you like," said Master Yuan amiably. "Do come again—after the rain."

The dragon king returned to his underwater palace and reported his doings to the various aquatic deities. ". . . and I told him, if he's made the tiniest mistake, I'll smash up his shop and drive him out of the city."

"Good one, Great King!" guffawed his relatives. "You're the generalissimo of the water. Only you know how much rain there's going to be. That fortune-teller's going to be fried rice!"

The royal dragon family and the fishy ministers were still laughing when a voice rang out above them: "Imperial command incoming, O Dragon King!"

A muscular envoy in a golden robe landed, delivered a decree from the Jade Emperor, and took off again. "'The prince of Chang'an's rivers,'" the dragon read, "'is to summon thunder and rain tomorrow to irrigate the capital.'" The instructions then stipulated the *exact weather conditions*—down to the last drop of rain—predicted by the fortune-teller. The dragon king fainted with shock. "How can this mortal know so much?" he whispered hoarsely when he came to. "I'm going to lose!"

"Don't worry," soothed a shad councilor. "I have a cunning

plan that will shut this know-it-all up for good. Tomorrow, miss the timings and quantity of rain by just a touch. His prediction will be a little bit off and victory will be yours. Then you can drive him away all the same." Well pleased by this stratagem, the dragon king enjoyed a perfectly carefree evening.

The next day, the dragon king ordered the Duke of Wind, the Lord of Thunder, the Page Boy of Clouds, and the Dame of Lightning to stand with him above Chang'an. Clouds, thunder, and rain succeeded one another exactly two hours later than instructed, and only three feet and forty drops of water fell. The dragon king then dismissed his subordinates, returned to earth, transformed into the scholar of the previous day, and bashed his way into Yuan Shoucheng's shop, smashing his sign, writing brushes, and inkstone. When Master Yuan remained seated, perfectly impassive, the dragon king ripped the door off its hinges and threatened him with it: "Bogus prophet! Everything you told me about the rain today was wrong! How dare you sit there so high-and-mighty? Get out before I throw you out!"

Master Yuan laughed scornfully. "You don't scare me. But I'm worried for you. I know who you are: the local dragon king. By altering the times and quantity of rain, you've disobeyed the Jade Emperor and broken Heavenly law. Those are capital offenses, you know."

Suddenly trembling, the dragon king dropped the door and kneeled before Master Yuan. "I was only joking! And now I've gone and broken Heavenly law. What's to become of me? Save me, please!"

"You must plead your case with Taizong, emperor of the Tang. His prime minister Wei Zheng is scheduled to execute you tomorrow at three-quarters past noon."

The dragon king tearfully hovered over Chang'an until midnight, then came to land near the gate of the palace just in time to encounter the emperor as a mirage—for Taizong was dreaming at that very moment that he was taking a moonlight walk outside the palace. The dragon king kneeled before him. "Save me, Your Majesty! Having broken Heavenly law, I am due to be executed tomorrow by your prime minister."

"Of course I will intervene on your behalf with Wei Zheng," the imperial mirage promised. "Don't give it a moment's further thought." And the dragon king gratefully retreated.

The dream began to trouble Taizong as soon as he woke the next morning. Following the advice of his officials, he decided to keep Wei Zheng with him at court all day to prevent the prime minister from beheading any dragons. Now it just so happened that the previous night, Wei Zheng had also received a visitor in his sleep: a messenger from the Jade Emperor ordering him to carry out a dream execution of a local dragon king at three-quarters past noon. That morning, therefore, Wei Zheng had not gone to court, in order to bathe, to sharpen his magic sword for the impending execution, and to practice some calisthenics of the soul. After receiving an extraordinary summons from the emperor, however, he immediately hurried to the palace, where the emperor invited him to play chess. At three-quarters past noon, with the game still going on, Wei Zheng suddenly rested his head on the table and began snoring loudly. "Our prime minister works himself too hard!" the emperor remarked with a smile, letting him sleep. Soon after, though, Wei Zheng woke up again. Mortified that he had nodded off for no good reason in the emperor's presence, he warmly recommended that Taizong execute him ten thousand times. "No offense taken!" said the emperor, smiling again. "How about another game?"

Just as the two of them were rearranging the pieces, two ministers rushed in, holding a dragon's head dripping with blood. "The strangest thing, Your Majesty! This fell from the sky onto a street."

"What is the meaning of this, Wei Zheng?" asked the alarmed emperor.

"I fear I executed this dragon just now in my sleep."

"But you were completely motionless!" the emperor replied.

"I dreamed I traveled up to the execution ground in Heaven, pronounced judgment on the dragon, and decapitated him with one stroke of my sword. Hence its bleeding head falling from the sky just now," Wei Zheng explained.

On the one hand, the emperor was proud to have such a capable minister, whom Heaven trusted to carry out its commands even in his sleep. On the other, however, he felt guilty at his failure to save the dragon.

From that point, Taizong was haunted by his memory of the weeping dragon begging for his life; he felt exhausted and enervated, the sound of sobbing echoing in his ears. The moment Taizong fell into a fitful sleep that evening, the dragon king appeared before him, holding his dripping head. "Taizong! You promised to save me. So why did you order your prime minister to execute me? I'm going to sue you in Hell." Just as he began to tug the sweating emperor down to the underworld, Guanyin— who, recall, was in the neighborhood in search of her pilgrim and had herself been woken by the dragon's ghostly cries—batted the dragon away with her willow twig; the wretched beast took himself off, still sobbing, to file suit in purgatory.

Taizong woke with a start, shouting about ghosts; no one in the palace got much sleep that night. The next day the emperor did not appear for the early morning court session. Hours after it was due to start, the palace announced that the emperor was too ill to attend. Some five more days passed like this, until the queen mother asked the court physician for his opinion. "His Majesty's pulse is irregular and he rambles about ghosts," he informed the courtiers after completing his examination. "His viscera are severely weakened. I fear he will pass away within the week."

Taizong now summoned three of his ministers. "Since I was

eighteen, I have led armies all over the empire. Although I saw and did some terrible things, I was never haunted as I am now."

"To found the empire, you had to kill so many people," observed his ministers. "Why have you suddenly started to fear the dead?"

"Ghosts scream and throw bricks outside my window. I can just about get through the days, but the nights are unbearable."

"Fear not, Your Majesty. We will stand guard at the palace gate and get to the bottom of this business." That evening the ministers donned full, gleaming battle dress and, armed with bludgeons and battle-axes, watched over the palace gate; Taizong at last had a peaceful night's sleep. But his condition continued to deteriorate; the queen mother started making funeral arrangements, and the emperor handed over care of the state to his ministers. He then bathed, changed his clothes, and waited for the end.

Before he went, though, Wei Zheng had some words of comfort: "When you go down to Hell, be sure to seek out Cui Jue. He was a minister and close friend of your father, the late emperor. After he died, he became an infernal judge, superintending the ledgers of life and death. We often hold meetings in my dreams. Give him this letter, which reminds him that he owes me a favor—I guarantee he'll let you return to life." Placing the letter in his sleeve, the emperor closed his eyes and died. While the imperial family and courtiers put on their mourning clothes, the adventures of Taizong's soul began.

Chapter Eleven

Taizong's soul drifted hazily out of the palace. As he floated along, a company of imperial guards seemed to invite him on a hunt, but after Taizong had gone happily along with them for a good while, they suddenly vanished, leaving the emperor alone and disoriented amid a deserted landscape. "Great Emperor of the Tang!" a voice suddenly called out to him from some distance away. Following the direction of the voice, Taizong saw a man kneeling by the side of the road. Though he was dressed like an official—black gauze cap, silk robe, rhinoceros horn belt, white-soled boots—he had an unearthly look: a halo of light and mist surrounded him. He was carrying the Ledger of Life and Death. "Forgive me for not picking you up from your palace," the man apologized as Taizong approached.

"Who are you?" the emperor asked. "And why are you waiting for me?"

"Two weeks ago," the man explained, "a ghost dragon came to my court in the Palace of Hell to file suit against Your Majesty, on account of your having broken a promise to save him from execution. The Minister of Hell therefore sent his ghostly constables off to arrest you and try you in the Court of Hell. I would have escorted you down myself, but I got a little held up in the office. Hence my lateness—my apologies."

"Your name and rank?"

"My name is Cui Jue. On earth, I served your father as a county magistrate and then as vice president of the Board of Rites. Since starting in Hell, I've been a judge on the Capital of Death circuit."

"Enchanted." Taizong smiled, pulling Cui Jue to his feet. "My minister Wei Zheng told me all about you and asked me to pass on a letter." He fished it out of his sleeve and gave it to Cui Jue, who read out the contents:

I, Wei Zheng—who does not deserve your esteem—bow to my sworn brother, Cui Jue. I miss you and your conversation greatly; logistical obstacles—the fact that the worlds of Light and Darkness are separated by a gulf as wide as the heavens—have regrettably made face-to-face meetings hard to arrange of late. In the years since you died, I have prepared a few unworthy fruits and vegetables as sacrifices to you; I wonder if they have been to your taste. I am honored that you have deigned to visit me from time to time in dreams, and was delighted to learn of your infernal promotion. I'm writing now to inform you of the sudden demise of our brilliant emperor Taizong, whom I expect you will meet when his case comes up for review before the Court of Hell. In recognition of our friendship in the mortal world, I'd like to ask you the small favor of revoking His Majesty's death. Thank you for your time and consideration. Yours, etc., etc.

"Since my death, Wei Zheng has taken excellent care of my children and, moreover, written me an exquisitely polite letter," mused Cui Jue. "Please consider your death annulled forthwith!" Just as Taizong was thanking him, two flag-waving young men in blue robes approached, trilling out an invitation from the King of the Underworld for Taizong to visit the infernal palace. Taizong and Cui Jue followed the young men into a huge metropolis, past a golden-lettered welcome sign that read THE CAPITAL OF DARKNESS: A FINE CITY. Rather awkwardly, they passed on the street

Taizong's father, Li Yuan, and his two brothers, Jiancheng and Yuanji. Painfully aware that while still the crown prince, Taizong had killed both of them in an ambush at the palace gate in order to blackmail their father into abdicating the throne to him, Jiancheng and Yuanji set upon Taizong. Only the intervention of a blue-faced, bucktoothed demon drove the vengeful brothers away.

After a few miles, they reached the Palace of Hell. It was a magnificent, green-tiled building, shrouded in crimson mists. Its doors had white jade sills and were fringed with scarlet silk lanterns. To the left and right of the entrance, respectively, a horde of bull- and horse-heads watched over the palace's comings and goings. As Taizong took this all in, the Ten Kings of the Underworld—with a tinkling of jade girdles and wafting of infernal incense—swished out to bow to their guest. "Your Majesty is the emperor of all men in the World of Light, while we are merely the kings of ghosts in the World of Darkness. After you—we insist."

"No, no—after you," countered Taizong. Eventually, after much demurring, he accompanied the kings into their reception hall, and all took their designated seats.

The Minister of Darkness began by ascertaining from Taizong the facts of the case of the unfortunate dragon. "He had committed a capital crime," Taizong self-justified, after explaining how Wei Zheng had executed the beast in his sleep. "It's not my fault it ended badly for him."

"The dragon's execution was preordained in his book of death and we've already sent him on to his next reincarnation. But even though all this was clearly stated in the terms and conditions of his birth, he still insisted on suing you down here for negligence or perjury or some such, which then required you to die so you could appear in the Court of the Underworld—process is process. Terribly sorry for the trouble." Cui Jue then consulted the section in the Ledger of Life and Death specifying the lifespans of kings. On reading that Taizong was originally due to die in his thirteenth—the current—year on the throne, Cui Jue changed his death date to the thirty-third year.

"Following a thorough and rigorous case review," King Yama told Taizong, "you've now another twenty years to live. Please return to the World of Light at your earliest convenience—Cui Jue and our Minister of Defense will escort you."

Seeing as he was there anyway, Taizong asked about the longevity of his family. "They've nothing to worry about except for your sister, who'll be paying us a visit very soon."

"Could I send you a token of my esteem after I return to my palace?" Taizong asked. "Some fruit, perhaps?"

"We've plenty of melons of various sorts," considered the kings, "but we have a hankering for pumpkins, as it happens."

"Consider it done." They all bowed to one another and went their separate ways.

Taizong noticed that the Minister of Defense seemed to be taking him a different way from the one he'd come in. "Are you sure this is right?" the emperor asked Cui Jue.

"There is a road into Hell, but no way out," the judge replied reassuringly. "You can leave only on the Wheel of Transmigration, so that's where we're headed. We thought we'd take you on the scenic route, to show you some of the sights of Hell as we go." After a few miles, they crossed the precipitous Mountain of Shade, crawling with ghosts and goblins, and garlanded with pitch-black demonic exhalations and monster-harboring thickets of thorns. They next came to a sprawl of government departments, all sites of indescribable grotesquerie echoing with cries of agony.

"What happens here?" asked Taizong.

"This is the Eighteen-Story Hell," explained Cui Jue. "It's a merciless honeycomb of torture chambers, injustice cells, and fiery pits. There's something for every sinner: liars, flatterers, swindlers, unfilial children, bullies, murderers. There's tongue-pulling, skin-shredding—and -peeling, for those gluttons for punishment out there—bone-exposing, tendon-severing, freezing, pounding, crushing, grinding, mutilation, evisceration, boiling oil, and of course oodles of blood. Does that answer your question?"

Taizong was too horrified to speak.

They now came to three parallel bridges. The first, made of gold, they led Taizong over. The bridge to one side was made of silver; a number of respectable, honest-looking individuals were walking across. The bridge on the other side was wreathed in howls and whimpers; icy winds and tides of blood churned around it. "What's that?" Taizong asked.

"The Bridge of No Alternative," Cui Jue replied, "where the barefoot, wild-haired souls of the damned have to cross. Underneath it runs the bone-chilling River Rancid. The bridge is several miles long and suspended a hundred feet above waves a thousand fathoms deep, but is only as wide as the span between thumb and index finger. No handrail, of course. Or lifeboats patrolling the waters below. The river's depths are populated by fiends hungry for humans—including a breed of iron dogs and brass serpents with a particular yen for women who bad-mouth their in-laws."

Taizong was, once more, speechless with terror.

Presently, Taizong and his guides reached the City of the Dead, where a crowd of broken ghosts—some with severed limbs, some headless, some with their backs snapped by the rack—clamored around Taizong: "Save us!" He tried to hide behind Cui Jue.

"These are the impoverished hungry ghosts of miscellaneous princes and gangsters," the judge explained, "who led wicked lives and currently have no hope of reincarnation because no one looks after their memory on earth. I can get you past them only if you give them some money."

"But you see that I came empty-handed," objected Taizong.

"A man in your world, Liang Xiang from Kaifeng in Henan, has deposited thirteen vaults of gold and silver in Hell. If you tell the infernal bankers who you are and I vouch for you, they're sure to advance you a loan, which we can give to the hungry ghosts."

Taizong promptly signed a chit, borrowed a roomful of gold and silver, and distributed it among the ghosts. "Let the emperor through," instructed Cui Jue. "When he returns to the world of the living, he'll hold a grand mass to enable your souls to be reborn. So I'll have no more trouble out of any of you." The ghosts obediently retreated, and Cui Jue led Taizong on.

A good way farther on, they reached the forking of the Six Paths of Karma. An infinite river of humanity—religious and secular—and of animals, birds, and ghosts flowed into the Wheel of Transmigration. The emperor looked questioningly at Cui Jue.

"When you return to life, do remind your fellow mortals about the Six Paths of Karma. The virtuous will become immortals, the loyal nobles. The filial will be blessed, the principled wealthy. The just will be reborn as humans, the cruel as demons." After leading the emperor up to the path of nobility, Cui Jue kowtowed in farewell. "Our Minister of Defense will accompany you a little farther. Don't forget about the mass to redeem those hungry ghosts. Your World of Light can be at peace only when the cries for vengeance down here have been stilled. Repent of your own wickedness and order your people to do good, to safeguard your dynasty and empire." Taizong promised faithfully, then the Minister of Defense helped him mount a black-maned chestnut horse and they galloped up to a riverbank. "Hurry back to Chang'an, while you still can," the minister urged him. When Taizong refused to move—he was staring, as if mesmerized, at a pair of golden carp—the minister grabbed one of his legs and yanked him into the river, whose fast-flowing current took him directly back to the mortal world.

In the court at Chang'an, meanwhile, a throng of officials and the palace women were gathered around the coffin of the emperor, discussing when to crown the prince emperor. "I wouldn't do anything too hasty if I were you," advised Wei Zheng. "News of the emperor's death will destabilize the empire. And anyway, I'm sure His Majesty will return to life in a day or so. Trust me—I know what I'm talking about."

Just as one of Wei Zheng's colleagues was countering that spilled water was lost forever, a cry came from inside the casket: "You're drowning me!"

The entire court fled for cover except for Wei Zheng and three ministers who plucked up the courage to engage with the coffin. "Is there something bothering Your Majesty? Coffin drapes not to your liking perhaps?"

"What did I tell you?" exclaimed Wei Zheng. "He's coming back to life!"

The lid was lifted to reveal the emperor sitting up inside, still shouting about being drowned. "Don't worry, Your Majesty," the brave ministers reassured him. "We're here now. What's wrong?"

"The Minister of Defense in Hell just now pushed me into a river while I was watching two golden carp," he explained. Wei Zheng quickly ordered some medicinal broth and rice porridge. A couple of portions later, the emperor—after three days and nights of being dead—felt quite himself again.

The next day the courtiers swapped their mourning clothes for their usual red, black, purple, and gold court outfits, and listened admiringly to the emperor—magnificent in a dark yellow robe— recount his time in the underworld. Seized with a new determination to rule virtuously, Taizong then declared a general amnesty for the empire's prisoners and granted all those under sentence of death a year's stay of execution, to give them time to go home and put their affairs in order, before returning to the execution ground to receive their just deserts. Taizong then legislated for the welfare of orphans and married some three thousand palace women to military officers. He also issued an edict informing his subjects about the inevitability of retribution for villainy and rewards for good works; and the empire became a universally better place.

Next, Taizong refunded the roomful of gold and silver that he had borrowed from the gentleman of Kaifeng. He turned out to be a humble water-seller who donated all his surplus income to alms-giving or burning paper money—that was how he had built up such an extraordinary fortune in the netherworld. Taizong then advertised for a volunteer to deliver the promised pumpkins to Hell. A few days later, a man called Liu Quan—from a wealthy family of central China—came forward. Not long before, he had scolded his wife for her indiscretion in giving a monk a gold hairpin at their front door, and she had promptly hanged herself in shame and anger, leaving behind a pair of grief-stricken young children. Liu Quan was so remorseful that he was more than happy to leave this world to become an infernal fruit courier. Following the emperor's instructions, he placed two pumpkins on his head and some money up his sleeve and swallowed poison.

Soon enough, his soul reached the Gate of Ghosts, the pumpkins still on his head. "Who dares approach?" roared the sentry.

"I come on the orders of Taizong of the Tang, to deliver pumpkins for the delectation of the Kings of Hell." Now all smiles, the demonic doorman ushered him into the Palace of Darkness, where Liu Quan presented the pumpkins "as a token of the emperor's gratitude for his holiday in Hell."

A delighted King Yama beamed. "Your emperor is a man of his word!" He then politely asked Liu Quan about himself. On hearing Liu's tragic story, the ministers of Hell immediately had Liu's wife, Li Cuilian, shown in. While the couple had a touching reunion, King Yama consulted the Ledger of Life and Death and discovered that an administrative error had been made, for both Li and Liu were supposed to live to ripe old ages, and quickly asked a clerk to restore them to life.

But there was a hitch, the minion revealed: "Because Li's been dead too long, her soul no longer has a body to go back to."

"Not a problem," determined King Yama. "The emperor's sister Yuying is due to die at any moment now. Cuilian can take her body." And the administrator led Liu Quan and his wife away, to implement this technically complex reincarnation procedure.

Chapter Twelve

The infernal assistant swirled Liu Quan and Li Cuilian out of Hell and into the imperial palace in Chang'an, where Princess Yuying was taking a walk. Yama's envoy knocked her to the ground, pulled out her soul, inserted Cuilian's into the still-warm body, and swirled back to Hell and out of our story.

As soon as the palace maids saw that the princess had collapsed and died, they rushed to report it to the throne room. Taizong merely sighed phlegmatically, for King Yama had told him his sister did not have long to live. But when the residents of the palace approached her body to pay their respects, they saw that she was still breathing. "Stop crying!" hushed the emperor. "You'll startle her." Lifting her head, he called out to wake her.

The "princess" rolled over and opened her eyes. "Who are you? Get your hands off me!"

"I am your brother, the emperor."

"My brother's no emperor! My name is Cuilian, Li Cuilian. I committed suicide three months ago, when my husband scolded me for showing my face outside the front door. After my husband delivered some pumpkins to Hell, King Yama took pity on us and decided to bring us back to life. But Liu Quan ran ahead, and when I tried to keep up with him I tripped and fell. Stop manhandling me, ruffian!"

"Delirious," pronounced Taizong. "She must have bumped her head in the fall." He ordered the princess to be carried inside and given some restorative medicine. Back in the throne room, one of the emperor's aides announced that Liu Quan, so recently deceased, was back outside the gate, awaiting instructions. The amazed emperor had him shown in. "How did the pumpkin presentation go?" he wanted to know.

"Very well," Liu Quan replied. "King Yama was very touched that you'd remembered him." He then reported Yama's decision to bring him and his wife back to life, borrowing the body of the princess. "But I mislaid my wife somewhere between the regions of light and dark."

The emperor smiled broadly. "So that's why my sister was acting so strangely just now. Her soul has been replaced by that of Liu Quan's wife. Of course!"

In another part of the palace, the revived princess was making her presence felt. "I don't need any medicine! And who chose those garish yellow tiles all over this place? And those vulgar decorations? Let me out!" A team of palace ladies and eunuchs guided her to the throne room, where Taizong asked if Liu Quan was her husband. "We were betrothed as children, and I'm the mother of his son and daughter. Of course he's my husband!" She now turned to Liu Quan. "Where did you run off to? Why didn't you wait for me? I tripped while trying to keep up, and the next thing I knew, I was surrounded by all these crazy people." Liu Quan had no idea how to respond: this woman sounded exactly like his wife but looked nothing like her.

Taizong now stepped in, declaring that the living, his sister Yuying, had been exchanged for the dead, Cuilian. He gifted Liu Quan with all of his sister's clothes, jewelry, and cosmetics, exempted him from any future conscriptions, and sent the happy couple back to their home, where—reunited with their children—they lived happily and virtuously ever after.

Having cleared up this confusing business of resurrection-substitution, Taizong turned his attention to the grand Buddhist mass that he had promised the hungry ghosts he had encountered in the Region of Darkness. A heated court debate ensued about whether Buddhism constituted a corrupting foreign faith that urged gullible believers to focus on the possible rewards of a later existence rather than on the here and now; that undermined social hierarchies, between ruler and subject, father and son. For had not the Buddha abandoned parents, family, and ruler? Eventually, though, Taizong's highest ministers passed judgment, extolling the wisdom and compassion of the Buddha and the need for syncretic balance among the three teachings—Confucianism, Taoism, and Buddhism. Taizong then invited monks from all over the empire to Chang'an to take part in the mass and ruled that anyone who further criticized Buddhism would have their arms broken.

As to who should lead the mass, there was none as qualified as Guangrui's son Xuanzang: a vegetarian monk since childhood, word-perfect in thousands of sutras and hymns. After receiving a robe of knitted gold, Xuanzang began preparing for the mass. At the Temple of Transformation in Chang'an, monks were gathered, beds were made, platforms were built, music was rehearsed, and an auspicious date selected. On the appointed day, twelve hundred monks assembled to receive the emperor's magnificent cortege illuminated with red silk lanterns and thronged with guardsmen, soldiers, and splendidly dressed officials. When the cavalcade paused in front of the temple, the emperor ordered the music to stop, dismounted from his carriage, and went in to lead the worship. Inside the temple, the air was fragrant with sandalwood incense; vermilion trays were heaped with cakes, sweets, and fruit. Carrying lit incense sticks, all bowed three times while priests chanted sutras for the deliverance of the hungry ghosts. Xuanzang and the other monks in turn prostrated themselves before the emperor, who, after a vegetarian banquet, returned to his palace to await the conclusion of the mass seven days hence.

Let us return now to Guanyin, still in Chang'an looking for a scripture pilgrim. Just as she was beginning to despair of finding someone virtuous enough, she heard of the emperor's grand mass. When she discovered that its master of ceremonies was Riverflow, a child of Buddha whom she had personally dispatched into his present incarnation, she knew her search was at an end. As the next stage of her plan, she took to the streets of Chang'an with her disciple Hui'an, to hawk two of the Buddha's treasures: the decorated robe and the staff. The three magic hoops she stored up for use at a later point.

A dim-witted monk, insufficiently elevated to have been chosen to attend the grand mass but with a few ill-gotten coins to rub together, happened to stroll past Guanyin, who had transformed herself into a ragged, barefoot monk. His eye was immediately caught by the glowing robe. "How much, scab-face?"

"Five thousand ounces of silver for the robe, two thousand for the staff."

"You must be mad!" the birdbrained monk guffawed. "No one'll give you so much for that junk! Get away with you!" Without engaging further, the disguised Guanyin and Hui'an carried on their way, until they encountered the cortege of Taizong's chancellor, Xiao Yu, at the Gate of Eastern Resplendence.

When Guanyin refused to step aside to let him past, Xiao Yu reined in his horse; the luminous robe immediately caught his eye. "How much is it?" he asked.

"That depends," Guanyin replied. "Seven thousand is the price for the impious. But I will gift these items gratis to a faithful follower of the Buddha."

The minister now dismounted and treated Guanyin with the utmost courtesy. "Because our emperor is devoted to good works, the capital is currently celebrating a grand mass. This robe would be perfect for the officiating priest, Xuanzang."

Xiao Yu led her in to see the emperor. "What is special about this robe?" Taizong asked her.

"Made from ice-white silkworms and by immortal weavers, it protects the wearer from calamity. It glows with a magic aura bright enough to illuminate your mortal world."

"That does sound good," admitted the emperor. "And the staff?"

"A former prop of immortals, it laughs at the very idea of old age."

Taizong insisted on buying both for Xuanzang. But Guanyin refused payment, in recognition of the emperor's devotion to good works. When the emperor tried to thank her with a vegetarian banquet, she also declined and returned happily to her temple lodging. The emperor immediately summoned Xuanzang to the palace to try on the robe. It fit him perfectly.

The seventh day, the conclusion of the mass, swiftly arrived, and the emperor returned to the temple, followed by most of the capital's population. "Let's go and see what all the fuss is about," Guanyin said to Hui'an, "and whether this monk deserves our treasures and what he actually knows about Buddhism." When they arrived, Xuanzang was busy preaching about this and that: now the sutra of Life and Deliverance for the Dead, now the Heavenly Chronicle of Peace, now the Scroll of Merit Through Self-Cultivation. Pushing her way to the front, Guanyin thumped the platform. "Hey, you up there!" she heckled. "So you know a thing or two about Hinayana, the lesser vehicle of Buddhist enlightenment. But what can you tell me about Mahayana, the great vehicle?"

Xuanzang gladly jumped off the platform from which he had been speaking, to salute his challenger. "We know nothing of Mahayana. Please tell us more!"

"Hinayana is the doctrine of the confused; its followers will never ascend to Heaven. Only the Mahayana can break the endless cycles of transmigration. Fortunately, I possess three collections of these teachings: the Tripitaka."

At this point, the temple's security officer hauled off the two disguised mendicants to be interrogated by Taizong at the back of the temple. "You're the monk who brought us the robe, aren't you? Why are you breaking up the mass by arguing with our priest?"

"Your priest does not know the path to salvation," Guanyin told him without bowing first. "For that, you need my Tripitaka—the scriptures of the great vehicle."

"And where are they?" the emperor asked eagerly.

"In Thunderclap Monastery in India, the Western Heaven—the home of the Buddha. These teachings can unravel a hundred grievances and dispel unimagined calamities."

"Can you recite any of it from memory?"

Guanyin and Hui'an now rose up, took their actual forms, and hovered beatifically above the crowd on auspicious clouds.

"How wonderful!" gasped all present—including the emperor—kneeling, bowing, and burning incense. Taizong called quickly for a skilled painter to sketch a true likeness of the Bodhisattva, but as soon as the artist lifted his brush, the vision vaporized, leaving only a slip of paper drifting down on the breeze. On it was written the following message:

> Greetings, Emperor of the Tang!
> 108,000 miles west of here, wonderful texts speak of the Mahayana. Once distributed throughout your empire, these sutras will deliver the ghosts of the damned from Hell. He who is willing to seek them will become a golden Buddha.

"Let's pause the mass and our pursuit of virtue until someone has brought back these miraculous scriptures," decided the emperor.

"But who will go?" asked his officials.

"Though entirely useless," Xuanzang instantly spoke up, "I volunteer to fetch these treasures that will secure the empire in perpetuity."

The emperor immediately raised Xuanzang to his feet and bowed four times to him. "For such sacrifice and service, we will become brothers."

"I swear on my life to reach the Western Heaven," Xuanzang responded, overwhelmed. "If not, I will never return home and instead pass straight to Hell."

The beaming emperor now returned to the palace, to prepare Xuanzang's travel documents and await an auspicious day for his departure.

Xuanzang, meanwhile, went back to his own temple, which was buzzing with the news of his pledge. "Did you really volunteer to go to the Western Heaven?" one of his disciples asked him. "The way is full of tigers, leopards, demons, and monsters, wide rivers and high mountains. Will we ever see you again?"

"I have made a solemn oath," said Xuanzang. "I must repay the emperor's generosity by serving the country. If I fail, I will be damned to eternal perdition. Remember: The active mind conjures up demons; the stilled mind extinguishes them. I may be gone for two, three, seven years, or forever. But if the pine tree inside our gate points eastward, you'll know that I'll be back soon."

The next morning at court, Taizong wrote out a document describing the mission and stamped it with an imperial seal granting free passage to its bearer. "The stars are auspiciously aligned today for the start of a long journey," the Department of Astronomy reported.

The emperor immediately summoned Xuanzang into the throne room; presented him with his travel permit, a purple-gold begging bowl, two attendants, and a horse; and told him he should leave immediately. The emperor and his officials personally saw Xuanzang out of the city wall, where the monks from Xuanzang's temple were waiting with luggage containing winter and summer clothes. When all was ready for the pilgrim's departure, the emperor lifted a cup of wine. "Do you have a nickname that your friends call you by?" he asked.

"I fear I do not," apologized Xuanzang.

"Well, Guanyin called the scriptures you are seeking the Tripitaka. How about I call you that—one brother to another?"

The newly renamed Tripitaka thanked the emperor but was unwilling to drink the wine, for his religion dictated abstinence. "Make an exception today," the emperor insisted, "so that I can send you off properly." Tripitaka was about to drain the cup when Taizong gathered a pinch of earth from the ground and sprinkled it into the wine. He laughed at the confusion on Tripitaka's face. "When will you return from the west?"

"In three years," Tripitaka predicted optimistically.

"You have a long way to go," the emperor told him. "Cherish a pinch of dirt from your motherland above myriad ounces of foreign gold." Now understanding the gesture, Tripitaka drank the wine and set out from the city gate.

Chapter Thirteen

After a week or so of travel, Tripitaka and his two attendants left the empire of the Tang via the frontier town of Hezhou.* Impatient to be on his way that frosty, late autumn morning, Tripitaka had set out earlier than was perhaps wise, before sunrise. Having proceeded for a few dozen miles by moonlight, the three of them found their way forward blocked by a mountain range. Distracted by searching for the path and by fears that they had taken a wrong turn, they tripped and tumbled into a pit. Almost before they had time to panic properly, they heard a clamor of voices and a mob of about fifty monsters hauled them out. Back on level ground and trembling with fear, Tripitaka and his attendants beheld a fiendishly hideous demon king—flashing eyes, sawlike teeth, striped back, wiry whiskers, razor-sharp claws—seated in front of them. "Truss 'em up!" he roared. Just as the three prisoners were to be seasoned for dinner, it was announced that the Lord of Bear Mountain and the Bull-Hermit had arrived for a visit. Presently, two brawny individuals swaggered in and the monstrous king warmly received them. "How are you, gentlemen?" the host inquired of his guests.

"Oh, same old, same old," responded the Bull-Hermit. These pleasantries complete, the three of them sat down for a cordial chat.

*Linxia in contemporary China.

But their airy persiflage was interrupted by one of Tripitaka's attendants mewling piteously because the ropes binding him were so tight. "Who's this?" asked the Lord of Bear Mountain.

"Self-delivering supper," replied the demon king.

The Bull-Hermit laughed. "May we stay for dinner?"

"Be my guests," responded the demon king.

"Let's eat two now," considered the ever-moderate Bear Mountain lord, "and save one for later." The demon king yelled to his retinue to gouge out the hearts and chop up the bodies of Tripitaka's two attendants. The guests were served the heads, hearts, and livers, the host got the limbs, and the rank-and-file ogres got whatever remained. The meal was over in a few noisy seconds. Tripitaka—facing his first ordeal since leaving Chang'an—almost died of fright.

At daybreak, the two visitors took their leave. "Always a pleasure. Our treat next time!"

While Tripitaka remained catatonic with horror, an old man with a staff suddenly appeared. With one wave of his hands, the ropes around Tripitaka snapped. He then blew on Tripitaka, who began to revive. "Thank you, oh, thank you!" Tripitaka cried, kneeling in gratitude.

"Up you get," responded the old man. "Do you have everything you came with?"

"My attendants were eaten by the monsters, and I don't know where my bags and horse have gotten to."

"There they are." The old man pointed behind Tripitaka.

"Where am I?" Tripitaka now asked, a little calmer.

"The Double-Fork Ridge, a favored haunt of tigers and wolves."

"How did you come to rescue me?"

"The three monsters-in-chief were just local demons; your primal purity protected you from their fangs. I'll point you on your way."

After they reached the main road again, Tripitaka turned to

thank the old man but found that his savior was floating upward on a vermilion-headed crane. After he had disappeared, a slip of paper fluttered down, on which was written:

I am the Planet Venus, sent from the west to rescue you. Magic disciples will soon join you to help you on your journey. Do not blame the scriptures for what lies ahead.

After bowing his thanks, Tripitaka carried on his sad and lonely way. For half a day he traversed the ridge without encountering another living soul, weakened by hunger and discouraged by the roughness of the path. His situation took another turn for the worse when his way forward was blocked by two growling tigers and several coiled snakes. With no idea what to do—the temple had offered no training course for this kind of encounter—Tripitaka resigned himself to certain death, while his terrified horse collapsed and refused to get up. At this moment of maximum desperation, however, Tripitaka's predators suddenly fled, as a plucky-looking, bearded man approached down the mountain. He was armed with a steel pitchfork and a bow and arrows, and wore a leopard-skin cap. Tripitaka fell to his knees. "Great king!"

"You've nothing to fear from me," the new arrival reassured Tripitaka, raising him to his feet. "I'm just a local hunter called Liu Boqin. I was out searching for some dinner. I hope I didn't scare you."

"I'm a Buddhist monk from the Tang empire, sent to fetch scriptures from the west. You saved me from those tigers and snakes! How can I ever thank you?"

"They know I'm a hunter," replied Boqin. "That's why they ran away as soon as they saw me. We are actually compatriots, you and I, for this bit of country still counts as part of the Tang empire. Come home with me to rest your horse. I'll see you on your way tomorrow." Tripitaka happily accepted.

After one hill, the wind started up again. "Stay there," Boqin said. "Where there's a wind, there's a wildcat. That's your dinner on its way over here." Tripitaka, as usual, was paralyzed with fear while the indomitable Boqin faced off with a tiger, which tried to flee as soon as it saw the hunter. "Where do you think you're going?" thundered Boqin, attacking the animal with his trident. Eventually, after a couple of hours' struggle, the tiger grew tired, and he dispatched it by driving the pitchfork through its chest. Perfectly composed, Boqin dragged the blood-soaked carcass by the ear back to his village, which turned out to be a rather picturesque settlement with a stone bridge and white-walled houses. On arriving home, the hunter introduced his mother and his wife to Tripitaka and his mission.

"Tomorrow is the anniversary of your father's death," the old lady observed. "Could our visitor recite some scriptures for the occasion?" A filial son, Boqin immediately set to preparing incense and paper money for an ancestral ceremony.

Night quickly fell, and servants produced several steaming platters of freshly cooked tiger meat. Boqin invited Tripitaka to help himself; there would be rice to follow. "I'm afraid I've never touched meat in my life," the embarrassed Tripitaka explained.

"Oh, dear," responded Boqin. "I fear we can't cook you anything vegetarian because our pots and pans are covered in tiger grease."

"Please don't worry," Tripitaka assured him. "You just saved my life. Starving is better than being tiger food."

"Leave this to me," Boqin's mother told her son. She immediately ordered her daughter-in-law to burn the fat off a small pan, scrub it clean, and purify it with boiling water, then boil some wild mountain vegetables into a broth, cook some yellow millet with corn, and serve up two bowlfuls of dried vegetables alongside. As Tripitaka thanked her and sat down to eat, Boqin set up his own banquet at another part of the table. It was a modest spread: some unsauced bowls of tiger meat, alongside dishes of musk deer, snake, fox and rabbit flesh, and strips of venison jerky.

The following morning, the family asked Tripitaka to begin the mass for Boqin's father. After washing his hands, Tripitaka lit incense in the family shrine, bowed, and struck his wooden fish— a percussion instrument to accompany rituals—and spent the rest of the day reciting sutras. When evening came around once again, more incense was burned, along with paper gods and horses, and a written prayer for delivering the dead.

That night, the soul of Boqin's father visited all of the members of his family in their dreams. "I won't lie to you," he told them, "it's been rough in the ranks of the damned and the unreincarnated. But things are looking up. Now that Tripitaka's sutras have canceled out my sins, King Yama has approved my transmigratory transfer to a noble family in China. Do warmly thank Tripitaka on my behalf and see him safely on his way. Must dash, about to be reincarnated."

On waking, the family rushed to thank Tripitaka, who was delighted to hear about the dream message. He refused the ounce of silver they tried to press on him and asked instead that Boqin escort him part of the way west. Boqin's mother baked him some biscuits for the journey, and the two men set out with three servants.

After traveling for half a day, they came to a mountain so high that it seemed to stretch up to the sky. Boqin began skipping up the slope as if it were flat ground. Halfway across, though, he stopped. "You must go on alone from here," he told Tripitaka, "for this is the Mountain of Two Frontiers: the eastern side belongs to the Tang, the western half to the Tartars. I'm not allowed to cross the border, and in any case I have no authority over the Tartar wolves."

Just as the timorous Tripitaka began to weep and tug at the hunter's sleeves, a voice boomed out from the base of the mountain: "Master! MASTER!"

Whose voice was it? Read on to find out.

Chapter Fourteen

"It must be that monkey trapped in a stone casket beneath the mountain," ventured one of Boqin's servants.

"Of course!" exclaimed Boqin. "Who else?"

"What monkey?" asked Tripitaka.

"Before the Tang emperor conquered the west and renamed this the Mountain of Two Frontiers, the ancients called it Five-Phases. Apparently, around the time that Wang Mang usurped the throne from the Han,* this mountain fell from Heaven with a magic monkey impervious to heat and cold trapped beneath it. Local spirits kept watch over him, feeding him iron pellets and copper juice when he got hungry and thirsty. Let's pay him a visit."

Back at the foot of the mountain, they discovered—as advertised—a stone casket containing a monkey; his head and hands had squeezed through the gaps, and he was gesticulating wildly. "What took you so long, Master? Get me out of here, and I'll keep you safe on your journey to the west." The monkey was not looking his best: his eyes blazed above hollow cheeks; his head was carpeted with lichen, grass, and moss; wisteria was growing out of his ears.

Boqin got close enough to pluck some of the grass from his

*AD 9–23.

temples and the sedge from his chin. "I've nothing to say to you," Monkey informed him saltily. "But send that monk over here."

"What for?" Tripitaka asked.

"I've some questions for you. Did the King of the East send you to seek scriptures in the west?"

"He did indeed. Why do you ask?"

"I am the Great Sage Equal to Heaven. Five hundred years ago I rebelled against the Jade Emperor and the Buddha pinned me underneath this mountain as punishment. A while back, Guanyin stopped by on her journey east to find a scripture pilgrim. She said that if I swear off violence, worship the Law of the Buddha, and escort the scripture pilgrim to the west, the Buddha will reward me. I've been watching and waiting for you ever since."

Tripitaka beamed. "Well, that's wonderful. But how can I release you from this stone box? I have no ax or drill."

"Easy. The Buddha stuck a plaque on the top of the mountain engraved in gold. Lift that up, and out I pop."

Tripitaka asked Boqin to come with him. "D'you think he's telling the truth?" the hunter asked doubtfully.

"I swear!" yelped Monkey.

So Boqin and Tripitaka went up the mountain a second time, hauling themselves up on creepers. At the summit, they found a square stone slab, haloed with golden light and mists, bearing the gold inscription OM MANI PADME HUM. Facing west, Tripitaka kneeled next to it and prayed: "If this monkey is fated to be my disciple on my journey to the west, permit me to lift this stone and take him with me to Soul Mountain." He then lifted the stone with perfect ease, and a moment later a scented wind snatched it into the air.

"I am the jailer of Monkey," intoned a disembodied voice. "His punishment ends forthwith. I will return this seal to the Buddha." After kowtowing to Heaven, Tripitaka and Boqin made their way back down to the stone casket beneath the mountain to tell

Monkey the good news. "Best keep your distance while I break out," Monkey warned them.

Boqin led the party some five or six miles away. "Keep going!" Monkey called to them. After Tripitaka and the others had left the precincts of the mountain entirely, they heard a huge crash— as if the earth were splitting. Then a naked Monkey appeared, kneeling, before them. "Monkey is free!" After kowtowing four times to Tripitaka, he sprang up again. "Thanks for looking after my master," he hailed Boqin. "And for pulling grass off my face." He then gathered up Tripitaka's luggage and strapped it onto the back of the horse, who cowered with fear—given Monkey's past experience as a Heavenly stable hand, both mortal and immortal horses submitted to him.

"Now that you've acquired such an, um, distinguished disciple, I'll take my leave," Boqin said to Tripitaka.

"Deepest thanks." Tripitaka bowed to him. Boqin returned the bow and they went their separate ways.

Tripitaka and his new, still naked disciple set off across the Mountain of Two Frontiers. Soon enough, yet another tiger presented itself, snarling and swishing its tail. Tripitaka—on horseback—cowered; Monkey, by contrast, was delighted: "Don't worry, Master. He's just here to deliver some clothes." He pulled the needle-shaped iron out of his ear: with one wave, it became a thick cudgel. "Time to give my precious a little exercise, after five hundred years' rest." He strode up to the tiger. "Where do you think you're going?" While the tiger crouched, as if mesmerized, Monkey with one blow smashed its brains and teeth into a gory porridge. Tripitaka rolled off his horse in terror at Monkey's deadly speed.

Monkey now dragged the dead tiger over. "Do take a seat while I undress him."

"But he's not wearing any clothes," protested a puzzled Tripitaka.

Monkey pulled out a hair and with one magic breath turned it into a sharp, curved knife. With a few deft cuts, Monkey removed the tiger skin in one piece. After slicing off the head and paws, he was left with a large square. "Hmm, a little big," he considered, holding it against himself. After cutting it in two, he wrapped one of the pieces around his waist like a kilt and secured it with a belt made from a length of roadside vine. "Onward, Master!" he cried. "I'll borrow a needle and thread to sew it up properly at the next house we pass." With a twist of his fingers, the iron cudgel shrank back to the size of a needle, which he slipped inside his ear. He now shouldered the luggage himself and asked Tripitaka to mount the horse.

A question came to Tripitaka as they walked: "What happened to the cudgel you hit the tiger with?"

With a happy laugh, Monkey explained the provenance of the weapon and its name. "It came in pretty handy when I rebelled against Heaven, because I could shrink and grow it as required."

"And how come that tiger froze as soon as it saw you?" Tripitaka asked.

"I can defeat dragons and tigers, and churn rivers and oceans. I can read a person from one glance at their face; I can discern truth from sounds. I can grow as big as the universe or shrink to smaller than a hair. I have mastered infinite transformations and can turn invisible and visible at will. Killing that tiger was child's play. Give me a proper challenge and I'll show you what I'm made of." All this was music to Tripitaka's easily frightened ears, and the two of them barely noticed the day drawing in as they walked and chatted.

"It's getting late," observed Monkey. "There should be a house in that copse of trees ahead. Let's ask to spend the night." He marched up to the door. "Open up!" An old man leaning on a bamboo staff came to the door. One glance at Monkey—bulbous muzzle, red eyes, freshly flayed tiger-skin kilt—and the old man began babbling fearfully about demons.

"Don't be afraid, sir," Tripitaka reassured him. "I am a monk and he is my disciple."

The old man gazed, somewhat reassured, at Tripitaka's handsome, guileless face. "But what sort of temple accepts monks as ugly as that?"

Tripitaka now explained where he had come from and where he was going, and asked to stay for a night. "That eyesore of a disciple of yours doesn't look very Chinese to me," said the old man doubtfully.

"I'm the Great Sage Equal to Heaven, you dim geriatric," scolded Monkey. "And anyway, we've met plenty of times before. When you were young, you gathered firewood and carried vegetables right in front of me."

"What?"

"I'm the monkey from the stone casket on the Mountain of Two Frontiers. Recognize me now?"

"You do look a little familiar," conceded the old man. "But how did you get out?"

After Monkey had relayed his experiences of the past five hundred years, the old man called his wife and children together to join them for a convivial vegetarian meal. "One more thing," said Monkey. "As I haven't had a bath for five centuries, would you heat some water so that my master and I can wash?" Basins were duly brought in. "Oh, and could you lend me a needle and thread?" the freshly bathed Monkey continued. The old man quickly produced these items. Monkey slipped on the white shirt that Tripitaka had been wearing before his bath, neatly hemmed the bottom of the tiger-skin kilt, and tied it around his waist once more with the piece of vine. "How do I look?" he asked Tripitaka, parading about the room.

"Never better!" applauded the monk. "If you don't mind wearing secondhand things, you're welcome to keep that shirt."

"Thanks!" sang Monkey. "This has been easily the best day

I've had in half a millennium." And once he had found some hay for the horse, the entire household retired to bed.

The next day after breakfast, the two set out once more. On they went for months, traveling by day and resting at night, until one day in early winter six men jumped out at them from the side of the road, armed with spears, swords, and bows, and shouting, "Your money or your life!"

Dumb with fear, Tripitaka tumbled off the horse. Monkey picked him up off the ground. "Don't worry, Master. These nice men have come to give us all their clothes and money."

"Is there something wrong with your hearing?" Tripitaka asked him.

"You just look after our things," Monkey said soothingly, "while I go and have an exchange of views with them."

"But there are six of them to one of you. And you're an undersized monkey. How will you manage?"

Monkey sauntered up to them with his arms folded. "Why, may I ask, are you blocking our way?"

"We are the kings of this highway," they replied, "famed for our feats of wealth redistribution—to ourselves—though you seem inexplicably ignorant of our reputation. We are: Eyes-That-See-and-Delight, Ears-That-Hear-and-Rage, Nose-That-Smells-and-Loves, Tongue-That-Tastes-and-Desires, Mind-That-Sees-and-Lusts, and Body-That-Sustains-and-Suffers. Give us everything you possess or we'll smash you to a pulp."

"I see," mused Monkey. "Six hairy bandits. Hand over all *your* ill-gotten gains or I'll pulp *you*."

Snorting with a combination of amusement and rage, the highwaymen hacked at Monkey's head for a good ten minutes or so. Monkey was entirely unbothered. "A tough nut to crack, this one," observed one of the robbers.

Monkey giggled. "You must be tired after all that exercise. Let me show you this needle of mine."

While the robbers looked at one another in confusion—"Is he an acupuncturist? We're not ill!"—Monkey pulled the magic iron out from his ear and turned it into a thick iron cudgel.

"Monkey's turn!" he whooped. Though the robbers tried to flee, Monkey caught up with every one of them, beat them to death, stripped them of their clothes and valuables, and returned, beaming, to Tripitaka. "Job done, Master! Onward!"

"What horror have you committed?" gasped Tripitaka. "You could have just chased them away. How can you hope to become a Buddhist monk if you take lives so recklessly? What if someone bumped into you in a crowded city and you lashed out like this again? I'd be an accessory to the crime!"

"If I hadn't beaten them," Monkey argued back, "they would have beaten *you* to death."

"I would rather die than use violence on others," Tripitaka shot back primly.

"When I was King of Flower-Fruit Mountain five hundred years ago," Monkey pointed out, "I killed more people than I can remember. I'd never have gotten to be the Great Sage Equal to Heaven otherwise."

"Ha! And that's what got you pinned beneath a mountain for the last five centuries with only copper juice to drink. You'll never get to the west if you carry on like this."

Now, this monkey of ours had never taken well to being told off and immediately lost his temper. "If that's how you feel about it, fine!" he snapped and shot off into the air.

"Ach," Tripitaka sighed. "I just offered him a little constructive criticism and off he went in a huff. It seems that fate does not wish me to have a disciple. Even if I wanted him back, I have no idea how to summon him. I'll just have to go on alone."

His staff in one hand, the reins in the other, he plodded sadly on westward. Before long, he spotted coming down the mountain toward him an old woman holding a silk shirt and a patterned cap. As she approached, Tripitaka reined in his horse and stood to one side to let her pass, but she stopped for a chat. "What's a Buddhist monk like you doing alone on this road?" Tripitaka explained the purpose of his journey. "But the Buddha lives in Thunderclap Monastery in India, 108,000 miles from here. How on earth will you get there on your own?" she wondered.

"I did acquire a disciple not so long ago, but he was a rather unruly type. When I gave him some gentle advice, he flounced off."

"I'm just on my way back from visiting the temple where my late son was a monk. The abbot gave me this shirt and cap to remember him by. As you've a disciple, I'll pass them on to you."

"Thank you, but I don't think he's coming back."

"Which way did he go?" the old woman asked.

"Eastward, I think."

"I'm heading in that direction myself. I'll catch up with him and tell him to return. I also happen to know a useful little rhyme: True Words for Controlling the Mind, which I sometimes shorten to the Tight Hoop Spell. Memorize it secretly and don't tell it to another soul. Get him to put on the shirt and cap. Next time he misbehaves, recite the spell and he'll never disobey you again."

As Tripitaka bowed his thanks, the old woman turned into a beam of light and zapped eastward—only then did Tripitaka realize that his benefactor had been Guanyin. After scattering a few pinches of earth (a wilderness substitute for incense) and bowing worshipfully toward the east, he hid the shirt and cap in his pack and sat by the path, practicing the Tight Hoop Spell, which he soon memorized.

Meanwhile, Monkey had cloud-somersaulted straight to the Eastern Ocean. Pausing his cloud over the surface of the water, he parted the waves and dived down to the Water-Crystal Palace, where a flustered Aoguang, the dragon king, sprang up to greet him. After exchanging courtesies, the dragon invited Monkey to take a seat. "I did hear that your jail term was up—forgive me for being late to offer my congratulations. I imagine that you have returned to your old haunt on Flower-Fruit Mountain?"

"I did think of that, but then I decided to become a Buddhist monk. "

"Oh, really?" queried the dragon king.

"Well, I owed Guanyin a favor, and she said I should escort the Tang emperor's scripture pilgrim, Tripitaka, to the west."

"Good for you!" applauded the dragon king. "So what are you doing here, then?"

"Tripitaka didn't appreciate me. When I killed a few robbers who got in our way, he fussed and nagged at me. I can't be dealing with that sort of nonsense. So I decided to return to Flower-Fruit Mountain. I thought I'd drop in on you on the way there to cadge a cup of tea."

"I'm honored," responded the dragon king.

Their tea drunk, Monkey asked about the painting on the wall behind him: a deity of some kind sitting on a bridge and a young man presenting a shoe to him. "It's the story of the immortal Huang Shigong and the future founder of the Han dynasty, Zhang Liang," the dragon king explained. "Sitting on a bridge one day, Huang Shigong suddenly dropped one of his shoes and asked Zhang Liang—who happened to be nearby—to fetch it. Zhang not only retrieved it but even kneeled to put it back on Huang Shigong's foot. This happened twice more; each time Zhang Liang brought the shoe back without a trace of irritation. Impressed by Zhang's good humor, Huang gave him a book of celestial strategies, which Zhang used to found the Han dynasty. Afterward Zhang Liang retired to the mountains and studied to become a Taoist immortal. If you don't help Tripitaka, or learn to work hard and accept criticism, you'll always be more of a demon than an immortal." Monkey silently mulled over these words. "Only you can decide," the dragon king continued, "but don't jeopardize your long-term future in the pursuit of instant gratification."

"All right," Monkey capitulated. "I'll go back to the monk."

"Then I won't hold you up any longer," the dragon king concluded.

With a whoop of farewell, Monkey somersaulted out of the sea and back onto another cloud.

And who should Monkey run into on his way back but Guanyin? "What are you doing here?" she demanded. "Why aren't you looking after Tripitaka?"

Caught off balance for once, Monkey bowed from the edge of his cloud. "Well, yes, a monk did come by and save my life, and I did become his disciple. Then he scolded me for murdering people and I ran off. But don't worry, I'm heading back to him now."

"Hurry!" Guanyin urged him, and each went their separate ways.

An instant later, Monkey found Tripitaka—who was sitting despondently by the roadside—more or less where he'd left him. "Why aren't you on the move?" Monkey asked.

"I didn't dare advance without you," Tripitaka explained. "Maybe I was a little sharp just now. Where did you go?"

"Oh, I just dropped in on the Dragon King of the Eastern Ocean for a cup of tea."

"Buddhists don't lie. You've been gone less than an hour—how could you have gotten to the Eastern Ocean and back, and drunk a cup of tea, in that time?"

"I can travel 108,000 miles in a single cloud-somersault," said Monkey, smirking.

"You can just go off and get a cup of tea wherever you like," whined Tripitaka, "while I sit here and starve."

"I'll go and beg some food for you."

"No need for that," Tripitaka now said. "We've still got the biscuits that Boqin's mother baked for me. Fetch me some water and we'll set off after I've had a bite to eat."

While Monkey rummaged for the biscuits in the pack, the

luminescent shirt and patterned cap caught his eye. "Are these from the east?"

"Oh, they're just a couple of things I've had since I was a boy," Tripitaka lied glibly. "The cap enables you to recite scriptures without having to learn them. The shirt enables you to perform Buddhist rites without practicing them first."

"Let me try them, dear Master," wheedled Monkey.

"If they fit you, you're welcome to them," Tripitaka replied.

Monkey pulled off Tripitaka's old white shirt and replaced it with the silk one, which fit him perfectly. The instant that Monkey put on the cap, Tripitaka set down his biscuit and began silently reciting the Tight Hoop Spell. "Owwwwwww! My head hurts! My head hurts!" howled Monkey. After a few more renditions by the compassionate Tripitaka, Monkey was rolling around on the ground in pain, ripping at the cap. Fearing that he might break the golden hoop within, Tripitaka stopped his recital and the pain stopped, too. Monkey now touched his head. It felt like a golden wire was tightly wound about his crown, and however hard he tugged, it would not come off, as if it had taken root around his scalp. He pulled the staff out of his ear and tried desperately to prize off the hoop. Now afraid that Monkey might manage it, Tripitaka resumed his recitation until Monkey was somersaulting and cartwheeling in agony, eyes bulging, face and ears flushed scarlet. Taking pity on his disciple, Tripitaka desisted once more.

"You've cursed my head!" raged Monkey.

"That's a bit strong," protested Tripitaka. "I was only reciting the Tight Hoop Spell."

"Do it again," asked Monkey. Soon enough, he was begging Tripitaka to stop.

"Now will you listen to me?" asked Tripitaka.

"I will!"

"No more mischief?"

"I wouldn't dare!"

Monkey's heart, however, still plotted rebellion. The next instant, he turned the iron into a cudgel and was about to bring it down on Tripitaka's head when the Buddhist pilgrim gabbled the spell and Monkey collapsed helplessly to the ground once more. "Mercy! I've learned my lesson! I'll never try to sneak up and kill you again! Who taught you this trick, anyway?"

"An old woman I passed on the road just a moment ago."

"That's Guanyin, I'll bet. What's she got against me? I'm going to make her pay."

"Think about it," Tripitaka reasoned. "She was the one who taught me the spell. If you pick a fight with her, she'll turn your brain to soup."

There was wisdom in this, Monkey could see. He now kneeled before Tripitaka. "So she's tricked me into going west with you. You win this time, but you mustn't torture me for no good reason."

"All right," agreed Tripitaka. "Help me onto the horse and let's be on our way."

Dropping all further thoughts of insurrection, Monkey gathered himself and the luggage together, and the two of them carried on westward.

Chapter Fifteen

It was the dead of winter. A freezing north wind blew across the ice-coated landscape, over hanging cliffs, rocky precipices, and rugged mountain paths. One day, while crossing Serpent's Coil Mountain, the travelers reached the bank of a stream. Just as Monkey was wondering aloud whether they had reached the famous Brook of Eagle's Sorrow, a dragon surged out of the water and made for Tripitaka. Monkey managed to drag Tripitaka to safety, but the dragon swallowed the horse and harness whole and disappeared back into the stream. After settling Tripitaka on safe high ground, Monkey returned to discover the bags still on the bank but the horse gone. A quick aerial reconnaissance confirmed that the horse had entirely vanished. "I'm sure that dragon ate the horse," he concluded, upon returning to solid ground.

Tripitaka crumpled instantly, fountaining tears. "A thousand mountains and myriad rivers lie ahead! How can I go on? Misery and woe!"

Monkey found his master's terror extremely irritating. "Calm down, for goodness' sake. I'll have a word with that dragon to give us our horse back."

"Don't leave me!" Tripitaka implored. "What if he suddenly appears and snatches me?"

"You are totally useless!" Monkey fulminated. "First you want a horse, then you won't let me fetch you one. Why don't we just sit here watching our bags till we get old and die?"

"Don't be so tetchy, Monkey," a chorus of voices called from above. "And do stop blubbing, Tripitaka. We are spirits sent by Guanyin to offer you secret protection."

While Tripitaka bowed, Monkey busied himself with administrative matters. "I want your names and ranks so I can put together a register for the guardian spirit protection rota." The forty-odd deities obediently recited back their names and occupations; the Gods of Darkness and Light volunteered for the first shift. "The rest of you can get lost for the time being," Monkey told them. "Take good care of Tripitaka while I go after that damn dragon." He tightened his vine belt, hitched up his tiger-skin kilt, and stood guard by a bulge in the stream, armed with his staff. "Lawless loach!" he yelled at the water. "Give me back my horse!"

Having thoroughly eaten the horse, the dragon was at this moment lying on the bed of the brook, nurturing his humors and cultivating his digestive juices. When this abusive demand reached his ears, though, his heart caught fire and he leaped back out of the churning stream. "Who dares insult me?" Without pausing for formalities, Monkey whacked the dragon's head with his staff, while his opponent fought back with teeth and claws. After a long and frenzied engagement, the dragon eventually grew tired and retreated back to the bed of the stream. Monkey continued to heap vitriol upon him, but the dragon suddenly developed hearing difficulties.

Monkey went back to Tripitaka and made a full report. "That day you killed the tiger, you said you could defeat any animal," Tripitaka needled him. "Why not this dragon?"

Monkey was very susceptible to this kind of provocation. "Enough!" he bellowed. "I'll go have a few more words with him." He bounded back to the stream. Mustering his magic powers, he churned the calm waters of Eagle's Sorrow until they resembled the turbid, zigzagging waves of the Yellow River at high tide, in order to flush the dragon out.

When you're stuck at the bottom of a well, someone's bound to drop a rock on your head, the unfortunate creature thought to himself. *Barely a year after I escaped execution in Heaven, here I am being harassed by this churlish demon.* He decided to re-emerge to have it out with Monkey. "Who are you and why are you persecuting me?"

"Never mind that. Just give me back my horse and I'll let you be!" Monkey demanded.

"It's a bit late for that—I'm digesting it."

"In that case, it's an eye for an eye."

After a few more rounds of battle, the dragon—who was, after all, a rather small specimen—escaped by turning into a water snake and vanishing into the grassy undergrowth. Monkey was so enraged by this disappearing trick that smoke poured out of his seven apertures. Reciting a spell, he summoned the local earth and mountain spirits, who promptly kneeled before him. "Show me your shanks and I'll give you each five blows of my staff to vent my feelings."

"Forgive us for not organizing a welcome party," they wailed obsequiously. "We'd no idea you'd been released from Five-Phases Mountain."

"All right, I'll let you off then," conceded Monkey. "But tell me where that fiendish dragon came from and why he ate my master's horse."

The spirits were nonplussed. "You have a master? We always thought you were a primordial being of the first rank, insubordinate to heaven and earth."

"That's the old Monkey. Guanyin released me from my five hundred years of torment only on the condition that I escort the Tang emperor's monk—my master—to India to fetch scriptures. That's why I'm here. Keep up."

"We see. Well, a while back Guanyin saved a jade dragon from execution on condition that he join your pilgrimage and sent him here to behave himself until the scripture seekers picked him up en route. When he's hungry, he usually grabs the odd bird or deer. He's meant to be on your side; how has he ended up eating your horse? But anyway, just ask Guanyin to get him to surrender and we're sure you'll all get along famously."

Monkey relayed all this to Tripitaka. Hardly had the indomitable monk begun to mewl about how hungry and cold he would get waiting for Monkey to return when one of his protectors, the Golden-Headed Guardian, intervened from midair: "Don't stir yourself. I'll fetch her."

"Much obliged!" Monkey shouted back. "Quick as you can!"

Thanks to a speedy cloud transportation system, the guardian soon reached the South Sea and asked to be shown in to Guanyin in her Purple Bamboo Grove. "Tripitaka and Monkey are in a fix: they've lost their horse at the Brook of Eagle's Sorrow on Serpent's Coil Mountain. The local deities said that a dragon you'd sent to the stream had eaten it, so Monkey requests that you subdue the lizard and get them back their horse."

"That creature is the son of Aorun of the Western Ocean," Guanyin replied. "After he set fire to the palace and its luminous pearls, his father accused him of being unfilial and the Heavenly Court condemned him to death. I asked the Jade Emperor to send him down to earth instead, to carry Tripitaka to India. What's he playing at, eating their horse? I'd better go and sort out this mess myself."

Traveling by auspicious light, the two made their way to Serpent's Coil Mountain. It was business as usual there, with Monkey standing on the bank of the stream hurling abuse into the water. As soon as the Golden-Headed Guardian informed Monkey of Guanyin's arrival, Monkey sprang into the air and began railing at her. "Some Mistress of Mercy you are! What have you got against me?"

"You red-buttocked stable monkey! All that trouble I took to send a scripture pilgrim to save you, and not a word of thanks!"

"That's rich. When you saw me the other day, couldn't you have just told me to behave myself? Why did you have to tell Tripitaka to trick me into putting on that tight hoop, so he can torment me whenever he feels like it?"

"An unruly monkey like you has to be restrained somehow, otherwise you'll never reform. You need to experience a touch of adversity before you become an enlightened Buddhist," she told him.

"All right, let's call it quits over the torture hoop. But why did you send that wretched dragon to eat my master's horse? That was a touch of adversity too far."

"I personally intervened with the Jade Emperor to have this dragon wait for you here to carry the scripture pilgrim west. Do you really think an ordinary Chinese horse can carry you all the way to the Buddha's Soul Mountain?"

"Well, we've not gotten off on the right foot and he's too scared to come out. So what do I do now?"

"Stand on the bank," Guanyin instructed Monkey, "and shout: 'Come out, Third Prince Jade Dragon, son of Aorun. Guanyin's here to see you.' That should do the trick."

After two such summonses, the little dragon leaped out of the water onto a cloud. "Thank you for saving my life," he said, bowing to Guanyin. "But I'm still waiting for that pilgrim of yours to show up."

"Why, this is his senior disciple." Guanyin gestured toward Monkey.

"Him? But he's my sworn enemy. Just because I got hungry and ate his horse yesterday, he's been making my life hell. He never said a word about scriptures."

"You weren't exactly fulsome with the pleasantries yourself," retorted Monkey.

"I asked who you were," countered the dragon, "but you just kept yelling about your horse."

"Monkey-brain!" scolded Guanyin. "You can't manage this quest alone. Along the way, you'll collect other disciples to help you. If anyone asks, tell them you're on a scripture pilgrimage, and we can avoid any more of this unpleasantness."

As Monkey took this on board with surprising serenity, Guanyin dipped a willow branch into her vase of sweet dew, sprinkled it over the little dragon, and blew an immortal breath over him. The dragon transformed into a horse identical to the one he had eaten. "After you have redeemed your sin through this pilgrimage, you will become a golden Buddha," Guanyin told him. The little dragon meekly accepted his mission. Guanyin now turned to Monkey. "Take this horse to Tripitaka. I'm going back to the South Sea."

Monkey clung fast to her. "I can't do it! The road to the west is too treacherous and this monk is too useless. This quest will be the end of me."

"In centuries past," chided Guanyin, "you were hungry for enlightenment. Do not waste your gifts now that Heaven has forgiven your previous transgressions. You need faith and perseverance to reach nirvana. If you find yourself in mortal danger, call on Heaven and Earth and they will hear you. If you are in truly dire straits, I will personally come to your rescue. Come here: I have one more magic power to give you." Picking three leaves from her willow branch, she placed them on the back of Monkey's head. "Those leaves have turned into three hairs with life-saving power. When all seems hopeless, they will not fail you." A little mollified, Monkey thanked Guanyin, who disappeared amid swirling colored mists and scented breezes, and led the new horse to Tripitaka.

Chapter Sixteen

For a few months they journeyed peacefully on, meeting only bar-
barians, Muslims, wolves, tigers, leopards, larcenous monks, and
the Taoist Bear Spirit of Black Wind Mountain. The days passed
into early spring: peach and apricot blossoms lit up the forests,
willows budded, and birds chattered. As dusk fell one evening,
Tripitaka spotted a settlement up ahead. It looked like a pleasant, prosperous place: a cluster of thatched houses, neat bamboo
fences, and willow-edged paths. Well-fed pigs and chickens dozed
in pens and coops; cows milled peacefully about. "How about asking to spend a night there before we go on?" Tripitaka suggested.

After a brief look around, Monkey agreed. At the entrance to
the village, they met a young man, dressed in a blue jacket,
rolled-up trousers, and straw sandals. He had an umbrella in his
hand and a pack on his back, and was clearly in a tearing hurry
when Monkey grabbed him to ask a question: "What's the name
of this village?"

"Can't you ask someone else?" the man snapped back, trying
to struggle free.

"Calm down." Monkey smiled genially. "Something's clearly
eating you. If you help us, maybe we can help you."

"It never rains but it pours!" the man raged. "I'm being tormented by my relatives, and now this monkey's joining in."

"If you can prize open my paw," proposed Monkey, "I'll let you go." Try as he might—pummeling and scratching—the testy young man could not escape from Monkey's grip.

"Look," Tripitaka intervened, "someone else is coming. Let's ask him instead and let this one go."

"Where's the fun in that?" Monkey twinkled.

Realizing that resistance was futile, Monkey's captive finally became informative: "This is the village of Gao, in the kingdom of Tibet. Most of the inhabitants are called Gao, hence the name. Now can I go?"

"You're clearly on your way somewhere. First tell us where you're going and why." And so the hapless passerby told his tale.

"My name is Gao Cai, and I'm a relative of Mr. Gao, the biggest landowner around here. Three years ago, a monster moved in with him and demanded his youngest daughter, only seventeen at the time and not yet betrothed, in marriage. My illustrious kinsman was unhappy about this on a couple of levels. For one, having a demon as a son-in-law made the family look bad, and for another it meant Mr. Gao had no hope of hobnobbing with his in-laws. The monster first ignored Mr. Gao's request to have the marriage annulled, then locked up the daughter, his wife, at the back of the house and for the past half year hasn't allowed her any contact with her family. So Mr. Gao gave me a few ounces of silver and told me to find an exorcist to get rid of his problem in-law. I haven't had a moment's peace since. The three or four I've hired so far have all turned out to be bunglers. He's just given me a roasting and told me to find someone better. And then you held me up with your questions. Now do you see why I'm not in the best of moods? And can I go, finally?"

"Your luck has turned, " said Monkey. "It just so happens we are doctors in demonology. Go and tell your clansman that we are holy monks sent by the emperor of the east to fetch Buddhist scriptures from the west, with a particular specialty in defeating monsters and subduing fiends."

"Truly?" Gao Cai looked doubtful.

"Lead on," commanded Monkey.

Not having any better ideas, Gao Cai picked up his things and took the two of them to his front door. "Stay out here while I announce you."

Gao Cai ran directly into the venerable Mr. Gao. "What are you doing back here, you waste of space?" the irritable elder greeted him. The ill-starred Gao Cai explained the encounter he had just had at the entrance to the village. "If they are who they say," Mr. Gao mused, "they should have remarkable powers." After quickly donning a black silk head-wrap, a scallion-white robe of Sichuan silk cinched with a dark green sash, and a pair of rough hide boots, the head of the house strode out to greet his guests. "Your holiness!" he exclaimed to Tripitaka, bowing. Then he spotted the less attractive—hideous, even—Monkey, to whom he did not extend the same courtesy.

"How about a hello?" asked Monkey.

"I've already got one demon in the family," Mr. Gao hissed at Gao Cai, "and now you've brought this horror to my door."

"Don't judge a book by its cover," Monkey preached. "I'm ugly but useful. I'll overlook your hurtful personal comments for the time being and devote myself to expelling your unwanted son-in-law and reuniting you with your daughter." Still shaking with fear, the old man had no choice but to invite them in.

Free as you like, Monkey sauntered into the house, tethered the horse to a pillar, and drew up a couple of chairs for himself and Tripitaka. "You certainly know how to make yourself at home," observed old Mr. Gao. "Anyway, I understand from my junior kinsman here that you have come from the Land of the East."

"Indeed," replied Tripitaka. "My emperor has commissioned me to seek scriptures from the Buddha in India. We would much appreciate a night's lodging before we go on tomorrow."

"Then why did you say you were in the monster-capturing business?" asked Mr. Gao.

"We thought we might as well capture the odd monster while we're about it, just for fun," intervened Monkey. "How many do you have for us?"

"Heavens! How many do you think I could cope with? Just the one, my son-in-law. That's more than enough!"

"Tell me about this troublesome relative," Monkey requested.

"Before he moved in, we never had a problem with phantoms, ghosts, ghouls, spirits, or fiends in this village," Mr. Gao explained. "The only blot on my happiness was the lack of a son. But I have three daughters: in order of age, Fragrant Orchid, Jade Orchid, and Emerald Orchid. The older two left to live with their in-laws after marriage, but we always hoped that the husband of the third would marry into our clan and move in with us, to help out around the house, look after us in my old age, and continue the family name. Three years ago, a passably good-looking, if slightly stout, fellow turned up at our door. He said he came from Fuling Mountain and his surname was Pig. He had no family of his own and offered himself as a live-in son-in-law. Seeing as he came with no strings attached, I took him in. He's been a hard worker, I'll grant you. He's so strong he doesn't need any animals or tools on the farm. He starts early and comes home late. Truth to tell, we were pretty happy with the arrangement in the beginning. But then the trouble started up. First, his appearance began to change. His nose and ears started to grow, and a forest of bristles sprang up at the back of his head. He put on weight. To put it bluntly, he looked more and more like a pig. His appetite has become monstrous, too. He puts away between three and five pecks of rice at one sitting. A snack is at least a hundred bread rolls. Just as well he's a vegetarian. If he demanded meat and wine, he'd have eaten and drunk me out of house and home in six months."

"Maybe he needs to eat a lot because he works so hard," Tripitaka suggested.

"His appetite's actually the least of my worries," resumed Mr. Gao. "He's also fond of riding the wind and stirs up an almighty mess of stones and dirt whenever he comes and goes. Terrible nuisance for me and my neighbors. And then he locked up my youngest daughter, Emerald Orchid, in the back room of the house. I haven't seen her for half a year and don't know whether she's dead or alive. Hence my suspicion that he's a demon and my search for a reliable exorcist."

"Don't worry, old man," Monkey said, grinning. "Before the night's out, I'll capture him, have him sign the divorce papers, and return your daughter to you."

"Forget the paper trail," said Mr. Gao. "Just get rid of him for me. Or my relatives will never speak to me again."

"Consider it done," Monkey reassured him.

By the time they had eaten, night was drawing in. "Do you need any weapons or reinforcements?" Mr. Gao asked Monkey.

"Just me and my staff," replied Monkey, removing the magic iron from his ear. With one wave, it grew into a substantial cudgel. "Onward!" When they reached the door to the monster's room, Monkey asked for the key.

"If I had a key, I wouldn't need you, would I?" Mr. Gao sighed.

"Just my little joke," Monkey chortled, noting that the lock had been sealed with molten copper. It gave way with one irritable blow of his staff. Inside, it was pitch dark. "Call out to your daughter," Monkey instructed.

"Emerald Orchid!" Mr. Gao cried nervously.

"Father," came a weak reply, "I'm over here."

Despite the darkness, Monkey could discern a beautiful but

unkempt girl: thin, pale, hair disheveled, face unwashed. As soon as she saw her father, she grabbed hold of him and began to wail. "Stop crying!" barked Monkey. "Where's the demon?"

"I don't know," she replied. "Since learning that Father wanted to exorcise him, he's taken to leaving early and coming home late, traveling by cloud and mist. But I've no idea where he goes."

"All right," said Monkey. "Take your daughter to safety, Mr. Gao, and I'll wait for your son-in-law here." Mr. Gao happily led his daughter away.

Monkey now transformed himself into the exact likeness of the girl and awaited the demon. Before long, a tornado-like wind blew up, scouring the village with dust and gravel. It subsided to reveal a genuinely hideous monster. He had a dark bristly face, with a long snout and huge ears. He was wearing a greenish-black cotton shirt and a patterned hankie of sorts on his head. Monkey lay on the bed moaning, pretending to be ill. Entirely taken in, the monster approached, took his "wife" in his arms, and demanded a kiss. *So it's horseplay he's after, is it?* thought Monkey, who treated the demon to one of his holds: a deft twist to the snout sent him crashing to the ground.

Dusting himself off, the monster now stood more circumspectly at the side of the bed. "You seem miffed with me today, my love. Is it because I'm back so late?"

"You're so uncouth," trilled Monkey. "I'm not feeling at all well today, but in you come demanding a kiss. Get undressed and go to sleep." The unsuspecting fiend did as he was told. Meanwhile, Monkey got up to sit on the chamber pot.

"Where are you, my sugarplum?" the monster asked, now in bed and unable to find his beloved.

"You go to sleep," Monkey told him. "I need to unburden myself." Then he began to sigh theatrically.

"What's wrong now?" asked the monster.

"All day, my parents made a terrible scene outside our door.

They said you were rude, ugly, and completely unpresentable as a son-in-law—that you've ruined the family name. They complained that they'd never met any of your relatives, and they've no idea where you go every day on all that cloud and fog. So I'm understandably not in the best of moods."

"I'm not a great looker," conceded the monster, "but we did have a full and frank prenuptial discussion about all this, after which they gave the marriage their blessing. Why are they going back over old ground now? I told them at the outset that I come from the Cloud-Path Cave on Fuling Mountain, my surname's Pig, and my given name's Stiff-Bristles. It's true I have a healthy appetite, but I pull my weight around on the farm, draining ditches, building walls, plowing fields, planting crops. You've nice things to wear, and flowers, fruit, and vegetables all year round. If they give you any more trouble, just remind them of all this."

At least I'm dealing with an honest variety of fiend, Monkey thought, smirking. *He's just told me everything I need for a full background check.* Out loud again: "Father's still trying to get you exorcised, you know."

"Don't lose any sleep over that!" Stiff-Bristles guffawed. "I know as many transformations as there are stars in the Big Dipper. I've also got a nine-pronged rake and friends in high places. Even if your family hired the Monster-Sweeping Patriarch of the Ninefold Heaven as a shaman, he'd swap sides as soon as I reminded him of our past acquaintance."

"Actually, they were talking about bringing in the Great Sage Equal to Heaven to get rid of you. You know, the one who rebelled against Heaven five hundred years ago?"

Three-tenths of the color instantly drained from the monster's face. "In that case, I'm off. Consider yourself divorced. That monkey is pretty talented." The demon was heading for the door when Monkey grabbed him.

"Recognize me now?" Monkey shook off his disguise, and

when Stiff-Bristles turned to face him, he was treated to a close-up view of the real Monkey's protruding teeth, flashing eyes, and hairy face. With a loud rip of his shirt, he slipped out of Monkey's grasp and escaped as a gust of wind and myriad beams of burning light.

Chapter Seventeen

Hotly pursued by Monkey, the light sped back to the pig's ancestral mountain, where the monster regained his earthly form, fished out his nine-pronged rake, and joined battle. "Cursed fiend!" hollered Monkey. "Where did you come from and how do you know my name? What powers do you have? Confess and I may spare your life." In between clashes, the pig-demon's full story came out: how his youth had been misspent in idleness and indulgence until, encountering the teachings of an immortal, he mastered the mysteries of alchemy and ascended to Heaven. There, the Jade Emperor appointed him Marshal of the Heavenly River—his top naval command—which was how he knew of Monkey. The rake he was fighting with was a handy, Heavenly piece of equipment—a gift from the Jade Emperor himself. Its handle was forged by Laozi, its nine prongs by the Gods of Darkness and Light. But then Stiff-Bristles had gotten reeling drunk at a peaches banquet—the celebration that, on a separate occasion, had also led to Monkey's downfall—and made repeated passes at Chang'e, the famous beauty who lives on the moon. Sentenced to death for rowdy behavior, he was reprieved at the eleventh hour thanks to the intervention of the Gold Star of Venus. Punishment was commuted to two thousand lashes and banishment to earth—at which point he took a wrong turn on the path to Karma and ended up being reborn as a hog.

Eventually, at dawn, the exhausted pig-monster turned into another gust of wind, swept inside his cave home, shut the door tightly behind him, and refused to re-emerge. *Tripitaka will be waiting for news,* thought Monkey. *I'd better update him before I come back to finish the job.*

Having spent the night talking of this and that with Mr. Gao, Tripitaka had not slept a wink. Just as he was starting to wonder about Monkey's whereabouts, the latter dropped into the court-yard and marched into the hall. He then summarized all he had learned and done: about the monster's true immortal identity and the fierce mountain battle. "We're much obliged to you for having chased the monster away," responded Mr. Gao. "But what if he comes back? I'd still rather you capture him, just in case. I'll give you half of everything I own."

"How about seeing things from the monster's side?" suggested Monkey. "Granted, he has a large appetite, but he's saved you a lot of money over the years. After all, he is an immortal and he's done a great deal of work around the farm without harming your daughter. Quite a catch, I'd say. How about a bit of live and let live?"

"But people will still say 'The Gaos have a demonic son-in-law.' It's embarrassing," Mr. Gao responded.

"Why don't you finish the job off?" Tripitaka asked Monkey.

Monkey giggled. "Just playing Yama's advocate. I'll bring him to heel, don't worry!"

He returned to the mountain in one leap. With a judicious application of his staff, he turned the pig's cave door to dust. "Come out, you rice bucket, and resume battle!"

The taunt woke the pig-monster from a deep sleep; freshly enraged, he ran to the cave entrance, dragging his rake behind him. "Breaking and entering is a capital offense!" he yelled at Monkey.

Monkey laughed back at him. "Pigs in glass houses shouldn't throw stones. You forced a girl into marriage! No matchmakers! No gifts!"

"Enough bristle-splitting," the pig-monster spat back. "I'm going to rake you till your soul melts and your spirit leaks away!"

"Here's my head," Monkey responded genially. "Let's see how much melting and leaking ensues."

The pig-monster brought the rake down with all his strength on Monkey's skull. Sparks flew, as it bounced straight off. "That's quite a head," the pig-monster muttered weakly.

"Back when I rebelled against Heaven," Monkey exulted, "I consumed the elixirs, peaches, and wine of immortality. After I was captured, the heavenly spirits chopped, sliced, skewered, and burned me. There wasn't even a speck of surface damage. A forty-nine-day roasting in Laozi's Brazier of Eight-Trigrams then gave me blazing eyes, a head of bronze, and arms of iron. Have another go—this is fun."

"But I thought you lived on Flower-Fruit Mountain when you weren't making life hell in Heaven. What are you doing all the way out here?"

"Monkey has mended his ways and converted from Taoism to Buddhism. I'm escorting a priest called Tripitaka from the Tang empire to collect scriptures from the Buddha in the west. We happened to ask for a night's lodging from old Mr. Gao, who immediately mentioned his daughter and asked me to arrest you."

Dropping his rake, Stiff-Bristles was suddenly all smiles. "A scripture pilgrim, you say? Could I trouble you for an introduction?" Seeing Monkey's puzzlement, he explained his change of tack. "Guanyin persuaded me, too, to convert to Buddhism and to help escort the scripture seeker to the west, to atone for my crime through good deeds. She gave me a religious name as well—Pig Awakened-to-Power; you can call me Pigsy. I've been waiting here for years. Why didn't you tell me you were his disciple instead of attacking me?"

"Don't double-deal me, pig. Swear to Heaven you're telling the truth."

The pig-monster kowtowed, banging his head against the ground like a pestle. "May I be minced into ten thousand pieces if I lie!"

Just to be on the safe side, Monkey confiscated the rake, turned one of his hairs into a rope with which to truss Stiff-Bristles, and dragged him back by the ear to Mr. Gao's place.

In an instant they were back in the village, where Mr. Gao and Tripitaka were overjoyed to see Monkey again. "That's my son-in-law!" exclaimed Mr. Gao.

The pig-monster fell to his knees before Tripitaka. "Forgive me, Master! If I'd only known that you were a guest of my father-in-law, I'd have paid my respects straightaway and we wouldn't have had any of this unpleasantness."

"How did you get him to surrender?" Tripitaka asked Monkey.

"You tell him, thickhead!" Monkey ordered Pigsy, whacking him with the handle of the rake, and the story tumbled out of the captive. Tripitaka immediately offered Guanyin a prayer of thanks and asked Monkey to untie their new disciple. With one shake of Monkey's body, the rope fell off and returned to him as a hair.

The pig-monster bowed again to Tripitaka, and then to Monkey, as the senior disciple. "I've been vegetarian since taking holy orders from Guanyin," Pigsy told Tripitaka. "I trust you won't mind if I start feasting on flesh again now that I've found you?

"Out of the question!" exclaimed Tripitaka.

After treating his guests to a decidedly vegetarian banquet, Mr. Gao produced a red lacquer tray heaped with two hundred ounces of gold and silver to thank Tripitaka and Monkey for solving his domestic problem. Tripitaka refused to accept it. "Wherever we go, we beg for food. We cannot accept money."

But Monkey gave a handful of the cash to Gao Cai, his original informant. "Thanks to you, we've gained a disciple. Take this—it'll keep you in sandals for a bit. Save any other monsters you meet for me!"

Pigsy was not prepared to be so austere. "You got a good few years of toil out of me," he said to Mr. Gao. "Monkey here ripped my shirt last night and my shoes are in pieces. Cough up for replacements, will you?" His ex-father-in-law could not comply fast enough.

Delighted with his fine new clothes, Pigsy began strutting around the courtyard. "Send my best to the in-laws! Look after the old wife! If the scripture thing doesn't work out, I'll come back to her."

"Stupid rice bucket!" fulminated Monkey.

"Always wise to have a plan B," justified Pigsy.

"Stop wasting time," chided Tripitaka. "We must be on our way." Pigsy shouldered the bags on a carrying pole, Tripitaka mounted the horse, and Monkey led the way to the west, his iron staff across his shoulders.

Chapter Eighteen

Summer came—the air scorching, the pomegranates ripe, the cicadas noisy—and went. Monkey carped at Pigsy a good deal, mostly about Pigsy's near-constant complaints of hunger ("We can't all drink wind and burp mist like you," Pigsy shot back), and Tripitaka needed rescuing from the Magic Mink of Yellow-Wind Cave.

Before they knew it, it was autumn again; the now-chilly cicadas chirped on wilting willows and the sun rose lower in the sky. The pilgrims presently encountered a vast, turbulent river. "Why is there no ferry to take us across?" asked an alarmed Tripitaka.

"It's too choppy for boats," observed Pigsy.

Monkey leaped into the air to scope out the situation. "This isn't going to be easy," he admitted. "It's at least eight hundred miles wide. Though I can cross the river in a fraction of a cloud-somersault, that's not an option for you, Master."

Heaving an anxious sigh, Tripitaka spotted a stone slab on the riverbank. The three of them gathered around to read it: THE RIVER OF FLOWING SAND: EIGHT HUNDRED MILES WIDE, THREE THOUSAND DEEP. EVERYTHING—EVEN FEATHERS AND PETALS—SINKS. As they processed this discouraging information, the river billowed into mountainous waves, and an appallingly ugly monster—wild red hair, burning eyes, bluish face, thunderclap roar, and a truly intimidating stave—surged out of the spray. A yellow goose-down cloak was draped over its shoulders, two bleached reeds were tied around its waist, and a necklace of nine skulls rattled around its neck. This tornado of a fiend went straight for Tripitaka. Monkey snatched Tripitaka off to higher, safer ground while Pigsy threw down the luggage, drew his rake, and engaged the monster on the riverbank. Some twenty clashes later, no clear winner had emerged. To begin with, Monkey kept watch over Tripitaka and the luggage, but soon he itched to join the fight. Ignoring Tripitaka's nervous protestations, Monkey leaped down onto the bank with a battle whoop just as the fight was reaching a fever pitch. But the moment he brought his staff down hard on the monster's head, the fiend spun around in a panic and dived back into the river and out of sight. "Who invited you to the party?" Pigsy raged. "The monster was getting tired and I would have had him in another few blows of my rake. When he saw you, he was so scared he ran away. Now what?"

"The fight looked so delicious, I just wanted to play with him a little," Monkey explained, laughing. "It's not my fault he turned out to be a bad sport."

Hand in hand, the two of them joked and joshed their way back to Tripitaka, to whom they reported the fiend's disappearance. "Seeing as there's no boat to take us across," Tripitaka mused, "we really need the help of that monster to get us safely over."

"Good point," conceded Monkey. "We'll catch him and get him to take you across the river, before we deal with him."

"Off you pop," said Pigsy. "I'll keep an eye on Master."

"I'm not the best one for this mission." Monkey smiled artfully. "I either need a bunch of spells to operate under the water or have to turn myself into a fish, shrimp, crab, or some such. I'm unbeatable on land and air, but water's not in my line at all. Whereas you . . ."

Pigsy took the bait. "True. When I was Marshal of the Heavenly

River," he reminisced, "I commanded an eighty-thousand-strong navy. I know a thing or two about fighting in the water. But I'm worried he's got a gang of relatives on the riverbed. What if they hang me out to dry?"

"Don't draw it out. Pretend to flee, lure him out into the open again, and I'll lend a paw."

"Good plan!" chimed Pigsy, who tugged off his shirt and shoes, grabbed his rake, and plunged into the water.

The monster had barely caught his breath when down hurtled Pigsy into his lair. "Who are you, fiend, and how dare you block our way?"

"I'm no fiend," responded the fiend. "I was once an immortal, the Jade Emperor's General of Curtain-Drawing. I was chief of the Heavenly guardians of the throne, until I broke a crystal glass at the Peach Festival. The Jade Emperor was incandescent with rage, and I only just avoided execution. I was banished here, to the eastern shore of Flowing Sand, where I've survived solely by devouring woodcutters and fishermen unwise enough to approach the shoreline. On which subject, your arrival has made my stomach optimistic. Though you're mostly gristle, you'll make a decent ragout once I've caught and minced you."

"Rude, undiscriminating creature!" roared Pigsy. "How dare you call me gristly! I'll have you know I'm universally considered positively mouthwatering. Anyway, the only thing you're going to eat is my rake!" Battle was rejoined, even more ferociously than before, on the surface of the river. This time the collateral damage was heavy: carps and perches lost scales, turtle shells were shattered, and red shrimps and purple crabs were flattened.

Desperate but not daring to join the fight, Monkey guarded Tripitaka until—four hours into the battle—he saw Pigsy make a theatrically weak swing of his rake and retreat back onto the riverbank. As soon as the fiend reappeared on dry land, Monkey abandoned Tripitaka, leaped down onto the bank, and smashed his staff down on the head of the fiend, who, once more, dived straight back into the water. "You just did it again!" howled Pigsy. "Couldn't you have waited until I lured him onto higher ground, then blocked his route back to the river? We won't see head nor tail of him for a good while now."

"Cool it, half-wit," said Monkey amiably. "Let's have another word with Tripitaka."

"You must be exhausted," Tripitaka comforted Pigsy when the two of them returned. "What shall we do now?"

"It's getting late," said Monkey. "I'll go and find you a bite to eat, then we'll turn in for the night and come up with a new plan tomorrow." With a quick cloud-somersault, he hurtled north, begged a bowl of food from a family, and sped back to give it to his master.

"That was quick!" exclaimed Tripitaka. "Why don't we ask the person who gave you the food to help us across the river? Surely that would be better than wrangling with that monster."

Monkey laughed. "They're about six thousand miles away. What will they know about this river?" Pigsy was very skeptical that Monkey had traveled so far, so fast. "What do you know?" retorted Monkey. "One cloud-somersault carries me 108,000 miles. A nod of my head was enough for this round trip."

"If it's so easy for you, why have we been wasting our time wrangling with this monster here? Why don't you put Master on your shoulders and nod your way over the river?"

"You can ride the clouds, right?" Monkey shot back. "Why don't *you* take Master across?"

"Master's mortal flesh and bones are heavier than Mount Tai. How could I take him cloud-riding with me? No, we need your cloud-somersaulting here."

"My cloud-somersaulting is pretty much the same as your cloud-riding except that I can travel farther and faster. I can't carry him any more than you can. As the old saying goes: 'It's easier to topple Mount Tai than to lift a human off the mortal earth.' Tripitaka has to cross all these foreign lands himself if he is to escape the bitter sea of mortality; he has to take every difficult step himself. We are his guardians: we can protect him, but we can't suffer these hardships for him, neither can we go and pick up the scriptures ourselves. If we were to go alone, the Buddha wouldn't hand them over to the likes of you or me." Thus mulling over the enormity of their task, the three of them had something to eat, then spent the night on the shore of Flowing Sand.

"Now what?" Tripitaka asked the next morning.

"Same as yesterday," Monkey pronounced. "Pigsy goes into the river." Pigsy was understandably reluctant. "This time, I promise to control myself," Monkey reassured him. "Get him onto dry land and I'll block his escape route into the river."

Back Pigsy went with his rake, bursting in just as the fiend was waking up. The monster immediately jumped up and the battle restarted, both combatants energetically insulting the other's weapon, until Pigsy feigned defeat once more and returned to the surface. "Come and fight me on solid ground, wretch!" hollered Pigsy invitingly.

"I know you're just going to get that assistant of yours involved again," responded the monster. "I'm staying in the water." While the two of them squabbled, Monkey swooped down at the monster, like an eagle after his prey, but the fiend heard the whistle of the wind, spotted Monkey hurtling toward him, and disappeared back into the river.

Tripitaka now began to weep. "How will we ever get across?" he sniveled.

"You stay here with Tripitaka," said Monkey to Pigsy. "I'm going to the South Sea, to find Guanyin. The scripture pilgrimage was her bright idea. Now we're in a fix at Flowing Sand and she's the only one who can help us. Anyway, going to see her can't be worse than battling that monster."

"True words," Pigsy pondered. "Make sure you put in a good word for me."

"Quickly!" urged Tripitaka.

Within an hour, a cloud-somersault had taken Monkey to the South Sea, where he was ushered in to see Guanyin (who happened to be busy in the Cave of Tidal Sounds with the Pearl-Bearing Dragon Girl, admiring the flowers in the Pool of Precious Lotus). Monkey bowed deeply. "Why aren't you with Tripitaka?" Guanyin wanted to know.

Monkey updated her on the acquisition of Pigsy, the obstacle of the Flowing Sand, Pigsy's triple battle with the river monster (whom Monkey described as "not bad at martial arts"), and the stalemate that had resulted. "Hence my visit. Will you help us?"

"Why didn't you just tell that monster that you were off to seek scriptures with Tripitaka?" Guanyin asked.

"The water's not my strong point," Monkey replied, "so Pigsy dived alone into his lair. While they were trying to kill each other, he and the fiend chatted about this and that but didn't, I imagine, get onto the subject of scripture-fetching."

"The monster of Flowing Sand," said Guanyin, sighing, "is an incarnation of the Jade Emperor's former General of Curtain-Drawing, who also converted to Buddhism—under the religious nickname of Sandy—when I ordered him to await the scripture pilgrim and escort him to India. If you'd told him at the outset what you were doing, there'd have been none of this trouble."

"Well, he's currently lurking at the bottom of the river refusing to come out, and my master has no way of crossing the river. How do we bring the fiend—I mean, fellow disciple—around?"

Calling for Hui'an, Guanyin pulled a red gourd out of her sleeve. "Go with Monkey to Flowing Sand," she instructed. "Shout 'Sandy' and he'll come out. Get him to surrender to Tripitaka, then arrange that skull necklace he's wearing around this gourd, which will transform into a boat of enlightenment to carry them over the river."

Hui'an and Monkey cloud-traveled back to the river. As soon as he saw them, Pigsy began to thank Hui'an over-effusively for introducing him to Guanyin a few years back. "No time for that," Monkey interrupted. "Let's get this creature out of the river."

After Monkey had quickly explained to his two traveling companions that the fiend was Tripitaka's third and final disciple, Hui'an took up position on a cloud above the river. "Sandy!" he called. "The pilgrim is waiting for you."

On hearing his religious name, the terrified fiend lurking on the riverbed knew that the messenger had to be from Guanyin. Rushing to the surface, he smiled and bowed at Hui'an, who passed on the instructions about the boat and pointed out Tripitaka on the riverbank. Sandy shuddered when he spotted Pigsy standing nearby. "That rude creature has been terrorizing me since yesterday. Why didn't he tell me he was part of the scripture pilgrimage? And that monkey tried to kill me three times. I'm not going anywhere near them."

"There's nothing to be afraid of," Hui'an reassured him. "Those are your fellow disciples, all recruited by Guanyin. Look, I'll make the introductions."

Finally agreeing to put away his staff, Sandy clambered onto the riverbank and kneeled before Tripitaka. "Sorry about that business before," he muttered.

Pigsy was unwilling to let bygones be bygones. "You blackguard! Why did you spend the last two days fighting me instead of submitting to Tripitaka here?"

Monkey was more forgiving. "We should have told him who we were," he said, smiling.

"No more time to waste," urged Hui'an. "Let's make this boat of enlightenment." Sandy floated the ring of skulls around the gourd on the surface of the river, and the gourd transformed into a steady little skiff. Pigsy and Sandy embarked with Tripitaka, standing protectively to his left and right, Monkey and the dragon-horse followed behind on some passing mist, and Hui'an floated protectively directly overhead. And so Tripitaka glided uneventfully across Flowing Sand and stepped safely onto dry land on the other side.

Descending from his auspicious cloud, Hui'an gathered up the gourd and returned to Guanyin; the skulls dissolved into nine curls of dark wind and silently disappeared.

Chapter Nineteen

After a series of remarkable events—Pigsy falling into the Buddha's honey-trap; a piqued Monkey demolishing a holy tree laden with magical fruits resembling newborn babies; Pigsy, Tripitaka, and Sandy being lacquered, and Monkey being fried by the outraged keeper of the tree—the team of disciples made peace with the immortal horticulturalist in question, restored themselves with plenty of ginseng and cinnabar, and set off once more for the west.

Soon they came to another tall mountain. "The way ahead is steep and treacherous," observed Tripitaka, "I fear the horse will slip. Take care, all of you."

"Don't worry, Master!" cheered Monkey. Our hero led the way, opening a path onto a high ridge. Before them lay yet another mountain range running with streams, tigers, wolves, deer, foxes, rabbits, and a thousand-foot python and a one-hundred-thousand-foot hydra, both of whom busily belched horrendous miasma. Just as Tripitaka was beginning to whimper, Monkey waved his staff and all the wild beasts scattered like so many rodents.

Onward they journeyed to the summit, at which moment Tripitaka chose to say: "I've not had anything to eat all day. Go and beg me some food."

"Did you walk up here with your eyes shut?" Monkey responded affably. "This mountain is completely uninhabited. Even if we had money to spend, there'd be no one to sell us food."

Tripitaka now turned petulant. "Are you forgetting who rescued you from that stone casket beneath the Mountain of Two
Frontiers? You owe me, Monkey! Get me something to eat before
this pestilential mountain finishes me off."

"All right, all right," said Monkey. "I know how ticklish you
are—one step out of line and you start that head-squeezing spell.
Rest a while and I'll go and forage."

Leaping onto the clouds, Monkey inspected the pilgrims' sur-
roundings. The area was densely forested but, as he had said,
uninhabited. The only glimmer of possibility was a patch of
pinkish-red dots on a mountain due south. "There may be some
mountain peaches to be had," Monkey reported back. "I'll go and
pick them."

"Peaches!" enthused Tripitaka. "It's not often a Buddhist monk
gets to eat peaches!" And off Monkey hurtled with the begging
bowl.

But as the saying goes: a large mountain must have a monster—
and this one was no exception. Monkey's departure aroused the
fiend in question. Traveling on dark winds, she spotted—from the
edge of the clouds—Tripitaka seated on the ground. "What luck!
What luck!" she rejoiced. "My family has been talking for years
about a monk from the east traveling west to fetch scriptures.
This monk has cultivated himself through ten pure existences. His
flesh has powerful life-prolonging properties. And here he is, on
my mountain!" But the covetous monster dared not approach
while Tripitaka was guarded by the formidable-looking Pigsy and
Sandy, who after all had once worked for the Jade Emperor. "I'll
play a good joke on them," said the monster to herself.

In a mountain hollow, this virtuoso fiend transformed herself
into a ravishingly beautiful girl—bright eyes, red lips, white teeth,
moonlike visage, delicate hands, tiny feet—wearing an emerald
silk dress. In her left hand she carried a blue sandstone pot and
in her right a green porcelain vase. She then set her course directly

for the travelers. And as soon as she came into view, Tripitaka could not take his eyes off her. "Monkey said the mountain was uninhabited. But this looks remarkably like a human being approaching."

"You stay here with Sandy," Pigsy told him. "I'll investigate." He set down his rake, straightened his shirt, and sauntered over, trying his best to look debonair. The "girl" was even more gorgeous close up: porcelain skin, flawless bone structure, almond eyes, gently curvaceous. The mere sight of her scrambled the lustful Pigsy's brain. "Beautiful lady!" he babbled. "Where are you going and what are you carrying?" It was clearer than the day itself that she was a fiend, but Pigsy's mortal desires blinded him to the obvious.

"Why, hello, sir!" she simpered at him. "This pot contains fragrant rice and the vase fried gluten. I'm here to fulfill my sole desire in life: to feed mendicant Buddhists."

Pigsy scurried back like a delirious hog to Tripitaka. "Heaven truly rewards the virtuous! Who knows where that monkey's gone for those peaches, which will probably give you wind, anyway. Here's someone actually bringing us food!"

Tripitaka jumped to his feet and pressed his hands together to greet the girl. "Where do you live, madam? What brings you here?" For even this Buddhist master did not recognize the fiend for what she was.

"This is White Tiger Mountain," she glibly told him. "My home is directly west of here. My parents are devout Buddhists and always taught me to give food to monks. I am their only child. When I married, my husband moved in with my parents, to look after them in their old age, so we all live together still."

"But Confucius said: 'Do not travel far while your parents are alive.' Why didn't you send your husband instead? Why are you, a married woman, wandering out here on your own, without even a servant?" Tripitaka asked. "Most unseemly!"

"My husband is in the north, digging the fields with a few laborers," she embroidered further with a coy smile. "I cooked this food to deliver to them. As it's the busy season for farming right now, there's no one except me to run this errand. But when I ran into you, I was reminded of my parents' love of Buddhists and decided to donate it to you instead. Unless you feel it is unworthy of you . . . ?"

"Another disciple of mine has gone to pick peaches and is due back any moment. And if I ate that rice of yours, wouldn't your husband scold you?"

The girl laid it on even thicker. "When it comes to piety, my parents are mere dabblers compared with my husband. He's forever building bridges, repairing roads, and caring for the old and needy. When he hears that I gave his rice to a Buddhist monk, he'll love me more than ever."

Still Tripitaka wouldn't touch the rice—to Pigsy's exasperation. *Ditherer!* Pigsy thought furiously, pouting. *A ready-to-eat meal with its own delectable delivery service, and he won't touch it. If we wait much longer, that monkey will come back and we'll have to divide it among the four of us.*

Just as Pigsy was about to bury his snout in the pot, Monkey somersaulted back to the group, the alms bowl filled with freshly picked peaches, and instantly recognized the girl for the monster she was. He put the bowl down and was about to smash her hard on the head when Tripitaka pulled him back, appalled. "This woman's a fiend in disguise," Monkey explained. "She's come to trick you."

"Nonsense!" objected Tripitaka. "She's our benefactor—she's brought us food."

Monkey laughed. "You know nothing. When I was a full-time demon back at Water-Curtain Cave, if I wanted to snack on human flesh, I, too, would change myself into something irresistible: gold, silver, a beautiful woman—that kind of thing. I'd lure anyone stupid enough back to the cave and gobble as much of them as I felt like—steaming or boiling them first, of course—then sun-dry the leftovers for a rainy day. If I'd returned just a moment later, you'd have been monk-meat." Still Tripitaka refused to believe it. "I see what's happened here," mused Monkey. "Her beauty has aroused mortal lusts in you. That's fine. Pigsy will cut wood, Sandy will gather thatch, and I'll build you a love nest, where the two of you can consummate your love for each other. We'll all go our separate ways and forget about those pesky sutras. What d'you say?"

While Tripitaka, who after all had lived a very sheltered life, flushed scarlet at the suggestion, Monkey lost patience with the situation and smashed his staff down on the fiend's head. But she had a trick or two up her sleeve—including the Corpse Liberation spell. A split second before Monkey landed the blow, her spirit escaped, leaving a fake corpse—resembling the beautiful girl—on the ground. "You just killed an innocent person!" Tripitaka sputtered.

"Calm down," Monkey told his master. "Look what was in those pots of hers." Peering inside, Sandy and Tripitaka found writhing maggots instead of rice, and frogs and toads instead of fried gluten.

Tripitaka would have started to believe Monkey, if a spiteful and hungry Pigsy had not decided to make mischief at this point. "She was just a farm girl, delivering food to her husband in the fields. Monkey was spoiling for a fight and hit her harder than he meant to. Once he'd killed her, he was worried you'd say the headache sutra, so he tried to trick you by putting a spell on the food."

As bad luck would have it, Tripitaka allowed himself to be swayed by Pigsy and set to reciting the sutra. "Owah!" howled Monkey. "Stop it!"

"You're incorrigible!" raged Tripitaka. "Buddhists are supposed to protect the lives of the tiniest creature, and you've just gone and beaten to death an innocent civilian. I don't want you on this pilgrimage. Leave me now!"

"You'll never get to India without me."

"Only Heaven can decide that. If I'm destined to be broiled by one or another monster, so be it. Go away!"

"But I haven't yet repaid your kindness in releasing me from that mountain. My name will be mud through all posterity if I don't escort you to the west."

Moved by Monkey's piteous pleading, Tripitaka softened his tone. "All right, I'll forgive you this time. But one more misstep and I'll say the sutra twenty times."

"You can say it thirty times!" rejoiced Monkey. "I'll never hit anyone again." He helped Tripitaka back onto the horse and gave him the peaches; for an empty stomach never helps in these situations.

Meanwhile, the monster was fulminating in the clouds above them. "That ape is justly famous. I was so close! If that priest had taken just one sniff of that pot, I would have had him. The monkey not only robbed me of my lunch but also almost smashed me into a fiend fritter. But I'm not about to give up now. There's more fun to be had with them."

The monster landed on another mountain slope a little way ahead of the pilgrims and this time transformed herself into a bony, wrinkled old woman, limping along on a bamboo cane with a curved handle and weeping copiously. Pigsy saw her first. "Uh-oh, it's the mother of that girl Monkey beat to death. She must be looking for her daughter."

"Ridiculous!" Monkey snorted. "That girl was about eighteen. This old woman's at least eighty. How could she have had a child at the age of sixty? Another phony for sure. I'll go and investigate."

Recognizing the fiend at a glance, this time Monkey didn't stop to chat but immediately smashed her over the head with his staff. As before, though, the monster's spirit escaped just in time, leaving behind a bogus, aged corpse. Falling off his horse in fright, Tripitaka lay on the ground reciting the headache spell twenty times over. Poor Monkey's head was cinched like an hourglass. "Mercy! Mercy!" he pleaded, rolling about in agony.

"I've tried turning you to the good," fumed Tripitaka, "yet you persist in beating people to death."

"But she was a monster."

"Absurd! You see monsters everywhere. You're incorrigibly wicked. Be gone!"

"All right, all right," Monkey said. "Just one thing before I go, though."

"He wants his share of the luggage," Pigsy sniped. "Fob him off with an old hat or shirt."

"Keep your snout out of it!" shouted Monkey, hopping up and down in a fury. "I haven't known a moment's covetousness since I swore my Buddhist oath of poverty. I don't want anything to do with the rotten luggage."

"So what is it, then?" asked Tripitaka.

"Five centuries ago, I was the overlord of seventy-two cave monsters and forty-seven thousand lesser fiends. I cut quite a figure, with my purple-gold crown, my ocher robe, my jade belt, my cloud-hopping shoes, and my staff. But now that I've got this gold hoop stuck on my head, I'm embarrassed to face my old associates. As one last act of kindness, could you remove the hoop and put it on someone else's head?"

"But Guanyin taught me only the Tight Hoop Spell; she never mentioned any Loose Hoop Spell."

"In that case," said Monkey, sighing, "you'd better keep me with you."

So Tripitaka decided to forgive him one more time. "But this time, no more violence."

"Absolutely!" Monkey assured Tripitaka, helping him back onto the horse and leading the way forward.

Back to the fiend, now, who had somehow escaped Monkey's second strike and was still hovering overhead, exclaiming at Monkey's acumen. "Those monks are moving westward fast and will be out of my power in another forty miles. If another monster succeeds in capturing them where I failed, I'll be a laughingstock. Let's have one more go at them."

She descended to another dip in the mountain out of sight of the travelers and this time disguised herself as an old man, with long white hair and a beard, chanting a sutra as he walked toward Tripitaka and the others. "How pious the west is!" Tripitaka rejoiced at the sight of him.

"I wouldn't celebrate if I were you," Pigsy warned him. "He's coming after us because Monkey killed his daughter and his wife. You'll be executed, I'll be conscripted into the army, and Sandy will be condemned to hard labor. Of course, Monkey will slip away through some magic trick or other, leaving us to take the blame."

"Stop scaring Tripitaka, idiot," Monkey told him. "Leave this to me." Concealing his staff, he walked up to the monster. "Where are you going, sir? And why are you reciting sutras?"

Here the monster miscalculated: she thought she'd finally fooled Monkey. Out she came with her subterfuge: "This is my ancestral home. I have spent my life doing good works and feeding mendicant monks, and reading and reciting the sutras. I sent my daughter to deliver food to my son-in-law in the fields this morning, but I fear she was waylaid by a tiger. My wife, who went out looking for her, has not returned either. I came to look for them both. If they are dead, I must gather their bones for burial in the family grave."

Our hero laughed mirthlessly. "You've picked the wrong monkey to monkey with today, fiend!" He now mulled his options: *To smash or not to smash*, he pondered. *That is the question. If I don't smash her, she'll carry on with her tricks. If I do smash her,*

Master will recite that headache sutra again. Then again, if I don't smash her she'll find a chance to capture Master and then I'll have to rescue him, with no end of trouble to myself . . . . Hmmm, best to smash her. I'll find a way to talk Tripitaka around. As a precautionary measure, Monkey first summoned the local mountain gods before him: "This monster has played three tricks on my master, and this time I want to finish her off. Don't let her escape again." The intimidated spirits stood guard on the edge of the clouds while Monkey dispatched the monster with one blow of his staff.

Witnessing this at a distance, Tripitaka was speechless with horror. "Oh, well played, Monkey!" chortled Pigsy. "Three murders and it's not even lunchtime."

Just as Tripitaka was about to start the headache spell again, Monkey rushed over to stop him. "Come and see who the old man really was." A powder-white skeleton lay on the ground.

"How can this be?" Tripitaka gasped. "You only killed him a moment ago."

"These are the remains of a demon that specialized in seducing innocent passersby. I finally succeeded in killing her just now and this is her true form. Look closer." Monkey pointed out four words written on the spine: THE WHITE-BONE DEMON. This time, Tripitaka really would have believed Monkey if the crafty Pigsy hadn't stirred things up again.

"He's just beaten someone to death and is humbugging you with magic of some sort because he's afraid of that spell of yours," he needled. The gullible Tripitaka was once more taken in and promptly began the headache spell, breaking off only to issue Monkey's marching orders.

This time Monkey, too, had had enough. "Don't worry, I'm going, seeing as you believe this idiot over me. Though I don't fancy your chances without me."

"What arrogance!" raged Tripitaka. "Pigsy and Sandy can manage perfectly well on their own."

"Without me, they wouldn't even be here! Well, such is life. 'After the rabbits have been killed, the dog gets fried,' as the saying goes. There's still the matter of the headache spell, though. Next time you're in danger, and Pigsy and Sandy can't help, you'll recite it to bring me back. So why don't we just carry on as we were?"

Ever more incensed by Monkey's suave reasoning, Tripitaka ordered Sandy to take paper and brush out of the luggage, then wrote a letter of banishment. "Here's your expulsion in writing. If I ever ask for you again, I deserve to burn in Hell. Clear enough for you?"

"As day," said Monkey, tucking the letter up his sleeve. "But at least allow me to bow to you, as we part for the last time." When Tripitaka turned his back on him, Monkey plucked three hairs from the back of his head and turned each into a replica Monkey. Surrounding Tripitaka on all sides, the four monkeys bowed, so whichever way Tripitaka turned, he had to accept an obeisance from one of them.

The ceremonials over, Monkey retrieved his hairs and had a word with Sandy. "You're a decent sort. Beware of Pigsy's nonsense and take care on the road ahead. If a monster happens to capture Tripitaka, just say that his senior disciple is Monkey. That'll scare them off."

"I refuse to trade on the name of a murderer," Tripitaka said primly. "Go away!"

Swallowing his anger at the injustice, Monkey somersaulted dolefully over the ocean. Pausing his cloud to gaze down at the water, he thought of Tripitaka, and tears rolled down his cheeks.

Chapter Twenty

Soon enough, though, Monkey was back on Flower-Fruit Mountain, smashing to a pulp an army of hunters that had been preying on his little monkey subjects and once more enjoying a carefree life of pleasure, coconut wine, and plentiful fruit.

Tripitaka, meanwhile, rode on westward; Pigsy led the way and Sandy brought up the rear with the luggage. On leaving behind White Tiger Mountain, they came upon a forest dense with creepers, cypresses, and pines. "We must be careful!" warned Tripitaka. "I fear demons and wild beasts lurk within." Pigsy cleared a path with his rake and led the party into the forest. Soon, Tripitaka spoke up again: "Pigsy, I'm still hungry. Find me something to eat, will you?"

"I pledge to draw fire from ice and oil from snow in my quest for lunch!" Pigsy declaimed. And off he went with the begging bowl and a touch of melodrama.

After walking ten miles without encountering a single human soul (though there was no shortage of tigers and wolves), Pigsy began to find the going tough. "When Monkey was still with us, he always managed to keep Tripitaka happy. Now that it's my turn, I see it's not so easy. Honestly, it's like looking after a child. How on earth am I going to feed him?" A little farther on and he began to feel drowsy. "If I head back now and tell him I couldn't find anything, he won't believe that I walked far enough. I'll fill in the time with a little snooze—just an hour or two—then go back to give him the bad news." The moment he put his head down on the grass, he began to snore.

By now, Tripitaka was starting to fret. "Where on earth could that Pigsy have gotten to?" he asked Sandy, his eye twitching.

"When that hog finds a generous benefactor," Sandy remarked, "he'll forget about you and concentrate on filling that big belly of his. We won't see him again till he's taken care of himself."

"True," conceded Tripitaka mournfully. "But what shall we do while we wait? It's getting dark, and we can't sleep out in this forest. We'd better find a roof for the night."

"Fear not," said Sandy. "You stay here and I'll retrieve him."

Left alone in the forest, Tripitaka became increasingly tired and melancholy, and decided to go for a walk to keep his spirits up. Rambling along the narrow, densely forested paths and gazing at the wild grasses and flowers, he quickly lost his way. Although he thought he was heading in the same westerly direction as his disciples, he instead circled around to the south. Eventually emerging from the forest, he saw before him a jeweled pagoda, its dome gleaming with the rays of the setting sun, set amid a landscape of flowering meadows, white blossom trees, fragrant pines, purple bamboo, and clear streams, all alive with monkeys and magpies. "How did I not spot this place before? Where there's a pagoda, a monastery's never far away. I'll go and beg a night's lodging."

Tripitaka was now in mortal danger. Lifting up a mottled bamboo curtain over the entrance, he discovered inside an indigo-faced monster asleep on a stone couch, its huge mouth agape, revealing long, white fangs. It had bouffant red sideburns, a stubbly purple beard reminiscent of a sprouting lychee, a parrot's beak of a nose, bowl-shaped fists, and enormous, varicose-blue feet. Dressed in a lemon-yellow robe, the monster grasped tightly—even while asleep—a gleaming sword.

Tripitaka immediately backed out of the pagoda, his body and limbs weak with fear. But the monster had perceived the movement with its fiendish golden eyes. "Who's at the door, little ones?" he shouted to his army of goblins.

"A deliciously soft-skinned monk," a lookout quickly reported back. "A proper tender morsel."

The monster roared with laughter. "A fly landing on a serpent's head—a self-delivering meal. Bring him back to me, and I'll reward you well."

They went after Tripitaka like a swarm of bees and hauled him back to the monster, who immediately began interrogating him. "Where are you from and where are you going?"

Tripitaka explained that he was the envoy of the Tang emperor, heading west to seek scriptures from the Buddha. "Please forgive me for barging in on Your Marvelousness. When I return to the east, I will record your illustriousness for posterity."

"Ha!" exulted the monster. "The subject of a great empire—I thought you looked unusually succulent. What a stroke of luck that you presented yourself to me; you're clearly destined to be my dinner. Tie him up, imps!" They bound Tripitaka tightly to the Pillar of Ultimate Peace, a name that some demonic wag had given to the pagoda's execution post. "How many companions do you have? You'd never dare go to India on your own."

As soon as the monster picked up his sword, Tripitaka told all: "Great king, I have two disciples, Pigsy and Sandy, who've gone begging for food. We've luggage and a horse, too, somewhere in the forest."

"Even better!" The monster rejoiced some more. "Three Buddhists plus a horse! A square meal at last."

"Shall we go capture the others?" offered the subordinate goblins.

"No need," said the monster. "Just shut the door and the others will come looking for their master as soon as they're back from fetching food. Then we can deal with them on home ground."

Sandy, meanwhile, had wandered some ten miles out of the forest without catching a glimpse of Pigsy. As he stood on a large mound looking around him, he suddenly heard mumbling at ground level. Parting the grass with his staff, whom should he discover but his revered elder disciple sleep-babbling. "You idiot!" Sandy yanked hard on one of Pigsy's large ears. "You're meant to be begging food for Tripitaka, not napping your head off."

Pigsy bolted up. "What time is it?"

"Time to get up! Tripitaka says we should forget about food and just find somewhere to sleep."

A bleary Pigsy made his way back into the forest with Sandy. There, of course, they discovered that Tripitaka had disappeared. "It's all your fault for not coming back sooner with something to eat," complained Sandy. "I'll bet you a basket of scriptures Tripitaka's been kidnapped by a monster."

"A monster in a forest?" scoffed Pigsy. "Ridiculous. He must have gone sightseeing. We'll find him soon enough." The two of them scooped up the luggage and the horse, and made their way out of the woods in search of Tripitaka.

It just so happened that Tripitaka was not yet destined to be dinner, for the two disciples soon spotted the pagoda's golden light. "Scrumptious news!" exclaimed Pigsy. "Tripitaka is doubtless inside that pagoda right now, stuffing his face. Let's go before Tripitaka finishes it all off!"

"We don't know what sort of a place this is," cautioned Sandy. "Let's do a little reconnaissance first." Approaching, they discovered over the front door an inscribed slab of white jade. "'Residence of Lord Yellow-Robe, Cave of the Tidal Moon, Casserole Mountain,'" read Sandy. "This is no temple. This is the den of a monster. If Tripitaka's inside . . ."

"Don't worry!" said Pigsy. "You see to the horse and the luggage, and I'll find out what's what. Open up!" he bellowed, lifting his rake above his head.

The goblin on sentry duty ran to report to the monster king: "Two monks at the door. One with big ears and a snout, the other with the most miserable face I've ever seen."

"Aha!" chortled the monster. "As expected, our main course's disciples—also known as starter and dessert. Let's give them a warm welcome. Bring me my armor!"

Buckled into a golden cuirass, Yellow-Robe—for it was he—swaggered out, sword in hand. "How dare you kick up such a rumpus at my door!"

"I'm the representative of the Tang empire," Pigsy somewhat embellished his status on the quest, "traveling west to seek scriptures. My master is the emperor's own brother. If you've got him inside there, hand him over now or I'll let my rake do the talking."

"Oh, yes, I've a Buddhist monk in here. I was just rustling up some human dumplings for him. Do join us."

His mouth watering, Pigsy was about to take up the invitation when Sandy pulled him back. "He's lying. Tripitaka's not allowed to eat human flesh, and neither are we." Realizing his mistake, Pigsy smashed his rake down on the monster's face. Narrowly dodging the blow, the monster blocked the rake with his sword and the three of them leaped into battle among the clouds, churning up cloud and fog and pulverizing cliff faces. In truth, Yellow-Robe was more than a match for the two of them and could easily have added Pigsy and Sandy to that evening's menu had it not been for Guanyin's forty-some guardian spirits, still watching over Tripitaka and his disciples.

While Pigsy, Sandy, and Yellow-Robe were relandscaping the surrounding area, back inside the cave Tripitaka was tearfully bemoaning his abandonment by his disciples. "Oh, Pigsy, where are you filling your belly? Oh, Sandy, how will you learn of my terrible sufferings in the clutches of this monster? When will you rescue me? When will we reach Soul Mountain?"

Just then, a woman of about thirty appeared. "Where did you come from?" she asked, leaning against the Pillar of Ultimate Peace. "Why are you tied to this post?"

"Why waste your breath?" he answered through tear-clouded eyes. "I am doomed—doomed! Just eat me and put me out of my misery."

"I'm no cannibal!" protested the woman. "I'm the third daughter of the king of Precious Image, a citadel about three hundred miles west of here, and my name is Baihuaxiu—Hundred Flowers' Shame. Thirteen years ago, this monster carried me off in a tornado and forced me to be his wife and have his children. In all this time, I've not been able to send any message to, much less see, my parents. But why has he captured you?"

Tripitaka explained his mission and the misstep that had brought him there. "Now your husband is after my two disciples, so he can put us all in the same steamer."

The princess beamed. "Don't worry. Precious Image lies on your route westward. If you take a letter to my parents, I'll tell my husband to spare your life." Tripitaka naturally agreed.

The princess quickly wrote and sealed a letter, then untied Tripitaka. "Thank you," he said, taking the note. "I promise to deliver it. But will your parents believe the letter is from you, after so many years of silence?"

"Don't worry. They'll know." Tripitaka lodged the letter deep in his sleeve and made for the door. The princess pulled him back. "You can't go out the front! My husband's goblins are all there, cheering on their king, who's fighting your disciples. They'll tear you apart the moment they see you. Best to go out the back. But wait for me to talk my husband around. If he agrees to let you go, your disciples can go with you." Tripitaka kowtowed his thanks, slipped out of the back door, and hid in some bramble bushes.

That clever princess now pushed her way through the throng of mini-fiends in front of the cave, directly beneath the theater of battle. "Lord Yellow-Robe!" she shouted.

The devoted monster instantly abandoned Pigsy and Sandy, descended to earth, and took the princess's hand. "What is it, darling?"

"While asleep just now, I dreamed of a god in golden armor."

"And?" the monster asked.

"When I was a child growing up in the palace, I vowed secretly that if I married a noble husband, I would go up into the mountains to care for Buddhist monks. We've been so happy the past thirteen years that I forgot to mention it. But the god in my dream demanded that I make good on my vow; even though it was just a dream, he shouted so angrily that I woke up. As I was hurrying to tell you about it, I happened to see a monk tied to a post inside our house. Spare his life, for my sake, so I can fulfill my vow. Please?"

"Honestly," chided the monster, "I thought it was something important. All right, all right. Humans are ten a penny and this one's nothing special; I can capture some others for my dinner. Let him go. Hey, you, pig, up there!" he now shouted, brandishing his sword. "The battle's off. I promised my wife I'd spare your master. Pick him up at the back door and carry on to the west. I won't be so easy on you a second time!"

Enormously relieved, Pigsy and Sandy gathered up the horse and luggage, scurried to the back of the cave, scooped Tripitaka onto the horse, and ran away as fast as they could. Proceeding along a main road, the two disciples bickered relentlessly, each blaming the other for the Yellow-Robe catastrophe, with Tripitaka trying to keep the peace.

After two hundred and ninety-nine ill-tempered miles, the beautiful city-state of Precious Image rose up before them, its formidable walls set amid high, forested mountains and neatly farmed fields. Music—chimes, drums, pipes, and flutes—floated up from its many towers and palaces. The city's thoroughfares teemed with chariots and vigorous, well-dressed youths. The scene more than compared with the finest cities of China; Tripitaka's heart almost burst with homesickness.

After lodging his disciples, horse, and luggage in a posthouse, Tripitaka made his way to court and requested an audience with the king, for the purposes of having their travel documents stamped. Delighted by the news of a visitor from an empire as great as the Tang, the king immediately summoned Tripitaka into his presence. "Exquisite!" the courtiers exclaimed at Tripitaka's elaborate rituals of homage to the king. "Clearly a traveler from a civilized country!"

"And what has brought you here?" asked the king.

Tripitaka explained the mission that his emperor had given him. "Now that I have reached Your Majesty's kingdom, I must trouble you to stamp our travel documents."

"Show me the papers that the Tang Son of Heaven gave you." Tripitaka presented the document with both hands, unfolding it on the imperial desk. It recounted the reasons for the emperor's resolve to dispatch a scripture pilgrim: the mysterious death of the river dragon, the emperor's sojourn in the underworld, his release and celebration of a mass, and Guanyin's revelation of the existence of Buddha's scriptures in the far west. "We hope," it concluded, "that this document will allow our pilgrim to pass through the many kingdoms of the west."

The king stamped the document with his jade seal and returned it to Tripitaka. Thanking the king, Tripitaka explained the other purpose of his journey to court. "I also have a letter for you from a member of your family."

"What do you mean?" asked the king.

"On my journey here, I happened to meet your third daughter, who has been kidnapped by the Yellow-Robe fiend of the Cave of the Tidal Moon on Casserole Mountain, and she asked me to pass on this letter to you."

The king's eyes filled with tears. "After losing our princess thirteen years ago, we cashiered countless officials and beat to death innumerable palace maids and eunuchs. For we thought that she had wandered out of the palace and lost her way. And now it turns out she was kidnapped by a monster!" Tripitaka presented the letter he had tucked inside his sleeve. Too overcome to open the letter, the king handed it to the director of the Literary Academy, who read it out to a rapt court audience:

> Your unfilial daughter Hundred Flowers' Shame touches her head to the ground a hundred times before her father, the king. Thirteen years ago, a blue-faced demon in a yellow robe appeared on a fragrant tornado and carried me away to his mountain fastness. For thirteen years he has forced me to be his wife, and to bear two demon children. I hesitated to insult you with this news, but I thought you ought to know, in case I should die in captivity. Just now, I chanced upon this monk, who had been taken prisoner by the monster, and secured the monk's release so that he might deliver this letter. Take pity on me, Father, and send your best generals to Casserole Mountain to apprehend Yellow-Robe and rescue your daughter. Excuse my haste—I will tell you more when we meet again. Your treacherous daughter kowtows some more.

By the end of this reading, everyone in the court was sobbing their hearts out. On finally collecting himself, the king asked his officials for volunteers to capture the monster and rescue his daughter. In fact, he asked several times, but there was no response—as if the entire court had been turned to clay. The irritated king began to weep again, at which point a mass of officials prostrated themselves before him. "This letter from the princess," they argued, "is rather sudden and we have not yet been able to fully research her situation. Moreover, your ministers are mere mortals, who have only studied conventional military tactics and formations. We have no practical experience at all of monster-fiends who come and go on fragrant winds, and we do not rate our chances of success highly. However, we have in our midst a scripture pilgrim from the east, a holy monk from a superior country, an individual whose wisdom and power can subdue dragons and tigers, gods and demons. Let's give him the job; this is definitely the plan of plans."

The king now quickly turned back to Tripitaka. "If you manage to capture this monster and rescue my daughter, you needn't journey on to the Buddha. You can stay here and share my throne. What do you say?"

"I know nothing of subduing monsters," a panicked Tripitaka protested. "All I'm good for is reciting sutras."

"Without demon-taming skills, how on earth do you think you're going to make it to the west?" asked the king.

"I have two talented disciples whose job it is to protect me," Tripitaka admitted.

"How careless of you," chided the king, "not to bring them with you to court."

"The two of them," apologized Tripitaka, "are rather unconventional in their looks. I didn't dare bring them here without authorization, for fear they might frighten Your Majesty. The first, Pigsy, has a long snout and tusks, a bristly head and fanlike ears. His belly is so vast it stirs up the wind when he walks. The second, Sandy, is twelve feet tall and three arm spans wide. He has a blue face, burning eyes, and a row of nails for teeth."

The king laughed. "Do you think I'm that easily scared? Call them in."

"I smell a banquet!" rejoiced Pigsy when the king's invitation reached the posthouse. "Let's fill our faces and head off tomorrow."

"We'll see," Sandy ruminated pessimistically. The two of them headed to court, fully armed, and made a perfunctory bow before the throne.

"Ugly *and* rude!" muttered the assembled officials. "Why on earth aren't they kowtowing?"

"You can take us or leave us," responded Pigsy, on hearing their murmurings. "We might not be much to look at, but we have our uses."

The king, meanwhile, was so terrified by the sight of Pigsy and Sandy that he fell off his royal couch and needed his attendants to help him back up. "Messrs. Pigsy and Sandy," he asked when he had recovered a little, "which of you is best at defeating monsters?"

"Me!" volunteered Pigsy, without thinking through the consequences of his boast. "I used to be in charge of the Jade Emperor's navy. Since we started on our journey from the east, I've been the pilgrimage's top demon defeater."

"So you must be skilled in the art of transformation," reasoned the king. "Turn into something big."

After making a magic sign and chanting a spell, Pigsy shot up to eighty or ninety feet tall. "When will you stop?" asked one of the king's rattled generals.

"Depends on the wind direction," Pigsy bragged mindlessly. "If it's southerly, I'll punch a hole in the sky!"

"No need for that," said the king weakly. "Come back to earth." Pigsy returned to his original height. "And what weapons do you use for fighting demons?"

"A rake," Pigsy responded, producing the trusty item. "Guaranteed tiger-, wolf-, dragon-, and sea-serpent-proof."

Somewhat dubious about what he presumed was a glorified garden tool, the king called for wine to toast Pigsy. "When you have captured the monster and rescued my daughter, we will reward you with a huge banquet and a thousand pieces of gold."

Once Pigsy had emptied the cup, clouds began to grow under his feet and he soared into the air.

"When Yellow-Robe captured you," Sandy quietly observed to Tripitaka, "Pigsy and I together could barely fight him to a standstill. I'm frankly worried about his chances."

"Good thinking," agreed Tripitaka. "You go give him a hand."

Sandy then soared off on his own cloud. Unsettled by all this levitation, the king clutched at Tripitaka and begged him to sit and chat a while.

Zooming along on auspicious clouds, Pigsy and Sandy soon landed back at the entrance to the cave, and Pigsy announced their return by smashing a sizable hole in the stone door. "Bad news, great king!" the sentry goblins reported to Yellow-Robe. "Big Snout and Sulky Chops have broken our door down."

"What are they doing back here?" he wondered. "Didn't I just spare their master?"

"Maybe," speculated one of the imps, "they forgot something and have come to pick it up."

"Nonsense!" snorted the monster. "Why would they smash the door just to pick up lost property? No, there's something else behind this." Grabbing his armor and sword, he strode out to confront them. "What is it now?"

"So—kidnap the princess of Precious Image and force her to be your wife, would you?" roared Pigsy. "I'm on a royal mission to capture you. Save me some trouble and tie yourself up."

Utterly enraged by this little speech, Yellow-Robe brought his sword down as hard as he could on Pigsy's head. Pigsy fought back with his rake, assisted by Sandy. But after fewer than ten clashes, Pigsy was so exhausted that he could barely lift his weapon. During their first battle, Pigsy and Sandy had only managed to fight Yellow-Robe to a stalemate due to the presence of Guanyin's guardian spirits, who'd been there to protect Tripitaka. Now, of course, they were all watching over Tripitaka in Precious

Image, and so Yellow-Robe soon bested the two disciples. "Need the toilet," Pigsy told Sandy. "You carry on." Pigsy dived into a bush without a backward glance at Sandy and refused to come out again. With Pigsy's hasty departure from the battlefield, Yellow-Robe quickly captured Sandy and dragged him into the cave, where goblins bound him tightly.

Chapter Twenty-One

Back inside the cave, Yellow-Robe neither killed nor beat nor swore at his prisoner. For the monster was puzzled. "That monk I captured was from a civilized country and ought to understand common decency. I can't believe he would have sent his disciples back to capture me after I'd spared his life . . . I know! That wife of mine must have somehow sent a letter back home." He charged off to have it out with her. "Treacherous bitch!" spat the monster. "Have I not looked after you well and loved you deeply? Have I not dressed you in gold and brocade and satisfied your every whim? And yet you think only of your parents!"

The terrified princess instantly kneeled. "What are you talking about, darling?"

"I was all ready to enjoy that nice savory monk, but you insisted on releasing him. You must have given him a secret message to deliver to your family. Why else would his disciples be back here demanding your return on the king's orders? Let's ask that miserable second disciple if I'm right." Dragging the princess by her thick, lustrous hair, Yellow-Robe threw her to the ground in front of Sandy. "Was it because of this woman's letter that the king sent you back here?"

It's true that she wrote a letter, Sandy thought. *But she also saved Tripitaka. If I tell him, he'll kill her, and that's no way to return a favor. I might as well make a living sacrifice of myself.*

"What letter, you churlish fiend?" he shouted back at the monster. "Tripitaka happened to see the princess while he was a captive here. When he got to Precious Image to have his travel papers stamped, the king showed him her portrait and asked if he'd come across her on his travels. When my master described your wife, the king knew it was his daughter and ordered us to bring her back to the palace. If you're going to kill anyone, kill me—not your innocent wife."

Impressed by Sandy's vehemence, Yellow-Robe threw down his sword and lifted the princess off the ground. Tenderly straightening her hair and jewelry, he escorted her to a seat, whispering sweet nothings into her ear. "Please untie Sandy's ropes," the princess asked her husband, taking advantage of his good mood.

Yellow-Robe agreed, ordering his imps to lock him up instead. *One good turn deserves another*, Sandy thought with a smile.

Yellow-Robe now indulged the princess with wine and food. When they were both well on the way to being drunk, he changed into a brightly colored robe and strapped a sword to his waist. "You enjoy yourself here. Look after the children and don't let our guest escape. I'm going to spend some time with my in-laws."

The princess was not at all sure this was a good idea. "My father has lived a very sheltered life and has never met anyone even remotely as grotesque-looking as you. You'd scare the wits out of him." Taking the point, her husband transformed into a handsome young man, dressed in a white silk robe and patterned black boots. "Bravo!" said the princess, applauding. "Remember, though, that you'll get invited to a great many banquets. Maintain the disguise, however drunk you get. You're quite a lot less fetching in reality."

"Yes, yes," said the monster. "I know what I'm doing."

Hopping onto a cloud, he soon reached Precious Image and had himself announced to the court as the king's third son-in-law. "Ah, the monster," deduced the royal ministers.

"Shall we invite him in?" asked the king.

"This monster," Tripitaka explained, "is a formidable character. He'll come whether you invite him or not. I advise the path of
least resistance."

When Yellow-Robe approached and paid elaborate homage to
the king, the court was mesmerized by his good looks—none saw
through to the monster inside. The king was all over him. "Where
are you from? Why didn't you come to visit us sooner?"

"I'm a hunter by profession, from the Cave of the Tidal Moon
on Casserole Mountain, three hundred miles east of here."

"Three hundred miles! How on earth did my daughter end up
there?"

"Thirteen years ago," the crafty monster extemporized, "I
was hunting with my servants in the mountains when we saw a
large tiger with a young girl on its back. I shot the tiger with a
single arrow and saved the girl's life with nourishing hot drinks.
Because she claimed she was an ordinary girl and seemed fond of
me, we were married soon after. She never once mentioned that
she was a princess. Had I known, I would never have dared to
marry her without your consent. I'd originally planned to slaughter
the tiger for our wedding feast, but the princess begged me to spare
its life, as it had brought us together. So I let it go. But the tiger
recovered from its wound and became an evil spirit. It ate the
pilgrims from the Tang empire that everyone's talking about, stole
their travel papers, and impersonated one of them to deceive my
revered father-in-law. There he is"—he pointed to Tripitaka—
"sitting on your very own brocade cushion: the tiger that kidnapped
your daughter."

The dim-witted king found this story entirely plausible. "But
how can you tell this is the same tiger?"

"Tigers are my specialty. How would I not know one when I
see one?"

"Make him appear in his true form," ordered the king. The

monster approached Tripitaka, muttered the eye-dimming spell, and spat a mouthful of water over the monk. Everyone in the court now saw Tripitaka only as a ferocious tiger with lightning eyes, hooked claws, sawlike teeth, and appalling, meaty breath. While the king melted into a puddle of fear and most of his courtiers fled for safety, a handful of brave army officers began hacking at the "tiger" with their weapons. If it hadn't been for all his Heavenly guardians creating a protective force field around him, Tripitaka would have been cut to pieces. Eventually, by evening, the panic had subsided, and the "tiger" was clapped in irons and locked in an iron cage.

The king then ordered the royal catering department to drum up a lavish banquet to thank his son-in-law for saving him from the specious Buddhist. That evening, eighteen palace ladies sang, danced, and plied the monster with drink in the Hall of Silver Peace. Yellow-Robe enjoyed himself thoroughly until, at the end of the second watch, he started to enjoy himself too much, and the mischief began. Drunk as an owl, he began to laugh hysterically and changed back into his true form. Seizing a nearby girl strumming the lute, he bit her head clean off. The surviving seventeen palace ladies fled for their lives, their lutes and zithers crashing to the ground as they ran. Because they were well trained, though, none of them screamed, for fear of disturbing the king so late at night. The unruffled monster of Casserole Mountain stayed on in the banquet hall having a fine time of it, alternating gulps of wine with bites from the bleeding corpse next to him.

A little earlier that night, rumors about Tripitaka being a tiger-spirit had spread through the city, eventually reaching the post-house where the pilgrims' dragon-horse was munching hay. "That monster must have played a trick on him," the horse mused. "But what's to be done? Monkey's long gone, and we've no news of either Pigsy or Sandy." By ten o'clock that evening, the white horse resolved to mount his own rescue mission. Shaking off his harness, he turned back into a dragon and flew toward the palace, where he soon spotted the monster sitting alone at a banquet table gorging on wine and human flesh. "So he's shown his true colors," muttered the little dragon. "As I'm the only pilgrim in sight, I might as well have some fun with him."

The dragon now turned into a beautiful palace lady and entered the hall. "Please don't hurt me, Your Magnificence," she said, bowing to the horror. "I've come to pour wine for you." Using the magic of Liquid Restriction, the dragon poured a cup of wine that rose up in the shape of a thirteen-story pagoda with a pointed roof. The entranced monster glugged the whole lot down, took another bite of the corpse, demanded a song, then accepted a second oversize goblet of drink.

"Can you dance?" he now asked the disguised dragon.

"A little, but it would be better if I had something to dance with."

The monster promptly unbuckled his sword and handed the blade over. The dragon-lady began a dance of extraordinary intricacy, moving the sword now to the left, now to the right, now up, now down. When the monster was utterly mesmerized, she suddenly broke off and thrust the sword hard at him. Only narrowly dodging the blow, the monster grabbed a wrought-iron candelabrum weighing eighty or ninety pounds, and the two of them battled their way out of the hall and into the air, where the palace lady changed back into a dragon. Eventually, though, the dragon—who was a somewhat petite creature, recall—grew tired. In desperation, he hurled the sword at the monster, who promptly caught it and, with his other hand, threw the candelabrum at the dragon. Caught off balance, the dragon took a blow to one of his hind legs. Falling out of the sky, he was saved only by the palace moat into which he plunged, immediately becoming invisible to the monster. Shrugging his shoulders, the monster returned to the Hall of Silver Peace with sword and candelabrum to drink himself into oblivion. The little dragon waited an hour, then dragged himself back to the posthouse, where he changed back into a horse and lay down feeling very sorry for himself. Things looked bad for the band of pilgrims: Monkey was who knew where; the horse was wounded and bedraggled; Pigsy and Sandy were lost on maneuvers.

On which subject: Pigsy, you will remember, had abandoned Sandy for a clump of bushes and fallen asleep snout-down. Waking up around midnight, surrounded by near-total silence, he felt thoroughly disoriented. *I'd like to rescue Sandy, of course,* he thought, rubbing his eyes, *but it's hard to clap with one hand, as it were. I'll report back to Tripitaka first. If I can wangle a few reinforcements, I'll come back for Sandy tomorrow.*

Pigsy cloud-traveled back to the posthouse. There he found only the white horse, soaked to the skin and with a massive bruise on one of his legs. "This is not good," he worried. "How did that lazy horse of ours get roughed up?"

"Pigsy!" the horse suddenly cried out.

"A talking horse!" Pigsy stammered. "Never a good sign." He was so terrified at the animal's sudden acquisition of human speech that he would have fled from the posthouse if the horse had not bitten hold of his robe.

"Do you know that Tripitaka's in terrible trouble?"

"Er, no."

"Of course you don't!" snapped the horse. "You and Sandy were so busy showing off in front of the king that it never crossed your mind that the monster would get the better of you both. While the two of you were doing Heaven knows what, the monster came to court disguised as a handsome young hunter, convinced the king that he was his dream son-in-law, turned our master into a fierce tiger, and had him locked up in a cage. When I had no word from you in two days, I took matters into my own hooves. I changed into a palace lady, tried to kill the monster in a sword dance, took a nasty blow to my hind leg with a candle-holder, and hid in the moat for an hour."

All this was a lot for Pigsy to take in. "Can you move at all?" he eventually asked.

"What if I can?" asked the dragon-horse.

"Then you can go back to the ocean and I'll take the luggage and go back to my wife in Gao Village."

The horse fastened his teeth even harder into Pigsy's robe. "Pull yourself together! We can't give up. You must go to Flower-Fruit Mountain and get Monkey back."

"I'm not the best person for this mission," Pigsy equivocated. "Monkey and I didn't part on the best of terms. For some reason, he blames me for his falling-out with Tripitaka. That staff of his is dangerous, you know."

"He'll have gotten over all that," the horse reasoned. "Don't tell him that Tripitaka's in danger—just that Master's missing him. When we've lured him back with flattery and he sees what's going on, he'll want to save the day. Go! Go now!"

Still nursing a sinking feeling, Pigsy cloud-traveled east. Luck was on his side: the winds were favorable, and Pigsy simply stuck out his enormous ears and sped across the ocean. Landing on Flower-Fruit at sunrise, he heard a voice in a nearby valley. Approaching, he saw that it was Monkey addressing, from a stone boulder, a host of twelve hundred monkeys, all of whom were busy kowtowing. Impressed but also nervous about encountering Monkey again, Pigsy tried to go undercover by creeping into the kowtowing throng. Monkey spotted the intruder instantly and ordered his swarm of monkeys to drag him up to the front. "Who are you? Where's your name card?"

The embarrassed Pigsy now looked Monkey full in the face. "This snout ring a bell?"

"Pigsy." Monkey laughed. "We meet again."

Pigsy was heartened by this; it was a conversational entrée, at least. "Tripitaka is missing you!" he blurted out.

"Last time we met," countered Monkey, "he swore to Heaven that he never wanted to see me again."

"Just now he said Sandy and I were useless and told me to fetch you back," lied Pigsy.

Monkey changed the subject. "Let me show you around, Pigsy." Ignoring Pigsy's protestations that time was getting on and they really needed to go back, Monkey led him by the hand around the beautiful mountains, forests, and caves of Flower-Fruit.

"What a place!" Pigsy sighed, reflecting that it would be difficult to lure Monkey back to the hardships of the pilgrimage. After a breakfast of grapes, pears, loquats, and strawberries, Pigsy repeated that it was time to leave.

"Well, it's been fun," Monkey said. "So long, now."

"You're not coming back with me?"

"Why would I? Life is good here. Tell Tripitaka to forget all about me."

Pigsy made as if to leave amicably. But he began muttering as soon as he set off down the mountain: "Suit yourself, monstrous monkey!"

Little did he know that Monkey had secretly dispatched two of his most agile little followers to spy on Pigsy; they promptly reported back their visitor's sour fulminations. Monkey angrily ordered them to drag the bad-tempered hog back. They then deposited their captive in front of Monkey, who had resumed his place on the boulder. "All right, you pointless pig: what bother has Tripitaka gotten himself into that he needs me to rescue him from? Don't make me beat it out of you."

Pigsy told Monkey everything: his mission to find food, his nap, Tripitaka's misstep into Yellow-Robe's pagoda, their escape to Precious Image, Pigsy and Sandy's return to rescue the princess, his nap, Sandy's capture, the horse's sword dance . . . "And then the talking horse told me to bring you back, and that's where we are."

"Idiot!" snapped Monkey. "Didn't I tell you to frighten any incidental demons by telling them that I'm Tripitaka's senior disciple?"

Here Pigsy had his stroke of genius. "Funny you should say that. As soon as I mentioned you, the monster became even more bumptious. 'Monster,' I said to him, 'don't you lay a finger on my master, for I have a senior disciple with an advanced degree in demon-defeating. When Monkey shows up, you'll be dead before you've picked a burial ground.' He was not bothered in the slightest. 'I'll skin him alive, pull out his tendons, gnaw his bones, and eat his heart! I'll mince the rest of him, then quick-fry the lot!' is what he said. I just thought you ought to know," Pigsy finished serenely.

As anticipated, Monkey began tugging his ears and scratching his cheeks in fury. "Who is this outrageous fiend?"

"His name's Yellow-Robe."

"We're leaving now," Monkey declared. "That monster is begging for a beating. I'll smash him to smithereens, then pick up where I left off here in Flower-Fruit."

"Good idea," approved Pigsy. "Revenge first, long-term life plans second."

Monkey rushed into the cave and put his pilgrim's clothes—the silk shirt and the tiger-skin kilt—back on. "Where are you going?" his little monkeys clamored. "Stay with us and enjoy yourself!"

"Heaven and earth have fated me to be this monk's disciple," Monkey admonished them. "He didn't really banish me—he just wanted me to have a little holiday. Look after this mountain of ours, and be sure to plant the willows and pines in the right season. When I've been to India and delivered the scriptures back to the Land of the East, I'll return to our monkey paradise."

Monkey and Pigsy cloud-traveled across the Great Eastern

Ocean, pausing only briefly for Monkey to wash off what he called his "demonic odor," so as not to disgust Tripitaka when they met again. Soon, Yellow-Robe's golden pagoda came into view. "That's where Sandy's being held, though the monster's not there right now," Pigsy explained. Spotting two boys—one a little older than nine, the other about seven—playing a variation of hockey outside, Monkey swooped down, grabbed them by their hair, and carried them off screaming.

The princess ran out to see Monkey standing on a cliff, making as if to smash her sons to the ground. "Who are you and why have you snatched my children?" she screeched. "Their father has a nasty temper on him—if you hurt a hair on their heads, he'll make you pay."

"I—and you should know this already—am Monkey, Tripitaka's chief and most charismatic disciple. Release Sandy and you'll get your boys back."

The princess rushed back inside to untie Sandy, explaining that a monkey had shown up to demand his release. An ecstatic Sandy ran outside to acclaim his rescuer. "You're a sight for sore eyes, Monkey!"

"Ha!" Monkey greeted him back. "Why didn't you put in a good word for me when Tripitaka was chanting that spell?"

"Forgive and forget?" Sandy suggested hopefully.

Monkey now invited him to hop onto the cliff, where Pigsy—who had been hovering overhead—also joined them, making sympathetic noises about Sandy's ordeal and filling Sandy in on recent events in Precious Image. "Enough talking," interrupted Monkey. "Time for action. You two, take these boys into the city and throw them from a great height onto the ground in front of the throne. Tell anyone who asks that they're Yellow-Robe's sons. As soon as the monster hears of this, he'll rush back here. I don't want to fight him in the city because it'll make a terrible mess of the place."

"Are you trying to get us killed?" Pigsy snorted. "If we drop these boys to the ground, they'll become people-patties, and the monster will kill us in revenge, while you're sitting pretty at a safe distance."

"Just draw him out here," Monkey advised, "and I'll deal with him." Buoyed by Monkey's confidence, the two of them sped off with the boys.

Meanwhile, Monkey came down from the cliff to have a word with the princess. "Faithless monkey!" she rebuked him. "You promised to return my boys if I released Sandy. Where have those associates of yours taken them now?"

"Don't worry," Monkey said with a smile. "The boys have gone to pay a long-overdue visit to their grandfather. And while we're on the subject of faithlessness, for the last thirteen years you've committed the greatest crime there is: neglecting your parents. How could you have abandoned them to take up with a monster?"

The princess flushed scarlet at the reproach. "But what could I do? Yellow-Robe kidnapped me here and kept me under close guard. And because we were so far from the palace, there was no one to take a letter from me. I contemplated suicide but then feared that my parents might think I'd eloped. You're right, though. I betrayed their love and care for me. I'm a terrible person." Tears streamed down her face.

"Cheer up," said Monkey. "Pigsy also told me that you saved Tripitaka and sent him off with a letter to your parents. How about I defeat the monster and take you back to Precious Image? You can marry someone more appropriate and look after your parents in their old age."

"But you're just a stringy little shrimp," objected the princess. "What chance do you stand against the likes of Yellow-Robe?"

Monkey laughed at her doubts. "'A urine bubble is large but weightless; a steelyard is small but weighs a thousand pounds.' I may be small, but I punch above my weight. Hide away while I finish him off, then I'll take you back to the palace." With the princess out of sight, Monkey transformed himself into her exact likeness and went into the cave to await the monster.

Back in Precious Image, Pigsy and Sandy had, according to the plan, smashed the two boys to the ground in front of the throne, leaving a hideous hash of blood and bones. "Behold the sons of the monster Yellow-Robe!" Pigsy shouted down to the horrified courtiers.

Still sleeping off the wine in the Hall of Silver Peace, the monster blearily heard someone calling his name. He rolled over and saw Pigsy and Sandy hovering above the clouds and hollering about his sons. *Isn't Sandy meant to be tied up at home? How have those two got hold of my boys? Are they spoiling for a fight? I've a beast of a hangover, though, and my battling mightn't be up to scratch. I'll head home first, find out whether those really were my boys, then settle with them.* Back he went without even a word of farewell to the king. By this point the court knew full well that he was a monster. After Yellow-Robe had eaten one of the palace ladies during the night, at daybreak the seventeen survivors had reported the whole incident to the king. And when their visitor flew off without a courteous leave-taking—well, that finally confirmed them in their supposition that he was no gentleman.

In the guise of Yellow-Robe's wife, Monkey prepared a proper performance for the monster's return to the cave: bawling, footstamping, chest-pounding—the works. Entirely taken in, the monster rushed to embrace his "wife" and to find out what was distressing her so. After she sobbed out the story of Pigsy kidnapping their sons, the monster was maddened by rage. "So those *were* my sons he killed in front of the palace! He will pay with his life! But can I do anything for you first, my dearest love?"

"Actually, yes. You can"—here, Monkey became his real self again and pulled out his magic iron—"eat my staff!"

The sight of his beautiful wife transforming into a wizened monkey warrior shook even the fearsome Yellow-Robe. "Goodness, darling—you certainly look . . . different."

"Disgusting fiend!" Monkey scolded him. "Don't you recognize me?"

"You look a *little* familiar," stalled the monster. "No, it's gone. You'll have to remind me."

"Know then that I am Monkey, chief disciple of Tripitaka."

"Not possible!" protested Yellow-Robe. "There's only Pigsy and Sandy. No one ever mentioned a—what was the name again?—Monkey."

"Don't play the innocent with me. I know full well that you bad-mouthed me behind my back."

"What?" asked Yellow-Robe.

"Pigsy told me."

"You'd believe a pig over a demon?"

"Enough! At any rate, you've been positively inhospitable today, and in my book that's grounds for a beating."

Yellow-Robe now properly lost his temper, chasing Monkey out of the cave. "How dare you harass me in my own home!" The two waged battle on a nearby mountaintop until the monster misread a Monkey feint and Monkey smashed his staff down on Yellow-Robe's head. The monster instantly vanished without a trace.

Concluding that his foe had to be a deity of some sort—only immortals could pull off this kind of top-notch disappearing trick—Monkey somersaulted up to Heaven and demanded a full roll call of all the spirits. Eventually, it was discovered that the Wood-Wolf Star had been absent without leave for thirteen days—thirteen years in earthly time. On the orders of the Jade Emperor, Wood-Wolf's astral colleagues recited a spell to draw him out of his present hiding place, in a mountain stream. As the errant constellation approached the gate of Heaven, Monkey was

all for bashing him some more; it was only thanks to the intervention of Wood-Wolf's celestial colleagues that he made it as far as
a hearing in front of the Jade Emperor.

"Why," asked the emperor, "did you abandon Heaven for the
mortal world?"

"Forgive me, Your Majesty," Wood-Wolf beseeched, kowtowing. "The princess of Precious Image is no ordinary woman—she
is the Jade Lady in charge of heavenly incense. When she asked me
to have an affair with her, I refused her on the grounds that it
might anger you. Then she said we should elope to the mortal
world and immediately took over the body of the princess of Precious Image. After she'd gone to all this trouble, it seemed rude not
to play along, so I turned into a monster, occupied a mountain,
kidnapped her in a scented cyclone, and made her my wife for
thirteen years."

Taking a dim view of these shenanigans, the Jade Emperor
promptly demoted Wood-Wolf Star to fire-tending duties in the
Tushita Palace.

"Thanks and so long!" whooped Monkey.

"Still haven't learned any manners, Monkey?" snarked one of
the Heavenly courtiers.

The Jade Emperor was phlegmatic. "We count ourselves lucky
if he leaves Heaven without wrecking the show."

Monkey returned to earth on a beam of auspicious light and
gave a full report to the princess (whose body the goddess had
now vacated), Pigsy, and Sandy (the last two had returned to Casserole Mountain, in search of some more fiends to harass). Then
with the judicious application of some ground-shortening magic,
the four of them returned to the palace in Precious Image, where
the princess bowed reverently to her parents, and Monkey explained that she had been possessed by a jade incense attendant
in love with the Wood-Wolf Star.

"All's well that ends well," said the king. "Now let's go and see

Tripitaka." They proceeded to another part of the palace, where officials produced the cage and loosened the "tiger's" chains.

Monkey giggled. "Aren't you the stripy one."

"Don't tease him," Pigsy urged. "Undo the spell."

"You're the favorite," Monkey replied. "You undo it. Anyway, didn't I say I'd go back to Flower-Fruit after defeating the monster?"

Sandy now kneeled before him. "If we had the power to rescue Tripitaka, why would we have needed to fetch you back?"

"All right, all right." Monkey chanted a spell, spat a mouthful of water over the tiger, and Tripitaka reappeared before them. Master and Monkey were joyfully reunited.

"I owe you my life!" Tripitaka exclaimed. "When we return to China, I'll tell the Tang emperor that you are my best and favorite disciple."

"Don't mention it!" Monkey shrugged, laughing. "Just don't give me any more headaches, all right?" And after a lavish feast at the court of Precious Image, the four pilgrims set off again for the west.

Chapter Twenty-Two

Soon enough, another mountain loomed up before the travelers. A woodcutter on a ledge on its lower slope stopped work as soon as he saw them approach. "Pilgrims, beware!" he shouted down to them. "This mountain is infested with demons that specialize in eating travelers to the west."

Tripitaka began trembling so violently that he almost fell off the horse. "Relax!" said Monkey. "I'll find out more."

Up Monkey went. "These monsters, then: are they professionals or amateurs?"

The woodcutter laughed mirthlessly. "Deep in this mountain lies the Lotus-Flower Cave, home to two monsters determined to have you for dinner."

"What luck!" responded Monkey cheerfully. "Do you know how they plan to eat us?"

"I beg your pardon?" asked the nonplussed woodcutter.

"I see you are inexperienced in such matters. If they start with the head, I'll be dead in one bite—all good. After that, they can fry, sauté, braise, or boil me—it wouldn't matter one bit. But if they start with my feet, well, I might still be alive even when they get to my pelvis. And that would be—literally—a pain."

"You're overthinking this. The monsters will catch you, pop you in a steamer, then eat you whole."

"Better still! Just a touch of stuffiness, then it'll all be over."

"Beware, flippant monkey! Beware! These monsters have five treasures of incomparable magic power. Beware!"

The imperturbable Monkey now strolled back to the others. "Nothing to worry about," he reported to Tripitaka. "The odd demon or two, that's all. The locals seem a little high-strung, but with me to protect you, you've nothing to worry about. Onward!"

"Why did that woodcutter disappear so suddenly?" Tripitaka asked a few seconds later.

Looking around, Monkey immediately spotted a Heavenly guardian perched on top of the clouds and somersaulted over. "Tricky little wretch!" Monkey berated him. "If you've something to say, just spit it out. No need to sneak about in fancy dress."

"Please believe me that these demons are exceptionally powerful," the terrified deity implored him. "You'll need every ounce of that cleverness of yours to keep Tripitaka safe. One slip, and the pilgrimage will be over."

"Yes, yes—now get lost."

But Monkey weighed the spirit's words carefully all the same as he made his way back to the group. *If I tell Tripitaka the truth about the immortal's warnings, he's such a weakling he'll burst into tears and refuse to go on. But if I hide the information from him to keep us on the move and these monsters do succeed in capturing him, I'll have to go to the trouble of rescuing him yet again. I know: I'll send Pigsy on ahead to test the waters. If he defeats the monsters solo, good for him. If he's captured, then I'll come to the rescue again and further burnish my demon-defeating credentials.* On returning to the others, Monkey cleverly offered Pigsy two choices of task: either begging for food for Tripitaka or patrolling the mountain. Remembering what had happened the last time he was sent foraging, Pigsy opted—albeit grudgingly— to go on reconnaissance.

"Useless Tripitaka!" he muttered to himself as he trudged off.

"Scheming Monkey! Miserable Sandy! You're all fine and dandy, while I wear out my feet on this cursed mountain."

Now this mountain did indeed contain a Lotus-Flower Cave, home to two fiends who answered to the names Great King Golden Horn and Great King Silver Horn. That very day, their conversation turned to the scripture pilgrims. "I recently heard," remarked Golden Horn, "that the emperor of the Tang has dispatched a monk to seek scriptures from the Buddha in the west. This monk has four companions: Monkey, Pigsy, Sandy, and a horse. Capture them for me, would you?"

"Do I have to?" Silver Horn yawned. "It's not hard to catch the odd human for our dinner. Let these pilgrims go."

"Listen," said Golden Horn seriously. "This one is the result of ten successive reincarnations as a monk, through which his yang energy has been preserved entirely intact. One taste of his flesh will preserve us for thousands of years."

"Ha!" exclaimed Silver Horn. "So if we eat that monk, we no longer need to practice longevity exercises or guzzle nasty alchemical formulas? What are we waiting for?"

"Steady," cautioned Golden Horn. "You don't want to grab the wrong monk—even flesh-eating demons like to avoid collateral damage. Take with you these named portraits of the monk and his disciples, which you can use to check the identities of any pilgrims you encounter." Likenesses in hand, Silver Horn set out with thirty goblins in tow.

It wasn't long before the band of fiends chanced upon Pigsy; some of their number quickly recognized him from his portrait. "Great king! Long snout, huge ears—it's Pigsy for sure!"

Pigsy immediately tried to bury his snout in his chest.

"Lift your chin up so we can get a good look at you," ordered Silver Horn.

"Can't," mumbled Pigsy. "Birth defect." But when Silver Horn told his army of fiends to pull it up with hooks, Pigsy immediately obliged. "All right, it's a snout! What of it?"

Immediately confirming that it was Pigsy, Silver Horn charged. But Pigsy wasn't willing to go quietly. Seizing his rake (which Silver Horn loudly disparaged as a pilfered gardening implement), the enraged Pigsy fought with a reckless ferocity, flapping his ears, spitting, whooping. But then Silver Horn summoned his thirty fiends as backup, and Pigsy panicked as they swarmed toward him. Turning to flee, he tripped over a vine and the goblins were all over him in a moment and hauled him back to the cave. "We caught one, brother!" announced Silver Horn.

Golden Horn rushed over to see, but his delight quickly turned to disappointment. "You got the wrong one. This one's worthless."

"Couldn't agree more," chipped in Pigsy. "Better let me go."

Silver Horn disagreed. "He's still one of the pilgrims. Let's soak him in the pool at the back of the cave, peel off his hide and bristles, then salt and sun-dry him. He'll slip down nicely with a cup of wine on a rainy day." The goblins tossed Pigsy into the pool and left him to pickle.

Back on the mountainside, the other pilgrims had gotten tired of waiting for Pigsy to return and so set off after him. Silver Horn now returned to the hunt and spied on the pilgrims' progress from a mountaintop, devising a cunning plan to get Tripitaka away from the ever-victorious Monkey. He transformed himself into an elderly Taoist—white hair, yellow shoes, silk-sashed gown—with a broken, bleeding leg and hid in the bushes ahead of the pilgrims. "Save me, oh, save me!" he cried, crawling out of the roadside vegetation as they approached.

"Where are you from, sir?" Tripitaka asked. "And what has happened to your leg?"

"I am a priest in a temple to the west of this mountain," explained the "Taoist." "I was walking back last night from distributing blessings when a tiger attacked me. I tripped while running away, and have been lost out here ever since. Please help me get back to my temple!"

"We are both men of religion," answered Tripitaka. "Of course I must help you. Sandy, you carry this gentleman."

"Oh, not that face full of misery!" protested the fiend. "My poor nerves couldn't take it."

"All right, you carry him, Monkey," decided Tripitaka.

"Ha!" muttered Monkey, as he took the Taoist onto his back. "You have underestimated me, shameless fiend. Tripitaka might not see through you, but I read you like a book. My master's not on your menu."

"I've no idea what you're talking about," the monster replied primly.

"Manners, Monkey!" chided Tripitaka, overhearing some of their exchange.

After five or so miles, Tripitaka and Sandy disappeared out of view in a fold of the mountain and Monkey was all ready to dash the monster to the ground. But the fiend was a step ahead of him: deploying the Moving Mountains magic, he brought Mount Meru—the five-peaked center of the Buddhist universe—directly down on Monkey's left shoulder. "Piffling mountain," Monkey observed with a giggle. With another spell, the fiend summoned Mount Emei, another sacred peak, from west China. Monkey caught the second mountain on his right shoulder and began to sprint after Tripitaka. Now sweating with panic, the fiend recited one more spell to summon Mount Tai—a third sacred peak, this time from the east—which caught Monkey full on the head and finally pinned him to the ground.

With Monkey taken care of, the fiend hitched a ride on a gale to catch up with Tripitaka. Hovering overhead, Silver Horn tucked Sandy under one monstrous armpit, Tripitaka under the other, and with another magic gust of wind the three were back in Lotus-Flower Cave. "I've got them, brother!" exulted Silver Horn.

"Wrong again," said Golden Horn, sighing. "Capturing the monk's all very well, but we can't eat him until we've secured the monkey. If we eat his master while he's still at large, he'll make our lives hell."

"That monkey isn't going anywhere," boasted Silver Horn. "Right now, he's pinned beneath three mountains."

"Wonderful!" rejoiced Golden Horn. "Dinnertime! Goblins, wine!" The three prisoners were strung up ready for the pot: Pigsy on the east side of the cave, Sandy on the west, Tripitaka in between them. "Three monks in two trips," he congratulated his brother. "What say we get Monkey along, too, to add to the steamer?"

"Just send Cunning Devil and Wily Worm here," Silver Horn replied with a grin. He gave the two minions a crimson-gold calabash and a mutton-jade vase. "Take these treasures to the top of the mountain, turn them upside down, and shout 'Monkey!' If he answers to his name, he'll be sucked inside one of them. Seal the container with this tag labeled 'For the Urgent Attention of Laozi.' He'll be slime in an hour and three-quarters."

Back on the mountaintop, pinned beneath three notable geographical features, Monkey was not ready to go quietly. He wailed so loudly that the Golden-Headed Guardian and the Protectors of the Five Directions, whom Guanyin had deputized to escort the pilgrimage, the god of the mountain, and the spirit of the soil held a conference about it. "Do you know who you've got trapped beneath these mountains?" Golden-Headed Guardian asked the local divinities.

They shook their heads.

"Monkey, formerly known as the Great Sage Equal to Heaven, who caused such a rumpus in Heaven five centuries ago. What on earth were you thinking of, lending that fiend those mountains to crush him? If Monkey ever escapes, you're all dead meat."

The resident deities went ashen. "We had no idea. We were just following the Moving Mountain spell we heard."

"What's done is done. You'll just have to plead ignorance and hope he doesn't puree you after we release him."

After a brief further discussion, the local spirits nervously approached and introduced themselves to Monkey. "What of it?" responded Monkey, not in the mood for small talk.

"Permit us to remove the mountains from your head and shoulders and beg-your-pardon-for-the-inconvenience-none-intended."

"Go ahead. No hard feelings."

The relieved deities recited some spells and the mountains returned to their homes. Monkey instantly sprang up. Pausing only to hitch up his tiger-skin kilt, he whipped out his staff. "Show me your shanks! Two strokes each for favoring a monster over Monkey."

"But these mountain demons are just too powerful," protested the spirits. "We have to be at their beck and call."

"Outrageous!" cried Monkey. "Even in my most outlandish moments I *never* ordered a local deity around." (He omitted to mention here that he might have urinated on the hand of the Buddha.) Two shafts of light coming from a nearby valley suddenly distracted him. "What's that?"

"Some goblins, I suspect, with the monsters' treasures, here to capture you."

"Finally, some fun!" exclaimed Monkey. "A question, quickly: who would be their favorite sort of visitor?"

"They're obsessed with elixirs—a Taoist, therefore."

"I'll postpone your beating for another day. Monkey has other business for now." The deities did not wait for him to change his mind.

Monkey transformed himself into the very image of an old Taoist priest—patchwork robe, hair pulled up in two topknots—

and reclined by the roadside, awaiting the imps. As they approached, he introduced himself by sticking out his golden-hooped staff for one of the goblins to trip over. "If my kings weren't so fond of Taoists, I'd punch your lights out!" whined the imp, who had gone flying.

Monkey smiled sweetly. "Oh, tripping people up when we first meet them is just a custom of my country."

"You can't be from around here, then."

"Indeed not. I hail from Mount Penglai, the island of the immortals."

"Then you must be—an immortal!" The imp quickly swallowed his anger. "Pardon our ignorance."

"No offense taken. Now, I've landed here on this mountain in search of followers to impart my immortal wisdom to. Do I have any volunteers?"

"Me! Me!" squeaked Cunning Devil and Wily Worm.

"And where were you going just now, my little ones?" Monkey asked.

"Our great kings Golden Horn and Silver Horn have ordered us to capture Monkey," Cunning Devil replied.

"Tripitaka's disciple?" Monkey smoothly interpolated. "That mannerless ape has crossed me one too many times. I'll lend a hand."

"No need," said the imp. "Our king has already pinned the monkey down. All we've got to do is bottle him up in these two treasures of ours."

"How do they work?" asked Monkey.

The goblin described the process, finishing with the all-important outcome: "In one and three-quarter hours, the monkey will be slime."

Secretly shaken, Monkey smiled genially. "May I see?" The unsuspecting goblins immediately presented the vase and the calabash. Marveling at them, Monkey first thought of cloud-somersaulting away with them, then devised a more subtle plan. "Would you like to see my treasure, too?"

"Do show, do show!" squealed the imps. Pulling a hair from his tail, Monkey instantly transformed it into an identical crimson-gold calabash, some seventeen inches tall.

"It certainly looks impressive," admitted Wily Worm, "but is it as powerful as ours? Each of our treasures can store up to a thousand people."

"Mine can bottle up Heaven," boasted Monkey. "If I give you a demonstration, will you swap mine for your two treasures?"

"Done!" the goblins agreed.

Monkey turned around and summoned a handful of deities, whom he ordered to report to the Jade Emperor on the jeopardy currently facing the pilgrimage. "To get out of this pickle, I need to entice a pair of imps to give me their magic containers. I beg His Majesty with greatest reverence to swallow up Heaven for an hour so that I can seal the deal with the goblins. Oh, and tell him that if he doesn't say yes, I'll bring my bashing fist back to his throne room."

Just as the Jade Emperor was fulminating at the insolence of it, Monkey's old friend Prince Nezha stepped forward. "It can be done, Your Majesty. If successful, Monkey's pilgrimage will bring great blessings. We should help him."

"But how?" asked the Jade Emperor.

"Unfurl a black banner across the sun, the moon, and the stars. The earth will be sunk in darkness and those goblins will be tricked into thinking that Monkey has swallowed up Heaven." Not seeing a better option, the Jade Emperor agreed.

Soon enough, one of Monkey's emissary deities returned and whispered the plan in his ear. "And now," Monkey announced to the expectant goblins, "I will store up Heaven!" He muttered some mumbo jumbo and hurled the specious gourd high into the sky, where it spent the next bit of time drifting here and there on the different winds (for it was only as heavy as a single monkey hair); at this cue, Nezha shook out the black banner, smothering sun, moon, and stars. It was as if the universe had suddenly been doused in ink. "And that," said Monkey, "is how you bottle up Heaven."

"It was midday just a moment ago! How can it be night already?" squawked the imps. "Where are you? Where are we?"

Seeing that he'd well and truly duped them, Monkey declaimed some more mumbo jumbo as a cue to Nezha to roll up the banner, restore the midday sunshine, and return the fake calabash to earth.

"A marvel!" exclaimed the little imps, quickly swapping their treasures for Monkey's forgery. Monkey somersaulted up to Heaven to thank Nezha for his help, then hovered in the sky above the imps, watching what they did next.

Chapter Twenty-Three

The goblins were so busy scrapping with each other over who would get to try out the gourd first that they did not notice for some while that Monkey had vanished. "Hey, he said he'd teach us immortality after we'd swapped treasures!" complained Wily Worm.

"Forget it," said Cunning Devil. "We've lucked out with this new treasure of ours. Let's have a go at bottling Heaven." He threw it into the air; it immediately fell back down to the ground.

"What's wrong?" Wily Worm yelped in alarm. "Give it here and I'll have a go. You forgot the spell." Up the calabash went and down it came again, before the "incantation" was even out of his mouth. "It's a fake!" screeched the imps.

Seeing from midair that the game was up, Monkey summoned back the hair that had been the gourd, leaving the two little imps suddenly empty-handed. "Give me back the calabash," demanded Cunning Devil.

"I thought you had it," replied Wily Worm. After a bout of frantic, fruitless searching, the two goblins started to panic. "What are we to do?" shrieked Wily Worm. "Our king told us to capture Monkey with those treasures, and now we have neither Monkey nor the treasures. He'll beat us to death, for sure."

Then Cunning Devil came up with a plan. "King Silver Horn has a soft spot for you. I'll put the blame on you and maybe he'll let both of us off."

After the imps set off for home, Monkey turned into a fly to follow them. (The treasures, like his staff, shrank with him.) After the imps entered the cave, Monkey perched on the door frame to listen to their confession. "This must be the work of Monkey," thundered Golden Horn. "Some idiot spirit's released him and now he's got our treasures."

"Calm down, brother," soothed Silver Horn. "We still have two of the others: the Sword of Seven Stars and the inferno-generating Palm-Leaf Fan. The Golden Rope is in the safekeeping of our beloved mother, in Dragon-Squashing Cave on Squashing-Dragon Mountain. Let's send another couple of fiends to fetch it and invite Mother to the monk banquet while we're at it. Out of my sight, you useless lumps!" shouted Silver Horn at Cunning Devil and Wily Worm, who could hardly believe their luck. "Send in some competent goblins instead." In came imps three and four, Mountain Tiger and Lounging Dragon. "Go and invite our mother to dinner, and ask her to bring the Golden Rope with her. Don't mess this up."

Off the two new goblins raced, with Monkey-as-fly buzzing in pursuit. Two or three miles into the journey, Monkey turned himself into another goblin and pretended to be running to catch up with them. "Wait for me!" he called. "Silver Horn sent me to remind you to hurry." On they ran, until Lounging Dragon pointed out a forest up ahead as their destination. Figuring that he could find his way from here, Monkey held back a little, allowing the two goblins to run ahead, then smashed them both to mincemeat. After scraping them up into some roadside bushes, he turned himself into Lounging Dragon and one of his hairs into Mountain Tiger and soon found his way to a double stone door in the forest.

"Who are you?" asked a female janitor-demon.

"We've come from Lotus-Flower Cave. Kings Golden Horn and Silver Horn invite their mother Monstress Dowager to a banquet of an exceptionally succulent monk from the Tang empire. They also ask if she could bring her Golden Rope to capture a troublesome monkey."

"What filial sons!" exclaimed the mother-fiend as soon as she heard, calling at once for her sedan chair. The party set off immediately: two attendants to carry the monster, plus the two goblins impersonated by Monkey.

After five or so miles, "Lounging Dragon" plucked a hair from his chest and transformed it into an enormous flatbread, then sat down and began to nibble on it. "Can we have some, too?" asked the carriers, pausing for a rest. As they approached, Monkey pounded both into mush. Disturbed by the whimpers of pain, the Monstress Dowager looked out of the sedan and was also pulverized by Monkey, who quickly located and tucked up his sleeve the Golden Rope. Then he transformed himself into the old woman, plucked three more hairs to stand in for the rest of the goblin party, and carried on toward Lotus-Flower Cave.

Soon enough this curious ensemble reached their destination, and Monkey swaggered into the cave, in grandiloquent imitation of the dowager, to a resplendent reception: the cave's full detail of fiends, drums, and flutes, wisps of perfumed smoke from an enormous urn, and kowtows from Golden Horn and Silver Horn.

Pigsy suddenly giggled.

"What's so funny?" Sandy asked sourly.

"It's our mutual friend."

"Who?"

"Monkey!"

"How d'you know?"

"When he bent over to return the monsters' greetings, his tail rode up. Being hung up on this high beam certainly gives you perspective."

Sandy shushed him. "Let's hear what they're saying."

"We have neglected you recently, dearest Mother," one of the brothers began. "Today we captured an unusually virtuous and tender monk, and plan to steam him for your delectation. He's rich in longevity."

"I don't really feel like monk today. What I fancy is a nice bit of pig's ear. D'you have anything like that?"

"Curse you!" spat Pigsy. "How about I tell them their mother's grown a tail?"

This outburst unfortunately blew Monkey's cover. Some patrol goblins also happened to rush in at this moment with more bad news: "Disaster, great king! Monkey has beaten your mother to death and infiltrated the cave in disguise." Unsheathing his Sword of Seven Stars, one of the kings slashed at the face of Monkey, who transformed himself this time into red light and escaped the cave as ether, which he thoroughly enjoyed. Silver Horn pulled on his armor—a wrought-iron suit, cinched at the waist with a dragon's tendon—strode out of the cave, and hurled himself into combat with Monkey on the edge of the clouds.

After a while, Monkey tried to settle the fight by lassoing his opponent with the Golden Rope. But here Monkey was out of his depth. Just as the noose settled around Silver Horn's head, the demon recited a loose-rope spell. The monster then seized hold of one end and, before Monkey could do his body-thinning magic, lassoed him with a tight-rope spell. In an instant Monkey was comprehensively trussed with an inescapable gold ring enclosing him around his neck. The monster also dealt him seven or eight blows to the head with his sword, to which Monkey was entirely indifferent. "All right, you hardheaded ape," said the demon, "back to the cave where I'll beat you some more. But first I want my other two treasures back." After a careful search, Silver Horn took back the gourd and the vase, then used one end of the rope as a leash to lead Monkey back to the cave. He and Golden Horn tied Monkey to a pillar and went back to their drinking.

"Looks like you won't be nibbling my ears anytime soon!"

Pigsy chortled down at Monkey from the beam. But Monkey was already busy with an escape plan. When no one was paying attention, he turned his staff into a steel file, sawed his way out of the neck ring, turned a hair into a specious Monkey still tied to the pillar, and changed himself into a goblin.

"Phony Monkey alert!" Pigsy trilled.

"Pigsy's just making a fuss," the Monkey-goblin explained to the kings, "because Monkey's refusing to use magic to escape."

"Tricksy devil!" said Silver Horn. "Give him twenty strokes on the snout."

"Gently now," warned Pigsy as Monkey approached with a stick, "or I'll rat you out again."

"I'm trying to get us all out of this hole," hissed Monkey. "Why do you keep on giving me away? Anyway, how come you're the only one in this caveful of fiends who can still recognize me?"

"Your art of seventy-two transformations doesn't reach as far as your red buttocks. They're a bit of a giveaway."

Monkey then shuffled over to the kitchen to rub his bottom against the charcoal burned onto the base of a pot while Pigsy giggled some more.

Monkey now plotted to take back the treasures. "Monkey has frayed that Golden Rope," the Monkey-goblin informed the kings. "How about I replace it with something thicker?"

"Good idea," responded the demon, undoing a lion-buckled belt and handing it to the fake goblin. Monkey reattached his phony self to the pillar with the belt, slipped the Golden Rope up his sleeve, and turned another hair into a fake Golden Rope, which he handed back to the demon. Busy guzzling wine, the demon put it away without noticing.

Now in possession of one of the treasures, Monkey sprang out of the cave door and changed back to his true form. "Fiends!" he shouted. "Know that Yeknom is here!"

"Who?" asked a startled Golden Horn.

MONKEY KING   213

"Don't worry," soothed Silver Horn. "I'll prepare the calabash so we can bottle up our unexpected visitor if necessary." Just outside the door, he encountered an ever-so-slightly-shorter replica of Monkey.

"I am the brother of Monkey," said Monkey. "I'm here to reckon with his captors."

Silver Horn yawned. "I suppose you want to fight me now. Well, I'm not playing that game. I'll call your name instead. Will you answer to it?"

"Ten thousand times!"

The demon leaped into the air, holding the calabash upside down, and roared: "Yeknom!"

Monkey now hesitated, knowing the power of the gourd.

"Answer!" cried the fiend.

"My ears are a little blocked today. Speak up, would you?"

"YEKNOM!"

Monkey experienced some inner turmoil: *My real name is Monkey; Yeknom is just an alias. If I answer to a false name, will I still be sucked inside?* He soon found out. Answering to Yeknom, he was swallowed whole and the calabash was taped up. It turned out that Monkey had been overthinking the matter. The gourd didn't bother checking your identity: as long as you answered back, it had you.

Inside the gourd it was perfectly dark. Unworried about the calabash's power over him—forty-nine days in Laozi's brazier had only made him stronger—Monkey concentrated on following what was going on outside. "All good," he heard Silver Horn tell Golden Horn. "I've got Monkey's brother inside."

"Sit down and take your ease, excellent brother." Golden Horn said jubilantly. "When we can hear monkey-slime sloshing around inside, we'll take the seal off."

First, Monkey thought of hoaxing the monsters by urinating inside the gourd to generate a liquid sound effect, but rethought when he considered what a smelly mess it would make of his shirt. *I'll gargle instead*, he decided. Bored of waiting for the monsters to remember to shake the gourd, Monkey resorted to some amateur dramatics to accelerate matters: "Oh, goodness! What's happened to my shins?" No response from the demons. "My pelvis is pus!"

"He must be almost done," reflected Golden Horn. "Let's take a look."

Monkey plucked a hair and transformed it into a half monkey stuck to the bottom of the gourd, while changing his real self into a cicada perched near the rim of the calabash. The instant that Silver Horn lifted the seal, Monkey flew out and instantly transformed again into Lounging Dragon, who had met such a sticky end earlier. Panicked by glimpsing the partially dissolved body inside the gourd, the monster didn't wait to verify that it was Monkey. "He's not finished, quickly put the stopper back on." Back went the seal with Monkey sniggering on the outside.

Golden Horn poured his brother a full cup of wine. "Let me toast your success in capturing Tripitaka, Pigsy, Sandy, Monkey, and Monkey's brother Yeknom." Anxious to take the proffered cup respectfully, with two hands, Silver Horn passed the gourd to Lounging Dragon—the disguised Monkey. While the two brothers politely toasted each other, Monkey had time to tuck the treasure up his sleeve and turn another of his hairs into a replica. The toasts complete, Silver Horn took back the gourd without checking it over, while Monkey slipped out of the room.

Returning to his true form outside the cave, Monkey now tried another grand entrance. "Open up, monsters! It's Nomyek, brother of Monkey and Yeknom!"

"How can that Monkey have so many damn brothers?" asked Golden Horn.

"Relax," reassured Silver Horn. "This calabash can bottle up a thousand people. I'll deal with him straightaway." And out he strode to receive his visitor. "I won't fight you," Silver Horn told Nomyek. "But I will call your name. Will you answer to it?"

"Happy to oblige." Monkey chuckled. "But if I call *your* name, will *you* answer to it?"

"I want to call your name," revealed the disingenuous fiend, "so that my calabash here will swallow you up. Why do you want to call my name?"

"Because I have my own humble calabash," replied Monkey.

"Let's see," said the monster. Monkey waved it in front of Silver Horn, then shook it back up his sleeve, afraid that the monster would grab it. "Extraordinary," wondered a flustered Silver Horn. "The exact likeness of mine. Where did it come from?"

Having no idea, Monkey threw the question back at his interlocutor: "Where did *yours* come from?"

Silver Horn earnestly embarked on an exhaustive account of the calabash's origins: "When primeval chaos divided, heaven and earth were created. The Supreme Primordial Venerable Patriarch died and was reborn as the goddess Nüwa. She smelted stones to mend the heavens to save the world. When she came to the crack at the base of Kunlun Mountain, she found this crimson-gold gourd growing on a tendril of immortal vine and passed it to Laozi for safekeeping."

"That's where mine came from, too," Monkey glibly interpolated. "Let's try them out—you go first."

"Nomyek!" the fiend duly cried, leaping into the air. Monkey replied almost a dozen times, but nothing happened. The demon returned to the ground, stamping his feet in vexation.

"Monkey's . . . I mean . . . Nomyek's turn," Monkey now announced. He somersaulted into the air, pointed the mouth of the calabash downward, toward the demon, and shouted, "Great King Silver Horn!" The latter felt honor bound to respond and was promptly swallowed by the gourd, which Monkey then sealed with the designated stopper. "Happy dissolving!" cheered Monkey, and the gourd soon began to make a sloshing sound, suggesting that Silver Horn was already slime, although Monkey was not about to open the gourd rashly to check. "In case you're pissing or gargling, I'll leave you in there for another seven days or so—just to make sure."

Monkey stood at the cave entrance, shaking the bottle loudly. Golden Horn and his little fiends soon worked out who was inside. "Excellent brother!" Golden Horn wailed, collapsing to the ground. "When you and I left Heaven for the mortal world, we planned to live as powerful kings in this mountain cave. And now we are parted forever!" The caveful of goblins sobbed in solidarity.

"Buck up, fiends!" shouted Pigsy from his beam. "That's the power of Monkey for you. But what's done is done—your brother's dead and that's the end of it. Scrub your pots and cook up some pancakes. Once we've eaten, we'll be delighted to cheer you up with a nice sutra."

Pigsy's intervention enraged Golden Horn. "How dare you make fun of me? Goblins, steam this pig till he's tender. I'll deal with that Monkey once I've filled my stomach."

Just as Pigsy was getting worried, a gastronomically minded fiend intervened: "He won't taste good steamed."

"Thank the Buddha!" chimed Pigsy. "Some sense at last."

"You need to skin him first," the goblin continued.

But Golden Horn had already lost patience with this exchange. "Forget about Pigsy. Bring me the Sword of Seven Stars." He then stormed out of the cave with three hundred fiends to face Monkey, who pulled a handful of hairs from his left armpit, chewed them into pieces, and spat them out. Each fragment became a replica Monkey, punching and biting Golden Horn and the fiends into flight. Monkey next somersaulted back into the abandoned cave, scooped up two of the other treasures—the mutton-jade vase and the Palm-Leaf Fan—and cut his fellow pilgrims down from their various beams. The reunited travelers had a hearty meal of the rice, noodles, and vegetables that they found in the cave and rested overnight.

The following day, Monkey was ordering Sandy to get things ready for their departure when an army of goblins whirled up from the southwest. For Golden Horn had mustered not only his mother's household of female demons but also the fiendish retinue of a maternal uncle of his. The monsters were no match, though, for the combined forces of Monkey, Pigsy, and Sandy. Pigsy dispatched the uncle with his rake, and when the surrounded Golden Horn turned to flee, Monkey produced the jade vase, aimed its mouth at the demon, and cried, "Great King Golden Horn!" Thinking that one of his demon soldiers was calling him, Golden Horn answered and was immediately swallowed by the vase, with the mouth then stoppered shut. The Sword of Seven Stars—the last treasure—clattered to the ground and was collected by Monkey.

The three disciples returned to the cave in time for breakfast. But just as they were preparing to set off for the west, a blind man suddenly appeared and grabbed the reins of the horse. Immediately recognizing his old friend Laozi, the Taoist patriarch, Monkey bowed. Laozi now floated up to a jade throne suspended in the air above them. "I want my treasures back, Monkey."

Monkey rose level with him. "Which treasures would those be?"

"The calabash I use for storing elixir, the vase for holy water, the Sword of Seven Stars for tempering demons, the Palm-Leaf Fan for stoking my eternal flames, and the Golden Rope—I use the rope to hold my robe together, actually. Golden Horn and Silver Horn are two of my brazier attendants. I've been looking all over for them, since they stole my treasures and fled to the mortal world."

"That was a bit slack, allowing your servants to become demons," Monkey needled the Taoist founder.

"It was out of my hands," Laozi explained. "Guanyin kept on pestering me for them, because she needed them to generate some demonic adversity to test your resolve."

Unbelievable! thought Monkey. *She told me she'd come and rescue us if we got into a pickle. And here she is, harassing us with monsters! Damn her to a husbandless eternity!* He grudgingly returned the objects to Laozi, who unsealed the gourd and the vase and poured out the divine ether inside. One wave of his finger transformed the ether back into his servants, and the three of them drifted heavenward, haloed by auspicious light.

Chapter Twenty-Four

After a couple of weeks in the plains, the pilgrims found themselves approaching another vertiginous mountain. As they picked their way up its lower slopes, a hungry-looking red fireball whizzed toward them. When Monkey, Pigsy, and Sandy looked back after following its progress past them, they discovered that Tripitaka had disappeared. While Pigsy immediately concluded that this was a sign from above that they should give up on the whole enterprise, Monkey was busy summoning the local spirits to investigate what had happened. When the deities arrived, they were in a sorry state: their clothes in tatters, their trousers seatless and unhemmed.

"Tell me about the monsters in this mountain," Monkey requested.

"There's only the one, but he's worn us ragged, always extorting bribes or chores out of us. As Heaven runs a cashless economy, our only way of getting the demon off our backs is to pay him and his goons off with the odd mountain deer. And when we don't have anything for them, they smash up our temples and rip our clothes."

"Who is he, and where does he live?" asked Monkey.

"We know him by the name of Red Boy, son of King Bull Demon and Princess Iron-Fan, and he lives in Fire-Cloud Cave, where he has perfected the art of demonic flames."

Monkey now returned, beaming, to his comrades. "Nothing to worry about here," he told them. "Tripitaka'll be fine—he's been captured by one of my relatives. When I was the king of Flower-Fruit Mountain, I swore blood brotherhood with one King Bull Demon—his son's the fireball who kidnapped Tripitaka. I'm sure he'll release Tripitaka to his favorite uncle."

Sandy was dubious. "You've not seen this relative of yours for at least five hundred years or—I imagine—sent him birthday gifts or greetings. Are you sure he'll remember you?"

"Look," said Monkey, "he might not lay on a banquet for us, but he'll give us back our spiritual leader, for sure."

Within a few days, they found their way to Fire-Cloud Cave. Monkey and Pigsy approached, while Sandy guarded the luggage and the horse from a distance. "Tell your master to produce Tripitaka," Monkey ordered some goblins on military maneuvers in front of the cave, "or we'll raze this place to the ground."

Inside the cave, things were not looking good for Tripitaka. Red Boy—who had transformed from a fireball into a demon of striking beauty, with porcelain-white skin, scarlet lips, and ebony hair—was overseeing while his goblin menials stripped Tripitaka, hog-tied him, and scrubbed him clean, ready for the steamer. As soon as Red Boy learned of his unexpected visitors, he strode out of the cave with his lance. "Who dares approach Fire-Cloud Cave?" he roared.

"Well met, nephew!" Monkey hailed him heartily. "That monk you seized when you were a fireball just now—hand him back, will you? There's a good boy."

"I've no idea who you are or what you're talking about, monkey-face," Red Boy responded, not very encouragingly.

"You know me—your father's blood brother from five hundred years ago. There were seven of us, with Dragon-Monster, Roc-Fiend, Lion-Camel, Macaque, and Giant-Ape. True, you weren't born at the time. But I'm amazed your father's not told you all about me."

Red Boy responded to Uncle Monkey's trip down memory lane by trying to stab him with his fire-tipped lance. "Rude little beast!" exclaimed Monkey, fighting back with his staff. After Pigsy joined in, delivering a massive blow to Red Boy's head, the latter retreated to the entrance of the cave, recited a spell, and blew out a blazing trail of fire enshrouding the entire cave. While Pigsy fled, yelping something about not wanting to be roast pork, Monkey tried to fight through the inferno, but Red Boy blew smoke hard into his eyes. Smarting at the blaze, Monkey dived straight into a mountain stream and immediately fainted at the shock of the cold water.

Having watched his dive, Pigsy and Sandy dragged Monkey out and massaged him back to life. "This is demonic fire," Monkey gasped after he had come to. "I can't fight it. We need help from Guanyin. But I'm too weak to cloud-somersault right now."

"I'll go," volunteered Pigsy.

Unfortunately, Red Boy—celebrating his victory over Monkey back in the cave—happened to spot Pigsy heading south and quickly deduced that he was on his way to see Guanyin. He decided there and then to capture Pigsy by stealth, steam him till he was flaky, and enjoy him with wine. Taking a shortcut to the South Sea, Red Boy turned into a bogus Guanyin and lay in wait for Pigsy, who was instantly taken in and explained that he had come to beg for help with the unruly Red Boy. "Of course," answered "Guanyin." "Follow me." Red Boy led him straight back to the cave, where goblins seized him and popped him into a leather bag, ready for the steamer.

Awaiting Pigsy's return in a nearby forest, Monkey sneezed. "A bad omen," he fretted to Sandy. "I fear Pigsy has taken a wrong turn. I'm going to the cave to investigate." The sentries rushed at him as he approached; too weak to fight, Monkey changed himself into a piece of gold cloth and fluttered down by the side of the road. Thinking that Monkey had dropped it in flight, one of the goblins picked it up and brought it back inside the cave, where Monkey could hear Pigsy raging from inside the leather bag. Just as he was trying to devise a rescue plan, Monkey overheard Red Boy sending six goblins out to deliver an invitation to his father, Monkey's old comrade King Bull Demon, to partake with him of the life-prolonging Tripitaka. Smelling an opportunity, Monkey turned into a fly and buzzed after them out of the cave.

Monkey soon overtook the emissaries and, ten miles ahead of them, transformed himself into the exact likeness of his former friend Bull Demon, then waited in a fold of the mountain, pretending to be on a hunting expedition. "How kind," cooed the specious Bull Demon on intercepting the goblins and learning of their purpose, and the seven of them returned to Red Boy's cave, where Monkey was treated to a full ceremonial welcome. "Be careful with this Tripitaka," he warned Red Boy, after sitting down. "I understand that his disciple is the famous Monkey who rebelled against Heaven. Back in the day, he saw off one hundred thousand celestial soldiers."

"Big deal," dismissed Red Boy. "I already burned him to a frazzle."

"Don't underestimate his powers of transformation, though."

"I'd spot him the moment he stepped through my door."

"But what if he becomes a fly, mosquito, flea, or bee?"

"He wouldn't dare!" gloated Red Boy.

Bull Demon now changed the subject. "About dinner. Good of you to invite me to share the monk with you, but I can't today. Now that I'm getting older, your mother's always after me to be a better demon. So I've decided to keep vegetarian four days in every month. I'll be back to meat tomorrow. Let's reconvene then."

Curious, thought Red Boy. *My father's never said no to a juicy human in a thousand years. And how could being a vegetarian a few days a month possibly atone for all the evil he has commit-ted?* Leaving Bull Demon for a moment, Red Boy went to quiz the goblins he had sent to fetch his father. "Where did you find him?"

"On the side of the road."

"You mean you didn't pick him up from his house? I fear, then, that we have an impostor. Prepare your weapons while I question him some more to establish the truth of the matter."

Red Boy now returned to his bogus father. "Actually, I also invited you here because I wanted to ask you something. The other day, when I was taking a turn around the Ninefold Heaven, I happened to bump into the Jade Emperor's alchemist and pre-ceptor."

"Oh, yes?" Monkey asked, feigning polite interest.

"He was struck by the regularity of my features and wanted to know the exact hour, month, and year of my birth so that he could tell my fortune. I couldn't supply the details he required, but I thought you'd be sure to know."

Monkey smiled to himself at Red Boy's cunning. "The old memory's not what it once was," he stalled his "son" genially. "I'll ask your mother when I get home."

There's no way my father wouldn't know this, Red Boy thought. *The old man's always carrying on about my time of birth. A phony, for sure.* Out loud he said: "Goblins, attack!"

Monkey instantly became his real self again. "The youth of today!" he teased Red Boy. "Attacking their own fathers!"

Temporarily wrong-footed by this nonsensical accusation of unfiliality, Red Boy looked away in embarrassment, and Monkey exited the cave as a beam of golden light. "Start steaming that monk!" roared an enraged Red Boy.

Outside the cave, Monkey strolled jauntily back to Sandy in the forest, chuckling away. "You've been gone for ages," Sandy greeted him. "I trust you've rescued Tripitaka?"

"I've got good news and bad news. The good news is I played an excellent joke on Red Boy and bluffed him into thinking I was his father. The bad news is that not only is Tripitaka being stripped and scrubbed for the steamer, but Pigsy's also been captured and is being marinated in a bag suspended from the roof of the cave, ready for slow-cooking."

"Stop wasting your time on pointless pranks!" Sandy chided him. "Tripitaka is in mortal danger."

"Don't worry. I feel like a new monkey after that lark. I'm more than well enough to ask for Guanyin's help myself."

"Hurry!" urged Sandy. "That demon now has a serious grudge against you."

In less than an hour, Monkey was in the South Sea, summarizing the pilgrimage's latest predicament to Guanyin. "Why didn't you tell me sooner?" the goddess reproached him.

"I was too badly burned by Red Boy's fire to come myself and sent Pigsy instead. But he was intercepted en route by Red Boy, who disguised himself as you and tricked Pigsy into going to his cave, where Pigsy is currently being prepared for the steamer."

Guanyin immediately flew into a rage. "How dare that demon impersonate me!" She threw her vase into the sea. Even Monkey was taken aback to witness her temper. "Shame about the vase, too," he noted regretfully. But an instant later, it reappeared, borne back up by the fierce black tortoise of the wind and the waves—the vase's dedicated guardian. Guanyin asked Monkey to collect it.

Monkey swooped down but discovered he could not move it an inch. "I've not been well, you know," he told Guanyin embarrassedly.

"It now contains an oceanful of water, drawn from all the seas, rivers, and lakes of the world—no wonder you couldn't lift it," she told him, stooping to pick it up with the greatest ease. Monkey bowed respectfully. "The water in this vase is magic dew, able to extinguish Red Boy's demonic fire. But how to get it to where it needs to be? You can't take it yourself. I could send my assistant, the Dragon Girl, but I fear you'd try to steal it off her. Leave a deposit here, to ensure you bring it back. I'll accept one of the life-saving hairs I gave you at the start of the quest."

"What a suspicious mind you have," Monkey reproached her. "I'd rather not give you one of those hairs—you're all fingers and thumbs and might break it. Why don't you just bring the vase yourself?"

"Oh, all right," she said, sighing. "Come on. After you."

Monkey explained that he didn't want to cloud-somersault first, as he was afraid his kilt would ride up and Guanyin would see his bottom. She instructed Monkey instead to climb onto a lotus petal floating on the ocean and with one gentle exhalation blew him all the way back to the other shore—to the continent of the quest. She next borrowed from Heaven the thirty-six constellation swords, out of which she built a platform to carry her across the ocean, concealing the points of the weapons beneath flowers and leaves. Then she and Hui'an followed Monkey across the sea, with a white parrot as their advance guard. In a moment, they all reached the top of Red Boy's mountain. Guanyin first ordered the local spirits to evacuate the area of all living creatures within three hundred miles, then emptied her vase of its ocean. "If I had this power," Monkey reflected, "I wouldn't have cared about saving all the local animals first."

Guanyin responded by dipping a twig in water and writing "delusion" on Monkey's palm. "Now draw the monster out of his cave and over here." She sat on her dais—constructed out of the concealed swords—to wait.

Monkey somersaulted to the entrance of the cave. When knocking did not get the door open, Monkey punched a hole in it with his staff. Red Boy immediately charged into the fray, but after a few minutes Monkey fled back to Guanyin and hid in her divine aura.

"Who are you?" Red Boy rudely quizzed her. "Monkey's side-kick?"

When Guanyin did not reply, Red Boy drove his lance at her heart, upon which she vanished into a ray of golden light.

"Why did you give up so easily?" demanded Monkey.

"Watch what he does next," she shushed him.

Red Boy was very pleased with himself. "That Guanyin was completely useless. I'll try out her dais for myself." The moment he sat down, arms and legs folded, Guanyin shouted "Disappear!" and the flowers and leaves that had been concealing the swords vanished, leaving Red Boy sitting on thirty-six heavenly points. From below, Hui'an struck the handles hundreds of times so that they pierced Red Boy's legs over and over again. When the demon tried to pull out the swords, Guanyin recited a spell to turn the blades into hooks that held fast to his body. Red Boy finally begged for mercy. "I did not realize how powerful you were, Guanyin. Spare me and I'll follow your Buddhist laws."

"You promise to take the commandments?"

Red Boy nodded, desperate to live. Guanyin shaved off almost all his hair except for three tufts plaited into tiny braids. "Disappear!" she then called, and the swords fell away, leaving Red Boy completely unscarred. But as soon as the swords and the pain had gone, and Red Boy realized he had been given a truly undignified hairstyle, he lunged again at Guanyin with his lance. Guanyin produced another golden circlet from her sleeve—partner to Monkey's headache hoop. With one wave, it became five rings. When she threw them at Red Boy, one attached to his head, the other four to his hands and feet. "Now time for the spell—no, not yours," she reassured Monkey, spotting his look of horror. "This one's just for Red Boy." As she recited, the demonic boy scratched his cheeks and ears, curled himself into a ball, and writhed this way and that. When Guanyin stopped after several recitations,

Red Boy discovered that there were golden hoops around his neck, wrists, and ankles—no amount of tugging dislodged them.

"How d'you like your bracelets of good behavior?" Monkey taunted him. When Red Boy charged at Monkey with his lance, Guanyin merely shouted "Close!" and Red Boy's wrists fastened tightly to his sides. With one more spell, Guanyin's vase scooped up all the water it had disgorged.

"The boy wants educating," Guanyin told Monkey. "I'll take him back to the South Sea now, to train him as my attendant. You go and rescue the others." And off Monkey went, for a happy reunion with Sandy, Tripitaka, and Pigsy.

But this was not the last that Monkey and his fellow pilgrims would hear of Red Boy and his family.

Chapter Twenty-Five

Soon spring came again, and as the pilgrims were proceeding along a road fringed with willows and blossom trees, they suddenly heard a deafening clamor of voices. Before Tripitaka had had time to wonder what it was, Monkey leaped into the air to scope out the surrounding area. In the distance he saw a moated city, haloed with light. *Looks pleasant and peaceful enough,* he thought. *So where's the noise coming from?* Just then, the source of the din came into view: a crowd of ragged Buddhist monks on a beach outside the city, straining to pull a cart, calling on the Buddha for help. Monkey now saw that the cart was filled with building materials—tiles, wood, mud bricks, and the like—and being hauled up an impossibly steep, narrow cliffside path. Just as he was wondering how they had ended up doing this kind of hard labor, Monkey saw two young Taoists, dressed in bright brocades and silks, swagger over to the building site. The appearance of the Taoists seemed to terrify the Buddhists, who redoubled their efforts with the cart. *Let's take a closer look,* he thought.

Landing near the beach, Monkey transformed himself into a wandering Taoist and bowed before the two young men. "I have traveled here from far away," he told them. "Is there any kind soul in the city from whom I could beg a little something to eat?"

The young men laughed at the question. "Everyone in this city, from the king down to the most ordinary subjects, is devoted to Taoism—people bow and gift us food whenever they see us."

"What's the name of this city, and how did its ruler come to be so pious?"

"The place is called Cart-Slow. Twenty years ago, there was a terrible drought and all the crops failed. Just as things were getting desperate, three Taoist masters descended from Heaven and saved us all. They now rule over us."

"What are their names?" asked Monkey.

"In order of seniority: Tiger-Strength Great Immortal, Deer-Strength Great Immortal, and Goat-Strength Great Immortal. They can summon the wind and the rain as easily as turning over their hands. If they point at water, it turns into oil; stones become gold. The awestruck king worships them."

"May I meet these famous Taoists?"

"Of course—as easy as blowing away ashes. We just need to check that those lazy Buddhists aren't slacking off." Monkey raised an eyebrow. "During the drought," one of the young men explained, "the Buddhists competed with the Taoists in praying for rain, but their sutras were completely useless. So the king destroyed all the monasteries and images of the Buddha and gave all the monks to us as slaves. This group here is meant to be moving construction materials, but they're bone idle."

"May I question the slaves myself? One of the reasons I ended up here is that I'm looking for a long-lost uncle who left home as a child to become a monk. He might have gotten stuck here."

"Be our guest!" said one of the young men expansively. "When you're done, we'll go into the city together."

The moment the monks saw Monkey approach dressed as a Taoist, they began frantically kowtowing. "No need for that," Monkey told them. "I'm not a foreman. But I am wondering why you've allowed yourselves to be enslaved by Taoists."

"The king here is an evil, gullible man," one of the Buddhists told Monkey. "The Taoists who now control the city seduced him twenty years ago with their rain spells and turned us into slaves."

"I see," said Monkey. "But why don't you just run away?"

"The Taoists have distributed portraits of us all across the kingdom and offer large rewards to anyone who captures an escaped monk. It's hopeless. More than half of us have already died from overwork or suicide. We've tried to kill ourselves, too, but our knives were too blunt and our nooses broke. It seems that Heaven is determined to torment us. When we go to sleep at night, the gods tell us to hold on for a monk from the Tang empire, for he has a disciple, a monkey, with miraculous magic powers and a low tolerance for injustice. They say that he will destroy the Taoists and restore Buddhism in Cart-Slow."

Delighted by this flattering write-up, Monkey turned back to the young Taoists. "Did you find your uncle?" one of them asked him.

"They're all my uncles," Monkey told them. "I want you to release them all."

"Are you mad?" the young man asked. "If we release them all, we won't have any servants."

After Monkey's request had been refused three times, he smashed the two Taoists to a pulp. "What have you done?" the horrified Buddhists asked Monkey. "The king treats Taoists like his own family, and we'll be accused of their murder."

"You've nothing to worry about," said Monkey, laughing, "for I am—Is that a flying iguana?" As they turned their heads to look, he changed back into his true form. "—Monkey, disciple of Tripitaka from the Tang empire, here to save you all." He flung the cart between the two passes, where it smashed to pieces, and hurled the bricks and timber back down the hill. "Tomorrow I will go and see the king and destroy the Taoists."

Tired of waiting for Monkey, Tripitaka now caught up with him and learned about the situation in Cart-Slow. "One Buddhist monastery in the city survived the king's purge, because it houses a portrait of his father," a monk-slave told them. "How about you stay there for the night?" After the pilgrims entered the city, they were shunned by everyone they encountered until they reached the Well of Wisdom Monastery, whose elderly monk kneeled before Monkey and acclaimed him his savior.

"Back on your feet!" Monkey laughed. "Let's see if I can get you some results tomorrow."

That night, though, Monkey could not sleep a wink. Around eleven o'clock, he heard gongs and flutes nearby. He quietly pulled on his clothes and leaped into the air to see what was going on. Due south, a Taoist temple was ablaze with lamps and candles. Inside a chamber hung with yellow silk brocade scrolls, three elderly priests in full ceremonial dress—Tiger-Strength, Deer-Strength, and Goat-Strength, Monkey surmised—officiated before tables groaning with sumptuous comestibles. Below them a crew of seven or eight hundred lesser Taoists were beating drums and bells, shaking incense and mumbling prayers. *I feel like playing a little joke on them,* Monkey thought, *but I might need some backup. Better bring Pigsy and Sandy along.*

Monkey returned to the monastery, where Pigsy and Sandy were fast asleep in the same bed. "Get up!" Monkey whispered to Sandy. "Let's go and have some fun."

"Sleep's fun," Sandy grumbled groggily.

"The Taoists nearby have filled their temple with steamed buns as big as barrels and cakes weighing fifty or sixty pounds apiece."

Pigsy sat bolt upright. "Did someone say steamed buns as big as barrels?"

"Don't wake Tripitaka," Monkey shushed him. "Just come with me."

The other two disciples quickly dressed and cloud-traveled to the temple. As soon as Pigsy saw the lights, he was all for going straight down there. "Be patient," Monkey restrained him. "Wait until they've gone."

"But when will that be?"

"Leave that to me," said Monkey.

Making a magic twist of his fingers, Monkey muttered a spell. When he exhaled, a mini cyclone hit the temple, blowing out all the lights. Tiger-Strength promptly dissolved the assembly, telling everyone to reconvene in the morning. The moment the Taoists had scattered, our three pilgrims dashed into the main hall, where Pigsy immediately stuffed one of the cakes into his mouth. "Where are your manners?" scolded Monkey, rapping Pigsy's trotter with his staff. "We should eat sitting down. How about over there?" Monkey pointed out a dais on which statues of the Taoist Trinity— the Three Pure Ones: the Jade Pure One, the Supreme Pure One, and Monkey's old friend Laozi—rested.

"Make way for Pigsy!" shouted Pigsy, shoving Laozi onto the floor with his snout. Monkey and Sandy barged the other statues off the platform, and the three of them each transformed into the effigy they had just displaced.

"But where to hide the evidence?" Monkey wondered. "Judging by the terrible smell, I suspect behind that door over there is a Bureau of Rice Reincarnation. Stash the real statues in there, would you?"

Pigsy swung the statues over his shoulder and kicked open the door specified by Monkey, where he found an enormous latrine. "That Monkey truly is a master of language," Pigsy noted with a chuckle. "Bureau of Rice Reincarnation indeed! At ease, gentlemen," he addressed the statues. "You've been sitting up there for so long, you probably need the toilet. Enjoy the sewage, Pure Ones!" He then hurled them into the latrine so hard that the splash back soaked his clothes.

"Success?" asked Monkey as Pigsy returned.

"Apart from my freshly fragranced robe."

"Pile in," said Monkey, giggling, "though it looks like we won't make a clean getaway now." Pigsy and Sandy sat down and filled their faces with enormous steamed buns, dumplings, cakes, fritters, and steamed pastries, while Monkey—who was not overly fond of cooked food—nibbled on a few pieces of fruit, just to be sociable. Soon enough, all the food was gone; the three disciples chatted and digested a while on top of the dais.

As bad luck would have it, though, a young Taoist in the temple's eastern dormitory chose that moment to remember that he had left his handbell in the hall and that he would get in trouble with the Taoist elders if he lost it. Dashing back, he managed to locate the bell and was about to leave when he heard the sound of someone breathing. Thoroughly rattled, he slipped on a lychee pit, went flying, and smashed the bell to pieces. Pigsy burst out laughing, at which point the terrified boy raised the alarm and all the temple's residents reconvened in the hall, with lamps and torches.

Chapter Twenty-Six

Monkey pinched Sandy and Pigsy to get them to pipe down and hold still. The Taoists carefully searched the hall but found nothing except the three gilded clay statues. "Strange," mused Tiger-Strength. "There's no sign of thieves, but all the offerings have gone."

"The peels and pits are still here; who could have eaten the fruit?" wondered Deer-Strength.

"The Three Pure Ones have visited us, to reward our piety," concluded Goat-Strength. "They must still be here. Let's ask them for some holy water and golden elixir to present to the king." The junior Taoists immediately formed two lines and set to reciting scripture, while Tiger-Strength put on his ceremonial robe, held aloft his jade tablet, and began an elaborate dancing prayer.

Listening to this performance, Pigsy grew highly uneasy. "We should have left as soon as we finished eating," he hissed at Monkey. "How are we going to get out of this mess?"

Monkey pinched him again to shut him up. "Lesser immortals!" he suddenly boomed out. "Cease your prayers. As we came directly from the Great Grand Festival of Immortal Peaches, we don't have any elixir or holy water on us. We'll bring you some next time."

"The Pure Ones have descended to earth!" the overexcited Taoists babbled. "Pray give us an immortal formula before you go!"

Now Deer-Strength embarked upon another painstaking supplication for holy water, while his underlings prayed, piped, and drummed.

"They're at it again," whispered Sandy. "Now what?"

"I'd still rather not leave you any holy water," Monkey intoned to his devoted audience. "The path to immortality should not be an easy one."

"Do, please do!" begged the Taoists, frantically kowtowing.

"Oh, all right then," Monkey capitulated. "Bring us some containers." The thirsty Tiger-Strength produced an enormous vat, Deer-Strength a basin, while Goat-Strength emptied some flowers from a pot and presented that. "So that Heaven's mysteries may be preserved, all of you leave and shutter the windows and doors while we make you some pious potion."

After the Taoists had exited, Monkey lifted his tiger-skin kilt and filled the flowerpot with atrocious-smelling urine. "This is easily the most fun I've ever had with you, Monkey," chortled Pigsy, who now let loose a torrential cascade, quickly filling the basin to the brim, while Sandy rather anticlimactically filled only half the vat. The "Three Pure Ones" then took their seats once more. "Your holy water is ready," they chorused.

Reentering, the Taoists first kowtowed effusively, then poured the contents of the basin and the flowerpot into the vat. "Bring me a goblet, disciples," ordered Tiger-Strength. He scooped out a cupful, took a large swig, then wiped his mouth and smacked his lips.

"Well?" quizzed Deer-Strength. "Is it delectable?"

"Not exactly," replied Tiger-Strength, puckering. "It's quite a particular taste."

"Let me try it," said Goat-Strength, taking a big gulp. "It tastes . . . a lot like pig urine."

Hearing this, Monkey realized the game was up and decided to go out with style. "Taoist dimwits! Know that we are Buddhist monks from the great Tang empire. Having enjoyed the food you so kindly left for us, we decided to leave you a token of our gratitude. In case you hadn't worked it out, that's piss in the vat, not holy water." The assembled Taoists immediately locked the door, gathered up pitchforks, rakes, brooms, tiles, rocks—anything they could lay their hands on—and hurled themselves at the impostors. Monkey grabbed Sandy with his left hand and Pigsy with his right, crashed through the door, and rode his cloud straight back to the Well of Wisdom. Anxious not to disturb Tripitaka, they repaired quietly to bed and slept soundly until dawn.

When day broke, Tripitaka dressed in his brocade robe and told his disciples that they needed to go to court to have their travel documents stamped. The three of them pulled on their clothes and braced themselves for trouble.

As anticipated, as soon as the four pilgrims were presented to the throne, the king's face darkened. "Why haven't these Buddhists been arrested?"

"They come from the Tang empire in China," a royal tutor intervened, "a great country some ten thousand miles from here. The road to China is infested with monsters and fiends. These monks must have extraordinary magical powers to have undertaken such a journey. I beg Your Majesty to allow them through."

Just as the king had agreed to look at their travel papers, however, the official keeper of the door announced the arrival of the three state preceptors. The flustered king immediately put the documents away, stood up, and ordered his attendants to set out stools with embroidered seats. The three chief Taoists—the pilgrims' nemeses from the night before—strutted up to the throne, while the king and his courtiers bowed deeply. "To what do we owe this unexpected honor?" asked the king.

The Taoists glared at Tripitaka and company without responding to the king. "Where did those four come from?"

"They're Buddhists from the Tang empire, headed for India.

They're here to have their travel documents approved," the king responded.

"Ha!" The Taoists clapped their hands with grim satisfaction.

"Have they offended you in some way?" asked the king in alarm.

Tiger-Strength now informed the king about how the disciples had so far spent their time in Cart-Slow. "Yesterday, they killed two of our disciples outside the city gate, released the monk-slaves, destroyed a cart, broke into our temple at night, smashed the statues of the Three Pure Ones, and ate all our offerings. After convincing us that *they* were the Three Pure Ones, they claimed that their urine was holy water, had us drink a mouthful, then escaped. And now we meet again."

The enraged king was all for executing them there and then, but Monkey played for time with a stream of judicial consciousness. "Where are the witnesses to our murdering those disciples, destroying the cart, or releasing the prisoners? Even if we did murder them—which we didn't—only two of us should pay with our lives. And as we're strangers in the city, how would we find their temple, at night, and with full bladders? How do they know it was us? How do we know it wasn't you? I call for a full public inquiry!" The king's limited intellect was thoroughly befuddled by Monkey's quick-fire defense.

At this moment of maximum confusion, the keeper of the door reappeared. "A party of petitioners from the countryside are outside the gate, Your Majesty."

"Let them in," said the king.

Thirty or forty village elders now entered and began kowtowing. "There's been no rain all spring, and we fear that there will be famine by summer. We beg the state preceptors to pray for rain."

The king now turned back to Tripitaka and his disciples. "When we last held a rain-making contest, the city's Buddhists failed to produce a single drop, while these Taoists saved us from our

misery. You've so far dedicated yourselves to outraging our esteemed advisers. We will grant you a temporary amnesty if you
agree to a rain-making contest with our Taoist masters. If you
succeed in bringing rain, I will pardon you and let you continue on
your journey to the west. Fail and you will be publicly executed."

"You're on!" whooped Monkey.

As soon as the rain-making altar had been built, Tiger-Strength
swaggered up to it. "How rude!" teased Monkey. "Guests first,
surely? But if you insist on elbowing your way to the front, talk
me through what you're going to do and when we should expect
rain from you. I don't want you claiming credit for *my* rain."
(Here, the king started to feel a grudging admiration for Monkey's spirit.)

"See this ritual tablet?" said Tiger-Strength. "One tap will bring
wind; two, clouds; three, thunder and lightning; four, rain; five,
clear skies again."

"Looking forward to it," said Monkey, smiling.

Tiger-Strength now climbed to the top of the altar—some thirty
feet high—followed by Tripitaka and his disciples. The altar fluttered with banners bearing the names of constellations. A gold
tablet engraved with the names of the thunder gods was propped
up against a brazier filled with billowing incense and flanked by
candles. A large supporting staff of Taoist priests struck pillars and
wrote screeds. Holding a sword, Tiger-Strength chanted a spell,
burned a charm, and banged his ritual tablet. A breeze instantly
started up. "Not good!" worried Pigsy.

Monkey shushed him. "You two, look after Tripitaka. I'll take
care of this." He plucked out a hair, blew magic breath onto it,
and turned it into a phony Monkey standing next to Tripitaka.
The real Monkey soared into the air. "Who's in charge of the
wind up here?" he yelled. A panicked Old Woman of the Wind
and her sidekick twisted their wind bag shut and bowed before
Monkey. "Here I am," snapped Monkey, "doing my best to pro-

tect this Tang monk on his way to fetch scriptures, stuck in a rain-making contest with deviant Taoists, and I find you helping them, not me. I'll let you off this time if you stop the wind immediately. But if I see the merest flutter of that Tiger-Strength's whiskers, you'll each get twenty of the best from my iron staff."

"Understood!" replied the old woman, and the wind instantly subsided.

"You blew it!" Pigsy jeered at Tiger-Strength. "Our turn."

The Taoist now burned another charm, and banged his tablet a second time. This time, the sky clouded over. "Who's in charge of the clouds?" Monkey yelled again. A panicked Cloud-Pusher and Fog-Spreader bowed before him. Once Monkey had issued the same threat as before, the two cloud controllers gathered up their weather effects and the sun blazed in a cloudless sky.

"Loser!" Pigsy taunted Tiger-Strength some more.

By this point the Taoist was starting to get anxious. He let down his hair, recited another spell, burned yet another charm, and banged his tablet again. This performance immediately drew the Thunder Duke and the Dame of Lightning out of the South Gate of Heaven. Both bowed before Monkey, who once more explained the situation and demanded to know why the deities were helping his rival. "That Taoist knows what he's doing," said the Thunder Duke. "As soon as he heard the rain summons, the Jade Emperor dispatched a rain-making decree to the office of the Primordial Heavenly Lord of the All-Pervasive Thunderclap in the Nine Heavens, who then delegated us to provide some thunder and lightning."

"Well, as you're here, just hold fire a bit and you can help me instead," Monkey told him.

The Taoist went into a frenzy of incense-throwing, charm-burning, spell-reciting, and tablet-banging. Next to be intercepted by Monkey in the skies overhead were the Dragon Kings of the Four Oceans. "Where d'you think you're going?" he roared. The four kings—Aoguang, Aoshun, Aoqin, and Aorun—bowed and listened to Monkey's summary of events. "I trust I can count on your support?" Monkey concluded.

"Unconditionally!" said the dragon kings.

Monkey then addressed the crowd of immortals he had apprehended: "The Taoist has struck his tablet four times, and now it's my turn. As I don't have any of his tricks up my sleeve, I'm going to need your help to win the contest."

"Your wish is our command," pledged the Thunder Duke. "But we'll need a sign from you, otherwise the thunder and rain will be all mixed up, and you'll lose marks on presentation."

"I'll use my staff," said Monkey.

"Not the staff!" cried the terrified immortals.

"Not to hit you with," explained Monkey. "Look: the first time I point it up to the sky, make some wind. Second time, bring out the clouds. Third time, I want thunder and lightning. Fourth time, rain. Fifth, sunshine. Got that?"

"Consider it done!" the deities assured him.

Staff training delivered, Monkey returned to the altar and retrieved his specious self. (The magic was beyond the vision of the mortals on the scene.) "Time's up!" he told Tiger-Strength. "You've had your chance; now it's mine."

The Taoist sulkily retreated back to the king, who wanted to know why there had been no rain: "The dragon kings weren't at home," Tiger-Strength self-justified.

"Ha!" snorted Monkey, loud enough for the king to hear. "I bet they'll be at home for us Buddhists." Monkey now addressed Tripitaka. "Time to play."

"But I haven't the first idea how to pray for rain," the monk worried.

"He's setting you up!" Pigsy giggled. "When you don't bring rain, they'll pop you on a pyre and burn you to a crisp."

"Just recite sutras," Monkey told Tripitaka, ignoring Pigsy. "I'll manage the rest."

Tripitaka sat down in the middle of the altar and silently recited. When he judged that Tripitaka had finished, Monkey pulled out his staff, grew it to six feet long, and pointed it at the sky. The Old Woman of the Wind and her assistant immediately opened their bag and a gale gusted through the city: trees snapped, tiles and bricks fell off buildings, doors were ripped off their hinges, courtiers lost the embroidered tassels from their gold caps, and the palace ladies' hairdos collapsed.

Monkey pointed his staff again, and Cloud-Pusher and Fog-Spreader enveloped Cart-Slow in mist. He twirled his staff a third time: crazy gold snakes of lightning threaded the sky; the thunder seemed loud enough to shatter the city. He conducted with his staff a fourth time. At this, the dragon kings let loose a torrent of rain—it was as if the Yangtze River had been rolled out and up, then hurled back down at the ground. The precipitation was so heavy that by noon the king begged for a respite. Monkey pointed his staff one more time, and out came the sun. "Wonderful!" the king and officials gasped. "Even at the height of their powers, our Taoist ministers could not persuade the weather to change from rain to shine just like that." And the king prepared to stamp the pilgrims' papers.

"Not so fast!" Tiger-Strength objected. "This downpour was my doing. When I burned my charms and banged my tablet, the gods must have been out and about somewhere. They rushed back as soon as they could but not until the Buddhist had pushed me out of the way and taken credit for all my hard work." The witless king wavered once more.

"Forget this trivial magic show," interrupted Monkey. "The four dragon kings are hovering above us right now, waiting for my order to withdraw. If our Taoist here can order them to appear, he can take credit for the rain."

"Ooh, I'd love to see a dragon!" exclaimed the susceptible king.

The Taoists knew they had no such authority over the dragons and declined the contest. "But we'd like to see you try," they challenged Monkey sullenly.

"Show yourselves, dragons!" Monkey called up to the sky. The dragon kings immediately soared and circled around the city, their silver scales shining like mirrors, their whiskers fluttering like fine white silk threads.

"Thank you for your visit," the king called up to the sky, after burning incense to the fantastical creatures. "You may retire now."

"You heard him," said Monkey. "Off you go." And the immortals obediently returned home.

Chapter Twenty-Seven

Awestruck by Monkey's command of the dragons, the king immediately stamped the travelers' travel papers with the royal seal. But the three Taoists intervened before he could hand them back. "We have protected you and your kingdom for twenty long years. And now these murderous monks have destroyed our reputation with a few cheap conjuring tricks and a rain shower. We wish to challenge them to another competition—meditation, this time. We will build two pedestals, each fifty tables high; the contestants must float up on a cloud and sit immobile for an agreed-on number of hours."

The king now put the proposition to the travelers. Monkey, for once, had nothing to say for himself. "What's wrong?" asked Pigsy.

"It's like this," explained Monkey. "Kicking Heaven to pieces, churning oceans, carrying mountains, chasing the moon, changing the course of stars and planets—these are all child's play to me. You can cut off my head and chop it into pieces, split my stomach, and gouge out my heart—none of those unusual manipulations hold any dread for me. But please don't ask me to sit still. Padlock me to an iron pillar and I'll find a way to wriggle. I just can't do it."

"But I can," piped up Tripitaka.

"Wonderful news!" rejoiced Monkey. "For how long at a time?"

"Not very long, I'm afraid. No more than two or three years."

"We'll never get to India if you sit there for that long. A few hours will do nicely."

"But how am I to get up there?" Tripitaka asked.

"I'll take care of that," Monkey reassured him.

Within an hour, one tower of tables tottered to the left and another to the right of the palace. While Tiger-Strength floated up to the top of one, Monkey turned one of his hairs into a specious version of himself back on the ground, changed into a rainbow-colored cloud, and delivered Tripitaka onto the other meditation platform. Back on the ground, Monkey then transformed into a cricket and perched next to Pigsy's oversize ear. "Keep an eye on Tripitaka," he whispered, "and don't try talking to the fake Monkey—he's terribly dull." Pigsy giggled his assent.

Meanwhile, Deer-Strength was evaluating the two competitive meditators. Finding them evenly matched, he decided to give his brother a helping hand. He plucked a hair from his head, rolled it into a ball, and flicked it onto Tripitaka's scalp, where it turned into a large bedbug that promptly sank its fangs into that delicious expanse of bare skin. Tripitaka's head began to itch and then throb with pain. The rules of the meditation contest did not permit Tripitaka to move his hands, but the itch was so maddening that he began to rub his head against his shoulder.

"What's wrong with him?" wondered Sandy at the base of the pedestal.

Chirping away, Monkey flew onto Tripitaka's head, where he discovered a bean-sized bedbug making a meal of Tripitaka's scalp. Monkey butted it away and gave Tripitaka's scalp a few soothing scratches. Tripitaka sat straight-backed again. "I'll bet that bug was a gift from the Taoists," mused Monkey. "Well, two can play at that game." Turning into a seven-inch caterpillar, he launched an attack on Tiger-Strength's upper lip. The Taoist promptly rolled off the altar and tumbled to the ground, where he was saved from certain death by landing on a group of courtiers. While the king ordered Tiger-Strength to be taken off for a restorative wash and comb, Monkey became an auspicious cloud once more and bore Tripitaka back down before the throne, where he was declared the victor.

But just as the king was finally about to let them go, Deer-Strength made another petition. "My brother must have caught a cold and sneezed up there—the Buddhist didn't win fair and square. I now challenge them to a contest of Guess What's Inside the Box. If the Buddhists can outguess me, then let them go. If not, then let them suffer the consequences of their actions." Yet again, the weak-willed king allowed himself to be persuaded and asked the queen to place a treasure inside a red lacquer chest. The box was then set before the throne.

"Who wants to go first?" demanded the king.

"Monkey," Tripitaka whispered, "what should I say?"

Monkey changed back into a cricket and perched on Tripitaka's head. "Don't worry," he chirped. "I'll pop in to take a look." Squeezing through a crack in the bottom of the box, he found a ceremonial jacket and skirt on a red lacquered tray. Biting his tongue, he sprayed a mouthful of blood over them, and they immediately changed into a cracked old cup. As a final coup de grâce, Monkey gifted the cup with a bladderful of urine, then squeezed back out of the box and returned to Tripitaka's earside. "Say it's an old chipped cup," he buzzed.

"Really?" said Tripitaka doubtfully. "Didn't he ask the queen to choose a treasure?"

"I swear," Monkey assured him.

Just as Tripitaka stepped forward to guess, Deer-Strength interrupted: "I'll go first. I see inside the box . . . a ceremonial jacket and skirt."

"I see an old chipped cup," countered Tripitaka.

Just as the king was about to arrest Tripitaka for impertinence, an attendant opened the box and brought out the cup. "Who put this here?" barked the furious king.

"I put a jacket and skirt inside," said the queen. "How could they have been replaced by this cup?"

Deciding to hide something in the box himself, the king disappeared into his garden, chose an enormous peach, and returned for another round of guessing. "Now what?" whispered Tripitaka to Monkey.

"I'll take another look," chirped the cricket and squeezed through the crack a second time. Now, our monkey had long had a weakness for peaches, and as soon as he saw this succulent specimen he switched back to his true self and devoured the peach so thoroughly that not a scrap of fruit remained. Leaving the stone inside the box, he became the cricket again and returned to Tripitaka's ear. "Guess a peach stone," he buzzed.

"Are you sure?"

"Word of honor," Monkey replied.

This time, Goat-Strength got in first. "The box contains a peach."

"Not quite," countered Tripitaka. "A peach stone."

"Victory to the Taoists!" roared the king.

"Please, Your Majesty," Tripitaka begged, "first look inside the box." The attendant lifted out of the box a perfectly clean peach pit.

"Let them go," the frightened king told the Taoists. "This can only be the work of ghosts."

("He has no idea how many peaches that monkey has eaten in his time," Pigsy sniggered at Sandy.)

Tiger-Strength now returned to the throne room, freshly washed and combed after his tumble. "This Buddhist can move objects by magic," he whispered to the king, "but not people. Let me expose the limits of his power by locking one of our young disciples in the box." After the boy had climbed in, Tripitaka was asked to guess its contents. In the time-honored fashion, Monkey squeezed inside the box once more and turned into a Taoist elder.

"Where did you come from?" asked the startled boy.

"Never mind that. I have an important message. The Chinese monk saw you get into the box, so I'm here to shave your head to make you look like a Buddhist. When he says there's a Taoist in the box, we'll be able to prove him wrong."

"Whatever it takes to win," said the boy.

Monkey turned his staff into a razor and shaved the boy bald, then turned the boy's pale green silk robe into a brown Buddhist one. "Listen carefully to what's going on outside," he told the boy. "As soon as you hear someone say 'It's a Buddhist monk,' jump out of the box, chanting the Buddha's name." Monkey became a cricket once more, buzzed back to Tripitaka, and told him what to say.

Tiger-Strength went first, guessing that the box contained a Taoist. "It's a Buddhist monk," second-guessed Tripitaka, and the boy immediately sprang out of the box, reciting the Buddha's name over and over. The spellbound courtiers broke into cheers; the three Taoists were struck dumb with amazement.

"Ghosts!" the king rasped. "How can that boy have gone in a Taoist and come out a Buddhist? We must let these Buddhists go."

"We challenge them one more time," announced Tiger-Strength, "to a tripartite contest of head cutting, heart gouging, and bathing in boiling oil."

"What luck!" Monkey laughed. "Three of my favorite things. Cut my head off and I'll still talk the hind legs off a donkey. Rip up my stomach and it'll heal smooth as a dumpling. And as for bathing in hot oil: what could be better for the skin?" He now stepped forward to address the king. "A few years back, I learned a little trick for having my head cut off from a wandering Zen master. I've been dying ever since to find out whether it works."

"Are you sure about this?" asked the king. "Beheading's not usually a two-way street."

"Let him try!" urged Tiger-Strength. Once more, the idiotic king caved in to the Taoists and ordered his guards to prepare the execution ground.

"Me first!" chirruped Monkey, as soon as it was ready.

"I hope you know what you're doing," Tripitaka said to him.

"Fuss, fuss!" Monkey beamed, skipping off to the block where the executioner bound him. Down came the sword and off went Monkey's head, rolling some forty paces away, with the help of a hefty kick from the executioner. But here events took a turn for the strange, for the severed stump of Monkey's neck refused to bleed. "Come back, head!" shouted a voice from deep inside Monkey's stomach.

The flustered Deer-Strength began chanting bribe spells at the local spirits: "If you keep hold of that head, I'll get the king to turn your threadbare shrines into magnificent temples and your clay idols into gold statues." The spirits quietly accepted the deal.

"Head, you get back here now!" ordered Monkey. The head stayed put, as if it had grown roots. An exasperated Monkey now broke free of the ropes binding him, roared "Grow!" and sprouted another head.

This extraordinary news had barely been reported back to the court when in sashayed Monkey. "Greetings and salutations," he coolly greeted Tripitaka.

"Did it hurt?" the monk asked.

"No more than a tickle," answered Monkey.

"Did it leave a scar?" Pigsy wanted to know.

"Feel for yourself," Monkey invited him.

"Amazing!" Pigsy giggled. "Perfectly healed!"

The king was now desperate to get rid of the pilgrims. "Consider yourselves pardoned. Take your papers and leave."

"We're not in a tearing hurry," replied Monkey. "We'll stay

long enough to see your Taoist here have his head cut off, too. It's good to be open to new experiences."

And like Monkey a few moments earlier, Tiger-Strength was bound and beheaded. Once again, the executioner kicked the head some forty paces away; once again, the severed neck did not bleed and the beheadee cried: "Come back, head!" But then Monkey turned one of his hairs into a yellow dog that dashed up, seized the head in its mouth, galloped to the royal moat, and hurled it in, where it sank without a trace. When the head refused to return after three calls, Tiger-Strength's neck began to bleed, for unlike Monkey he was unable to generate a whole new head. An instant later, he toppled lifelessly into the dust and transformed into a headless tiger.

The king turned ashen on learning of Tiger-Strength's death. "I now challenge this Buddhist sorcerer to a heart-gouging contest!" raged Deer-Strength.

"I've been having some terrible stomachaches recently," reflected Monkey. "Too many steamed rolls, probably. Or it might be worms. I'd be much obliged if you could rip open my stomach so I can give my heart, liver, spleen, lungs, kidneys, stomach, gallbladder, intestines, and bladder a good spring cleaning before I go to see the Buddha. Just don't tie my hands—I'll need them free to sluice my vital organs."

He swaggered back to the execution ground and leaned nonchalantly against a stake. Loosening his shirt, he exposed his stomach, and with one drag of his dagger, the executioner sliced open Monkey's abdomen. After a little rummaging, Monkey pulled out his intestines, carefully examined them, then coiled them back inside, pulled the edges of his skin together, and blew magic breath over the seam, and his stomach was perfectly grafted together once more. The shocked king once more pressed the pilgrims to leave: "Here are your papers. We won't detain you any further."

"Not so fast," said Monkey. "Your Deer-Strength owes us a touch of heart gouging, no?"

Now it was Deer-Strength's turn to swagger to the execution ground, where he, too, was tied to the post. The dagger again sliced open his stomach and, like Monkey, he played with his intestines for a while. At this moment, however, Monkey turned one of his hairs into a hungry eagle, which swooped down, snatched the exposed intestines, and flew off toward the horizon. Deer-Strength's life quickly dripped out of his empty, ripped stomach. When the executioner approached to check on the corpse, he discovered that it had become that of a white-haired deer.

"More Buddhist sorcery," said Goat-Strength, when he and the king learned what had happened. "I will now avenge my brothers by challenging this diabolical monkey to a bath in boiling oil." So the king ordered a cauldron full of fragrant oil to be set over a fire.

"Such hospitality!" rejoiced Monkey. "I haven't washed for days and I'm itching all over. A bath in boiling oil will be just the thing for scalding the problem away."

When the oil began to bubble, an attendant invited Monkey to take a dip. Pausing only to remove his shirt and kilt—"so that I can really enjoy myself in there"—he dived into the cauldron and splashed happily about.

"This Monkey is really something," Pigsy said admiringly to Sandy.

But when Monkey saw them whispering together, he thought they were mocking him while he was taking a bath in boiling oil for the good of the pilgrimage. "Let's see how Pigsy enjoys a bit of heat himself," he muttered vengefully and suddenly executed a dive to the bottom of the cauldron, where he disappeared from view by turning into a nail the size of a date stone.

"Sire," the presiding officer reported, "the monk has been fried to death." The delighted king ordered Monkey's bones to be fished

out for an examination. The officer dredged about in the oil with
an iron sieve, but the tiny nail kept on slipping through the holes.
"He must have completely melted."

"Seize those monks!" commanded the king, and guards immediately tackled Pigsy to the ground and bound his hands.

"If Your Majesty wishes me to die, so be it," quavered Tripitaka. "But allow me first to present some porridge and paper
horses to the cauldron, to sustain my disciple in the afterlife."

"You Chinese certainly look out for each other," observed the
king. "All right."

The offerings obtained, Tripitaka spoke his eulogy into the
cauldron: "Monkey, you always gave me love and protection. We
hoped to find enlightenment together and yet today you have per-
ished. I know your spirit is on Soul Mountain with the Buddha."

"That was rubbish," panted Pigsy, still pinioned to the ground.
"My turn now. You waste of space! You're dead and as deep-fried
as a doughnut!"

Furious at this tirade of abuse, Monkey regained his true form
and stood up in the cauldron, dripping with oil. "You're the waste
of space! How dare you bad-mouth me!"

"You almost frightened me to death," Tripitaka exclaimed.

Afraid that he might be accused of lying to the throne, the responsible official tried to cover himself. "He's still dead. This is
just his disembodied soul."

An outraged Monkey jumped out of the cauldron, shook the
oil off his body, pulled on his clothes, and with one blow of his
staff turned the offending official into a meatball. "Ha! Could a
disembodied soul do that?"

Just as the king was trying to exit the throne room amid the
prevailing pandemonium, Monkey grabbed him back. "Don't forget, it's bathtime for Goat-Strength here."

Goat-Strength undressed, jumped into the cauldron, and began
splashing about. Testing the temperature of the oil, Monkey

discovered that it felt icy cold. "It was boiling hot when I was in there. Could one of those slippery dragon kings be at work?" Monkey leaped into the air and summoned the dragon king of the Northern Ocean. "How dare you lend this Taoist a freezing dragon, you horned earthworm!"

"I wouldn't dare," stammered the unfortunate Aoshun. "Here's how it is. The antelope spirit—part of the goat family, you know—that is masquerading as this Taoist has learned, among other things, how to conjure a cold dragon, which is currently coiled around the base of this cauldron and keeping the oil cool. I'll arrest that chilly lizard now, and Goat-Strength will be fried to a crisp. But please don't hit me!"

"Go!" Monkey snapped. "Before I change my mind." The dragon king swept the cold dragon off the base of the cauldron and back to the sea. Returning to the palace, Monkey—along with Tripitaka, Pigsy, and Sandy—watched as Goat-Strength slipped and struggled in the rapidly heating oil. Soon enough, his flesh, skin, and bones were fried into oblivion.

The king took the death of his third Taoist adviser badly, curling up on a table and fountaining tears until nightfall. "Gone!" he wailed. "Gone! My hopes of immortality!"

"How stupid can a king be?" an irritated Monkey eventually scolded him. "Those Taoists were animal spirits: a tiger, a deer, and an antelope. Fish the bones of the last one out of the cauldron if you don't believe me. In another year or two, they would have done away with you and taken your kingdom for themselves. We did you a favor getting rid of them. What are you crying for? Give us back our travel documents and send us on our way." The king finally collected himself, especially when his officials confirmed Monkey's identification of Goat-Strength as an antelope, and summoned the Buddhist monks back into the city. After a huge feast the next day, the returned monks kneeled along both sides of the road as the king and his courtiers escorted the pilgrims out of the city gate. Monkey addressed some parting words to the people of Cart-Slow: "I admit it now: I freed these monks, smashed the cart they were pulling, and pulverized their perverse Taoist masters. The lesson for you all? Don't worship false religions and respect the unity of the three faiths. Only this will guarantee the peace and prosperity of your kingdom." The king thanked the pilgrims once more and saw them off on the road to the west.

Chapter Twenty-Eight

As summer turned to autumn, the pilgrims approached the River to Heaven. After a quick aerial reconnaissance, Monkey estimated that it was at least four hundred miles wide. Just as Tripitaka was settling into a crying fit, a voice rose up from the water: "I'll take the four of you across." A moment later, an elderly, scabby-headed turtle emerged out of the depths and clambered onto the riverbank, revealing a huge, round white shell about forty feet in circumference.

"On we get," said Monkey.

"Is it safe?' Tripitaka worried.

"Think about it," Monkey reasoned with him, "a creature who's gone to the trouble of learning human speech wouldn't lie. Don't forget the horse." Following Monkey's direction, the band of travelers climbed onto the turtle's shell. Just in case the turtle did have any mischief in mind, Monkey untied his belt and threaded it through the turtle's nose to serve as a rein. He stood with one foot on the turtle's back, the other on its head, one hand grasping his staff, the other the makeshift rein. "Watch yourself, turtle," he muttered. "One false move and you'll taste my staff." The turtle glided out onto the water's surface as if it were solid, level ground. In less than a day, the disciples reached the other side of the river, perfectly safe and dry.

After disembarking, Tripitaka placed his palms together in

thanks. "You must be exhausted, venerable turtle, and we have nothing to reward you with. I'll be sure to bring you something back from India."

"No need," the turtle responded, "but perhaps in India you could help answer a question I have, for I understand that the Buddha is birthless and deathless, and knows past and future. I have cultivated myself for thirteen hundred years, thereby lengthening my life, lightening my body and learning human speech. But I still cannot escape my turtle shell. When you see the Buddha, could you ask him how I could acquire a human body?"

"I absolutely will," Tripitaka promised. The turtle then slid back into the water and the pilgrims carried on their way.

Chapter Twenty-Nine

As bad luck would have it, the travelers presently came to another river, though fortunately this one was a good deal narrower than the previous one. Tripitaka spotted some distance away a few thatched huts beneath the shade of some jade-green weeping willows. "Surely there'll be a boat over there," speculated Monkey.

Pigsy decided to take the initiative. "Hey!" he hollered. "Boat needed! Over here!"

Out from beneath one of the willows creaked a brightly painted paddleboat. As it approached the stretch of bank where the pilgrims were standing, Tripitaka realized it was being rowed by an old woman dressed in black silk shoes, a patched coat, and a grubby skirt. "Hop on," she told the pilgrims.

"Are you in charge of this boat?" Monkey asked. "Where's the ferryman?"

The woman merely smiled and pulled out the gangplank. Sandy carried the luggage on, Monkey helped Tripitaka embark, and Pigsy led the horse into the boat, taking up the plank after everyone was in. The woman then rowed the boat quickly across the river.

On the other side, Tripitaka asked Sandy to open one of the bundles and take out a few coppers to pay the woman for her trouble. She accepted the offering without haggling, tied the boat to a post on the bank, and disappeared into a nearby house, chortling away to herself. Gazing at the clear water, Tripitaka suddenly felt thirsty. "Get the bowl and scoop me some water, would you?" he asked Pigsy.

"I could use a drink myself," Pigsy replied. Tripitaka drank less than half the water that Pigsy bailed; Pigsy then finished the rest and helped Tripitaka back onto the horse.

The pilgrims had barely traveled for an hour when Tripitaka started to whimper. "My stomach aches!"

"Mine, too!" complained Pigsy.

"Could it be the cold water you just drank?" wondered Sandy.

"I feel terrible!" cried Tripitaka.

"Owwww!" echoed Pigsy.

As the pain grew steadily more unbearable, their stomachs began to swell. When they rubbed their abdomens, there seemed to be a blood clot or a mysterious lump ricocheting madly about inside them. Before long, Tripitaka was in agony. As soon as Monkey spotted a cottage at the roadside up ahead, he advised stopping there. "We'll ask for some hot water and whether there's an apothecary nearby where I could get you both some stomach medicine."

Tripitaka spurred the horse on and they arrived there shortly. An old woman was sitting outside on the grass, weaving hemp. "We're pilgrims from the Tang empire," Monkey told her. "My teacher here is the emperor's brother. Since drinking water from the river we just crossed, he's had a horrible stomachache."

The old woman hiccupped with laughter. "Hilarious. That's the best thing I've heard all day. Come inside and I'll explain."

By now, Tripitaka and Pigsy needed to lean heavily on the other two to stagger into the cottage, where they sat down, groaning with pain, their stomachs protruding, their faces waxen and contorted. "We'd be most grateful," Monkey asked the old woman, "if you could get us some hot water."

Ignoring the request, the giggling old woman rushed into the next room. "Here's some fun!" she could be heard saying. "Come and see what I just brought in." A handful of middle-aged women, gurgling with laughter, now clattered into the pilgrims' room.

Monkey bared his teeth, terrifying them into retreat, then grabbed hold of their hostess. "Get me some hot water now, if you want to live!"

"Hot water won't help your friends, Mr. Monkey," the old woman said, trembling. "Let go of me and I'll explain." Monkey relented and she began. "You're in Western Liang, also known as the Land of Women. There are no men here, and that's why we were so tickled when you turned up. I'm afraid it's very bad news that your friends drank from that river. It's called the Mother-and-Child River. Women around here don't touch its water until they're past their twentieth birthday because it brings on labor. Just outside our capital, there's a Receiving-Maleness Posthouse, to the side of which runs the Embryo-Reflecting Spring. Three days after a woman has drunk from the river, she goes and looks at her reflection in the spring. If she sees a double reflection, it means birth is imminent. Your friends have clearly fallen pregnant after drinking from Mother-and-Child and are due to give birth any moment now. What good will hot water do?"

"Calamity!" yelped Tripitaka, turning white, while Pigsy— sitting on the ground—bent over, trying to spread his legs. "But we're men! How can we have children? We don't have birth canals. Where's the baby going to come out?"

"A ripe melon will find a way to drop," said Monkey, grinning, "as the proverb goes. Maybe it'll burst out of your armpit."

Pigsy now doubled over with pain and fear. "Doom! I'm doomed!"

"Don't roll about so!" Sandy laughed, also enjoying himself tremendously. "You'll damage the umbilical cord. Or your water might break."

Pigsy's eyes welled with tears. "Ask if there are any decent midwives around here. The contractions are coming faster. The baby could come any minute. Hurry up!"

"Is there a doctor around here that could sell us some abortion medicine?" the unhappy Tripitaka asked.

"The only thing that will end the pregnancy is water from Abortion Spring, inside Child-Destroying Cave on Dissolving-Maleness Mountain," the old woman went on. "But it's not easy to get. A few years ago, a Taoist calling himself the True Immortal of Wish Fulfillment occupied the cave and now controls access to Abortion Spring. Anyone who wants a cup of water has to grovel and gift him with money, food, and wine. You beggar-monks don't have a hope. I suggest you prepare yourselves for parenthood."

But Monkey was very interested in Abortion Spring. "How far is it from here to Dissolving-Maleness?"

"About three thousand miles," replied the old woman.

"Marvelous," said Monkey. "Don't worry, Tripitaka. I'll be back with some of that water before you can say 'It's a beautiful baby girl.' Sandy, you're in charge while I'm away. If these people mistreat our teacher, feel free to terrorize them in any way you like."

"Try to get as much water as you can," the woman requested, presenting Monkey with a porcelain bowl, "so that we can keep some for emergencies."

Monkey cloud-somersaulted off into the horizon, while the old woman called the household together to heat some rice and hot water for their guests.

Not long into his cloud-somersault, Monkey encountered an exceptionally lovely mountain, dappled with brooks and canyons, carpeted in emerald-green forest and inhabited by wild geese, deer, and monkeys. As he took in the scene, he spotted a rather handsome building on the shaded side of the mountain. It looked like a perfect retreat for a recluse: a thatched house approached by a bridge over a stream. In a moment, Monkey was at the gate; just inside, an elderly Taoist sat cross-legged on an expanse of green grass. Monkey set his porcelain bowl down and approached to make inquiries. "What brings you to our humble temple?" the Taoist asked.

"I am a poor monk sent by the Tang empire to fetch scriptures from the west. Because my master mistakenly drank from the Mother-and-Child River, he is in terrible labor pain and due to give birth at any moment. I understand that his only hope is to drink water from Abortion Spring, which is located within your temple. I've therefore come to pay my respects to the True Immortal of Wish Fulfillment and beg a little water. Would you mind taking me in to see him?"

"You've come to the right place," said the Taoist, smiling, "and I'm Wish Fulfillment's senior disciple. What's your name, so I can announce you?"

"I am Monkey, disciple of Tripitaka."

"And your gifts are . . . where?"

"I am a mendicant monk. I have no gifts."

The Taoist laughed. "Are you mad? My master's never given water to anyone for free. When you've drummed up some donations, I'll show you in. Till then, hop off."

"When he learns it's Monkey asking, he'll be so thrilled he'll probably turn the whole spring over to me."

The Taoist disciple reluctantly went inside to announce Monkey's arrival to Wish Fulfillment, who was doing his zither practice. The instant the immortal—a formidable sight, with flame-red hair, beard, eyes, and lips—heard the name Monkey, he went puce with rage. Jumping off his zither couch, he changed into full Taoist regalia—red and gold robe, brocade-trimmed shoes, embroidered stockings—and marched out of the temple door, twirling a long-handled golden hook. "WHERE IS THAT MONKEY?"

"Your humble servant," Monkey greeted him, putting his palms together and bowing.

"Monkey—we meet at last," the immortal responded, laughing mirthlessly.

Monkey looked nonplussed.

"Don't you recognize me?" Wish Fulfillment segued.

"Should I?"

"Is your teacher Tripitaka of the Tang?" thundered the glowering immortal.

"The very same."

"Does the name Red Boy ring any bells for you?"

"Red Boy of Fire-Cloud Cave by Desiccated Pine Stream on Roaring Mountain? Why do you ask?"

"He is my nephew, son of my brother, King Bull Demon, who sometime ago sent me a letter explaining that you, Monkey, had brought misery and doom on Red Boy. And here you are, knocking at my door. Vengeance will be mine!"

"You are mistaken, sir," soothed Monkey with a smile. "Your elder brother is my very good friend. Indeed, a mere five hundred years ago we were in a band of seven sworn brothers. Excuse my not knowing the family connection. Let me reassure you, your nephew is in an excellent place right now. Guanyin has made him her senior attendant-administrator-thingummy. Definitely a step up in the world."

"Wretched monkey!" screamed the immortal. "My nephew was a king and now he's a slave! Eat my hook!"

"Are you sure you don't want to just give me some of that water?" asked Monkey, blocking the blow.

"The nerve! If you can defeat me, you can have the water. If not, I'll make revenge sauce of you."

"All right, you bastard," Monkey snapped back. "If you want a fight, you've got it."

The immortal made a good showing at the start, swiping his hook at Monkey like a mantis. Eventually, though, Wish Fulfillment grew tired and fled the scene, trailing his hook behind him. Abandoning the chase, Monkey went straight into the temple, kicking down the door in search of the spring, accessible through a well in the courtyard. Just as he was about to bail some water, however, the immortal suddenly reappeared and fastened his hook around one of Monkey's legs; Monkey fell flat on his muzzle. Scrambling to his feet, he made a second attempt to lower the bucket with his right hand, while fending off the hook with his left, but Wish Fulfillment struck again. This time, the bucket tumbled into the well as Monkey lost his balance. "This fellow needs to learn some manners," Monkey muttered, clambering back up and wildly hammering his opponent with blows of his staff. Although the immortal fled again, Monkey was stuck: rope and bucket were lost, and the hook could return at any moment. *I need an assistant,* he thought, reversing his cloud to the village.

Back at the cottage, it was business as usual: Tripitaka moaning and Pigsy babbling about their contractions. "Have you got the water?" asked Sandy eagerly when Monkey reappeared.

"Oh, woe," wailed Tripitaka on learning of Wish Fulfillment's frosty reception of Monkey.

Monkey shrugged. "It's all fine. I just need some backup from Sandy. I'll fight the immortal while Sandy gets the water."

"But the two of us are ill," worried Tripitaka. "Who will look after us?"

"Don't worry," reassured the old woman. "We'll take care of you. We wouldn't dream of harming such illustrious visitors."

"What harm could you women do to us?" Monkey snorted scornfully.

"You were lucky to have come straight to my door," said their hostess, smiling. "If you'd wandered into another house, they'd have torn you to pieces."

"W-what do you mean?" whimpered Pigsy.

"The five of us here are all too old to have thoughts of romance, so we wouldn't lay a finger on you. But if you'd stumbled into a house of young women, they'd have forced you to have sex and killed you if you put up any resistance. Then they'd have skinned you and turned you into perfume bags."

"I'd be safe at least." Pigsy sighed in relief. "I'm far too smelly to make perfume out of. The other three are deliciously fragrant though; can't recommend them highly enough."

"Save your breath," Monkey told him, laughing, "for giving birth."

"There's no time to waste," urged the woman. "Go get that water."

Pausing only to borrow a bucket and two ropes, Sandy and Monkey got on their clouds and were soon back at Dissolving-Maleness Mountain. At the entrance to the temple, Monkey told Sandy to go and hide with the bucket and ropes. "I'll provoke a battle, and once we're in the thick of it, sneak in and get the water."

"Understood," said Sandy.

Staff in hand, Monkey went up to the front door. "Open up!"

"It's that rude Monkey again," Wish Fulfillment's assistant told him.

The immortal emerged with a wide, confident smile and his hook at the ready. "Outrageous ape! What are you doing back here?"

"I already told you—I need some of that water," replied Monkey.

"No presents, no water," Wish Fulfillment countered. Monkey now drew his antagonist into battle farther down the mountain, while Sandy dashed inside with the bucket and filled it to the brim, breaking the arm of the assistant in the process, then ran back out and onto his cloud. "Leave him!" he shouted to Monkey, who was still in the thick of battle. "I've got the water."

Monkey blocked the hook with his staff. "No hard feelings, now that I've got what I came for. But no more fleecing innocent passersby." Though Wish Fulfillment tried another couple of hook swipes at Monkey's legs, Monkey danced out of reach, then grabbed the hook and smashed it to pieces. He hopped back onto his own cloud, caught up with Sandy, and the two of them returned in triumph. "How's it going, big belly?" Monkey teased Pigsy, who was desperately hugging the door frame.

"Have you got it?" pleaded the desperate Pigsy.

Monkey would have had some more fun with him, but Sandy was more magnanimous. "Abortion water to the rescue!"

The old woman half-filled a cup with the water. "Sip this slowly; one mouthful should be enough to end the pregnancy."

"Just pass the bucket," gasped Pigsy.

"If you drink the whole thing," said the woman, "it'll dissolve your entire digestive system." On learning this, Pigsy behaved with uncharacteristic moderation around the water.

Within about twenty minutes, the two of them felt sharp cramps and their intestines began to growl, after which Pigsy lost control of his bowels and bladder; Tripitaka also retired to empty his system. After a few bowel movements, the pain stopped and the swelling gradually subsided as the balls of blood and flesh dissolved. The old woman's family then cooked the two unfortunates some restorative rice porridge. Tripitaka ate two bowls, while Pigsy polished off a dozen and still asked for more. "If you're not careful," Monkey said, laughing, "you'll get a postpartum sandbag belly."

"Will you leave me the rest of the water?" the old woman now asked the pilgrims. After checking that Pigsy and Tripitaka had fully recovered, Monkey said that she was more than welcome to it. "This'll pay for my funeral!" she said happily, decanting the leftovers into a porcelain jar and burying it in her back garden. After a feast of a meal, all retired for the night. The following dawn, the disciples—their bodies miraculously free of pregnancies—thanked the woman and her family for their hospitality and set out again.

Chapter Thirty

In another forty or so miles, the band of pilgrims approached a flourishing city. "The capital of the Land of Women, I presume," observed Tripitaka. "Best behavior, all of you."

They entered the city through a road leading in from the east gate. As forewarned, all the locals were women: they wore long skirts and short jackets; their faces were powdered and their hair oiled. The street was crowded with traders, but as soon as they saw the four new arrivals, they stopped what they were doing and crowded exuberantly around: "Seeds! Man seeds!"

Even Pigsy—whom Heaven had punished for his licentiousness—began to panic at the intensity of the female attention. "I'm just a pig!" he cried out. "Nothing to see here!"

"Your face is your best protection," Monkey kindly observed. Pigsy unfurled his massive, palm-leaf ears, pouted his snout, and whooped out a battle cry. The women promptly scattered in terror, but still—from a safe distance—gazed hungrily at Tripitaka. Eventually able to move forward, the pilgrims noted that the houses were built in neat, regular rows and the shops lavishly supplied with rice, salt, wine, and tea.

After they had gone on a while, a female official approached them. "Strangers are not permitted to enter the city without authorization. Please register at the posthouse up ahead and I will announce your arrival to the queen. When your travel documents have been approved, you will be allowed to proceed."

Tripitaka read the sign on the building she pointed to: THE RECEIVING-MALENESS POSTHOUSE. "Just as the old woman said," he observed to Monkey.

"Better go and check for a double reflection in the Embryo-Reflecting Spring," Sandy teased Pigsy.

"Shut up!" Pigsy whined. "That water finished off the pregnancy."

"Shush, Pigsy," Tripitaka chided. "Don't draw attention to yourself."

The official ordered tea for the travelers, found out from them who they were and where they were going, then immediately left to report to the queen. "Since the beginning of time," the monarch mused on learning of the pilgrims' arrival, "our country's rulers have never possessed a man. And now Heaven has sent us a brother of the Tang emperor. We will persuade him to marry me and produce children to perpetuate the dynasty." Her officials all thought this an excellent plan.

"But you might be a little . . . underwhelmed by the appearance of some of the monk's disciples," the clerk from the posthouse warned her.

"What do you mean?" asked the queen.

"The emperor's brother is as beautiful as China is great. His three disciples, however, are unsightly, to say the least. Demonically ugly would be closer to the truth."

"In that case," judged the queen, "let us fill them with food, stamp their travel documents, and send them on westward, while we keep the emperor's brother here. Any objections?"

"A perfect course of action," murmured the officials. "Let us dispatch the Grand Preceptor as matchmaker and the posthouse clerk as mistress of ceremonies."

Tripitaka and his disciples were just enjoying their dinner in the posthouse when the Grand Preceptor and the clerk arrived. After exchanging a few courtesies, the two officials made the queen's proposal of marriage.

"Goodness me!" exclaimed a flustered Tripitaka.

"This is the opportunity of a lifetime," the preceptor urged him. "She brings with her Western Liang as a dowry. Say yes and I'll give her the happy news straightaway."

Seeing that Tripitaka seemed to have lost the power of speech, Pigsy decided to stick his snout in. "Tell your queen that my master is a Buddhist ascetic totally uninterested in wealth or beauty. Let him go on to the west, and I'll marry your queen. How about it?"

Now it was the Grand Preceptor's turn to be rendered speechless.

"You're not exactly the queen's type," the clerk managed to stammer.

"Beggars can't be choosers," Pigsy retorted, laughing. "As the proverb has it: Thick willow for baskets, thin for barrels. In other words: a man is a man is a man."

"Pipe down," Monkey interjected. "Let Tripitaka decide for himself."

"What should I do?" Tripitaka asked Monkey.

"Perhaps you'd best stay here," Monkey replied. "These sorts of opportunities don't grow on trees."

"But then who will fetch the scriptures from the west?"

"Our ruler only wants you," the preceptor told Tripitaka. "After the wedding banquet, your disciples can carry on to the west."

"Ideal," said Monkey. "Tripitaka will stay here and live happily ever after. We'll go fetch the scriptures, then call in here on our way back to top up our supplies for the journey home." Preceptor and clerk gushed their thanks to Monkey.

"Fine words don't cook no rice," Pigsy reminded them. "Tell that queen of yours to get going on the wedding banquet. And a few drinks to toast the engagement."

"Forthwith!" promised the delighted preceptor, who set off back to the palace with the clerk.

As soon as the women had left, a furious Tripitaka grabbed Monkey. "What are you playing at? How can you marry me off while you three go on to the west? I'd rather die!"

"I know, I know," Monkey soothed him. "But given that we're in a tight corner here, we have to fight plots with plots."

"What?" asked Tripitaka.

"If you refuse them," Monkey expanded, "at best they won't stamp our papers and let us continue our journey. At worst, they might try to chop us up into those famous perfume bags, in which case we'd have to fight back and might end up wiping them all out—Pigsy, Sandy, and I are quite powerful, you know. Although I'm not overly fond of them for what they're doing right now, they're just humans, not demons. You are a compassionate person and wouldn't be able to bear the guilt of slaughtering so many people."

"Well said," Tripitaka considered. "But what if the queen forces me to sleep with her? I would lose both my chastity and my masculine yang essence."

"Here's the plan. Now that we've agreed to the marriage, she'll do things by the book, sending her carriage to escort you to the palace. Once there, ask her to stamp, sign, and return our travel documents. You should also make sure there's a banquet, to celebrate the wedding and send us off. At the end of the feast, insist on seeing us out of the city before you consummate the marriage. When we reach the outskirts, I'll freeze them all with my immobility magic while Sandy helps you onto the horse and we carry on to the west. After we've traveled a day and a night, I'll recite the spell to release them and they can return to the city. They'll be unharmed and you'll preserve your primordial chastity. Win-win. This stratagem is called 'Escaping the net through a sham marriage.'"

Tripitaka immediately forgot all his worries. "Monkey, you're brilliant!"

Meanwhile, the Grand Preceptor and clerk rushed into the palace to report the success of their mission, "Wedded bliss will soon be yours! And your fiancé's second disciple particularly asks for wine." The elated queen gave orders for the wedding banquet and set out in the carriage to meet her fiancé. The royal cortege was absolutely the equal of China's: shaded by pearl-encrusted screens and enveloped in exotic, billowing scents and harmonious music. The queen's officials were a sight to behold, bedecked with gold and jade pendants. The instant that the Grand Preceptor pointed out Tripitaka to the queen, she was smitten by his beautiful eyes, pearly teeth, and noble ears. Blushing scarlet, Tripitaka was too embarrassed even to look her in the face. Pigsy by contrast boldly looked the queen up and down and found her to be very easy on the eyes: kingfisher-blue eyebrows, skin like white mutton-jade, cherry-red lips, golden hair piled into a chignon and gleaming with jade and pearl pins. Her eyes were pool-like, her fingers long and elegant. Gold pendants tinkled at every movement of her willowy waist and delicate lotus feet. He drooled at the very sight of her.

The queen seized hold of Tripitaka. "Please mount the dragon chariot, imperial beloved, so that we may become husband and wife in my palace of golden bells."

By this point, Tripitaka was shaking so much he could barely stand up, as if he were drunk or mad. "Control yourself," hissed Monkey. "Get into the carriage and get our travel documents stamped and signed so that we can get out of here." Tears now streamed down Tripitaka's face. "Don't be sad," Monkey urged him out loud. "Live a little, why not?" Wiping his tears away, Tripitaka did his best to smile and stepped into the carriage, which set off back to the east wing of the palace, where the royal couple was greeted by a choir of pipes and singers, two lines of beautiful palace women, and a sumptuous banquet. The queen toasted her guests with a jade cupful of wine; Monkey threw Tripitaka a look, to signify that he should return the compliment.

The ceremonials completed, the music stopped and Pigsy welcomed the banquet into his stomach: corn, steamed bread, cakes, mushrooms, bamboo shoots, cabbage, seaweed, turnips, and yams, all washed down with half a dozen cups of wine. "More food, more wine, quickly!" he shouted. "We scripture-seekers need to keep up our strength." The queen ordered an array of extraordinary vessels: parrot cups with cormorant-shaped ladles, golden beakers, crystal basins, and amber goblets. They were filled with the finest wines, and all drank a round.

Rising from the table, Tripitaka bowed to the queen. "Thank you for this extraordinary banquet, Your Majesty. We've all drunk quite enough. Please stamp my disciples' papers and send them on their way while it is still light." Leading Tripitaka by the hand, the queen dismissed the banquet and proceeded to the throne room, where she stamped the documents with her own seal, signed her name, and passed them back to Monkey. She then tried to press upon the three disciples gold, silver, and brocade for their journey. Monkey refused them all, for Buddhist mendicants were not permitted such riches. "Take six pints of rice at least," she suggested instead.

This Pigsy instantly accepted: "It'll do me for one meal."

"I would like to see them off personally," Tripitaka now told the queen, "as I have some advice for them about their journey to the west." The unsuspecting queen called once more for her carriage and, snuggling fragrantly up to Tripitaka, rode out with him to the western outskirts of the city, through streets lined with city dwellers eager to catch a glimpse of the royal couple.

When they were ready for the send-off, the three disciples stood before the carriage and chorused: "No need to come any further, Your Majesty. We'll say our good-byes here."

Tripitaka got out of the carriage. "Your Majesty, please return to your capital and allow me to carry on my journey west."

The queen paled with shock. "What are you talking about? I've promised you my kingdom. Your reign is due to start tomorrow. You've eaten the wedding feast!"

Pigsy lost his temper here. "Let Tripitaka go, you powdered skeleton!"

But just as the intimidated queen stumbled back into the carriage and Sandy was helping Tripitaka onto the horse, a girl rushed out of the crowd. "Where do you think you're going, you beautiful Buddhist? You and I have some love to make!" And before Sandy could beat her off with his staff, and Monkey and Pigsy could perform their immobility spells, she and Tripitaka disappeared into a whirlwind. Tripitaka's romantic adventures, it seems, were taking him out of the frying pan and into the fire.

Chapter Thirty-One

Monkey leaped into the clouds, from where he could see a roiling mass of dust and wind careering toward the northwest. "Hop on a cloud and follow me!" he shouted down to Pigsy and Sandy, who sprang up to join him, leaving the frightened and chastened women of Western Liang behind. The three pilgrims chased the cyclone all the way to a high mountain, where they found a shiny green stone slab screening two stone doors with the inscription CAVE OF THE LUTE, MOUNTAIN OF THE TOXIC ENEMY. Rash as ever, Pigsy wanted to smash the door down with his rake. "Not so fast," warned Monkey. "We have no idea whether this door has anything to do with our kidnapper. In case it doesn't, we don't want to get on the wrong side of the owner. You two stay out here. I'll snoop around inside before we decide on our next step."

"Good thinking, Monkey!" applauded Sandy. "Calm under pressure."

Making a magic sign with his fingers and reciting a spell, Monkey transformed into a very convincing bee. His gossamer wings whirring, the bee-monkey slipped between the two stone doors and promptly came upon a flower-bedecked pavilion, in the center of which sat a female fiend surrounded by girls in colorful embroidered silks. They all seemed in high spirits, chatting away about something or other. Monkey softly approached and perched on the pavilion's trellis to hear what was going on. At that instant, two more girls appeared on the scene, carrying two platters of steaming bread. "One platter contains buns stuffed with human flesh," they explained to their mistress, "the other red bean paste."

"Bring our guest out for some refreshments," ordered the beaming fiend. A few of the girls disappeared and then came back with Tripitaka, who was looking dreadful. His face was sallow, his lips white, and his eyes red and swollen with crying.

Emerging from the pavilion, the fiend extended her fingers—long and slender as ten spring onions—to Tripitaka. "Relax, beloved. My place isn't as luxurious as the queen's palace, but it's a lot more peaceful—perfect for chanting sutras and growing old together." Tripitaka said nothing. "Don't vex yourself," resumed the fiend. "I noticed you didn't eat much at your first wedding banquet of the day, so I've prepared you a little snack of human and red bean pastries. You'll feel better if you eat something. Girls, some hot tea, to wash down our priest's buns."

Tiring of this exchange, Monkey resumed his true form and whipped out his staff. The fiend blew out a mouthful of misty light that engulfed the pavilion. "Keep Tripitaka safe!" she enjoined her maidservants, then grabbed an enormous steel fork. "Outrageous monkey!" she bellowed. "How dare you barge into my home and spy on me?"

The two of them fought their way out of the cave, at which point Pigsy sprang into action. "Stand back, Monkey! Prepare for Pigsy!"

With another battle cry, the fiend now snorted fire from her nose and puffed smoke from her mouth; somehow, her single trident had become three, which she passed among too many hands for Monkey and Pigsy to count. "I know who you are," she taunted, "but you don't know who I am. Even the Buddha fears me." The battle went on until nightfall, at which point the fiend suddenly jumped into the air and stabbed Monkey hard on the head.

"Agony!" howled Monkey, fleeing in pain. Seeing him retreat, Pigsy followed, trailing his rake. The fiend returned triumphantly to the cave and tidied away her tridents.

"I feel terrible!" groaned Monkey, gripping his head, his face contorted with pain.

"It was going so well," Pigsy asked him. "Why did you suddenly run away yelping with pain?"

"Ow! Ow!" Monkey responded.

"Have you got a headache?" asked Sandy.

"No!" replied Monkey, hopping about. "I don't know what she stabbed my head with, but the pain was so unbearable I had to retreat."

"You're always boasting about your head," Pigsy said, smirking, "about how you toughened it up through meditation and whatnot. How come it can't stand a little tap with a trident?"

"True." Monkey was puzzled. "After I stole and ate the peaches of immortality, drank the heavenly wine and Laozi's golden elixir, and caused chaos in Heaven, the Jade Emperor ordered me to be killed." ("Oh, really?" Pigsy interpolated. "You never mentioned that.") "His divine executioners hacked at me with knives, axes, hammers, and swords, thunderbolts and fire, then Laozi smelted me in his Brazier of Eight Trigrams for forty-nine days. Not a scratch on the old head. What on earth did that fiend use on me today? I feel awful."

"Maybe you've got a head carbuncle," speculated a delighted Pigsy.

"Stop joking," Sandy chided him. "It's getting late, Monkey's hurt his head, and we've no idea whether Tripitaka is dead or alive. What are we to do?"

"Tripitaka's fine," said Monkey, explaining what he'd seen behind the stone doors.

"Then let's find a sheltered spot to spend the night and recover our energies," advised Sandy. "We can decide what to do in the morning."

Back inside the cave, the female fiend shook off thoughts of battle and went back to smiling pleasantly. "Make sure the front and back doors are locked," she ordered her maids, appointing two as sentries to prevent Monkey from sneaking in again. "Light some candles and incense in the bedroom for a bit of ambience," she told some other servants. "Tonight, Tripitaka and I are going to make beautiful love." When Tripitaka was delivered to her, she enveloped him in her arms. Dumb with horror, Tripitaka's instinct was to refuse her, but he worried she might kill him for it. Shaking like jelly, then, he followed her into the fragrant bedroom. By this point, he was too horrified even to hear the fiend's sweet nothings. The demon began to disrobe, revealing a soft, scented body; Tripitaka wrapped his robe all the more tightly around himself. "I'll be the courtesan to your emperor," simpered the fiend.

"No, thank you," he responded. Back and forth they went deep into the night, with Tripitaka staunchly resisting the fiend's advances. Around midnight, she finally lost her temper, trussed her beloved up like a chicken, ordered her servants to dump him in the corridor, blew out the candles, and shut down the cave for the night.

Soon enough, day broke and Monkey got up and stretched. "My headache's gone," he rejoiced. "There's just a little itch left."

"Shall we ask her to give you another tap?" Pigsy teased.

"Get lost!" Monkey spat at him.

"On the general subject of heads," continued Pigsy, still in humorous mode, "Master must have let his hair down last night."

"Enough, both of you," chided Sandy. "We've got a fiend to deal with."

Leaving Sandy with the horse, Monkey and Pigsy leaped back

to the stone screen. "Stay here," Monkey instructed Pigsy. "I'm going in first to find out whether the fiend assaulted Master during the night. If he lost his virtue to her, the pilgrimage is off. If he resisted her, we'll fight the fiend to the death, rescue Master, and carry on to the west."

"Can a dried fish serve as a cat's pillow?" asked Pigsy rhetorically.

"Shut up while I go and investigate," retorted Monkey.

Changing back into a bee, Monkey flew inside the cave and found all the servants still fast asleep, exhausted by the previous night's bedroom kerfuffle. Flying deeper into the cave, Monkey heard Tripitaka moaning faintly and discovered the priest bound hand and foot in a corridor. "Master," he whispered, gently landing on Tripitaka's head.

"Can that be you, Monkey?" Tripitaka gasped. "Save me!"

"How were the nocturnal activities?" Monkey inquired.

"I would rather die!" Tripitaka shot back.

"She was all over you yesterday," Monkey pointed out. "Why has she turned on you now?"

"She tormented me for half the night," explained Tripitaka, "but I refused to go near her. When she realized she wouldn't get anywhere, she tied me up and left me here."

Monkey buzzed back out of the cave and filled Pigsy in on everything. "Excellent!" Pigsy chuckled. "Chastity to spare. To the rescue!"

Never one to beat around the bush, Pigsy smashed the stone doors with his rake. "Those two horrors from yesterday are back," cried the terrified sentries, rushing inside the cave.

The fiend, who was just emerging from her bedroom, immediately gave instructions. "Keep our imperial visitor safe in the back of the cave. I'll deal with our uninvited guests." She then seized her trident. "Outrageous monkey! Barbaric swine! How dare you break down my door!"

"That's our teacher you've got there," Monkey shouted back. "Release him now and we'll spare your life. Refuse and we'll flatten this mountain of yours." The fiend answered by snorting smoke and fire and charging with her trident. After a few rounds, she dealt Pigsy's snout the coup de grâce she'd given Monkey the previous day. Pigsy promptly fled in agony, his rake trailing behind him. Monkey himself made a false move with his staff and also fled in defeat. The victorious fiend told her servants to secure the doors with piles of rocks.

Standing guard by the horse, Sandy heard the most fearful grunting and snorting approach. Pigsy soon came into view. "This is the worst! The worst!" he wailed.

Monkey followed not far behind, giggling. "You thought I had a head carbuncle yesterday. Looks like you've got snout pox today!"

"Oh, the pain!" Pigsy resumed. "I can't bear it!"

The three of them were thus in a fix when they spotted an old woman approaching from the south, a green bamboo basket filled with vegetables over her arm. Monkey quickly noticed that the old woman was wreathed with fragrant mists. "Kowtow!" he shouted to his fellow disciples. "It's Guanyin!" The three of them fell to the ground.

Guanyin now floated into midair on her auspicious clouds and took her true form. "Forgive this shabby reception!" pleaded Monkey, rising up to meet her. "We've been rather tied up of late. We're dealing with a particularly unruly fiend here. A little help, perhaps?"

"This demon is a formidable scorpion-spirit," Guanyin told them. "Those tridents of hers are pincers, and she stabbed you with her tail-sting. One day she spied on the Buddha while he lectured in Thunderclap Monastery. When he tried to push her away, she stabbed his left thumb and fled here. Even he and I daren't go near her. Only the Star Lord Orionis can help you."

She then melted into a beam of golden light and returned to the South Sea.

Monkey passed on Guanyin's counsel to the other two. "I'll pop off to see Orionis right away."

"Ask that star lord of yours for some medicinal cakes for my lip while you're at it," grunted Pigsy.

"Buck up, Pigsy," Monkey told him, laughing. "You'll be right as rain tomorrow."

"Stop wasting time," Sandy urged. "Go now!"

Monkey arrived an instant later at the Palace of Light just as Orionis was returning, in a cloud of Heavenly fragrance, from some military maneuvers. He was quite a sight: dressed all in gold, waist cinched with a jeweled belt, a seven-star sword hanging from his robe. "To what do we owe this honor?" he asked. Monkey set out his predicament at the Cave of the Lute on the Mountain of the Toxic Enemy and Guanyin's recommendation of his services. "No time to offer you tea," Orionis apologized. "Let's go defeat this demon."

The two of them sped back to Toxic Enemy, where they found Pigsy still looking very sorry for himself. "What's wrong?" Orionis asked him.

"The fiend stabbed me on the mouth this morning, and it's horribly painful," Pigsy said.

The star lord stroked the injured snout, then blew on it, and the pain vanished. "Wonder of wonders!" rejoiced Pigsy, falling to his knees.

"Could you touch my head, too?" Monkey grinned.

"Nothing wrong with you, is there?" asked Orionis.

"I was stung yesterday. Though the pain's gone, my scalp's still a bit itchy. I'm worried it might flare up when the weather turns damp."

Orionis performed the same service on Monkey, and the itch disappeared.

Fully recovered, Pigsy now turned ferocious. "Let's go and settle that hussy's hash."

"Good idea," agreed the star god. "You two draw her out of the cave, and I'll finish her off."

Monkey and Pigsy bounded back up the mountain. In no time at all, and shouting filthy abuse all the while, Pigsy had cleared the rocks piled up at the entrance to the cave. The little fiends announced the bad news to their mistress just as she was about to untie Tripitaka to feed him some tea and rice. She charged at Pigsy and Monkey with her trident; guessing that she might be about to deploy her sting a third time, the two pilgrims fled—with the fiend in hot pursuit—down the side of the mountain where Orionis stood waiting in his true form: a seven-foot, double-combed rooster. He crowed once and the fiend became a lute-sized scorpion. He crowed again and the scorpion collapsed and died.

Pigsy put his foot on her back. "So where's your stinger now?" He then pounded her into a paste with his rake.

After bowing their thanks to Orionis, who immediately headed off on a cloud, the pilgrims entered the cave, where the fiend's maids kneeled to receive them. "We aren't demons. We're women of Western Liang kidnapped by the scorpion. Your master is in a perfumed room at the back of the cave. Weeping, as usual."

"Dearest disciples, I'm so glad to see you!" exclaimed the monk through his tears. "Who was that woman?"

"Oh, just an enormous female scorpion," explained Pigsy, before describing how they vanquished her. "And now she's jam."

They made a meal of some noodles and rice they found in the cave, showed the kidnapped women the way down the mountain and back to Western Liang, burned the cave to ashes, and carried on toward the west.

Chapter Thirty-Two

Time flew like an arrow; the seasons passed back and forth like a weaver's shuttle. The dog days of summer gave way to the first frosts of autumn. But then the weather seemed to reverse itself: the autumn grew scalding. "How can this be?" wondered Tripitaka.

"We are approaching the kingdom of Sihali," Pigsy expounded knowledgeably. "Also known as Heaven's End, where the sun sets. Late every afternoon, the king sends people onto the city walls to beat drums and blow horns to block out the sound of the sea boiling—for when the sun drops into the ocean, it makes a deafening sizzle. Without music to block the noise, the city's children would all perish."

"Bunk!" scoffed Monkey. "We're still ages away from Sihali. And at the rate we're going, we might never get there."

"Then why is it so hot?" Pigsy asked. As they walked and squabbled, they came upon a large red house at the roadside.

"Go inside and find out what's going on with the weather," Tripitaka ordered Monkey.

Putting away his staff and trying his best to look normal, Monkey approached the house just as an old man emerged. The man wore a rough orange robe and a bluish-black bamboo hat. His eyes were blue, his face bronze, his beard matted, and his eyebrows white. The sudden appearance of Monkey startled him. "A monkey in a kilt! Where did you come from?" he yelled.

"Don't be afraid, sir," Monkey replied with a bow, and introduced his fellow travelers and the purpose of their journey. "We've just arrived and were wondering if you could tell us the name of this place and why it is so hot here."

The old man relaxed and smiled, revealing some gold teeth. "Excuse my rudeness just now; my eyes are not what they used to be. Please—come in, all of you." Monkey waved the others over; all bowed to the old man, who was as charmed by Tripitaka's beauty as he was horrified by the hideousness of Pigsy and Sandy. Yet he had little choice but to give them tea and a meal. "You've reached the country of Flame Mountain, where it is hot all year round. The mountain itself is sixty miles from here, blocking the way to the west and engulfing the surrounding area with fire. I suggest you pick a new destination for your pilgrimage—nothing can get past Flame Mountain."

While Tripitaka wallowed in fear and despair, a young man pushing a red cart appeared at the door. "Rice pudding for sale!"

Monkey plucked a hair, turned it into a copper penny, and exchanged it for a piece of steaming rice cake. "Hot, hot, hot!" he exclaimed, juggling the cake from one hand to the other.

"If you can't stand the heat, then stay out of Flame Mountain." the young man said with a smile.

"If it's so hot," wondered Monkey, "how did you grow rice for this pudding?"

"With the help of Princess Iron-Fan."

"Who?" Monkey asked.

"She's an immortal with a magic palm-leaf fan. One wave of it puts the fire out, a second brings a breeze, a third rain. That brief respite allows us to grow crops. Otherwise, nothing would grow around here—not even a blade of grass."

Monkey rushed back inside. Presenting Tripitaka with the pudding, he explained what the peddler had just told him. "We just need to get Iron-Fan's fan and then we can extinguish the mountain of flames. We'll be able to carry on our way and the locals will be able to enjoy a more temperate climate."

"But you don't have any gifts," the old man pointed out. "The locals have to prepare pigs, sheep, cash, exotic flowers and fruits, chickens, geese, and fine wine before begging for a wave of the fan."

"Just give me her address," Monkey said nonchalantly.

"She lives in Palm-Leaf Cave on Jade-Cloud Mountain—it's about fifteen hundred miles southwest of here."

"No worries!" Monkey grinned. "I'll be there and back before you know it."

"Let me pack you some biscuits for the journey. And watch for the wolves and tigers."

"I'll go as I am!" Monkey laughed, then vanished.

An instant later, Monkey parked his auspicious light beam on Jade-Cloud Mountain. Searching for Palm-Leaf Cave, he heard a woodcutter chopping timber and singing to himself in the forest. "Greetings!" said Monkey with a bow, rushing up. The woodcutter dropped his ax and returned the bow. "Is this Jade-Cloud Mountain?" Monkey asked.

"Indeed."

"And where might I find Palm-Leaf Cave?"

"You mean the home of Princess Iron-Fan, wife of King Bull Demon?"

Even Monkey was shaken by this revelation. "Not that family again." He sighed to himself. "I've had more than enough trouble from Red Boy and his bad-tempered uncle. And now I have to face his mother. I don't like my chances of getting the fan off her."

The woodcutter smiled. "Buddhists aren't supposed to worry about anything. Follow this path five or six miles to the east and you'll come to Palm-Leaf Cave." Deciding to confide in the woodcutter, Monkey told him about the pilgrimage and the feud with Iron-Fan's son. "Don't fret about your history with the family," the woodcutter comforted him. "Just concentrate on getting the fan, and I'm sure you'll succeed." Thanking him for his advice, Monkey went on his way.

He soon arrived at the entrance to Palm-Leaf Cave. The view over the mountain was spectacular: cool, shady bamboo forests, paths dense with flowers, moss-covered rocks. Wild cranes roosted on towering pines; orioles sang from weeping willows. "King Bull!" Monkey called through the door with as much bonhomie as he could muster. "It's your brother! Open up!" Out came a young girl carrying a flower basket and resting a hoe on her shoulder, radiating serenity. "Would you deliver a message to the princess?" Monkey asked her, palms pressed together. "I'm seeking scriptures in the west, but Flame Mountain is blocking my way. I've come to borrow the Palm-Leaf Fan."

"Of course," the girl replied. "And your name is?"

"Monkey."

The girl went back inside, knelt before her mistress, and announced their visitor and his purpose. As soon as she heard the name Monkey, Iron-Fan predictably flushed with rage. "How dare that damn monkey show his face here? Bring me my armor and weapons!" Plated up and wielding two blue-bladed swords, she strode out of the cave.

Monkey quickly sized her up: she was wearing a priest's robe of patchwork brocade (the waist cinched with a pair of tiger tendons), three-inch phoenix-bill shoes, and trousers with golden dragon-whisker knee fringes.

"WHERE'S THAT MONKEY?" she bellowed.

"Here I am, sister-in-law!" he announced with a bow.

"Pah!" hissed Iron-Fan. "What do you mean, sister-in-law? And stop bowing in that stupid way."

"Your husband and I have been sworn brothers these past five hundred years. I understand that you are his wife. That means I'm your brother-in-law."

"If we're family, then why did you persecute my son?"

Monkey opted to feign ignorance. "And your son would be ... ?"

"Red Boy of Fire-Cloud Cave by Desiccated Pine Stream on Roaring Mountain. Name ring a bell? Just when I was wondering how to destroy you, here you come knocking at my door. Prepare to die!"

Monkey tried to smile his way out of it. "Surely some mistake. Monkey was not in the wrong. Your dear son had captured my teacher, Tripitaka, and was planning either to steam or boil him. Guanyin then rescued Tripitaka and gave your dear son a senior position in her administration, where he is exempt from mortal cycles of birth and death, enjoying life as long as heaven and earth, sun and moon. Perhaps a thank-you is in order?"

"Smart-talking simian!" spat Iron-Fan. "Let me have a go at your head. If you survive, I'll give you the fan. If not, you can go and entertain King Yama with your backchat."

Monkey walked up to her. "Don't hold back. But you have to give me the fan when you're done." She hacked at him a dozen or so times, Monkey giggling all the while. Losing her nerve, Iron-Fan turned and made to flee. "Where are you going?" asked Monkey. "What about the fan?"

"It's not for lending!" retorted Iron-Fan.

Monkey now produced his staff and the two of them did their best to kill each other, like the affectionate in-laws they were. As night fell, however, Iron-Fan realized that Monkey would ultimately get the better of her in a straight fight, so she shook her Palm-Leaf Fan at him: a gust of freezing wind blew him away and she returned victoriously to her cave.

Monkey drifted all through the night—like a leaf in a cyclone—until he finally managed to cling to the summit of a mountain as day broke. After catching his breath, he discovered he'd been blown as far as the Lesser Sumeru Mountain, a sacred Buddhist peak. "What a woman!" Monkey sighed in admiration. "Now, how do I get back on course?" Remembering that the mountain was home to a Bodhisattva with substantial magic powers, one Lingji, he followed the sound of bells to present himself at Lingji's temple.

"Well done, Monkey!" Lingji congratulated him, hopping off his throne. "Back with the scriptures already?"

"Not exactly," replied Monkey.

"Then what are you doing here? This isn't on the road to the west."

Monkey explained his latest imbroglio, this time with Princess Iron-Fan. ". . . and that's how I ended up here. How far is it back to Flame Mountain from here?"

Lingji seemed to find this whole story enormously entertaining. "Princess Iron-Fan's Palm-Leaf Fan," he explained with a smile, "was created by heaven and earth back when chaos divided and Pan Gu built the universe. It's made of magic leaves of supreme yin—darkness and cold—which is why it can extinguish all fires. It can fan a single human eighty-four thousand miles. Sumeru's only fifty thousand miles from Flame Mountain, so you did very well to stop here."

"Impressive," admitted Monkey. "But now what am I to do?"

"Don't worry," Lingji consoled him. "Some years back, the Buddha gave me a treasure for this very situation: the wind-stilling elixir, which will enable you to resist her fan. You can then take the fan, extinguish the fire, and carry on to the west." He fished out of his sleeve the magic pellet, which he sewed firmly onto the underside of Monkey's collar. "Not a moment to lose!" Lingji urged him. "Jade-Cloud is that way, to the northwest."

After an instant's cloud-somersaulting, Monkey was back at Iron-Fan's door, banging on it with his staff. "Open up! Monkey wants the fan!"

This monkey must be quite something, thought a fearful Iron-Fan. *How can he be back so soon after I fanned him? This time, I'll fan him two or three times—that'll send him packing for good.* She stomped out of the cave again. "Still got that death wish, I see," she greeted her adversary.

"Play fair," Monkey said, smiling back. "Lend me the fan so we can get past that mountain. You'll have it back straight after."

She answered by charging at him again. Realizing after a few minutes that the fight wasn't going her way, Iron-Fan fanned him once more, but this time Monkey was completely unmovable. "Technical issue?" he inquired, with a grin. Panicking, Iron-Fan ran back inside the cave and locked the door.

Popping the wind-stilling elixir into his mouth, Monkey transformed into a tiny cricket and squeezed in through a crack in the door. Inside, Iron-Fan was shouting for tea. Her maidservant poured a bowl for her so quickly that bubbles formed on the surface. Monkey nimbly buzzed inside one of the bubbles. After the thirsty Iron-Fan gulped down the tea, Monkey changed back to his true self inside her stomach. "I want that fan!" he bellowed.

"Did you not shut the doors?" Iron-Fan asked her maids, growing pale with fright. "Why can I hear Monkey shouting at me?"

"The voice is coming from inside you," one of the servants told her.

"Monkey! What trick is this?" Iron-Fan demanded.

"This is no trick," Monkey argued. "I'm a fully qualified immortal with serious abilities. And I'm currently deploying some of them in your esteemed stomach. I've got a particularly scenic view of your lungs and liver. You must be hungry and thirsty after that fight, so here's a bowl for you to drink out of"—he stamped his foot hard on the base of her stomach—"and here's something for you to chew on"—he butted his head up toward Iron-Fan's heart.

The princess writhed on the ground, her face yellow with pain. "Spare me!"

"I'll spare you out of brotherly love. But I want the fan. Now."

"It's yours!" wailed Iron-Fan. "Just come out and get it."

"I want to set eyes on it first," demanded Monkey. Iron-Fan ordered her maids to hold it up; Monkey crept to the top of her throat to see it for himself. "All right," he said. "I'll leave by your mouth so I don't make a hole in your rib cage. Open wide." He then flew back out of the princess's mouth as a cricket, returned to his true form, seized the fan, and strode out. The maids couldn't get the door open fast enough.

Turning his cloud around, Monkey returned to the redbrick house. "Monkey's back!" Pigsy squealed in delight.

"Is this the fan?" Monkey asked the old man, producing his prize.

"The very same!"

"Marvelous Monkey!" exclaimed Tripitaka. "That can't have been easy."

"It was nothing," replied Monkey. "Would you believe it, though? That Princess Iron-Fan turned out to be the wife of King Bull Demon and the mother of Red Boy. She wasn't too pleased to see me." After hearing about Monkey's trials on his quest for the fan, Tripitaka thanked him profusely, then the disciples bade the old man farewell.

They proceeded west for another forty miles, getting progressively more roasted. "My trotters are on fire!" complained Pigsy.

"Stay where you are," Monkey told the others. "I'm going to fan the fire. When the rain has cooled the ground, we can cross the mountain." He fanned it once, but the flames raged even more fiercely. He fanned it a second time, and the blaze intensified a hundredfold. He waved it a third time, and the flames shot up as high as the eye could see. Although Monkey fled as fast as he could, the hair on his thighs was still singed to oblivion. "Run away!" he cried.

The party of pilgrims fled some twenty miles eastward before

Monkey started to rage at what had happened. "How did she trick me? If I'd run any slower, I'd have lost all my fur."

While Tripitaka wept inconsolably, Pigsy amused himself by provoking Monkey. "Aren't you supposed to be immune to flames?"

"Idiot!" Monkey lashed back. "Because I wasn't expecting the fire, I didn't have time to do the fire-repellent spell."

"Have a bite to eat, Monkey." A voice suddenly broke into their argument. "You'll feel better." Turning, the four of them saw an old man, caped and capped and leaning on a cane with a dragon's head. Following him was a demon with the beak of a hawk and the cheeks of a fish, carrying on his head a copper pot containing steamed cakes and yellow millet. "Allow me to introduce myself," the old man said, bowing. "I am the spirit of Flame Mountain. I thought you could use some refreshments."

"Do you think we're interested in food at a time like this?" barked Monkey. "How are we going to put this fire out so we can carry on to the west?"

"You're the one who set this fire burning, you know," the spirit pointed out.

"Poppycock! When did I go around starting fires?"

"Let me explain," replied the spirit. "This mountain did not exist until five hundred years ago, when you made all that trouble in Heaven and Laozi had to smelt you inside his Brazier of Eight Trigrams. When he opened it, you kicked over the brazier, dislodging a few burning bricks that fell onto this very spot and became Flame Mountain. I was the shift worker attending the brazier, and on grounds of professional negligence, Laozi banished me here, where I became the local spirit. You need the princess's fan to extinguish the fire."

"Isn't this it?" asked Monkey, picking it up from the side of the road, where he had left it. "It only made the blaze stronger."

"Ah." The spirit smiled. "She duped you with a fake. If you want the real one, you'll have to seek out King Bull Demon."

"Why?" asked Monkey, only half persuaded by the spirit's account of the mountain's origins.

"King Bull Demon is Princess Iron-Fan's husband. Some while ago, however, he left her and currently resides in Cloud-Scraper Cave on Thunder-Hoard Mountain. The cave's former master, a fox king, passed away at the ripe old age of ten thousand, leaving behind a daughter called Princess Jade-Face and an extraordinary fortune with no one to look after it. Two years ago, Jade-Face learned how powerful King Bull Demon was and offered him all of her fortune as dowry if he agreed to become her consort. So the king abandoned Iron-Fan and hasn't been back to visit her since. You'll only get ahold of that fan with his help. If you succeed, you'll not only extinguish the fire, enabling the pilgrimage to proceed, but also solve the region's appalling climate problems. And I'll be pardoned and allowed to return to work for Laozi in Heaven. Win-win-win."

"So where is this Thunder-Hoard Mountain?" Monkey asked.

"About three thousand miles due south of here."

Telling Pigsy and Sandy to look after Tripitaka, and the spirit to keep them all company, Monkey disappeared with a whoosh.

In less than an hour, Monkey landed on yet another spectacularly lovely mountain. After admiring the scenery for a while, he picked his way down from the summit. Quite lost, he encountered a beautiful young woman on the edge of a shady pine forest, holding a fragrant sprig of orchid. As soon as she noticed him, the girl was paralyzed with fear—for he was an unusual-looking creature. "W-where did you come from?" she said, trembling. "What do you want?"

Better not mention the fan outright, Monkey thought, *in case she's related to old Bull Demon. I'd better just say that he's wanted back home.* Out loud: "I'm looking for Cloud-Scraper Cave. Could you direct me there, please?"

"And what is your business there?" she asked.

"Princess Iron-Fan from Palm-Leaf Cave on Jade-Cloud Mountain has sent me to fetch King Bull Demon."

The girl immediately flew into a rage. "That worthless hag! In the two years Bull Demon's been living with me, he's sent her endless pearls, gold, silver, jade, silk, and satin as alimony so that she can live in the lap of luxury. And now she wants him to go and see her! Does she have no shame?"

By now, Monkey had deduced both that this was Princess Jade-Face and that she was profoundly irritating.

"Hypocrite!" he threw back at her. "You bought King Bull Demon with your own fortune!"

The terrified girl turned and fled on her tiny feet, with Monkey in pursuit, through the shady forest and all the way to Cloud-Scraper Cave. She dashed in and slammed the door behind her. While Monkey paused once more to admire the scenery, Jade-Face, panting and perspiring, made straight for the library, where King Bull Demon was quietly studying some elixir manuals. The girl flung herself at him and sobbed uncontrollably. "There, there," soothed King Bull Demon with a smile, "whatever's wrong, darling?"

"Don't 'darling' me!" complained the girl, now sufficiently recovered for some petulance. "You almost got me killed!"

"Why are you so angry with me?" said Bull Demon, laughing at her fury.

"I took you in because everyone said you were such a hero—I thought you'd protect me. But that first wife of yours has got you wrapped around her little finger!" Jade-Face now told him what had just happened while she was out picking orchids (leaving out some of the less-flattering personal comments she had made about Princess Iron-Fan), and finished with her being pursued all the way back to the cave by a terrifying monkey.

Bull Demon eventually calmed her down, but something struck him as fishy. "My first wife runs a very tight ship with an all-female staff," he mused. "I'm not at all convinced that she would have sent a hideous monkey demon as a messenger. Time to investigate." Strapping on a gold cuirass lined with silk brocade and an iron helmet polished to a bright silver, he strode out of the cave wielding a cast-iron cudgel to confront Monkey.

As he took in the splendiferousness of Bull Demon, Monkey had to admit that his blood brother from half a millennium ago had done well for himself. "Recognize me?" he asked Bull Demon.

"Monkey—am I right?"

"Right the first time! Long time, brother. I must say, you haven't aged a bit. My compliments!"

"Enough blandishments!" roared Bull Demon. "Why did you give my son Red Boy, of Fire-Cloud Cave by Desiccated Pine Stream on Roaring Mountain, such a hard time?"

"Not that again. Don't make me out to be the unreasonable one, old chap. Your son was about to eat my teacher. And now he's living the good life, up with Guanyin."

"All right, I'll let you off for that one. But why did you attack my concubine?"

"Oh, that." Monkey laughed. "I didn't know where to find you, so I asked her ever so nicely for some directions. Then she gave me a tongue-lashing and I might have been a *little* rough. How was I to know she was my sister-in-law? Would it help if I said I was sorry?"

"I'll spare you for old time's sake. Now beat it!"

"You are too kind," simpered Monkey. "But I'm afraid there is one other thing I need to beg of you."

"Don't push your luck, Monkey," growled Bull Demon.

"It's like this." Monkey carried on regardless. "There I was, escorting that Tang monk of mine to the west, and what do you know—there's a whopping Flame Mountain in our way. The locals told us that my esteemed sister-in-law Princess Iron-Fan happens to possess the Palm-Leaf Fan that can extinguish fire. But she's not so keen on us borrowing it. Be a compassionate bull demon and come with me now to Jade-Cloud Mountain, would you, and persuade her to lend us the fan? We'll return it in mint condition as soon as we're past that furnace."

"So that's what you're after?" Bull Demon exploded. "I'll bet you insulted my wife, too, and now you have the gall to ask for my help? This time you've gone too far, Monkey. Have a taste of my cudgel!"

"I really do need that fan," Monkey persevered.

"If you can hold your own against me," growled Bull Demon, "I'll tell my wife to lend it to you. If not, I'll kill you, just to cheer myself up."

"Good plan, brother. It's been centuries since we tested ourselves against each other—I've really missed our mortal combat."

When they were about a hundred clashes in—each fighting on their respective auspicious clouds—a voice called out from the summit of Thunder-Hoard Mountain: "Lord Bull Demon! My sovereign begs the pleasure of your company for dinner."

Bull Demon blocked and held Monkey's staff. "Hold on. Back after a banquet." Dropping down from the clouds, Bull Demon went back inside the cave. "Dearest wife," he told Princess Jade-Face, "our hairy visitor is the infamous Monkey. I drove him away with my cudgel, so he won't give you any more trouble. I'm off to have a drink with a friend." He then swapped his armor for a duck-green silk-velvet jacket, mounted a water-repellent, golden-eyed beast, ordered the servants to guard the door, and disappeared northwest into the cloud and fog.

After watching him leave, Monkey turned into a gust of wind and chased after his adversary until the latter disappeared amid the folds of a mountain. After a little exploration, Monkey discovered a deep, limpid pool. *I'll bet he dived in there,* he thought.

Transforming this time into a thirty-six-pound crab, Monkey leaped in and sank straight to the bottom, where he encountered a finely carved gateway, beneath which was tethered the water-repellent, golden-eyed beast. Walking through the portal, the monkey-crab discovered it was perfectly dry inside. He heard music coming from a banquet hall with scarlet walls, shell-studded towers, and golden roof tiles. Peeking in through a door-frame of milky jade, he took in a scene of aquatic revelry: whales singing, giant crabs dancing, tortoises piping, alligators drumming, and perch courtesans stroking jade zithers. Ensconced in the seat of honor was King Bull Demon, surrounded by dragons, all busy toasting one another. *Seeing as Bull Demon is enjoying himself so much, why should I hang around waiting for him?* mused Monkey. *It's not like he's going to lend me the fan himself. Better still to steal his golden-eyed beast, impersonate him, and fool his first wife into handing over the goods.*

Becoming Monkey once more, he untied the beast, hopped into the carved saddle, and rode straight back to the surface of the pool. There he transformed into the exact likeness of King Bull Demon, soared off to Palm-Leaf Cave, and demanded to be let in. "Your husband is back," two of the maids reported to Iron-Fan, who immediately tidied her hair and rushed out to greet him. Not realizing the deception, she took him by the hand, led him into the cave, and proceeded to make the most tremendous fuss over him. In no time at all, the two were chatting pleasantly over tea.

"It's been too long," offered "Bull Demon."

"Indeed!" returned Iron-Fan. "You've been so wrapped up in your new consort that you seem to have completely forgotten about me. What brings you here today?"

"How could I forget you? It's just that after moving in with Princess Jade-Face, I've been run ragged by one thing after another: my friends' problems, running another household. But I'm here to warn you about something. I just heard that Monkey is plotting to get your fan from you so that he can cross Flame Mountain. I still haven't forgiven him for what he did to our son. Tell me the moment he shows up here so that I can chop him into ten thousand pieces."

Iron-Fan now summarized her two encounters with Monkey, all the way up to her capitulation over his stomach calisthenics.

"What?" exploded her fake husband. "Monkey already has the fan?"

"Don't worry!" Iron-Fan smirked. "I fobbed him off with a fake."

"So where's the real fan?" asked Monkey.

"Still safe and sound in my possession." The maids now brought in some wine.

"Do drink up, my precious persimmon," Monkey cajoled her. "Thank you for looking after our home while I've been gone."

"Please don't mention it," replied Iron-Fan, refilling the cup.

After a few more rounds, Iron-Fan had been thoroughly disinhibited by drink. She edged closer to Monkey: she held his hand, rubbed his shoulder, whispered sweet nothings in his ear, flushed peach-pink, and undid her top buttons. They drank from the same cup; they ate fruit from each other's mouths. Monkey had no choice but to play along.

Seeing that her defenses were lowered, Monkey pressed on with his mission. "Where have you put the real fan, my little cauliflower? You must be careful with it. That Monkey, you know, is a master of disguise. He might try to trick you again."

"Here it is!" Iron-Fan giggled, spitting out an object the size of an almond leaf.

Monkey took it in his hand disbelievingly. *Can this really be it?* he wondered to himself.

Iron-Fan now rubbed her powdered cheek against his face. "Put the fan away and have another drink," she urged. "What are you thinking about?"

Monkey decided to seize the moment. "How can such a tiny thing extinguish fire?"

"Has that Jade-Face rotted your brain?" replied Iron-Fan, reckless from drink. "Surely you remember—twist the seventh red thread on the handle, chant the magic words 'hui-xu-he-xi-xi-chui-hu,' and it will grow twelve feet long and extinguish any blaze!"

Carefully committing these instructions to memory, Monkey popped the fan into his mouth, then rubbed his face and revealed his true identity. "Recognize me now?" he yelled at Iron-Fan. She was so shocked and ashamed by her sudden realization of Monkey's deception that she stumbled and fell, knocking over tables and chairs as she went. Completely indifferent to her distress, Monkey strode triumphantly out of the cave. He hopped onto a cloud that took him straight to the top of the mountain, where he spat out the fan and followed Iron-Fan's usage instructions. The good news was that it was clearly different from the earlier fake one: it immediately grew to twelve feet and was enveloped in an auspicious light and propitious vapors. The bad news was that Monkey had not thought to learn the magic for shrinking the fan back again, so he had no choice but to haul the thing back on his shoulders.

Meanwhile, Bull Demon was finally leaving his underwater banquet. Returning to the gateway, however, he discovered that his steed had vanished. "Who stole my water-repellent, golden-eyed beast?" he roared at the gathered spirits.

"It wasn't us!" they pleaded, falling to their knees. "We were all in the banqueting hall, singing, playing, and serving."

"Could an intruder have somehow got in?" wondered the dragon paterfamilias.

"I do recall seeing an unfamiliar crab wandering about," recalled one of his sons.

"I think I can guess what happened," Bull Demon said. "Before you invited me tonight, I was battling with Monkey, who wanted the Palm-Leaf Fan off me so that he could carry on his way west. He must have turned into a crab to follow me here, stolen my ride, and gone on to my wife's place to finagle the fan off her."

"Not—not the Monkey who turned Heaven upside down?" the watery spirits said, trembling.

"The very same," Bull Demon confirmed. "I'd advise you to avoid the road to the west for the time being."

Parting the water, King Bull Demon leaped out of the pool, hopped onto a yellow cloud, and made for Palm-Leaf Cave on Jade-Cloud Mountain, where he found his first wife wailing and raging, and the golden-eyed beast tethered outside. "You bastard!" Iron-Fan screamed at him. "How could you let that monkey steal your golden-eyed beast and your identity and humiliate me like that?"

"Where is he?" Bull Demon asked between gritted teeth.

"That damned ape tricked the fan off me, turned back into Monkey, and disappeared. I'm so angry I could die!"

"Calm down. I'll catch that monkey, get the fan back, then skin him, pulverize his bones, and gouge out his heart. Now, give me my weapons!"

"You don't keep your weapons here anymore," the maids pointed out.

"All right, give me my wife's weapons!" The maids handed over the two blue-bladed swords. Taking off the duck-green silk-velvet jacket he'd worn to the banquet, King Bull Demon tightened his belt and headed straight for Flame Mountain.

Soon enough, he caught up with Monkey, who was strolling merrily along toward Flame Mountain with the enormous fan on his shoulders. *So he even swindled my wife out of the trick for enlarging the fan?* Bull Demon thought. *No good asking him for it directly—he'll just fan me into oblivion. I understand that he has two comrades, a pig and a sand-spirit, both of whom I knew*

back when they were demons. I'm going to impersonate the pig,
to give that monkey a taste of his own medicine. I'll bet he's too
pleased with himself to recognize me. Bull Demon, you see, had
also mastered seventy-two transformations; he was pretty much
a match for Monkey in terms of skill set, though a little slower
and heavier on his feet. He turned himself into the exact likeness
of Pigsy, took a shortcut to get ahead, and made straight for the
self-satisfied simian.

Busy reflecting on how clever he was, Monkey didn't bother to
verify "Pigsy's" identity. "Where are you headed, Pigsy?" he asked.

"You were gone so long," answered the artful king, "that Tripitaka was worried you couldn't defeat Bull Demon, so he sent me
to help out."

"I've saved you the bother!" Monkey laughed. "I've got the
fan." Out came the whole story: the battle, the banquet, the bogus
romancing of Iron-Fan.

"That can't have been easy," said the uncharacteristically so-
licitous "Pigsy." "You must be exhausted. Let me carry the fan
for you." Monkey unthinkingly handed it over.

The bull demon was of course an authority on how to control
the fan. As soon as it was in his hands, he made a magic sign of
some sort and it was instantly as tiny as an almond leaf. "Recognize me now, wretched monkey?" he yelled, changing back to his
true form.

"What an idiot I've been!" Monkey berated himself, before pulling out his staff and bringing it down hard on Bull Demon's head.
After dodging the blow, Bull Demon fanned Monkey. Unbe-
knownst to him (and also to Monkey, in fact), after Monkey had
placed the wind-stilling elixir in his mouth while a cricket in Iron-
Fan's stomach, he had absentmindedly swallowed it and hence become utterly immovable. The appalled Bull Demon tossed the fan
into his mouth, so as to free up both hands to slash at Monkey.

While this pair of swindlers battled it out, spraying dust, dirt, sand, and rocks at each other, Tripitaka was still sitting by the road, oppressed by heat and thirst. "How strong is this King Bull Demon?" he asked the local spirit.

"His magic powers are infinite. He's an exact match for Monkey."

"Where *is* Monkey?" Tripitaka began to fret. "It doesn't take him any time to travel two thousand miles. But he's been gone for a whole day. He must be battling the bull demon. Pigsy, Sandy, which of you would like to go and help Monkey fight a bull demon with infinite magic powers? We really need that fan."

"I'd love to help," Pigsy replied, "but it's getting late, and I don't know the way."

"I do!" piped up the local spirit. "I can take you."

A resigned Pigsy hopped onto a fast easterly cloud with the spirit, until they heard a commotion of voices and wind: the battle between Monkey and Bull Demon. "Yoo-hoo, Monkey! It's me!" shouted Pigsy.

Monkey took out on Pigsy his annoyance at having fallen into Bull Demon's trap. "You've gone and properly messed things up here," he grumbled at Pigsy, who was nonplussed until Monkey explained Bull Demon's fraud through impersonation. Enraged at learning about the deception, Pigsy rushed at the bull demon, showering him with blows. Exhausted by a day's battle, Bull Demon turned into a swan and flew off; Monkey pursued him as a gyrfalcon, trying to peck the swan's eyes out. The bull demon went on the attack now as a yellow eagle; Monkey fought back as a black phoenix. Bull Demon next transformed into a musk deer; Monkey went after him as a hungry tiger. When Bull Demon became a leopard, Monkey pounced as a golden-eyed lion. Bull Demon was now a bear and Monkey an elephant, trying to wrap his python-like trunk around the bear.

With a hoot of laughter, Bull Demon returned to his true form, a huge white bull, ten thousand feet long, eight thousand feet high. Monkey also became his real self and grew to a hundred thousand feet. This time, the forty-odd guardian deities that had been detailed to watch over the pilgrims and Monkey's former antagonist Nezha pitched in to help Monkey. The outnumbered Bull Demon fled back to Iron-Fan's cave on Jade-Cloud, shutting himself inside. By this point, Iron-Fan was all for surrendering, but Bull Demon insisted on continuing to fight. An instant later, however, Pigsy smashed in the cave's second door. Leaving the fan in his wife's safekeeping, the bull demon escaped once more, but ran directly into the cosmic nets set up by a Buddhist warrior guardian from the Cliff of Mysterious Demons—for both the Buddha and the Jade Emperor had dispatched their people to bring Bull Demon to heel. With the help of three magical weapons—a wheel of immortal fire, a demon-reflecting mirror (to prevent Bull Demon from transforming again), and a lasso—Nezha finally apprehended King Bull Demon, then led him back to Iron-Fan, who, seeing the game was up, fell to her knees and surrendered the fan.

Back on the roadside where Tripitaka and Sandy were waiting, the sky lit up as Monkey and his heavenly reinforcements returned with the fan. Walking up to Flame Mountain, Monkey waved the fan once and the fire subsided; a second time and a cool breeze blew; a third time and drizzle fell from the sky. The helpful deities scattered and King Bull Demon was taken off in disgrace to see the Buddha. Iron-Fan now kneeled before Monkey and begged for her fan back. "I promise never to misbehave again. Please return my fan to me so that I may repent and begin a new life of religious study."

"First," answered Monkey, "tell me how to extinguish the fire permanently."

"You must fan the mountain forty-nine times," revealed Iron-Fan.

Monkey did so: the fire went out and the rain came. The next day he returned the fan to her. "I'm acting in good faith here. Don't let me down."

Bowing her thanks, Iron-Fan began a life of reclusive self-cultivation. The local spirit decided to stay on Flame Mountain after all, to look after the locals and live off their offerings. And the four pilgrims carried on to the west, the ground wet and cool beneath their feet.

Chapter Thirty-Three

Winter arrived again and the shivering disciples trudged on until they approached the gate of another unknown city. Just inside its outer wall, they found an elderly soldier huddled up, asleep, in the sun. Monkey shook him gently. Coming to with a start, the soldier immediately rolled to his knees and began kowtowing—for Monkey was an intimidating vision to wake up to. "Calm down," said Monkey. "I'm just a Buddhist monk from the east traveling west for scriptures. I'm a stranger here and want to know what this place is called."

The soldier got to his feet, yawning and stretching. "This city used to be the Kingdom of Bhikku, but the name changed recently to the City of Young Sons."

"And is there a king?" asked Monkey.

"Oh, yes."

"I wonder why they changed the name," Tripitaka mused when Monkey reported the conversation. "Let's go in and make inquiries." After passing through three sets of city gates, they reached a wide, thriving thoroughfare, bustling with attractive, well-dressed people. There were noisy wine shops, brightly decorated teahouses, and stores stuffed with gold and brocade. After browsing through the streets for some time, they began to notice that there was a coop big enough for geese and screened with multicolored satin curtains in front of each house. Monkey decided to investigate.

"Best not," said Tripitaka, pulling him back. "Remember how ugly you are—you'll scare the locals."

Monkey took his point. "Then I'll go in disguise." Transforming into a bee, he buzzed up to one of the coops and crawled through a gap in the curtains. Inside, he discovered a little boy sitting in the middle of the box. A visit to another ten or so coops revealed the same thing. Every box contained a little boy, between the ages of four and six: either playing, crying, eating fruit, or sleeping. Monkey revealed his findings to Tripitaka, who grew more perplexed than ever.

Following a bend in the street, they came to a government building called the Golden Pavilion Posthouse. "Let's ask here about the city, get the horse fed, and take a room for the night," said Tripitaka.

The postal-station master received them warmly, offering them tea and a meal, and prepared the guest room. "You can have your travel documents stamped at court first thing tomorrow," he told them.

After thanking him, Tripitaka had a question: "Could you tell me, please, how you rear children around here?"

"First, you need the father's sperm and the mother's blood," the stationmaster patiently explained. "Ten months after conception, the child will be born. After birth, the child drinks the mother's milk for three years, until they are weaned. You seem to have lived a very sheltered life."

"It's just that when I entered the city I noticed there was a coop containing a little boy in front of every house, and I wondered why."

The stationmaster immediately lowered his voice. "Don't ask about that, I beg you. Please go to bed and be on your way tomorrow." But Tripitaka refused to let the matter go. Finally giving in, the stationmaster dismissed all his attendants. When they were seated together, alone, beneath the lamplight, the stationmaster spoke quietly again. "This is the doing of our wicked king. This was once the Kingdom of Bhikku, but local songs have recently redubbed it the City of Young Sons. Three years ago, an old man passing himself off as a Taoist priest arrived, bringing with him a young girl, barely sixteen and as beautiful as Guanyin herself. He presented her as tribute to our king, who became so infatuated with her that he gave her the title Queen Beauty and ennobled the Taoist who brought her as the Royal Father-in-Law. Since then, the king has gorged himself day and night on her, completely ignoring all his other consorts. And now he is a physical wreck: exhausted, emaciated, unable to eat or drink, hovering between life and death. None of the palace doctors' medicines have worked. But the Royal Father-in-Law claims to know a prescription for long life, consisting of medicinal herbs gathered from distant isles—and a terrible supplement. He says that if his medicine is taken with a soup made from the hearts of 1,111 little boys, the king will live for a thousand years. The children in those coops have all been selected for slaughter. Their parents are too afraid of the king to even weep. Their only outlet for protest is satire—renaming this place the City of Young Sons. You mustn't mention any of this when you go to court tomorrow to have your travel documents checked."

The stationmaster retired for the night, but Tripitaka was left distraught with horror at the king's debauchery and cruelty. "Don't cry over other people's coffins," the pragmatic Pigsy advised him. "Ministers and sons should die if their kings and fathers ask it. It's none of our business if he wants to kill his own subjects. Let's get some sleep."

"Where's your compassion?" asked Tripitaka. "This deluded king is planning to eat human hearts to prolong his own life."

"Let's raise the matter with the king tomorrow at court," ventured Sandy, "and size up this Taoist at the same time."

"Sandy's right," agreed Monkey. "Try to sleep now, and

tomorrow I'll go with you to court. If the Taoist is just a foolish priest who believes that medicines can make you live forever, I will put him right. If he turns out to be a demon, I will destroy him to teach the king a lesson. Either way, I won't allow the king to kill any of those boys. I'm going to whisk them to a safe place outside the city this very night."

"Wonderful, Monkey!" exclaimed Tripitaka. "But please go now—there's not a moment to lose!"

After reminding Pigsy and Sandy to take care of Tripitaka, Monkey soared into the air and made a magic sign that summoned the pilgrimage's guardian deities, along with the city god, the local god, the god of the land, and a handful of other immortal administrators. "What's the emergency?" they asked, bowing and yawning. "It's the middle of the night."

"We have just learned about Bhikku's cruel king," Monkey explained. "He has been duped by a demon who has told him that eating the hearts of little boys will prolong his own life. While we come up with a plan to destroy this fiend, I want you to move the little boys inside their coops to some mountain valley or forest outside the city. I need you to keep them safe, fed, and happy for a day or two. When I've dealt with this demon, brought the king to his senses, and restored order to the kingdom, you can bring the boys back."

The obedient spirits descended onto the city, where the temperature suddenly plummeted with freezing fog and wind. While the parents took shelter from the cold, the gale swept up the 1,111 coops and the boys inside. By about midnight, every coop had been secreted outside the city walls.

Waking at dawn the next day, Tripitaka immediately dressed for his visit to court. "I'm coming, too," Monkey reminded him. "You might not be able to manage on your own."

"But you're not very good with protocol," Tripitaka worried. "You might offend the king."

"I'll go in disguise, then."

Tripitaka told Pigsy and Sandy to mind the luggage and the horse, and the stationmaster reminded Tripitaka in a whisper not to ask about matters that did not concern him. Then they set off for the court: Tripitaka resplendent in his brocade robe and gold-topped priest's hat and carrying their travel papers in a silk case, Monkey transformed into a tiny cricket and perched on top of Tripitaka's hat.

As soon as Tripitaka's visit was announced, the king invited him in for an audience, hoping to glean some wisdom from his exotic visitor. On entering the throne room, Tripitaka immediately noticed how torpid and emaciated the king was: he could barely gesture a greeting or finish a sentence. After Tripitaka presented the travel papers, the king tried and failed to focus on them, then listlessly signed, stamped, and handed them back.

Just as the king was about to ask about Tripitaka's quest for scriptures, an official announced the arrival of the Royal Father-in-Law. Supported by a young eunuch, the king got up from his throne to bow to the new arrival. Also rising to his feet, Tripitaka watched an elderly Taoist stride up to the throne. He wore a turban of pale yellow damask, a brown silk cloak patterned with plums and a blue braided sash; he grasped a nine-jointed rattan staff carved to resemble a coiled dragon. His face was jade smooth, his beard long and white; his eyes seemed to burn in their sockets. "The Royal Father-in-Law!" cried the courtiers.

"Divine presence!" wheezed the king, still bowing. "We are honored."

After the Taoist lounged on the embroidered couch to the left of the king, Tripitaka stepped forward to bow to him. "Where has this monk come from?" the Taoist asked the king, without returning the greeting. The king explained the pilgrimage and the stamping of the travel documents. "The way to the west is long and dark," said the Taoist, yawning. "Why bother?"

"Nirvana lies in the west," Tripitaka responded.

"Can the Buddha confer immortality?" the king asked.

"A Buddhist monk," explained Tripitaka, "acquires peace, knowledge, and enlightenment through meditation. He seeks immortality not through elixirs but through eliminating mortal desires."

"Pah!" snorted the Taoist, wagging his finger at Tripitaka. "Meditation gets you nothing but a sore bottom. Your precious nirvana still leaves you a rotting corpse. Taoism's your method if you want to live forever. We collect herbs, dance, clap, and generally milk the energies of heaven and earth, the sun and the moon, yin and yang, fire and water. Taoism is the greatest."

"Taoism is the greatest!" the king and his courtiers echoed, to Tripitaka's obvious discomfort. His religious preferences notwithstanding, the king still ordered his catering department to prepare a vegetarian banquet for the pilgrims before they resumed their journey westward.

Tripitaka was about to leave the palace when Monkey, now perched on his ear, buzzed: "That Taoist is a demon who has entrapped the king. Go back to the posthouse; I'll stick around to find out more."

While Tripitaka obediently returned to their lodgings, Monkey roosted on a kingfisher screen. The Commander of the Five Garrisons stepped forward to make a report. "Last night, sire, a cold wind blew away the coops containing the boys. All have vanished without a trace."

"Heaven is plotting to destroy me!" the frightened, angry king told the Taoist. "I've been on the brink of death all these months, and just as we were ready to gouge out these little boys' hearts for your divine prescription at midday today, they've disappeared."

"Calm down, Your Majesty," the Taoist said, smiling. "Heaven has just gifted you eternal life."

"What?" asked the confused king.

"As soon as I walked in, I spotted an ingredient much more effective than the hearts of 1,111 little boys. Those hearts would enable you to live only to a thousand; the new supplement I have in mind will sustain you for ten thousand years."

"What?" repeated the king, even more confused.

"That Buddhist monk, I saw immediately, has devoted himself to his faith for at least ten incarnations. He has conserved his masculine essence, his yang, all this time and is therefore ten thousand times more purely powerful than those little boys. If you wash down my medicine with a broth made from his heart, I guarantee you will live for ten millennia."

The doltish king instantly believed him. "Why didn't you say so earlier? I could have arrested him just now."

"He won't escape us," the Taoist replied silkily. "The Buddhists won't leave until they've eaten the meal prepared by the royal catering department. Send out an edict straightaway ordering the closure of all of the city gates, surround the postal station where they're staying with troops, and have them bring back the monk. First ask him nicely for his heart: promise him a state funeral and a temple, with guaranteed sacrifices. If he doesn't agree, just tie him up and gouge his heart out anyway. Child's play." As ever, the king followed his instructions to the letter.

Having overheard all of this, Monkey flew back to the postal station, where Tripitaka and the others were enjoying their royal feast. "Disaster!" he exclaimed, suddenly reappearing as Monkey.

Tripitaka promptly fainted. "Wake up!" urged Sandy, trying to get him upright.

Monkey reported everything he had learned and that the postal station was about to be surrounded by soldiers.

"You did a good thing rescuing those little boys," concluded Pigsy. "But now Tripitaka's going to be in the soup—literally."

"Whatever shall we do?" beseeched Tripitaka, sweating with fear.

"If we're to get out of this fix," considered Monkey, "we'll need to swap identities. You'll have to become my disciple for the day."

"If you can save my life," pledged Tripitaka, "I'll follow you to the ends of the earth."

"No time to waste," said Monkey. "Pigsy: mud." To avoid having to go outside—the soldiers could arrive at any moment—Pigsy pissed on a patch of the dirt floor, stirred it all together, and passed it to Monkey. Monkey molded this unlovely mixture over his face to fashion a mask, then pressed it onto Tripitaka's face. With a spell and a mouthful of magic breath, Tripitaka turned into the exact likeness of Monkey. Master and disciple then swapped clothes, and Monkey changed himself into Tripitaka— even Pigsy and Sandy couldn't tell the difference.

Once the exchange of identities was complete, they heard gongs and drums, and saw a forest of spears and swords approach— three thousand of the royal guard had surrounded the postal station. Next, an officer in a brocade uniform marched in and ordered the stationmaster to take him to Tripitaka. "The king requests another audience," the officer informed "Tripitaka" and manhandled him back to court under tight guard, where he was deposited before the throne.

"I have been ill for a long time," wheedled the king. "My Royal Father-in-Law has honored me by drawing up a prescription, for which we have all of the ingredients except one, which we need from you. If it cures me of my illness, we will build a temple in your honor, where we will make year-round sacrifices to your spirit."

"But I am just a poor monk. What could I possibly offer a king?"

"I want your heart."

"Could you be a little more specific?" the false Tripitaka responded without missing a beat. "I have quite a few of those. What color and shape do you want?"

"We want your black heart," intervened the Taoist, who'd been standing by listening all the while.

"Good, good," agreed "Tripitaka." "Bring me a knife so that I can cut open my chest. If I have a black heart in there, you're more than welcome to it." The delighted king thanked him and obtained from his attendant a curved dagger. "Tripitaka" untied his robe and opened his chest with a spectacular ripping sound. A great pile of hearts came tumbling out. All of the officials present—civil and military—paled.

"He's got a lot of heart, this Buddhist," observed the Taoist drily.

"Tripitaka" now scooped up the bleeding heap and sorted through it in full view of everyone: there was a red heart, a white heart, a yellow heart, an avaricious heart, a greedy heart, an envious heart, a petty heart, a competitive heart, an ambitious heart, a scornful heart, a murderous heart, a vicious heart, a fearful heart, a cautious heart, a depraved heart, a dark, nameless heart, and all manner of evil hearts—but no black heart.

The king was stupefied by this performance. "Take them away!" he finally managed to croak out.

Unable to control himself any longer, Monkey undid his magic and became his true self again. "You are blind!" he lectured the king. "Buddhist monks have good hearts. Your resident Taoist here is the only one with a black heart: his will do very well for the supplement. Let me cut open his chest straightaway to show you."

Now recognizing Monkey as the troublemaker who had attained such notoriety in the mortal and immortal worlds, the Taoist soared into the sky, hotly pursued by Monkey's cloud-somersault. "Where do you think you're going?" roared Monkey. The Taoist fought back with his coiled-dragon staff, and the battle raged above the city, sending its residents fleeing for cover. After about twenty clashes, it became clear that the fiend was no match for Monkey.

Vaporizing into a beam of cold light, the Taoist shot into a palace boudoir to sweep up the concubine who had so intoxicated the king, and then both vanished.

"Now you know what your Royal Father-in-Law is!" Monkey told the courtiers, returning to the palace. "Stop bowing!" he barked at them, as they prostrated themselves in gratitude. "Where's your imbecilic king?"

"He went and hid in the Hall of Prudence before the battle began," reported the officials.

"Quickly go and find him," Monkey ordered, "before those two demons kidnap him."

A few moments later, a handful of eunuchs helped the misguided king back into the throne room and the courtiers explained that Queen Beauty had disappeared along with the Royal Father-in-Law. The king bowed to Monkey. "I must say, though, you seem rather . . . different from this morning. You've lost your looks somewhat." Monkey laughingly introduced himself and explained the deception, revealing that Tripitaka and the other two disciples were back at the postal station. The grateful king asked the others to be brought to court.

Just as Tripitaka was thinking how nice it would be not to wear a mud mask lubricated with pig's urine, he heard a voice outside: "The King of Bhikku wishes to thank you at court."

"Cheer up!" exulted Pigsy. "I don't think they want your heart this time. Monkey must have triumphed!"

"But how can I return to the court with this stinky face on me?"

"We'll have to get Monkey's help on that," admitted Pigsy.

"Heavens above! What a bunch of horrors!" quavered the courtiers when the three of them emerged into the courtyard.

"Sandy and I were born like this," Pigsy explained. "But our master here will look much better once he's exfoliated."

As soon as they entered the throne room, Monkey ran up and with one magic breath restored Tripitaka to his true self. While the king gushed at Tripitaka—Buddha this, Buddha that—Monkey remained focused on the here and now. "Do you have that fiend's address? I must destroy him so that he doesn't come back to make any more trouble."

"I did ask him that when he first arrived three years ago," the embarrassed king replied. "He said he was from nearby—the village of Pure Magnificence on Willow Hill, about seventy miles south of here."

"Oh, and on the subject of missing persons: I was the one who hid the little boys," Monkey told him, smiling, "on the compassionate orders of my master. Pigsy—you come with me."

"Gladly," replied Pigsy, "but my stomach's so empty I haven't the strength."

"Quickly!" the king called out to the royal catering department.

Pigsy's stomach filled, he and Monkey traveled by cloud some seventy miles south of the city, then landed to look for the demon. There they found a stream, planted densely on both banks with thousands of willows, but no sign of a village of Pure Magnificence. Monkey promptly made a magic sign and chanted the sacred word *om*, which immediately drew out the local spirit, who knelt trembling before him. "The spirit of Willow Hill reporting for duty!"

"Calm down," said Monkey. "I'm not here to rough you up. Can you tell me where a village called Pure Magnificence is? It's meant to be around here somewhere."

"There's a cave by that name, but not a village." (Monkey arguably should have known better than to take directions from that witless king.) "Am I right that you've come from Bhikku?" the spirit asked next.

"Exactly." Monkey explained the situation and his current project of subduing a fiend last seen as a beam of cold light.

"Forgive me!" exclaimed the spirit. "As we're within the jurisdiction of Bhikku here, I ought to have protected the king from

this demon. But this fiend is so powerful that he would have made
my life a misery if I'd exposed him earlier, which is why he's been
able to make all this mischief. But you can handle him. Go up to
the willow with nine forked branches on the southern bank. Walk
three times clockwise, then three times counterclockwise around
it. Press your hands against the trunk and say 'Open' three times.
The cave will appear before you."

Monkey and Pigsy hopped across the stream and soon found the
tree. After stationing Pigsy about half a mile away, Monkey followed the spirit's instructions: the tree immediately vanished and
a double door creaked open. Dashing in, Monkey discovered a
cave with its own springlike microclimate: it was somehow bathed
in both sunlight and moonlight, luxuriant with flowers, moss, and
grasses, and fluttering with bees and butterflies. Behind a stone
screen, he saw the senior fiend and Queen Beauty in each other's
arms. Both were panting hard. "Three years' work, and just as we
were going to succeed, that ape came and ruined everything!"

"You presumptuous demons!" raged Monkey, charging at them.

The older fiend immediately let go of the beautiful one, grabbed
his dragon staff, and recommenced battle at the entrance to the
cave. "How dare you barge into my home!" he roared. "And why
do you care about the King of Bhikku?"

"I'm a Buddhist," Monkey shouted back. "How could I stand
by while all those little boys were killed?" The tumult—which
made a frightful mess of the exotic blooms, picturesque lichens,
and luminous mists—alerted Pigsy, who joined the fight as soon
as Monkey emerged, battling, from the cave. Once Pigsy joined
in, the fiend lost his nerve, turned back into a ray of cold light,
and beamed eastward, hotly pursued by his two combatants.
When Monkey and Pigsy caught up, they found a venerable immortal, the Old Star of the South Pole, pinning the beam down.

"Greetings, you old fathead!" Pigsy hailed him. "Did you catch
our fiend for us?"

"Indeed, but I trust you will both spare his life."

"Why?" Monkey asked.

"He happens to be a steed of mine," the Old Star said with a smile, "who ran away to pursue a demonic sideline. Sit!" he suddenly barked at the light beam, which immediately became a cowering, sniveling white deer. "The wretched creature had the nerve to steal my staff, too," muttered Old Star, picking up the coiled dragon stave. He hopped onto the deer and was about to leave when Monkey pulled him back.

"We still need to capture the deer's accomplice, the king's former concubine, then take the pair of them back to that idiot on the throne of Bhikku, so he can see them for what they really are." Monkey and Pigsy rushed back to the cave, where the trembling, unarmed girl did not have a chance to escape. Monkey smashed his staff down on her head; Pigsy dealt a second, crushing blow. In an instant, the beauty that had so befuddled the king morphed into a dead white vixen. "Don't mangle her anymore," Monkey instructed Pigsy. "We need the king to see her for what she really was." Pigsy dragged her by the tail out of the cave, where the Old Star was still scolding the deer for his various diabolical escapades.

Pausing only to order the local spirit to burn the cave to ashes, Monkey and company returned to the palace of Bhikku, where they exhibited the two former favorites before the king. Scarlet with embarrassment, the king muttered his thanks, then busied himself ordering the royal catering department to prepare another banquet for the visitors. After taking their seats, Tripitaka and Sandy asked how the Old Star had allowed his deer to cause so much trouble. "Oh, that," the Old Star replied with a laugh. "An immortal neighbor of mine dropped by for a game of chess, and the deer slipped away while we were playing."

At this moment, the banquet was served: a magnificent feast of dragon-shaped pastries, duck-shaped cakes, lion-shaped bonbons, and roll-shaped rolls. The brocade-draped tables were covered end to end with enormous chestnuts, lychees, peaches, dates, and persimmons; gold and silver bowls were heaped with fragrant rice. "You can have the fruit," Pigsy told Monkey after the toasts, "I'll handle the rest." He then demolished the entire banquet.

When Old Star got up to leave, the king kneeled to beg a cure for his illness. "Because I was so focused on recovering my deer," the immortal said, "I came without any elixirs. I'd have been delighted to pass a couple of nutritious formulas on to you, but your tendons and spirit have degenerated so much that no alchemy will have any effect. I do, however, have up my sleeve three fire dates, which go nicely with tea. You'd be welcome to them."

As soon as he ate them, the king felt his sickness lifting; these magic fruits later enabled him to live to a ripe old age.

"Could I have a few?" Pigsy asked. "I'm still a bit hungry."

"Afraid I've run out," Old Star apologized. "I'll send on some more when I get home." The immortal then leaped onto the deer and soared into the clouds.

"Time for us to be on our way, too," Tripitaka told his disciples. The king begged them to stay on longer as his counselors. "Less luxury and more charity," Tripitaka told him. "That's my only advice to you." Although Tripitaka absolutely refused the king's offer of gold and silver to cover their journey onward, the king insisted that he get into the royal carriage and be pushed through the streets and out of the city by the monarch and his courtiers. As the townsfolk came out to watch, another howling gale—the work of the friendly local spirits who had previously helped Monkey—deposited by the side of the road 1,111 coops, each containing a wailing little boy. Moments later, their ecstatic parents rushed up, hugging, kissing, and soothing their lost children.

Chapter Thirty-Four

After crossing the Mountain of Hidden Mists, the travelers approached another city. "Are we nearly there yet?" Tripitaka asked Monkey.

"Even if we're now on the outskirts of India," considered Monkey, "we could still be a long way from the Buddha's Thunderclap Monastery on Soul Mountain. Let's find out what this place is."

Once through the gates, the travelers found the streets deserted until they eventually came to a busy marketplace, which Pigsy barged through with his snout. "Who are you? Where are you from?" a handful of constables asked.

For fear that his disciples might make trouble, Tripitaka took over the talking, explaining their quest. "And what is this place called, I wonder?"

"You've reached Phoenix-Immortal, an outer prefecture of India. After several years of drought, the local prefect is advertising for a priest to pray for rain," a constable said, indicating a notice on a building nearby, which the pilgrims crowded round to read.

Our wells and rivers are dry. Our people are starving and forced to sell or abandon their children. The Prefect of Phoenix-Immortal in the Great Kingdom of India therefore seeks a master of religion to bring back the rain.

"Can any of you help?" Tripitaka asked his disciples.

"I can conjure the odd weather effect," said Monkey. "Overturning rivers, stirring up seas, changing the course of stars, belching fog and clouds, hunting down the moon while carrying a mountain, summoning wind and rain. Nothing spectacular."

The delighted officials informed their prefect, who warmly invited the travelers to his official residence, where he served them tea and a meal that Pigsy ate with terrifying, tigerish abandon, while their waiters scurried back and forth with soup and rice. When Pigsy was finally full, the prefect told his sorry tale: three years of drought had killed two-thirds of the population; the remaining third was weak with starvation. "I've heard enough," said Monkey. "Will you look after Tripitaka while I execute my plan?"

"Speaking of which," Sandy interjected, "what is your plan, Monkey?"

"Easy. You two stand by while I summon a dragon to make some rain." The prefect, meanwhile, burned some incense and Tripitaka kept himself busy reciting a sutra.

After a magic spell from Monkey, a dark cloud rose up from the east and landed gently in the courtyard, becoming Aoguang, the Dragon King of the Eastern Ocean. "What can I do for you, Monkey?"

"I wanted to know why you've refused to provide rain to this prefecture for several years."

"May I respectfully remind you that although I'm technically in charge of rainmaking, I can't make it happen without Heavenly authorization. It's more than my job's worth."

"That's a lame excuse," Monkey complained.

"Look," explained the dragon king. "Heaven's not approved it, and in any case I didn't bring my team of rainmakers with me. How about this: I'll go rally the troops while you apply for a rain permit from Heaven. When the Jade Emperor's signed off on it, you'll get every single specified drop."

Unable to find a reasonable counterargument, Monkey let Aoguang return to the ocean and told his fellow pilgrims that he had to make a trip to Heaven. In a single cloud-somersault, Monkey was at the West Gate. "Afternoon, Monkey," the duty patrol greeted him. "Got those scriptures yet?"

"Any day now," answered Monkey. "Thing is—we've just reached Phoenix-Immortal in India. There's been no rain for three years and the people are starving. I asked the dragon king to do what's necessary, but he told me I had to sort out some paperwork with the Jade Emperor first."

He then barged into the antechamber to the throne room. "What are you doing here?" asked the Four Heavenly Preceptors, barring his way. Monkey explained his mission—to request rain for Phoenix-Immortal. The preceptors glanced perfunctorily down at their gold tablets, then back up at Monkey. "Heaven says no."

"Let me see the Jade Emperor," Monkey insisted. "I'll talk him around." Sighing at the boldness of the creature, the preceptors showed him in.

"While on a tour of Heaven and Earth three years ago," pronounced the Jade Emperor, "we saw the prefect knock over a table of offerings and feed them to his dogs while uttering obscenities. As punishment, we created three impossible challenges in the Hall Draped with Fragrance—take Monkey to see them. Only when these have been completed will we grant the prefect rain; otherwise, he should put up and shut up."

The four preceptors led Monkey into the hall in question, where he found a hundred-foot rice pyramid and a two-hundred-foot noodle mountain. A chicken no bigger than a human fist pecked at the rice with very little commitment, while a Pekinese lapped lackadaisically at the noodles. To one side a golden lock—some fifteen inches long—was suspended over a tiny flame, which was barely singeing the lock's very substantial key. "What does all this mean?" Monkey asked.

"After the prefect's transgression against Heaven," the preceptors explained, "the Jade Emperor ruled that there will be no rain until the chicken has pecked all the rice, the dog has lapped up all the noodles, and the flame has burned through the lock." Even Monkey paled at the size of the tasks and exited the hall, too crestfallen to press the Jade Emperor again. "Take heart," the preceptors comforted him. "Virtue will overcome these challenges and melt Heaven's anger."

Monkey cloud-traveled back to India to confront the prefect. "You are the cause of your people's suffering! Three years ago you fed offerings to Heaven to your dogs. What were you thinking?"

The prefect instantly kneeled before him. "It's true. That day, I'd had an argument with my wife—she started it—and in a fury I smashed the offerings to the floor and let the dogs eat them up. I've felt terrible about it ever since. And now Heaven is punishing my people for it!"

"The Jade Emperor has established three monuments to your crime," Monkey told him, evoking the two starchy mountains— and their lethargic consumers—and the lock, all of which needed to be vanquished before rain would return.

Pigsy's eyes lit up, for this was his favorite kind of impossible challenge. "Leave it to me—I'll polish off the rice and noodles in a single sitting, smash the lock, and there's your rain!"

"No, Pigsy," Monkey chided him. "This is Heavenly retribution. You can't eat or bash it into submission."

"Then what *can* we do?" the still-kneeling prefect asked.

"It's actually quite straightforward," said Monkey. "We just need some serious piety. You must all worship and recite scriptures like there's no tomorrow. Otherwise, there is no tomorrow."

The prefect ordered Buddhist *and* Taoist clerics to conduct services for three days, then write and post detailed reports of the proceedings to Heaven by burning them. Every household in the city was ordered to burn incense and chant the Buddha's name, and soon the city was a chorus of virtue. "You two keep an eye on Tripitaka," Monkey told Pigsy and Sandy. "I'm going to report back to the Jade Emperor about Phoenix-Immortal's festival of piety."

As Monkey approached the gate to Heaven, he encountered a courier with an armful of Phoenix-Immortal's religious reports. "Good work, Monkey," the courier saluted him. "I'm just off to present these to the Jade Emperor right now. You can go straight to the Department of the Seasons and book the thunder gods. Once they've done their bit, rain will quickly follow."

Monkey redirected his cloud to the specified bureau, where the divinity on reception announced the visitor to their minister, who hurried out from behind a nine-phoenix cinnabar screen. "How can I help you, Monkey?" Monkey explained his mission: to request thunder for Phoenix-Immortal. "Is that authorized?" the celestial being queried. "I understand that three conditions have to be met first."

"I know. But the Four Heavenly Preceptors also told me that the prefect could expiate his offense through religious devotion. The inhabitants of the city have been ostentatiously holy for the past three days, and a courier has just delivered their documents of repentance to the Jade Emperor."

"In that case," replied the minister, "the four thunder dukes and the Dame of Lightning are yours for the day."

In the sky above Phoenix-Immortal, Monkey conducted the dignitaries as they generated flashes of purple-gold light and deafening peals of thunder. The locals—who had not seen anything like this for three long years—fell to their knees and cried out to the Buddha.

While Monkey conducted this display, the courier delivered the piety reports to the throne room. "And what of the Three Impossible Challenges?" the Jade Emperor now asked.

"The rice and noodles have vanished," a minion from the Hall Draped with Fragrance reported, "and the lock is broken."

"I hereby order," pronounced the emperor, "the Departments of Wind, Cloud, and Rain to release three feet and forty-two drops of rain." Once the Four Heavenly Preceptors had liaised with the departments in question, the magic bureaucracy released a torrent over Phoenix-Immortal: it was as if whole rivers and seas were pouring from the sky. The streets ran with water; dying plants and trees revived.

After every single drop of the allotted rain had fallen, Monkey choreographed a round of thanks to the thunder-, lightning-, and rain-spirits. "Step out from the clouds and reveal yourselves," he told the divine administrators, "so that they will lavish you with sacrifices." The clouds parted to reveal the silver-bearded dragon king, the beaked thunder god, the jade-faced Cloud-Boy, and the bouffant-eyebrowed Earl of Wind. After the deities had received the adulation of the crowds below for a couple of hours, Monkey dismissed them all back to Heaven: "Thanks for coming. I'll make sure these mortals keep up the worship. In return, be certain to give them rain every ten days. Don't forget—if you want those sacrifices!" The gods scattered and Monkey returned to earth.

"Our work's done here," Monkey told Tripitaka. "Time to pack up and move on." The people of the prefecture tried to shower the pilgrims with money and gifts—all of which were declined. A huge farewell party—with banners, streamers, and drums—gathered to send the pilgrims off; the locals followed them for about thirty miles before regretfully letting them go. After watching the pilgrims disappear into the horizon, they tearfully returned to their homes.

"Well," Tripitaka said to Monkey as they walked along, "this time you've really outdone yourself in compassion. What you did there was even more impressive than in Bhikku."

"At Bhikku," Sandy chimed in, "you saved 1,111 little boys. But in Phoenix-Immortal, you saved hundreds and thousands of people from starvation. Hurrah for Monkey's merciful magic!"

"Oh, yes, good show, Monkey," snarked Pigsy. "So how about showing my feet some mercy? You're always treading on my toes. Or making sure I'm the one who gets tied up and scrubbed for the steamer so that you can play the hero. Or you could at least have let us stay in Phoenix-Immortal for a few months, so that I could get a square meal or two under my belt. I'm wasting away here. But no—Monkey had to hurry us out of there."

"Do you ever think about anything except your stomach?" snapped Tripitaka. "Get a move on, and don't talk back!"

Pouting and muttering to himself, Pigsy trudged on.

Chapter Thirty-Five

The landscape was now covered with gemlike flowers, jadelike grasses, ancient cypresses, and emerald pines. Everyone they met hummed sutras as they walked and lavished the pilgrims with food. After another week's travel, a vertiginous complex of towers and pavilions rose up before them. "For the last fourteen years," Monkey told Tripitaka, "you've been asking me how much farther. Now we've reached the Buddha's Western Heaven and you don't even get off your horse." The startled Tripitaka tumbled to the ground as quickly as he could.

At the compound gate, the pilgrims were met by a young Taoist gatekeeper—a boy of exceptional beauty, dressed in a brocade robe. "Are you the scripture seekers from the east?"

While Tripitaka brushed the dust of the journey off his robe, Monkey made introductions. "This is Great Golden-Head, custodian of Jade-Truth Taoist temple at the foot of Soul Mountain."

The boy laughed. "That Guanyin has a very loose notion of time. Much longer than a decade ago, she told me to expect you in a couple of years. We meet at last!" Tripitaka bowed and thanked Great Golden-Head for his patience. The four pilgrims entered the temple and took tea and a meal, while the spirit asked his underlings to heat some scented water so that the pilgrims could bathe before meeting the Buddha.

After a night's rest in the temple, Tripitaka changed into his patchwork brocade robe and Vairocana hat, picked up his staff, and took leave of his immortal host. "You seem almost a different person from the ragged traveler of yesterday," said Great Golden-Head with a smile. "Today you resemble a true son of the Buddha! Let me show you where to go from here."

"No need," said Monkey. "I know my way around Thunderclap."

"You know the way through the clouds, but our wise monk here still can't fly. You must stick to the road." Great Golden-Head took Tripitaka by the hand and led him out of the temple's back door, behind which lay Soul Mountain. "Do you see a place, halfway up to Heaven, shrouded in auspicious light and hallowed mist? That is the spiritual home of the Buddha." Tripitaka began bowing at the very sight of it.

"Save your energy," Monkey advised, laughing. "We've a good long way to go still! If you insist on kowtowing all the way there, you'll give yourself a terrible headache."

Led by Monkey, the pilgrims climbed slowly up until they encountered a fast-flowing river, some eight miles wide, in an apparently deserted landscape. "This can't be the right way," Tripitaka objected. "There's no boat to take us across."

"See that bridge over there?" said Monkey. "It will take us to the other side."

Approaching the bridge, Tripitaka read the inscription on the tablet next to it: CROSSING TO THE CLOUDS. The bridge itself was a single narrow, slippery log, thronged with rainbows. He began shaking like jelly. "It's impossible! We have to find another way."

"Stay there," Monkey instructed with a giggle. "I'll show you how it's done." In one bound he was across. "Come on!" he shouted from the other side. Tripitaka, Pigsy, and Sandy flatly refused to move.

Monkey hopped back over and tugged at Pigsy, who hurled himself at the ground in protest. "I can't do it! I'll hitch a lift on some passing mist!"

"You can't cheat with cloud-travel in a place like this! Unless you walk across the bridge, you'll never become a Buddha."

"No skin off my snout. I like being a pig."

While the two of them pushed and tugged at each other, Tripitaka spotted a boat farther down the river. "Over here!" he cried. As the boat approached them on the bank, the pilgrims saw that it had no base; Monkey immediately realized that its pilot was the Guiding Buddha, but he said nothing to the others. "How can we cross in a bottomless boat?" panicked Tripitaka.

"This boat is immune to wind, waves, and time," the boatman informed him. "It has no end and no beginning, and carries its passengers to eternal peace and joy."

"Sounds perfect," said Monkey. "Hop on, everyone." When Tripitaka continued to hesitate, Monkey gave him a good shove; the Buddhist master promptly fell into the river. The boatman quickly fished him out, and the religious master stood on one side of the boat wringing his clothes out, stamping his shoes, and grumbling at Monkey, who was busy helping Sandy and Pigsy get the horse and luggage on board. As soon as the boatman began gently punting across the river, a corpse floated past. Monkey smiled at the terror-stricken Tripitaka. "Don't be afraid. It's you."

"So it is!" Pigsy and Sandy exclaimed, clapping their hands.

"Congratulations!" added the boatman.

They were soon safely across, and Tripitaka skipped lightly onto the bank. They had truly reached the other shore, breaking free of their mortal senses—sight, sound, smell, taste, touch, and thought. The boat and its pilot vanished.

The four of them sprang up Soul Mountain. Soon, Thunderclap Monastery came into view: its agate-brick, golden-tiled turrets rose up out of cliffs scented with orchids. Divine apes picked peaches in its orchards; white cranes perched on pine branches; phoenixes swooped and pirouetted amid palaces, pavilions, and towers. Practically dancing with excitement, Tripitaka approached the monastery gate, where he was stopped and asked for his credentials by the Buddha's Four Guardian Kings. "Wait here while we announce you."

Delighted to learn that the pilgrims had finally arrived, the Buddha mobilized his full complement of deities—the Eight Bodhisattvas, the Four Guardian Kings, the Five Hundred Arhats, the Three Thousand Protectors, the Eleven Great Orbs, and the Eighteen Custodians of Monasteries—to line up in two columns to greet the travelers, then issued to Tripitaka a golden decree of summons, which was passed back, from gate to gate, eventually reaching the pilgrims at the front entrance.

The pilgrims prostrated themselves three times before the Buddha in the Great Hero Hall and then to his attendants to the left and the right. They showed their travel papers to the Buddha, who examined them carefully. "The Great Emperor of the Tang commanded me to beg you for scriptures of salvation," Tripitaka said. "Please grant this wish, so that I may return to my country as soon as possible."

The Buddha opened his merciful mouth of mercy: "Due to the size, fertility, wealth, and populousness of your country, it is rife with greed, violence, licentiousness, bullying, and trickery. Your people do not follow the Buddha's teachings or cultivate good karma. They are disloyal, unfilial, mendacious, immoral, unkind, and cruel. Due to their thoroughgoing wickedness, after death your people are banished to the darkness of Hell, where they are pounded, pestled, pounded some more, then reincarnated as beasts, mostly of the furred and horned variety, so that they can repay their debts to society in their next existence by becoming

food for others. In sum, for the above reasons, they are condemned to eternal perdition in my Buddhist Hell, with no hope
of deliverance. Your Confucius preached benevolence, righteous-
ness, ritual, and wisdom; generations of your rulers have devised
all kinds of punishments—imprisonment, banishment, hanging,
beheading—to police the conduct of your people. None of this
has managed to curb the foolish, the blind, and the reckless. But
I have here three baskets of scriptures—15,144 scrolls in total—
that can release mortals from vexations, calamities, and transgressions. One set speaks of Heaven, one of Earth; the third
redeems the damned. The path to virtue and immortality, they
cover astronomy, geography, biography, birds, beasts, flowers,
trees, tools, and human affairs across the four continents of the
world. Given how far you've traveled, I'd love to give you the
entire set, but unfortunately your compatriots are just too stupid
to appreciate them." The Buddha now called to two of his attendants: "Take our four pilgrims here to the Pavilion of Treasures
and give them something to eat. Then choose a few scrolls for
them to take back to the east as a token of our compassion."

In the Pavilion of Treasures, the travelers fell upon an extraordinary, immortal feast of strange food and fragrant tea. Then the
two attendants led them up to the manuscripts room and showed
them cases and jeweled chests, all marked with red labels, on
which the titles of the different sutras (and the number of scrolls)
were written in neat, regular script. At this point the conversation
took a businesslike turn. "So what treats did you bring us from
China?" the guides quizzed the travelers. "Hand them over and
you'll get your scriptures."

"We—we didn't bring any," explained a nonplussed Tripitaka.
"It was such a long journey."

"Hilarious!" guffawed the Buddha's honored attendants. "If
we gave out the scriptures for free, our descendants would starve
to death."

Their finagling enraged Monkey. "I'm going to tell on you to the Buddha. He'll get you to cough up."

"Shut up!" snapped one of the attendants. "All right, come and get your scriptures."

Controlling their irritation—and Monkey—Pigsy and Sandy loaded the horse with scrolls, then piled the rest onto carrying poles. The pilgrims kowtowed their thanks to the Buddha, then set off back down the mountain.

Back in the Pavilion of Treasures, the Buddha of the Archive had heard and seen everything, including the fact that those two attendants had given the pilgrims the wordless versions of the scripture scrolls. *Most Chinese priests,* he thought, smiling, *are so benighted that they won't understand the value of the wordless scriptures, and all the effort of the pilgrimage will be wasted.* He called the duty librarian over. "Use your magic to catch up with Tripitaka. Get the wordless scriptures off him so that he comes back for the written versions. Hurry!" The librarian swept out of the monastery complex on a gale that scattered the complex's apes, cranes, and phoenixes, and snapped pines and bamboos.

As this fragrant wind churned around Tripitaka, he assumed it was just an auspicious omen from the Buddha. So he was caught completely unawares when a hand reached down and snatched all the scriptures from the horse's back. Tripitaka yelped in terror, Pigsy rolled on the ground, and Sandy stood frozen to the spot. It was left to Monkey to chase the larcenous hand into the air. Spotting Monkey closing in, the emissary feared a blow from that infamous staff. He therefore ripped open the bags of scriptures and scattered their contents over the dusty ground. Monkey immediately abandoned his pursuit and returned to earth to retrieve them.

Pigsy and Monkey gathered the scattered scriptures and brought them back to the weeping Tripitaka. "Oh, disciples!" Tripitaka wailed. "We are still persecuted by demons, even in the land of ultimate bliss!" To check for damage, Sandy unrolled one of the scriptures that his two fellow disciples were clutching to their chests and discovered that it was completely blank. He showed it to Tripitaka. "What can this mean?" he asked. Monkey opened another; again, a perfect blank. They unrolled every single one; all were blank.

"How can I take these back to the emperor?" Tripitaka wondered. "He would have my head for the insult."

"Just because we didn't have any presents for those attendants," Monkey deduced, "they've given us blank scrolls. Let's go straight back to the Buddha and accuse them of extortion *and* fraud— twice the fun."

The four of them slogged back up the mountain. They soon found themselves at the temple gates again. "Exchange or return?" the laughing attendants asked, ushering the four of them back into the Great Hero Hall, where Monkey proceeded to tear into the Buddha.

"Do you have any idea what we've been through the past fourteen years? And then your servants demanded a bribe and, when we refused, conned us with blank scrolls. I demand satisfaction!"

"Calm down," the Buddha said with a chuckle. "I knew perfectly well that those two would ask for a token of your esteem. You don't get something for nothing, you know—and certainly not scriptures of salvation. Not so long ago, a number of our priests recited scriptures to a human family to protect them from danger and help their dead escape Hell. But they asked for only three pecks and three pints of rice in payment. I told them they'd undersold themselves and that they'd as good as given away the family fortune. So this time around, when you refused to come up with the goods, they gave you blank scrolls. Actually, these blank scrolls are just as good and true as written ones. But seeing as you creatures from the east are too dim to see it, I suppose I'd better give you the ones with writing on them." He now turned once more to the original two attendants. "Select for them a few written scrolls."

Back the attendants and disciples went to the pavilion; again, the former demanded a "gift." This time Tripitaka asked Sandy to dig out the purple-gold alms bowl, which he then presented with both hands. "Due to our poverty and the length of our journey, we were unable to prepare any presents. But please accept as a token of our gratitude this alms bowl that the Tang emperor gave us to beg for food along the way. When we return to the Tang court with the true teachings, the emperor will be sure to reward you richly. Only this time, do give us the written versions."

One of the attendants smiled gently and took the bowl. The various orderlies in the pavilion began sniggering and nudging one another: "Outrageous! Imagine asking scripture seekers for a bribe!" The rapacious attendants now began to look rather embarrassed, but not enough to relinquish the bowl.

One of them set to digging out scrolls, which they passed to Tripitaka. "Check every one," Tripitaka instructed his disciples. "We don't want a repeat of last time." Every single one—5,048 in total, a full canon—contained writing. Tripitaka and his disciples returned to bow before the Buddha.

"These scriptures are priceless," the Buddha informed them. "After you deliver them to China, no one should touch them without fasting and bathing first. Worship them! They contain the mysteries of immortality, the Way, and myriad transformations."

Once more, Tripitaka set off down the mountain.

After the pilgrims had left, Guanyin stepped forward. "Fourteen years ago, you ordered me to find a seeker of scriptures in the east. Today, after 5,040 days he has completed the pilgrimage—just eight days short of the perfect canonical number of 5,048. May we consider my mission accomplished?"

"You have done well," replied the Buddha, then turned to eight warrior attendants. "Use your magic to carry Tripitaka back to the east. As soon as he has delivered the scriptures, bring him back here. You have eight days to accomplish this, to ensure the pilgrimage takes exactly 5,048 days. Do not be late!"

The attendants swept the pilgrims into the clouds and all hurtled eastward, buoyant with enlightenment.

Chapter Thirty-Six

Guanyin now held a summit at the gates to Thunderclap with the spirits she had deputized to escort the pilgrims. "You ordered us to protect Tripitaka on his journey to the west," they said to her. "Now that he has reached his destination, may we be discharged?"

"Of course," she agreed happily. "And how did the pilgrims behave on their journey?"

"With great dedication and determination," answered the deities, "through appalling trials, all cataloged here." They now handed over a dossier of calamities, which Guanyin perused. Every single unfortunate event was listed: from the tragedy of Tripitaka's parents to acquiring the three disciples, being captured multiple times, abducted by wind, tied up, impregnated, and married, as well as coming very close to being lacquered, minced, sautéed, steamed, pickled, cured, liquefied, and mated with various fiends.

"But Buddhist immortality can be attained only through nine times nine," fretted the Bodhisattva. "Tripitaka here has undergone just eighty ordeals. He's one short." She now turned to one of her subordinates. "Go after the Buddha's escorts and create one more torment. Fast as you can!"

After one day and night of express cloud-traveling, the envoy caught up and whispered some urgent instructions to the Buddha's chaperones, who smartly turned off the wind that had been carrying the pilgrims, and the four of them, plus the horse and the scriptures, instantly fell to the ground—for immortality is a stickler for arithmetic.

Tripitaka was terrified by the return to the profane ground, but the disciples seemed to find it hilarious. "More haste, less speed!" Pigsy chortled nonsensically.

"Sit on one beach for ten days, then cross nine in a day," Monkey added, "as the proverb says."

"Oh, shut up, both of you," snapped Tripitaka. "Where are we?"

"I recognize this place," said Sandy, looking about him. "Can you hear water?"

Monkey now jumped into the air to get an aerial view. "Ah, yes. We're on the west bank of the River to Heaven," he reported.

"I remember," said Tripitaka. "Last time, we were carried across by an ancient white turtle. But what shall we do this time?"

"The Buddha said the Chinese were liars and cheats," harrumphed Pigsy, no longer seeing the funny side. "Well, I'm not too impressed with his people either. They were meant to take us all the way back to the Tang empire. Why have they dumped us here in the middle of nowhere?"

"Stop whining," said Sandy. "Now that Tripitaka has shed his mortal form, he won't sink in the water. Let's use our magic to carry him across."

Monkey, however, knew that Tripitaka was one short of the sacred number of nine times nine ordeals and that was why they were marooned on this riverbank. "It won't work!" he told the others.

As they argued back and forth, a voice called out to them: "Over here!" The disciples now saw, on an otherwise deserted bank, a large white turtle poke its neck out of the water. "What took you so long, Tripitaka?"

"You're a sight for sore eyes, turtle!" Monkey hailed him with a grin. "Will you help us across again?" The turtle crawled out of the river, and Monkey told the others to get onto its back. As before, Monkey balanced one foot on the turtle's head and the other on its neck. "Off you go, turtle. Steady now."

Once again the elderly turtle stretched out its legs and glided through the water as if on flat ground, carrying the four disciples and the horse toward the eastern shore. On they went until, approaching the east bank that afternoon, the turtle spoke again: "When I carried you across the river all those years ago, I begged you to ask the Buddha when I would be permitted to take human form. I wonder what he said."

Now Tripitaka, upon reaching the Western Heaven, had been very taken up with bathing in fragrant water, feasting on divine delicacies, shedding his mortal form, meeting the Buddha, and the like. Of course he hadn't asked when the turtle would become human. He dared not lie; choosing instead to be economical with the truth, he fell silent. Instantly understanding what had happened, the turtle shook all its passengers into the river and dived down out of sight. It was just as well that Tripitaka had finally cast off his mortal body; otherwise, he would have sunk straight to the bottom. Pigsy, Sandy, and the horse, formerly a dragon, were of course perfectly at home in the water. A laughing Monkey, meanwhile, hauled Tripitaka out of the water and deposited him on the east bank. But clothes, scriptures, saddle, and bridle were soaked.

With the sun still high in the sky, the pilgrims spread out the scriptures to dry on some nearby boulders. To Tripitaka's dismay, when they tried to repack them, the scrolls of one sutra had stuck to the rocks and had to be torn off. For this reason, that sutra today remains incomplete, and the text can still be read on the boulder on which the scrolls were dried. "We should have been more careful," tutted Tripitaka.

"Nothing's perfect," Monkey said, laughing. "Not even Heaven and Earth. Now the sutra suits the flawed nature of the cosmos." They stopped briefly for a meal at a monastery, where Pigsy complained that losing his mortal frame had quite taken away his appetite (but he still managed to put away nine dishes and twenty to thirty steamed buns). Just as the pilgrims were searching for the road to the east, the Buddha's attendants called out to them from midair: "Follow us!" Tripitaka and the others rose weightlessly up into the second magic wind that the Buddha's attendants had generated.

In a matter of hours, Chang'an came into view. That day, the emperor happened to have climbed up to the Scripture Anticipation Tower that he had had built more than ten years previously. From this vantage point, he immediately noticed something unusual: fragrant winds and an auspicious haze emanating from the west.

"We've reached our destination," the Buddha's attendants told Tripitaka, still in midair. "But as the locals are actually quite intelligent, we fear they might recognize us if we escort you to earth. Probably best if you go down alone, deliver the scriptures, then meet us back here, and we'll return together to the Buddha."

"Tripitaka can't manage all those bags and the horse on his own," objected Monkey. "We'll escort him down, then bring him back."

"The Buddha said that the whole trip should take no more than eight days," worried one of the attendants. "We've been gone more than four already, and we're afraid that once Pigsy gets a sniff of the delights of the Tang empire, we'll never get him back to nirvana in time."

"Rude!" Pigsy laughed. "I'm up for imminent promotion to Buddhahood. Why would I want to linger in the mortal world? Wait for us here, and I'll be back before you know it to get canonized."

The pilgrims and their horse landed their cloud next to the Scripture Anticipation Tower, and the emperor and his officials immediately came down to receive them. Tripitaka prostrated

himself, but the emperor personally raised him up. "And who are
these people with you?" he asked.

"The disciples that I acquired along the way," Tripitaka replied.

The group made a triumphant entry into the city. Soon the capital buzzed with the news of Tripitaka's return. The monks at the
Temple of Immense Blessings—Tripitaka's old place in Chang'an—
guessed the news through another channel. On the day of Tripitaka's homecoming, they noticed that the pines by the temple gate
were pointing eastward. "Strange!" they cried. "There was no
wind last night strong enough to bend the tops of the trees."

"Put on your best robes!" exclaimed one of Tripitaka's former
disciples with a retentive memory. "Tripitaka is back." They all
hurried onto the city streets, where the news of Tripitaka's return
was confirmed by passersby. The monks ran to catch up with the
emperor's cortege and followed it to the gate of the court, where
Tripitaka went in and presented the scriptures to the emperor.

"How many are there?" Taizong wanted to know. "And how
did you acquire them?"

Tripitaka began at the end: with the demands of the Buddha's
attendants, the haggling over the going rate for the scripture hand-
over, and the subsequent sacrifice of the purple-gold begging bowl.
"In return, we received a full canon of scriptures: 5,048 scrolls."

The delighted emperor promptly ordered the imperial catering
department to prepare a banquet. Only then did he notice how
unusual-looking Tripitaka's disciples were. "Are they foreigners?"
he asked.

Tripitaka now introduced them properly. First, there was Monkey, the bringer of mischief of five hundred years past, now a
devoted Buddhist. "His protection was invaluable on the journey." Next came Pigsy, once a committed fiend from Tibet, sub-
sequently converted by Guanyin and subdued by Monkey. "He
carried the luggage and helped us cross rivers." Then Sandy, who
repented of his cannibalistic ways at the River of Flowing Sand.

Finally, Tripitaka explained that—although it looked identical—the horse was not the one the emperor had originally given him. "When we tried to cross the Brook of Eagle's Sorrow on Serpent's Coil Mountain, your horse was eaten by this horse. Except at the time, this horse was the princeling son of the Dragon King of the Western Ocean. He would have been executed for setting fire to some pearls but for the intervention of Guanyin, who changed him into a horse identical to the one he had eaten. He carried me over the most treacherous, precipitous terrain, and brought the scriptures back to Chang'an."

Taking all this in stride, Taizong asked how long the journey to the west was. "Guanyin told us it was 108,000 miles. I did not record the distance as I went along, but I know we traveled through fourteen winters and fourteen summers. Every day, we crossed mountains, forests, and fast, wide rivers. We passed through many kingdoms, whose rulers stamped and signed our travel papers." Tripitaka asked his disciples to present their documents to the emperor, who studied the seals of the faraway kingdoms through which the pilgrims had traveled: Precious Image, Cart-Slow, Western Liang, Bhikku, and many others.

Filing the documents away, the emperor led Tripitaka by the hand to the banquet. "How are your disciples' table manners?"

Tripitaka tried to answer diplomatically: "They all started out as fiends in the wilderness. Some imperial forbearance might be necessary."

The emperor just smiled. "To the feast!"

Gazing around the banquet hall, the pilgrims appreciated how great China truly was and how mediocre the kingdoms of the west were by comparison. The doorway was draped with embroidered brocade, the floor cushioned with red carpets. Exotic incense whirled about them as they were served extraordinary delicacies on gold and jade platters: sweet mushrooms, exotic seaweeds, sugarcoated taros, gingered bamboo, peppered radishes, shredded mustard melon, steamed breads, and honeyed pastries. There were heaps of walnuts, persimmons, lychees, chestnuts, dates, rabbit-head pears, pine nuts, lotus seeds, giant grapes, crab apples, plums, strawberries—every species of fruit, seed, and nut from all parts of the empire was represented. Crystal goblets and amber cups brimmed with wines and fragrant teas.

After a day of celebrations, the pilgrims paid a visit to the Temple of Immense Blessings, where Pigsy distinguished himself by not demanding refreshments or indeed making any kind of mischief. Monkey and Sandy also behaved themselves, for achieving Buddhist enlightenment had brought them inner peace.

At court the following morning, Tripitaka asked the emperor to make copies of the scriptures to distribute through the empire, so that the precious originals could be preserved. The emperor then requested Tripitaka to recite the Buddha's words. "We must go first to a place of worship," Tripitaka declared. "A palace is no place to speak holy texts." The emperor ordered his officials to carry the scrolls to the holiest temple in the empire: the Wild Goose Pagoda. There, Tripitaka clambered onto a dais and was about to begin his oration when a fragrant wind rose up.

"Drop the scrolls and follow us back to the west," cried the Buddha's time-keeping attendants from above. All the pilgrims— including the horse—floated into the air and soared westward. The startled Taizong and his officials bowed to the sky and pledged to circulate the texts that Tripitaka had traveled so far to obtain. They selected priests to convene a mass in the Wild Goose Pagoda Temple; the priests read scriptures to deliver the damned and celebrate the virtuous.

And so the Buddha's attendants and the pilgrims completed their round trip within the stipulated eight days. On returning to Soul Mountain, they were immediately ushered back to the Great Hero Hall and given jobs in the Thunderclap administration. The Buddha turned first to Tripitaka, "In a previous incarnation you were my second-favorite disciple. But because you didn't pay attention in one of my lectures, I demoted you to reincarnation in the east. Fortunately, you kept the faith by undertaking a journey of 108,000 miles to bring Buddhist teachings back to China. I therefore appoint you Sandalwood Buddha.

"Now, Monkey. We didn't get off to the best of starts, what with your urinating on my hand and my pinning you beneath the Five-Phases Mountain for five hundred years. Since then, however, you have embraced my teachings and truly distinguished yourself in defeating demons. For your unwavering loyalty, I appoint you Buddha Victorious in Struggle.

"Pigsy, you were once a water god of the Heavenly River, banished to the mortal world and reincarnated as a pig after you got drunk and propositioned the moon goddess. Fortunately, you converted to Buddhism and protected Tripitaka on his journey here. Unfortunately, you remained susceptible to greed and lust. Nonetheless, in recognition of your service carrying the bags, I'm still going to give you a job: Altar Service Attendant."

"What?" spluttered Pigsy. "They're both Buddhas! How come I'm a rotten service attendant?"

"Because you're still lazy and talk back, and retain an enormous appetite. Think about it. You'll get to clean up the offerings whenever there are Buddhist services, anywhere in the world.

"Sandy, you were the great General of Curtain-Drawing. Because you smashed a crystal cup during the Great Grand Festival of Immortal Peaches, you were banished to the River of Flowing Sand, where you compounded your sin by eating humans. Fortunately, you embraced our teachings and helped Tripitaka by leading the horse on the pilgrimage. I therefore appoint you Golden-Bodied Arhat."

The Buddha turned finally to the horse. "You were once the dragon prince of the Western Ocean until your father had you condemned to death for disobedience. But because you embraced our teachings and carried Tripitaka on his journey to the west, and then the scriptures back to the east, I hereby promote you to Heavenly Dragon of the Order of Eight Supernatural Beasts."

Once the pilgrims had kowtowed their thanks to the Buddha, the horse was pushed into the Dragon-Transforming Pool behind Soul Mountain, where it instantly shed its coat and grew horns, golden scales, and silver whiskers. Swathed in auspicious air and clouds, it soared out of the pool and roosted on one of the Pillars Supporting Heaven.

Monkey turned to Tripitaka. "Seeing as I'm a Buddha now, can't I smash that hoop stuck on my head? I don't want that so-called Bodhisattva to use it to play tricks on me or anyone else."

Tritpitaka smiled. "We needed the hoop only because there was no other way of bringing you to heel. Now that you've become a Buddha, it's disappeared of its own accord. Feel for yourself." Touching his head, Monkey discovered that the hoop had indeed vanished.

The newly promoted pilgrims joined with all the other divinities of Soul Mountain in chanting their praise of every Buddha and Bodhisattva, including the Buddha Victorious in Struggle and all the way down to the Altar Service Attendant, the Golden-Bodied Arhat, and the Heavenly Dragon of the Order of Eight Supernatural Beasts. "We dedicate ourselves," the heavenly chorus finished, "to the pure land of the Buddha, to repay compassion from above, and to save those below. Those who see and hear will be reborn and enlightened in the land of ultimate bliss."

Here ends the Journey to the West.